THE
3RD
WOMAN
JONATHAN FREEDLAND

HARPER

Harper
An imprint of HarperCollins*Publishers*
1 London Bridge Street,
London, SE1 9GF

www.harpercollins.co.uk

This paperback edition 2016
3

First published in Great Britain by HarperCollins*Publishers* 2015

A catalogue record for this book
is available from the British Library

ISBN: 978-0-00-741369-0

Typeset in Sabon by Palimpsest Book Production Limited, Falkirk, Stirlingshire

Printed and bound in Great Britain by
Clays Ltd, St Ives plc

MIX
Paper from
responsible sources
FSC C007454

FSC™ is a non-profit international organisation established to promote
the responsible management of the world's forests. Products carrying the
FSC label are independently certified to assure consumers that they come
from forests that are managed to meet the social, economic and
ecological needs of present and future generations,
and other controlled sources.

Find out more about HarperCollins and the environment at
www.harpercollins.co.uk/green

THE
3RD
WOMAN

...an Freedland is an award-winning journalist, No.1 best-
... author and broadcaster. He is the *Guardian*'s Executive
... for Opinion, and also writes a weekly column. He is a
... contributor to the *New York Times* and the *New York
...v of Books*, and he presents BBC Radio 4's contemporary
... series, *The Long View*. In 2014 he was awarded the
...l special prize for journalism.

...2006 he has published five internationally bestselling
... under the pseudonym Sam Bourne, which have sold over
...ion copies and been published in over 30 languages.

www.jonathanfreedland.com

🐦 @Freedland

📘 Facebook.com/JonathanFreedlandOfficial

Writing as Sam Bourne

For my sister Fiona, 1963–2014.

A woman of strength, wisdom, laughter and constant love

Prologue

It was the last day of January and the New Year was approaching. The city of Los Angeles had been winding down for more than a week. The only place still humming was the airport, as the expats headed home, crossing the ocean to see devoted fathers, doting mothers and the occasional abandoned wife. Offices were closing early: with no one on the end of the phone and no deals to be made, there was little point staying open. It was the second break in six weeks, but this one felt less wanted and somehow involuntary, the way a city falls quiet during a strike or a national day of mourning. Still, the red lanterns hanging from the lampposts and trees gave the city some welcome cheer, especially after dark.

Not that it gave her much comfort. The night had never been her time. She had always been a child of the early mornings, up with the sun. She lost interest in the sky once it was no longer blue. She was the same now, even in winter, running out into the morning as soon as it had broken.

Which was another reason why she hated having to do this. Working in this place was bad enough, but the time was worse. These were hours meant for sleep.

But she managed to be cheery to the girls when she said goodbye, throwing her clothes into a tote bag and slinging it over her shoulder in a single, well-practised movement. She gave the guy on the door a smile too even though her jaw felt strained from a night spent in a fixed expression of delight.

Walking to her car out in the lot, she kept her eyes down. She had learned that lesson early enough. Avoid eye contact inside if you could, but never, ever meet anyone's eye once you were outside.

She aimed the key fob at the car door but it made a useless, dull click. Three more goes, three more empty clicks. The battery on the damn thing was fading. Opening the car door manually, she got in, taking care to lock the door after her.

The drive back was quicker than usual, thanks to the New Year emptiness. She put on a music station, playing oldies, and tried to forget her evening's work. She looked in her rear-view mirror occasionally, but besides the smog there was precious little to see.

At the apartment building, she had her key in hand and the entrance door opened smoothly. Too tired to close it after her, she let it swing slowly shut. All the same, something made her glance over her shoulder but in the dark she saw nothing. This was why she hated working late at night: she was always jumping at shadows.

When the elevator opened on her floor and she nudged the key into the apartment's front door, he was ready for her. She had heard no sound, her first awareness of his presence being the gloved hand over her mouth. Her nostrils sought out the air denied to her mouth, filling instantly with the scent of unwashed leather and sweat. Worse was the breath. The urgent, hot breath of a stranger against her neck, then dispersing around it, as if enveloping her.

She tried to call out. Not a scream but a word. If her mouth had not been gagged it might have come out as 'What?'

All of that was in the first second. But now, in the moments that followed, there was time for fear. It sped through her, throbbing out from her heart through her veins, into her brain, which seemed to be filling with flashing red and yellow, and then into her legs, which became light and unsteady. But she did not fall. He had her in his grip.

She felt him use his weight to push the apartment door, already unlocked, wide open, his shove splintering wood off the frame. Once she was bundled inside, he closed the door – deliberately not letting it slam.

Now the scream rose, trying to force its way through her chest and into her throat, but it came up against the leather hand and seemed to be pushed back into her. She felt his left hand leave her shoulder and move, as if checking for something.

Instinctively she tried to wriggle free, but his right arm was too strong. It held her in place, sealing her mouth at the same time.

Now she heard a ripping noise: had he torn her clothes? The first, primeval, terror had been of death, that this man would kill her. But the second fear, coming in instant pursuit, was the horror that he would push his brute body into hers. She made a wordless calculation, a bargain almost: she would withstand a rape if he would let her live.

But the sound she had heard was not of torn clothing. She saw his left hand hover in front of her face, a piece of wide, silver-coloured masking tape spanned between its fingers. Expertly, he placed it over her mouth, leaving not so much as a split-second in which she could emit a sound.

Now he grabbed her wrists, containing them both in the grasp of a single hand. Still behind her, still not letting her glimpse his face, he pushed her towards the centre of the room, in front of the couch. He shoved the coffee table out of the way with one foot, then tripped her from behind, so that she was face down on the carpet with pressure on her back, a knee holding her in position.

This is it, she thought. *He'll rip my clothes off now and do it here, like this.* She told herself to send her mind elsewhere,

3

so that she could survive what was to follow. *Live through this*, she thought. *You can*. She closed her eyes and tried to shut down. *Live through this*.

But he had not finished his preparations. A strip of black cloth was placed over her eyes, then tied at the back. Next, this man – whose face she had not seen, whose voice she had not heard – flipped her over, firmly but not roughly. Perhaps he had sensed that her strategy for survival was to co-operate.

One wrist was pulled above her head, so that she looked like a child demanding the teacher's attention. A moment later, the wrist was encircled by a kind of plastic bracelet. Loose at first, but then she heard that distinctive zipping sound she remembered from childhood, the sound of a hardware-store cable tie. Her father would use them to bundle loose wires together, keeping them neat behind the TV set; they were impossible to break, he said. Now this man did the same to her right wrist. She was lying on the floor, gagged and blind-folded, with both her arms stretched upward and tied to a single leg of the couch.

She willed her mind to transport itself somewhere else. But the fear was making her teeth chatter. Nausea was working its way up from her stomach and into her mouth. *Please God, let this be over. Let this end, please God.*

It was all happening so fast, so . . . efficiently. There was no rage in this man's actions, just purpose and method, as if this were a safety drill and he was following an established procedure. One of his hands was now on her right arm, except the touch was not the rough leather she had felt over her mouth. It was light, just a fingertip, but not human skin. Sightless, she could not be sure of the material, but the hand was close enough to her face that she could smell it. It was latex. The man was wearing latex gloves. Now a new terror seized her.

He gripped her wrist again and then she felt it, the sharp puncture of a needle plunged into her right arm. She cried

4

out, hearing only the sound of a muffled exclamation that seemed to come from somewhere else entirely.

And then, in an instant, the fear melted away, to be replaced by a rapid, tingling rush, a wave of blissful comfort. She felt no pain at all, just a deep, wide, unexpected happiness. When the tape was removed from her mouth, she let out no scream. Perhaps she had succeeded in sending herself far away after all, onto the Malibu beach at dawn, where the sand was kissed by sun. Or into a clear-blue ocean. Or into a hammock on a desert island in the South Pacific. Or into a cabin in mid-winter, the amber glow warming her as she lay on the rug before a fire that popped and crackled.

She heard the distant sound of the cable tie being cut loose, its job now done. She sensed the blindfold coming away from her face. But she felt no urge to open her eyes or move her arms, even though she was now free. Every nerve, every synapse, from her toes to her fingernails, was dedicated instead to passing messages of pleasure to her brain. Her system was flooded with goodness; she was a crowd assembling on the mountain top at the moment of the Rapture, every face grinning with delight.

Now she felt the lightest, most fleeting sensation between her legs. A hand was peeling back her underwear. Something brushed against her. It did not penetrate. It did not even bother her. Rather something still and smooth was resting there, against her most intimate place. She felt her skin kissed by silk petals.

A second passed and she was in the sealed, safe hiding place before any of that, floating in the fluid that could nourish her and support her and where no one could disturb her. She was in her mother's womb, utterly content, breathing only love and love and love.

Chapter 1

Normally Madison Webb liked January. If you grew up used to golden California sun, winter could be a welcome novelty. The cold – not that it ever got truly cold in LA – made your nerves tingle, made you feel alive.

Not this January, though. She had spent the month confined to a place of steel and blank, windowless walls, one of those rare corners of LA compelled to operate throughout the Chinese New Year. It never stopped, day or night. She had been working here for three weeks, twenty shifts straight, taking her place alongside the scores of seamstresses hunched over their machines. Though the word 'seamstresses' was misleading. As Maddy would be explaining to the LA public very soon, the word suggested some ancient, artisan skill, while in reality she and the other women were on an assembly line, in place solely to mind the devices, ensuring the fabric was placed squarely in the slot and letting the pre-programmed, robotic arm do the rest. They were glorified machine parts themselves.

Except that machines, as she would put it in the first in a series of undercover reports on life in an LA sweatshop, would be treated better than these people, who had to stand at their work-stations for hours on end, raising their hands for a bathroom break, surrendering their phones as they arrived, lest they surreptitiously try to photograph this dingy basement where, starved of natural light and illuminated by a few naked lightbulbs, she felt her eyesight degraded by the day.

Being deprived of her phone had presented the most obvious obstacle, Maddy reflected now, as she fed a stretch of denim through the roller, ensuring its edges aligned before it submitted to the stitching needle. She had worked with Katharine Hu, the resident tech-genius in the office and Maddy's best friend there, to devise a concealed camera. Its lens was in the form of a button on her shirt. From there, it transmitted by means of a tiny wire to a digital recorder taped into the small of her back. It did the job well, giving a wide-angled view of everything she faced: turn 360 degrees and she could sweep the whole place. It picked up snatches of conversation with her fellow seamstresses and with Walker, the foreman – including a choice moment as he instructed one 'bitch' to get back to work.

With nearly two hundred hours of recordings, she knew she had enough to run a story that would have serious impact. The camera had caught in full the incident nearly a week ago when Walker had denied one of Maddy's co-workers a bathroom break, despite repeated requests. The woman's pleas had grown desperate, but he just bellowed at her, 'How many times do I have to say it, *shabi*? You been on your break already today.' He used that word often, but calling a woman a cunt in a room full of other women represented an escalation all the same.

When the other workers started yelling, Walker reached for the night-stick that completed his pseudo-military, brown-and-beige polyester uniform, the kind worn by private security guards in supermarkets. He didn't use the weapon but the threat of it was enough. The crying woman collapsed at the sight of it. A moment or two later a pool of liquid spread from her. At first they thought it was the urine she had been struggling to contain. But even in this light they could see it

7

was blood. One of the older women understood. 'That poor child,' she said, though whether she was referring to the woman or the baby she had just miscarried, Maddy could not tell. She had been near enough to film the whole scene. Edited, it would appear alongside the first article in the series.

She was writing in her head at this very moment, mentally typing out what would be the second section of the main piece. Everyone knew already that sweatshops like this one were rife across California, providing cheap labour, thanks mainly to migrants who had dashed across the Mexican border in the dead of night, to make or finish goods for the US or Latin American markets. That wasn't news. *LA Times* readers knew why it had happened too: these days the big Chinese corporations found it cheaper to make goods in LA than in Beijing or Shanghai, now that their own workers cost so much. What people didn't know was what it was actually *like* inside one of these dumps. That was her job. The stats and the economics she'd leave to the bean-counters on the business desk. What would get this story noticed was the human element, the unseen workers who were actually paying the price. Oh, that sounded quite good. Maybe she should use that in the intro. *The unseen workers—*

There was a coughing noise, not especially loud but insistent. It came from the woman opposite her on the production belt, an artificial throat-clearing designed to catch her attention. '*What?*' Madison mouthed. She glanced up at her machine, looking for a red light, warning of a malfunction. Her co-worker raised her eyebrows, indicating something about Maddy's appearance.

She looked down. Emerging from the third buttonhole of her shirt was a tiny piglet's tail of wire.

She tried to tuck it away, but it was too late. In four large strides, Walker had covered the distance between them – lumbering and unfit, but bulky enough to loom over her, filling the space around her.

8

'You give me that. Right now.'

'Give you what?' Maddy could hear her heart banging in her chest.

'You don't want to give me any *taidu* now, I warn you. Give it to me.'

'What, a loose thread on my shirt? You're ordering me to remove my clothes now, is that it, Walker? I'm not sure that's allowed.'

'Just give it to me and I'll tell you what's allowed.'

That he spoke quietly only made her more frightened. His everyday mode was shouting. This, he knew – and therefore she knew and all the women standing and watching, in silence, knew – was more serious.

She made an instant decision, or rather her hand made it before her brain could consider it. In a single movement, she yanked out the tiny camera and dropped it to the floor, crunching it underfoot the second it hit.

The foreman fell to his knees, trying to pick up the pieces: not an easy manoeuvre for a man his size. She watched, frozen, as the tiny fragments of now-shattered electronics collected in his palm. It was clear that he understood what they were. That was why he had not shouted. He had suspected the instant he caught sight of the wire. Recording device. His instructions must have been absolute: they were not tolerated under any circumstances.

Now, as he pulled himself up, she had a split-second to calculate. She had already got three weeks of material, downloaded from the camera each night and, thanks to Katharine, safely backed up. Even today's footage was preserved, held on the recorder strapped to her back, regardless of the electronic debris on the floor. There was nothing to be gained from attempting to stay here, from coming up with some bullshit explanation for the now-extinct gadget. What would she say? And, she knew, she would be saying it to someone other than Walker. There was only one thing she could do.

Swiftly, she grabbed the security tag that hung around the foreman's neck like a pendant, whipped it off and turned around and ran, past the work benches, heading for the stairs. She touched Walker's tag against the electronic panel the way she'd seen him release the women for their rationed visits to the bathroom.

'Stop right there, bitch!' Walker was shouting. 'You stop right there.' He was coming after her, the thud of each footstep getting louder. The door beeped. She tugged at it, but the handle wouldn't open. She held the damn card against the panel once more and this time, at last, the little light turned green, accompanied by another short, sharp and friendlier beep. She opened the door and stepped through.

But Walker had been fast, so that now his hand reached through and grabbed at her shoulder. He was strong, but she had one advantage. She swivelled to face him, grabbed the door and used all of her strength to slam it shut. His arm was caught between the door and the frame. He let out a loud yowl of pain and the arm retracted. She slammed the door again, hearing the reassuring click that meant it was electronically sealed.

Leaping up the stairs two at a time, she clutched at the rail as she reached the first landing and pulled herself onto the next flight, seeing daylight ahead. She would only have a few seconds. Walker was bound to have alerted security in reception by now.

Maddy was in the short corridor that led to the entrance of the building. From the outside it resembled nothing more than a low-rent import–export office. That was in her article, too. If you walked past it, you'd never know what horrors lay beneath.

She breathed deep, realizing she had no idea what to do next. She couldn't breeze out, not from here. Workers were allowed to exit only at prescribed times. They would stop her; they'd call down to Walker; they'd start checking the computer. She needed to think of something. Her head was pounding now. And she could hear sounds coming from below. Had Walker got the downstairs door open?

She had the merest inkling of a plan, no more than an instinct. Flinging the door open, her voice rising with panic, she bellowed at the man and woman manning the front desk. 'It's Walker! I think he's having a heart attack. Come quick!'

The pair sat frozen in that second of paralysis that strikes in every crisis. Maddy had seen it before. 'Come on!' she shouted. 'I think he might be dying.'

Now they jumped up, barrelling past her to get down the stairs. 'I'll call for an ambulance!' she shouted after them.

She had only a second to look behind the desk, at the grid of cubby-holes where they kept the women's confiscated phones. *Shit*. She couldn't see hers. She thought of simply rushing out there and then, but she'd be lost without it. Besides, if they found it once she'd gone, they'd instantly know who she was and what she'd been working on.

Commotion downstairs. They'd be back up here any second. She moved her eye along the slots one last time, trying to be methodical while her head was about to explode. *Calm, calm, calm*, she told herself. But it was a lie.

Then at last, the recognizable shape, the distinct colour of the case, lurking in the corner of the second last row. She grabbed it and rushed out of the door, into the open air.

The sound of the freeway was loud but unimaginably welcome. She had no idea how she would get away from here. She could hardly wait for a bus. Besides, she had left her wallet downstairs, tucked inside her now-abandoned bag.

As she began running towards the noise of the traffic, working out who she would call first – her editor to say they should run the story tonight or Katharine to apologize for the broken camera – she realized that she had only one thing on her besides her phone. She unclenched her fist to see Walker's pass now clammy in her hand. Good, she thought.

His photo ID would complement her article nicely: 'The brute behind the brutality.'

Seven hours later the story was ready to go, including a paragraph or two on her ejection from the sweatshop and accompanied online by several segments of video, with greatest prominence given to the miscarriage episode. 'How LA sweatshop conditions can mean the difference between life and death.' Use of the Walker photo had taken up nearly an hour's back-and-forth with the news editor. Howard Burke had worried about naming an individual.

'Fine to go after the company, Madison, but you're calling this guy a sadist.'

'That's because he *is* a sadist, Howard.'

'Yes, but even sadists can sue.'

'So let him sue! He'll lose. We have video of him causing a woman to lose her baby. Jeez, Howard, you're such—'

'What, Maddy? What am I "such a"? And tread carefully here, because this story is not going anywhere till I say so.'

There was a silence between them, a stand-off of several seconds broken by her.

'Asshole.'

'Excuse me?'

'You're such an asshole. That's what I was going to say. Before you interrupted me.'

The exchange that followed could be heard at the other end of the open-plan office.

Burke's frustration overflowing, he drove his fist through an office partition, which newsroom historians recorded was the second time he had performed that feat – the first some four years earlier, also prompted by a clash with Madison Webb.

It took the intervention of the executive editor herself to broker a compromise. Jane Goldstein summoned Maddy into her office, making her wait while she took evidence from

Howard over by the newsdesk. Clearly she had decided it was too risky to have them both in the same room at once.

It gave Maddy time to look at the boss's power wall, which was a departure from the usual ego mural. Instead of photos with assorted political bigwigs and worthies, Goldstein had displayed a series of framed front pages of the biggest story she – or any other American reporter since Ed Murrow – had ever covered. She'd won a stack of Pulitzers, back when that had been the name of the biggest prize in US journalism.

Maddy's phone vibrated. A message from a burnt-out former colleague who had left the *Times* to join a company in Encino making educational films.

Hey Maddy. Greetings from the slow lane. Am attaching my latest, for what it's worth. Not exactly Stanley Kubrick, but I'd love any feedback. We've been told to aim at Junior High level. The brief is to explain the origins of the 'situation', in as neutral a way as possible. Nothing loaded. Tell me anything you think needs changing, especially script. You're the writer!

With no sign of Goldstein, Maddy dutifully clicked the play button. From her phone's small speaker, the voiceover – deep, mid-Western, reliable – began.

The story starts on Capitol Hill. Congress had gathered to raise the 'debt ceiling', the amount of money the American government is allowed to borrow each year. But Congress couldn't agree. There was footage of the then-Speaker, banging his gavel, failing to bring order to the chamber.

After that, lenders around the world began to worry that a loan to America was a bad bet. The country's 'credit rating' began to slip, downgraded from double A-plus to double A and then to letters of the alphabet no one ever expected to see alongside a dollar sign. That came with a neat little graphic animation, the A turning to B turning to C. *But then the crisis deepened.*

On screen was a single word in bold, black capital letters:

DEFAULT. The voiceover continued. *The United States had to admit it couldn't pay the interest on the money it owed to, among others, China. In official language, the US Treasury announced a default on one of its bonds.*

Now there were images of Tiananmen Square. *Beijing had been prepared to tolerate that once, but when the deadlock in Congress threatened a second American default, China came down hard.* A shot of the *LA Times* front page of the time.

Maddy hit the pause button and splayed her fingers to zoom in on the image. She could just make out the byline: a young Jane Goldstein. The headline was stark:

China's Message to US: 'Enough is enough'

A copy of that same front page was here now, framed and on Goldstein's wall.

At the time the People's Republic of China was America's largest creditor, the country that lent it the most money. And so China insisted it had a special right to be paid back what it was owed. Beijing called for 'certainty' over US interest payments, insisting it would accept nothing less than 'a guaranteed revenue stream'. China said it was not prepared to wait in line behind other creditors – or even behind other claims on American tax dollars, such as defence or education. From now on, said Beijing, interest payments to China would have to be America's number one priority.

Maddy imagined the kids in class watching this story unfold. The voice, calm and reassuring, was taking them through the events that had shaped the country, and the times, they had grown up in.

But China was not prepared to leave the matter of repayment up to America. Beijing demanded the right to take the money it was owed at source. America had little option but

14

to say yes. There followed a clip of an exhausted US official emerging from late night talks saying, 'If China doesn't get what it wants, if it deems the US a bad risk, there'll be no country on earth willing to lend to us, except at extortionate rates.'

Experts declared that the entire American way of life – fuelled by debt for decades – was at risk. And so America accepted China's demand and granted the People's Republic direct access to its most regular stream of revenue: the custom duties it levied on goods coming into the US. From now on, a slice of that money would be handed over to Beijing the instant it was received.

But there was a problem: Beijing's demand for a Chinese presence in the so-called 'string of pearls' along the American west coast – the ports of San Diego, Los Angeles, Long Beach and San Francisco. China insisted such a presence was essential if it was to monitor import traffic effectively.

Now came a short, dubbed clip of a Beijing official saying, 'For this customs arrangement to work, the People's Republic needs to be assured it is receiving its rightful allocation, no more and no less.'

The US government said no. It insisted a physical presence was a 'red line'. Finally, after days of negotiation, the two sides reached a compromise. A small delegation of Chinese customs officials would be based on Port Authority premises – including in Los Angeles – but this presence would, the US government insisted, be only 'symbolic'.

Archive footage of a CBS News broadcast from a few months after that agreement, reporting Chinese claims of smuggling and tax-dodging by American firms, crimes they suspected were tolerated, if not encouraged, by the US authorities. *Beijing began to demand an increase in the number of Chinese inspectors based in Los Angeles and the other 'string of pearl' ports. Each demand was resisted at first by the US authorities – but each one was met in the end.*

Next came pictures of the notorious Summer Riots, a sequence that had been played a thousand times on TV news in the US and around the world. A group of Chinese customs men surrounded by an angry American crowd; the LAPD trying to hold back the mob, struggling and eventually failing. The narrator took up the story. *On that turbulent night, several rioters armed with clubs broke through, eventually killing two Chinese customs officers. The two men were lynched. The fallout was immediate. Washington acceded to Beijing's request that the People's Republic of China be allowed to protect its own people.* The film ended with the White House spokesperson insisting that no more than 'a light, private security detail' would be sent from China to LA and the other 'pearls'.

Maddy smiled a mirthless smile: everyone knew how that had turned out.

She was halfway through a reply to her former colleague – 'Think that covers all the bases' followed by a winking emoticon – when she looked up to see the editor striding in, three words into her sentence before she got through the door.

'OK, we run the Walker picture tomorrow.'

Short, roundish and in her mid-fifties, her hair a solid, unapologetic white, Goldstein exuded impatience. Her eyes, her posture said, *Come on, come on, get to the point*, even before you had said a word. Still, Maddy risked a redundant question. 'So not tonight?'

'Correct. Walker remains unnamed tonight. Maybe tomorrow too. Depends on the re-act to the first piece.'

'But—'

Goldstein peered over her spectacles in a way that drew instant silence from Maddy. 'You have thirty minutes to make any final changes – and I mean *final*, Madison – and then you're going to get the fuck out of this office, am I clear? You will not hang around and get up to your usual tricks, *capisce*?'

Maddy nodded.

'No looking over the desk's shoulder while they write the headlines, no arguing about the wording of a fucking caption, no getting in the way. Do we understand each other?'

Maddy managed a 'Yes'.

'Good. To recapitulate: the suck-ups on Gawker might think you're the greatest investigative journalist in America, but I do not want you within a three-mile radius of this office.'

Maddy was about to say a word in her defence, but Goldstein's solution actually made good sense: if a story went big, you needed to have a follow-up ready for the next day. Naming Walker and publishing his photo ID on day two would prove that they – she – had not used up all their ammo in the first raid. That Goldstein was perhaps one of a tiny handful of people on the *LA Times* she truly respected Maddy did not admit as a factor. She murmured a thank you and headed out – wholly unaware that when she next set foot in that office, her life – and the life of this city – would have turned upside down.

17

Chapter 2

LA tended not to be a late night town, but the Mail Room was different. Downtown, in that borderland between scuzzy and bohemian, it had gone through a spell as a gay hangout; the Male Room, Katharine called it, explaining why she and her fellow dykes – her word – steered clear of it. Though now enjoying a wider clientele, it still retained some of that edgier vibe. Unlike plenty of places in LA, the kitchen didn't close at eight and you didn't have to use a valet to park your car.

Maddy found a spot between a convertible, the roof down even now, in January, and an extravagant sports car with tinted windows. The high-rollers were clearly in; maybe a movie star, slumming it for the night, plus entourage. She considered texting Katharine to suggest they go somewhere else.

The speakers in her car – a battered, made-in-China Geely that had been feeling its age even when she got it – were relaying the voices of the police scanner, announcing the usual mayhem of properties burgled and bodies found: the legacy of her days on the crime beat. She stabbed at the button, found a music station, wound up the volume. Let the beat pump through her while she used the car mirror to fix her make-up. Remarkably, despite the stress, she didn't look too horrific. Her long, brown hair was tangled: she dragged a brush through it. But the dark circles under her green eyes were beyond cosmetic help: the concealer she dabbed on looked worse than the shadows.

Inside, she had that initial shudder of nerves, known to every person who ever arrived at a party on their own. She scanned the room, looking for a familiar face. Had she got here too late? Had Katharine and Enrica come here, tired of it and moved on? She dug into her pocket, her fingers searching out the reassurance of her phone.

While her head was down, she felt the clasp of a hand on her shoulder.

'Hey, you!'

It took her a second to place the face, then she had it: Charlie Hughes. They'd met straight after college.

'You look great, Maddy. What you doing here?'

'I thought I was going to be celebrating. But I can't see the people I'm meet—'

'Celebrating? That'd be nice. I'm here to do the very opposite.'

'The opposite? Why?'

'You know that script I've been working on for, like, years?' Charlie was a qualified, practising physician but that wasn't enough for him. Ever since he'd been hired as a consultant on a TV medical drama, Charlie had become obsessed with making it as a screenwriter. In LA, even the doctors wanted to be in pictures. 'The one about the monks and devils?'

'*Devil Monk*?'

'Yes! Wow, Maddy, I love that you remember that. See, it *does* have a memorable title. I told them.'

'Them?'

'The studio. They've cancelled the project.'

'Oh no. Why?'

'Usual story. Sent it to Beijing for "approval". Which always means disapproval.'

19

'What didn't they like?' God, she could do without this. She gazed over his shoulder, desperately seeking a glimpse of her friends.

'Said it wouldn't resonate with the Chinese public. It's such bullshit, Maddy. I told them the most particular stories are always the most universal. If it means something to someone in Peoria, it'll mean something to someone in Guangdong. The trouble is, if they won't distribute, no one will fund. It's the same story every time—'

She showed him glazed eyes, but it made no difference. He was off. So lost was he in his own tale – *narrative*, he'd call it – that he barely looked at her, fixing instead on some middle distance where those who had conspired to thwart his career were apparently gathered.

With an inward sigh, Maddy scoped the room. The group that caught the eye had occupied the club's prime spot, perhaps a dozen of them gathering against the wide picture window that made up the far wall. Their laughter was loudest, their clothes sparkling brightest. The women were nearly all blonde – the exception was a redhead – and, as far as Maddy could see, gorgeous. Cocktails in hand, they were throwing their heads back in laughter, showing off their long, laboriously tonged hair. The men were Chinese, wearing expensive jeans and pressed white shirts, set off against watches as bejewelled and shiny as any trinket worn by the women. Princelings, she concluded.

She hadn't realized the Mail Room had become a favoured hangout for that set, the pampered sons of the Chinese ruling elite who, thanks to the garrison and the attached military academy, had become a fixture of LA high society. Soon these rich boys would be the officer corps of the PLA, the People's Liberation Army. PLAyers, the gossip sites called them.

The redhead was losing a battle to stay upright, tugged down by her wrist to sit on the lap of a man whose broad grin just got broader. He ran his hand down the woman's back, resting it just above her buttocks. She was showing her teeth in a smile, but her eyes suggested she didn't find it funny.

Maddy contemplated the tableau they made, the Princelings and their would-be princesses, their Aston Martins and Ferraris cooling outside. She was surprised this place was expensive enough for them. Now that they were here, it soon would be.

Charlie broke into his own monologue to wave hello at one of the PLAyers.

'Is he an investor?' Maddy asked, surprised.

'I wish,' Charlie sighed. 'He's a patient. The thing is . . .'

Suddenly she caught sight of Katharine standing at full stretch in a corner, her mouth making an O of delight, waving her to come over. Maddy gave Charlie a parting peck on the cheek, mumbled a 'Good luck' and all but fled to Katharine and Enrica, standing in a cluster with a few others around a small, high table congested with cocktails.

She slowed down when she saw him. What on earth was he doing here? She thought it was going to be a night with the girls, or at least men she hadn't met, ideally gay. A night off. She gave Katharine a glare. But it was too late. He was already there, glass in hand, with his trademark embryonic smile. The beard was a new addition. When they lived together, she had always vetoed facial hair. But that was nearly nine months ago and now she saw it, she had to admit, it suited him.

'Leo.'

'Maddy. You look as stunning as ever.'

'Don't be slimy. Slimy never suited you.'

'I was being *charming*.'

'Yeah, well, charming never suited you either.'

'How would you like me to be?'

'Somewhere else?' She lowered her voice. 'Seriously, Leo. I thought we were going to give each other some space.'

'Come on, Maddy. Let's not ruin your big night.'

'How do you know about that?'

He nodded towards Katharine, then took a sip of his drink. The budding smile had blossomed in his eyes, which never left her. They were a warm brown. In the right mood, when his interest, or better still his passion, was engaged, they seemed to contain sparks of light that would careen around the iris, bouncing off each other. They were brightening now.

'What did she tell you? K, what did you—'

He reached for her wrist. 'Don't worry, she didn't tell me anything. Just that you've reeled in a big one. Big enough to win a Huawei.'

'Katharine doesn't know what's she's talking about,' Maddy retorted. But her shoulders dropped for the first time since she walked in here. She couldn't hide it: she'd been thinking this story had the potential to win a Huawei prize from the beginning, before she'd even written a word. It had just what the judges liked: investigation, risk, its target corruption – at just that mid-level where its exposure did not threaten those at the very top. In more than one sleepless hour, she had worded the imaginary citation.

'But you do, Maddy. And your face is telling me I'm right. You've landed a biggie.'

'Don't think you're going to get me to tell you by flattering me, because it won't work.'

'Why not?'

'Because I know you, Leo Harris. I know all your tricks. Leaking my exclusive to everyone else, so it makes no impact—'

'Not that again.'

'Don't worry. I'm not going to let you ruin this evening. I'm in a happy mood and I'm going to—'

'OK, just tell me one thing.'

'No.'

'Does it affect the mayor in any way at all?'

'No.'

'Do I need to worry about it in any way at all?'

'No.' She paused. 'Not really.'

'Not really? And I'm supposed to be reassured by that?'

'I mean, only in the sense that it's happening in this city. And,' she tilted her chin towards her chest and dropped her voice two octaves, '"Everything that happens in this city concerns—"'

'"—concerns the mayor." You see, Maddy, you *do* remember me.'

She said nothing but kept her eyes trained on his, brown and warm as a logfire. Seeing his pleasure, his tickled vanity, the thought came out of her mouth before she was even fully aware of it. 'You're such an asshole, Leo.'

'Let me get you a drink.'

He turned and headed towards the bar, leaving Maddy to the gaze of Katharine, simultaneously quizzical and reproachful. Her friend and colleague, shorter, older and always wiser in such matters, was wordlessly asking her what the hell she was doing. By means of her eyes alone, she said, *I thought we'd talked about this.*

Leo was back, handing Maddy a glass. Whisky, not wine. *I know you.* She downed it in one gulp.

'So,' he began again, as if drawing a line under the previous topic. 'I tell you what would win an *instant* Huawei.'

'What's that?'

'Inside the campaign of the next Governor of the great state of California. Unprecedented access, fly on the wall. *In the room.*'

'Are you offering me access to Berger's campaign?'

'No. I'm telling you what you *could've* had if you hadn't broken up with me.'

'Leo.'

'All right. If you hadn't decided we should have a "break".'

'*We* decided.'

'Whatever. The point is, the mayor's going to win, Maddy.

23

He's the most popular mayor in the history of Los Angeles.'

'Well, I'll just have to live with that, won't I?'

He shrugged. *Your loss.*

They were joined just then by an improbably tall, slender woman perched on four-inch heels, wearing a dress which appeared to be slashed to the waist. Her skin was tanned and flawless. She was, Maddy decided, either a professional model or twenty-three years old. Or possibly both. When she spoke, it was with an accent that suggested an expensive education.

'Aren't you going to introduce me, Leo?' The woman's smile was wide and white. She gave Maddy a look of unambiguous warmth, as if they were destined to be friends for life.

'This is Jade,' Leo mumbled.

A long moment passed before Madison extended her hand and, realizing Leo was not going to do it for her, offered her own name. The three smiled at each other mutely before Madison finally turned and said under her breath, 'Goodnight, Leo.'

He whispered back, 'Don't break my balls, Maddy.'

'I don't want to go anywhere near your balls, Leo. Have a good night.'

It was after midnight when Enrica announced that it was past her bedtime and that, unless Katharine wanted to deal with a woman no longer responsible for her actions, she needed to take her home. As Maddy followed them down the two flights of stairs, Katharine steadying her wife as she negotiated each step, she imagined what Leo would make of this sight: the lesbian couple, one Chinese-American, the other Latina, both committed Angelenos. It was a wonder he hadn't cast them in a Berger campaign ad ages ago.

Now, in the dead of night, Maddy was experiencing what was, to her, the rare sensation of having done what she had been told. She had gone out and gone back home and not phoned the desk once. She had not bothered Howard or

24

complained. She had not tried to tweak the odd sentence here and there. Nor had she exploited the fact that she knew all the relevant codes to go online and make the changes herself – an action that would squarely fall into the category defined by Goldstein as 'her usual tricks'. Sure, she had looked at the website a dozen times, she had checked Weibo, which was now humming with the story. But, by her standards, she had exercised remarkable restraint.

She stood in the shower, unmoving, not washing, letting the water envelop her. Prompted, perhaps, by the sensation of warmth on her skin, she found herself tingling, her hands' movements turning to caresses. Unbidden, came Leo – not the look of him so much as the sense of him, his presence. And the memory of his touch when he had been close to her, right here, in this shower, his body next to hers.

And yet she lacked the energy for what would ordinarily come next. What she wanted most of all was to fall into a deep, restoring sleep. But what else was new?

The water was turning cold. She stepped out, grabbed a towel and wandered into the living room. Or 'living room' as she would put it, in heavy quotes, were she writing a profile of somebody whose apartment looked like this. She assessed it now, with the detached eye of an observer. Outside lay the neighbourhood of Echo City, one part funky to two parts rundown. Inside, a large table, big enough to seat six or eight, entirely covered with paper, two laptops and a stack of filled notebooks, none arranged in any order except the one known exclusively to her. A couch, both ends taken up by piles of magazines and more papers, narrowing it into a seat for one.

Off to one side, through an open archway, the kitchen area, deceptively clean – not through fastidiousness so much as underuse. Even from here she could see there was a veneer of dust on the stove. The explanation lay in the trash can, filled almost exclusively by take-out cartons, deposited in a daily stream since she'd been on this story – and, she conceded to herself, long before.

For a moment Madison pictured how this place looked when she and Leo lived together. No tidier, but busier. Fuller. She enjoyed the memory, interrupted by that cut-glass accent. *This is Jade.*

She glanced down at her phone. So busy writing all afternoon and into the evening, she'd repeatedly ignored it when it rang. She'd not even checked her missed calls. But here they were: two from Howard, one from Katharine, both now obsolete, six from her older sister, Quincy, and one from her younger sister, Abigail.

She instantly thumbed Abigail's name and hovered over the 'Call' button. It was late and Abigail was no night owl. On the other hand, she was a teacher at elementary school: blessed with a job that allowed her to turn off her cell when she went to bed. No risk of waking her up, no matter how late. Maddy perched on the end of the couch, still in her towel, and pressed the button. It rang six times and then voicemail, her sister's voice so much younger, so much lighter, than her own.

No one leaves messages on these any more. But go on, you've come this far. Let me hear how you sound.

Maddy clicked off as soon as she heard the beep. She looked at the others, at Quincy's six attempts. That suggested low-level incandescence rather than full-blown rage. Maddy wondered what she had done wrong to offend her older sister this time, what rule or convention or supposedly widely understood sisterly duty she had violated or failed to comprehend. She would not listen to the voicemail, she didn't need to.

Her skin dry now, she followed the promise of sleep into the bedroom. Letting the towel fall off her, she slipped into the sheets, enjoying their cool. She had a dim awareness that she was following at least two elements of the recommended advice to insomniacs – a good shower and clean bedclothes. Such advice was in plentiful supply. She had been deluged with it over the years. Go to bed early, go to bed late. A bath, rather than a shower. Steaming hot or, better still, not hot. Eat a hearty meal, pasta is especially effective, at nine pm, or six pm, or noon, or even, in one version, seven am. A cup of warm milk. Not milk, whisky. Give up alcohol, give up wheat, give up meat. Stop smoking, start drinking. Start smoking, stop drinking. Exercise more, exercise less. Have you tried melatonin? Best to clear the head last thing at night by writing a to-do list. Never, ever write a to-do list: it will only set your mind racing. People are not clocks: they need to be wound down before sleep, not wound up. Thinking before bed was good, thinking before bed was very bad. One thing she knew for certain: contemplating all the myriad, contradictory methods of falling asleep could keep a person up at night.

Indeed, here she was, shattered, her arms, her hands, her eyes, her very fingertips aching for sleep – and still wide awake. None of it worked. None of it had ever worked. Pills could knock her out, but the price was too high: groggy and listless the next day. And she feared getting hooked: she knew herself too well to take the risk.

She had been up for twenty hours; all she was asking for was a few hours' rest. Even a few minutes. She closed her eyes.

Something like sleep came, the jumble of semi-conscious images that, for a normal person, usually presages sleep, a partial dream, like an overture to the main performance. She remembered that much from her childhood, back when she could rest effortlessly, surrendering to slumber the instant her head touched the pillow. But the voice in her head refused to fall silent. Here it was now, telling her she was still awake, stubbornly, maddeningly present.

She reached for her phone, letting out a glum sigh: *all right, you win*. She checked the *LA Times* site again, her story still the 'most read'. Then she clicked on the scanner app again, listening long enough to hear the police reporting several bodies found around town. One was not far from here, in Eagle Creek, another in North Hollywood.

Next, a long article on foreign policy: 'Yang's Grand Tour', detailing how the man tipped to be China's next president had just returned from an extended visit to the Middle East and analysing what this meant for the next phase of the country's ambition. The piece was suitably dense. Sure enough, it came close to sending her off, her mental field of vision behind her lidded eyes darkening at the edges, like the blurred border on an old silent movie. The dark surround spread, so that the image glimpsed by her mind's eye became smaller and smaller, until it was very nearly all black . . .

But she was watching it too closely, wanting it too much. She was conscious of her own slide into unconsciousness and so it didn't happen. She was, goddammit, still awake. She opened her eyes in surrender.

And then, for perhaps the thousandth time, she opened the drawer by her bed and pulled out the photograph.

She gazed at it now, looking first at her mother. She would have been what, thirty-eight or thirty-nine, when this picture was taken. Christ, less than ten years older than Maddy was now. Her mother's hair was brown, unstyled. She wore glasses too, of the unfashionable variety, as if trying to make herself look unattractive. Which would make a kind of sense.

Quincy was there, seventeen, tall, the seriousness already etched into her face. Beautiful in a stern way. Abigail was adorable of course, gap-toothed and smiling, aged six and sitting on Maddy's lap. As for Maddy herself, aged fourteen in this photograph, she was smiling too, but her expression was not happy, exactly: it contained too much knowledge of the world and of what life can do.

She reached out to touch her earlier self, but came up against the right-hand edge of the picture, sharp where she had methodically cut it all those years ago, excising the part she didn't want to see.

Later she would not be able to say when she had fallen asleep or even if she had. But the phone buzzed shortly after two am, making the bedside table shake. A name she recognized but which baffled her at this late hour: Detective Howe. A long-time source of hers from the crime beat, one who had been especially keen to remain on her contacts list. He called her once or twice a month: usually pretending to have a story, occasionally coming right out with it and asking her on a date. They had had lunch a couple of times, but she had never let it go further. And he had certainly never called in the middle of the night. One explanation surfaced. The sweatshop must have reported her for assault and Jeff was giving her a heads-up. Funny, she'd have thought they'd have wanted to avoid anything that would add to the publicity, especially after—

'Madison, is that you?'

'Yes. Jeff? Are you all right?'

'I'm OK. I'm downstairs. You need to let me in. Your buzzer's broken.'

'Jeff. It's two in the morning. I'm—'

'I know, Madison. Just let me in.' He was not drunk, she could tell that much. Something in his voice told her this was not what she had briefly feared; he was not about to make a scene, declaring his love for her, pleading to share her bed. She buzzed him in and waited.

When he appeared at her front door, she knew. His face alone told her: usually handsome, lean, his greying hair close-cropped, he now looked gaunt. She offered a greeting but her words sounded strange to her, clogged. Her mouth had dried. She noticed that she was cold. Her body temperature seemed to have dropped several degrees instantly.

'I'm so sorry, Madison. But I was on duty when I heard and I asked to do this myself. I thought it was better you hear this from me.'

She recognized that tone. She was becoming light-headed,

the blood draining from her brain and thumping back into her heart. 'Who?' was all she could say.

She saw Jeff's eyes begin to glisten. 'It's your sister. Abigail. She's been found dead.'

Chapter 3

Jeff waited while she threw on the first clothes she could find before leading her to his car. He spoke throughout, telling her what he knew but she digested almost none of it. The only words she heard were the ones that replayed themselves over and over. *It's your sister. Abigail. She's been found dead.*

She was plagued by pictures of Abigail as a child. No matter how hard she tried, she could not see her sister as an adult. One image recurred more than any other: Abigail aged five or six, clutching the doll Maddy herself had once played with, that had, like everything else, been handed down from sister to sister to sister. And in her head, variations on a sentence that would not quite form itself: *I let you down, Abigail. I let it happen again. It was never meant to happen again.*

They had been driving less than ten minutes when Maddy suddenly sat bolt-upright, heart pounding. It took a moment for her to understand. Even if only for a few seconds, she had fallen asleep. Microsleeps, they called them. They happened to all insomniacs. She knew she was especially vulnerable after a shock; it could prompt her system to shut down. It had happened once in college, after some jerk she had fallen for dumped her, the pain sending her into brief unconsciousness.

Arriving at LAPD headquarters helped. Like a muscle memory, she knew how to walk and talk and carry herself here. She shook off Jeff's attempts to guide her like the walking wounded, a hand on her waist. She made for the entrance, determined to function like Madison Webb, reporter.

Later she would struggle to remember the exact sequence of those next few hours, even though individual moments were etched in her memory. She remembered pleading with Jeff, asking him to pull whatever strings he could to break the usual protocol and allow her to visit the coroner's office. Once there, she would never forget the grey-white sheet pulled back to reveal the frozen mask of her sister's face, her lips a faded purple now, though Maddy had been told they were cold and blue when Abigail's housemate had found her. Nor would she forget the way the doctor on duty had lifted her sister's right arm, as casually as if it were the limb of a mannequin, gesturing to a fresh needle mark. And she would never forget his words, dully announcing to her the provisional verdict based on the state of the body when found: that the deceased had died of a drugs overdose, specifically caused by a massive injection of heroin into the bloodstream.

A silent, glared rebuke from Jeff had prompted the physician to apologize for his use of 'the deceased' about a woman who until a few hours ago had only ever been known as Abigail – a vital, joyful, beautiful force of nature. But there was no room in Maddy's heart for anger about that. She was too numb to feel anything as direct as anger. Besides, she had covered enough murders to know that that was how death worked. You could be energetic, smart and sexy, an Olympic athlete or a Nobel-prize-winning genius, but it made no difference: within a moment you became meat on a slab. The staff in the coroner's office spoke and acted the way they did because that was all they were looking at. They couldn't see Abigail. They could only see a corpse.

Finally, Jeff ensured Madison got to meet the detective assigned to the case, Barbara Miller, a former partner of his. Brisk and businesslike, she gave them an initial briefing, describing the way Abigail's body had been discovered: lying straight on the floor, on her back. An initial, brief search of the apartment could not confirm any forced entry. There were a few marks on the neck and back, but nothing that suggested a struggle.

It was past four in the morning when Maddy left, Jeff still at her side.

'Thank you,' she said, her voice a whisper.

'You don't have to thank me. You've just had the most terrible shock a person can have.'

'I don't believe it, you know.'

'I know. It's impossible to take in.' He opened the passenger door for her, touching her elbow as he eased her into the seat.

'I mean, I don't *believe* it. Not a single fucking word of it.'

'Of what?'

'What your friend the detective was implying. In there.'

'What was she implying?'

'Come on, Jeff. No "confirmed" sign of forced entry. "Nothing to suggest a struggle." I used to write that shit. We all know what it means. It means your friend thinks this was an "accident".' Maddy indicated quote marks with her eyebrows.

'I don't—'

'I've seen that look you guys get when you talk about this stuff. She's made up her mind that this was some kind of druggie sex game that went wrong.'

'She didn't say that.'

'She didn't have to. No forced entry, no struggle: it means *consent*. But I'm telling you, I know my sister, Jeff. I know who she is. She teaches elementary school, for Christ's sake. She is not a fucking *junkie*.'

Jeff said nothing, so Maddy said it for him. 'She was

murdered, Jeff. Not killed by accident. Murdered. Someone murdered my baby sister.'

Then the words she thought but did not say out loud: *I will find out who did this to you, Abigail. I broke one promise to you, but I will not break this one.*

Chapter 4

She woke from two hours of not-quite sleep – the fitful dozing that was often the closest she got to rest – with a momentary pause. It lasted less than a second, the most fleeting delay before she realized that the sense of a great, grave weight sunk onto her chest was not the product of a dream that would slip away, but of memory. She had remembered what had happened in the night, and her spirit sank with the recognition that it was no illusion or confusion, but real. Abigail was dead. She had not been able to save her.

She had refused Jeff Howe's offer to sleep on her couch, which meant she had to drive herself to Quincy's house in Brentwood. The long downhill ride along Huntley Avenue, the twists and turns, made her nauseous. Though she suspected that had less to do with the winding road – which was, in fact, remarkably free of the potholes that were standard in all but the richest, and usually expat Chinese, neighbourhoods of Los Angeles – and more to do with sickening anticipation of the duty that faced her.

The dashboard clock told her it was just before seven. Quincy would be up now, getting the kids ready for school.

She walked around the single BMW – an SUV – in the driveway. That meant Mark was already at the office. Some role in finance she struggled – or, rather, had not bothered – to understand. The dawn start was becoming rarer in LA these days: most began work later and carried on into the evening, so they could be on Beijing time. But it was a relief. She would need to be alone with Quincy.

She pressed the doorbell once and waited. She could hear her nephews squabbling, then her sister's voice: 'Juanita! Will you get that?'

The live-in maid; Maddy had forgotten about that. It still surprised her, the notion of anyone in her family being able to afford staff. When they grew up under the same roof, they could afford nothing.

The door opened to reveal Juanita's pursed lips. Suddenly, and for the first time, Maddy thought of what she looked like: sleepless and in stained jeans with a sweater holed below the armpit. Was the Mexican-Catholic maid judging her appearance – or would she have got that look of disapproval no matter how she was dressed, thanks to a sustained campaign of propaganda from her employer?

'Hello, Juanita,' she managed, stepping inside. 'Is Quincy around?'

'We're in here!' her sister called out, her voice full of capable good cheer, the mom busy with her brood.

Maddy thought of asking Juanita to call Quincy out so they could speak alone, but thought better of it. So, bracing herself, she entered the kitchen that was as big as her entire apartment, large enough for the boys to be throwing a softball to each other in one area, their play barely disturbing their sister as she sat, eating cereal, at the breakfast bar. Quincy was stationed at what she called 'the island', making waffles.

'Hi, Aunt Maddy,' said the younger of the two boys, raising a mitt in greeting. His child's smile stabbed at her heart. He was not much older than Abigail in the photograph.

Quincy looked up from the stove. 'What happened to you? You look awful.'

Maddy moved over to her sister, dropping her voice. 'We need to talk.'

'I know,' Quincy said, pulling at a wide drawer which noiselessly slid out to offer a vast range of cutlery. 'That's why I've been calling you. You know Mom has an appointment today, don't you? At Cedar Sinai? Mark arranged it, with a specialist he knows. The thing is, I can't take her. And it's very much your turn, isn't it? Why don't you put these on the table? It's *so* nice to see you. The kids haven't seen you for ages.' She handed her three plates and a small jug of maple syrup.

Maddy took them and put them straight down. 'Quincy, it's not that. It's something terrible. We have to talk. Away from here.'

Into the vast living room, the silent black of the enormous TV screen that filled one wall reflecting them as they faced one another. Quincy's brow was furrowed into a frown that said: *What have you done now?*

'It's Abigail. The police called me in the middle of the night. She was found . . . They found her. She's dead, Quincy.'

'What?'

'Don't make me say it again.'

'What are you talking about? I saw her on Sunday. She was here. She had lunch with us.'

'They say it was a heroin overdose.'

'Heroin? Abigail? Why would you say these things, Maddy? What's wrong with you?'

'I wish it wasn't true. But I've seen . . . I've seen her. I was there a few hours ago, at the coroner's office. It's not a mistake.'

Once Quincy surrendered to the truth, she crumpled. As she did so, she instantly managed to find what had eluded Maddy all night: tears. Quincy held her arms open to be hugged by her younger sister, and they stood together, Maddy's face growing wet from tears that were not her own.

'You should have told me,' were the first words Quincy managed.

'I couldn't do it over the phone.'

'You should have come here earlier. I should have known.'

'I couldn't wake you up in the middle of the night. It would have terrified the children.'

'It wasn't right that you had to know this on your own, Maddy.' After a few seconds, she spoke again. 'And where was she?'

'Like I said, in her apartment.'

'No. I mean *where*?'

Maddy hesitated, picturing the image supplied to her at the coroner's office and now seared into her mind: of Abigail, laid out on the floor. She should tell her. Quincy had a right to know. If Maddy had had to endure it, then they both should. Quincy had even said as much, that it was wrong for Maddy to carry this knowledge alone. Instead she said, 'I don't know. I'm not sure.'

At that, Quincy started sobbing again. Her son, Brett, was calling for her.

'I'm really sorry, but there's something I need to ask you,' Maddy began. 'About Abigail.'

Quincy stood up. 'I'm going to go over to Mom's now. I think we should go together.'

'No. I can't.'

'What do you mean, you "can't"?'

'I can't, Quincy.'

'Don't tell me you're going to work. Jesus.'

'Of course I'm not! For God's sake. But I need to find out what happened to Abigail. None of it—'

'Are you kidding? Let the police do that. Right now, you need to be with your family.'

'I can't do it, Quincy. I'm not going over there.'

'Christ, Maddy. I don't understand you at all, do you know that? At a time like this, your place—'

'Look, just tell me. Did Abigail do drugs? Is that possible?'

'Abigail? *Abigail?* I can't believe you'd even ask that. Of course not.'

'OK. Because what this means—'

'Where would she even get drugs from? She didn't mix in those kind of circles. And nor do I.'

'What the fuck is that supposed to mean?'

'Shhh. The children!'

'No.' Madison raised her voice louder, deliberately shouting out the word most likely to anger her sister. 'What. The. FUCK is that supposed to mean?'

'Nothing, Maddy. Nothing. We're all in shock. Ignore it, just ignore—'

'Are you saying that *I* mix in those kind of circles, that I hang out with junkies? Is that what you're saying? You can be a real *shabi* sometimes, you know, Quincy.'

'How dare you use that language in this house!'

'I can't believe it. You're blaming me!'

'I'm not. Of course I'm not, Maddy. I'm just saying that you, you know, sometimes showed Abigail a more urban lifestyle than—'

'More *urban*? What the hell is that supposed to mean? You mean because I don't live in Crestwood fucking Hills with an SUV and a Merc?'

'I think you should leave. I need to tell our mother that her daughter is dead.'

That stopped Maddy cold. She felt the rage ebb, leaving only exhaustion behind. 'I'm sorry, Quincy. I'm not thinking straight. I'm just so . . .' The sentence faded away.

Quincy looked at her with eyes that were raw. 'OK. But you're meant to be this great investigator, so brilliant at finding out the truth. But you don't even know the people right in front of you, do you? You think you're this big media star, Maddy, but guess what: you don't always know everything. Not about me. Not about Mom.' She paused, considering whether to continue. 'Not even about Abigail.'

Chapter 5

She felt an extra rebuke in the fact that she didn't have a key. Quincy probably had one, entrusted to her by Abigail in case of emergency. If Abigail had locked herself out or gone on vacation without turning the air-con off, who was she going to call? Madison didn't blame her younger sister. Truth is, she'd have done the same in her position: rely on the one you can rely on.

You don't always know everything. The words had stung her, replaying themselves as she had driven away from Quincy. So typical that, even now, her elder sister had managed to find a way to make Maddy feel excluded, as if she were somehow on the edge of the family, not privy to a knowledge shared by the other three women. Occasionally, Maddy felt that way, somehow lacking a clear place in the sibling line-up. Quincy was the eldest, Abigail the youngest but what was she? The middle sister? There wasn't even a name for that.

In her head and even, for one moment, out loud in the car – alone in the driving seat – Madison had rehearsed her comeback. *Truth is, Quincy, it's you who doesn't know everything. In fact, Quince, you know nothing. Thanks to us, you never did. You don't have the slightest idea what happened that day, do you?*

It was then that it struck her. With Abigail gone, and her mother in the state she was in, Madison was the only one left who knew. The only one left who remembered. The sensation of it left her queasy, as if she were at a great height looking down, her knees ready to buckle. It was like that thing they taught her in college, when she did a philosophy class: if a tree falls in the forest, and no one hears it, does it make a sound? If you are the last living soul to remember an event, did it even happen?

She considered the elevator but took the stairs, emerging onto the third floor to see the familiar yellow-and-black tape, barring her path to Abigail's front door. There was no one around to enforce it, but Madison halted all the same. The door was ajar and there were voices coming from inside. Madison stared at the door frame, noticing some scarring close to the lock. Leaning in, she could see that a very small part of the surround had splintered, so that two or three painted wood shards jutted forward. Was that fresh damage or had it been done weeks earlier? She could not be sure. *An initial, brief search of the apartment could not confirm any forced entry.*

'Hello?' she called out, still on the wrong side of the police tape. The voices inside stopped. A few moments later, the door opened wider to reveal a young, fair-haired police officer bulked out by his uniform. Over his shoulder, four paces back, stood Abigail's room-mate, Jessica. When she had first met her, whenever that was, Madison had marvelled at her bouncing hair and California Girl energy; she and Abigail looked as if they'd walked out of an orange juice commercial. But now Jessica's shoulders were rounded and her hair was limp.

'I'm Abigail Webb's sister,' Madison said, replying to the man's unspoken question. 'I won't touch anything,' she added as she lifted the tape and walked through the front door. By way of confirmation, Jessica stepped forward and opened her arms. Madison let herself be hugged, unsure whether she was receiving solace or administering it.

'I'm so sorry,' Jessica whispered, her cheeks wet against Maddy's hair.

'I'm sorry it was . . . I'm sorry you had to be here when . . .'

Once they had parted, Madison stepped back and looked at Jessica. She seemed crushed, as if the weight that had fallen on her had been physical. The police officer hovered nearby. They were still no more than a yard from the front door.

Maddy didn't want to ask her sister's friend to say it all over again, to make her re-live the moment of horror from several hours earlier. But she did, all the same.

Jessica started talking. 'I walked in, put on the light and there she was. Lying on her back. She was still and she looked . . . so strange.' Jessica's voice faltered. 'Her lips were blue. And her hair was real clammy.'

'Did you know straight away that she was dead?' Maddy said.

'I wasn't sure. At first I thought maybe she was breathing. Like tiny, faint breaths. I put my face by her mouth, to see if I could feel anything. And maybe I did. But it was just once. I waited and I didn't feel it again. And she was so cold . . .' Jessica's chin began to tremble.

Maddy pressed on. 'And you called the police right away?'

'Not right away. I tried talking to her. You know, "Abigail, wake up. It's me." I might have slapped her, I can't remember for sure. Her cheek was so cold.'

They talked for a moment or two longer when the police officer interrupted them. 'Miss?' He was looking at Jessica. 'Do you know this gentleman?'

They both turned around to see an older man, his face covered by a smog mask, filling the door frame.

'Daddy,' Jessica said, moving towards him. Only then did Madison notice the overnight bag packed by the front door.

42

Jessica turned around and said, 'I'm sorry, Madison. But my parents say it'll be best for me if I leave town for a few days. They think I need to be home.'

'Of course,' Maddy said, attempting to smile. 'Thanks, Jess.' She had heard Abigail refer to her that way, but it sounded wrong coming from her. As Jessica followed her father out of the door – explaining to him that he didn't need to wear the mask indoors – Madison called out to her once more. 'I'm sorry it had to be you.' Maddy knew as she said it that it could hardly have been anyone else. Certainly not her: she hadn't been inside this apartment for months. It might even have been a year.

Once Jessica and her father had gone, the police officer turned to Madison and murmured a quiet 'OK', as if to say this visit had no doubt been tough but her time was nearly up.

'I want to go into my sister's room.'

'I got very strict instructions, Miss. I'm not—'

'I know about your instructions and I know the rules. I'm allowed in, so long as you're present at all times to make sure I don't remove anything. The place has been photographed and dusted for prints already, right?'

'Yes, but have you checked this with—'

'If you have any problems at all, call the Chief of Police. Tell him this is what Madison Webb has requested.'

It was a gamble, but a low-risk one. She had met Doug Jarrett a few times, though he was hardly a contact: he'd been appointed to the top job just as she was leaving the crime beat. For all that, she reckoned her name was well-enough known around the LAPD that had this officer called her bluff and telephoned headquarters – which he wouldn't – she'd be OK.

He dipped his head in assent and she led the way, passing the living area and kitchen until she pushed open the door to the room that belonged to Abigail.

She stepped inside and was hit instantly by a wave of love and nostalgia that almost floored her. In just a few seconds, she was flooded by all things Abigail. On the bed were a couple of ethnic-style cushions Abigail had picked up on a trip to Santa Fe during her sophomore year. In the corner, the guitar she had taken up as a wannabe hippie in the eighth grade: Maddy only had to glance at it to hear again the sound of her sister strumming, out of time, to 'Nowhere Man'. On the wall, the familiar collage of postcards of recent art exhibitions. On the night table, a copy of the latest novel by the young Nigerian literary sensation whom Maddy had heard interviewed on NPR in the middle of the night. The book was opened and face down, suggesting that Abigail – unlike all the journalist bullshitters Maddy knew – was actually reading it. The bed was rumpled, each crease a reminder that not long ago a living, breathing person had slept in it.

The room too was messy, a pile of exercise clothes and underwear in one corner. On the desk was a pile of children's exercise books: all yellow, each one methodically laminated by hand. She opened one to see an infant's scrawl.

E is for England. England has a Queen. It rains a lot. They call soccer football.

And below it, Abigail's unmistakable hand in bright red.

Good job, Oscar! You've made E Week really fun.

Next to it, she had drawn a smiley face.

How strange that those children saw Abigail as their teacher; to Madison she was barely more than a child herself. She could see her younger sister in the tiny bathroom of their house in Beverlywood, an eleven-year-old girl styling her long fair hair with a pink hairbrush, trying, she said, to look like Maddy.

With effort, she could picture Abigail as a student, sweeping her hair back before heading out for a run round Circle Park: Abigail had gone through a phase of running barefoot, her hair trailing behind her. And Maddy remembered Abigail chewing on a plastic pen top, moving the hair away from her temple in concentration.

But the image that bobbed up again and again was the one she tried to push deep below the surface.

Madison looked at the framed mirror above the desk. She ignored her own reflection and looked instead at everything tucked into the edges, all the way around the border. More arty postcards – a Klimt and a Sargent – the odd note and several photographs. One in particular pulled her up short.

It was a picture of a man Maddy had not seen in years. So long, in fact, that she had almost forgotten his face. But there he was, broad-faced, his hair dark brown with only the odd strand of grey, his jaw strong, coming forward just enough to suggest a fighter: her father, a man so patriotic he had named his three daughters after American presidents. (Abigail was the closest he could get to Abe Lincoln.)

On the opposite side of the glass was a picture of similar vintage of their mother, young and kitted out in the fashion of the times: leggings, T-shirt slipping off the shoulder, big hair. Above it, two more. One of Quincy and Abigail together, at Abigail's graduation. The other a picture Maddy had not seen, though she instantly remembered the occasion: Thanksgiving at their mother's house five years earlier, Abigail and Maddy caught in a moment of genuinely unstoppable laughter, their faces hurting with the pleasure of it. Their mother must have taken the photograph; Quincy was in it, looking on and smiling but not caught up in the delirium.

There were other pictures. One with Jessica in college; another with Greg, a boyfriend of that era. And there, at the top right, something she had very nearly overlooked: a scribbled note. Only now did she realize that the scribble was her own.

Abigail, you have nothing to fear. You are smart, capable, energetic and light up any room just by walking into it.

That school will be SO lucky to have you. Knock 'em dead.
Maddy x

Madison stared at the note for far longer than it took to read it. She could scarcely remember writing it, though it could only have been ahead of Abigail's interview at the elementary school, which made it about three years old. Harder to absorb was that Abigail had kept it. It had been dashed off, the work of a few seconds. It was, Madison could see now, written on a Post-it. And yet Abigail had treasured it all this time.

Madison looked around, conscious of the policeman watching her, knowing his patience could expire at any moment. On the desk was a box spilling over with costume jewellery, alongside some loose items of make-up. It was no tidier than Abigail's childhood bedroom.

Something about the disorder hit Madison hard. It was the disorder of day-to-day life, of objects grabbed and put down in a hurry, of the random rush of someone alive. Yet here they were now: as still and silent as exhibits in a museum, never to be moved or used again. They were lifeless because they belonged to someone now dead. Madison felt as if a thick, toxic cloud were growing and spreading through her chest.

She took a last look around, seeing more confirmation of Abigail's deadness in every item: shoes tucked under the bed, a small shelf of novels, a hair-scrunchy next to the lamp. Each glimpse despatched a sharp stab of pain. She would quickly check the closet and leave.

Inside were more clothes than she was expecting; so many hangers on the rail that she could barely move them along. There were a couple of skirts she guessed Abigail wore for school, but the rest was strictly for going out: a succession of sparkling tops, different pairs of pants, including at least two pairs in leather, sheath dresses and skirts that were more micro than mini.

She thought of Quincy, blaming Madison for introducing Abigail to – what had she called it? – an 'urban lifestyle' and reflected it was true in a way. Just after Abigail had graduated college, she had stayed with Maddy for a few months while she found a job and somewhere to live. They had gone out together, Maddy introducing her younger sister to her crowd at the *Times*. Madison had had to expend a lot of energy that summer, diverting the attentions of reporters far too old, unattractive or married for her baby sister.

Abigail had not dressed like this then, neither of them had. Madison pulled out one hanger at random: a jacket with a high-end European label she recognized only from the fashion pages. She brought it closer to her eyes, to check it was genuine rather than one of the knock-offs you could pick up in Santee Alley. The stitching was usually the giveaway. Judging by that standard, this one was real. She put it back and saw another: equally expensive, equally authentic.

Quincy's voice was back inside her head. *You don't always know everything. Not even about Abigail.*

'Is there something you're looking for, Miss? Remember, there'll be some effects returned to you by the coroner's office.'

'Thanks,' she said, opening and closing drawers, hesitant to rifle through her sister's underwear. 'I'm nearly done.' She took a last look around, aware that everything in this room had once touched the skin of her young, beautiful sister – and that it never would again.

But what made her head throb was the puzzle she had just glimpsed, the puzzle her sister had left behind.

Chapter 6

Back in her apartment, she all but had to push Jeff out of the door. He had been waiting for her, sitting in his parked car, for God knows how long. He wanted to see how she was doing, he said, make sure she was OK. She allowed him to come up, accepted his offer of coffee, bought not made, and allowed him to place a portion of *youtiao* on the table, the sticks of fried bread which he knew she liked. But she would not let him comfort her any longer. She told him she needed to rest. He raised a sceptical eyebrow at that, which she ignored. She hoped he would believe that grief would succeed where meditation, Temazepam and the latest supposedly cure-all import from Shanghai, the saliva of a swallow, had all failed.

Once the door was closed, she cleared the desk, which meant lifting the piles of transcripts and documents about LA's secret warren of sweatshops off the table and putting them under it, where they could not distract her. She paused as she remembered Jane Goldstein's parting request for a follow-up story. Then she took a sip of coffee and powered up her trusted Lenovo laptop.

There, lodged in the corner of the screen, was the outline of her Day Two piece, drafted during the long stretch of sleepless nights when she worked at the sweatshop. Of course it was insane for her to think of her job now. Her inner Quincy was adamant: *Don't tell me you're going to work.* Easy coming from Quincy, who identified herself as an 'SAHM' on that hideously smug mothers' website: Stay at Home Mom. Besides, this story was almost written. It made no sense to leave it sitting here on the machine. All it required was a quick read-through. If she sent it over now, that would buy her time with Howard and Jane: she could then spend the next day or two undisturbed, getting on with what really mattered. She'd give it half an hour, no more.

Forty-five minutes later the piece was done. Not as polished as she would have liked; the newsdesk would have to check some of the numbers. But it would do. She pressed 'Send' and hoped no one would look too closely at the time-stamp on the email or work out when, exactly, and under what circumstances she had written it. She sought to suppress the rebuke that was rising within her and whose target was herself.

Enough of this, she told herself. This navel-gazing would do Abigail no good. She had to focus on what mattered. The first thing she looked up was 'heroin'. She read rapidly through the medical and science sites, about the physiology of an overdose, the chemical and neurological reactions. She didn't know precisely what she was looking for – just that she needed confirmation of her iron certainty that, if Abigail did have heroin in her bloodstream, she had played no part in putting it there.

Every word she read triggered a memory of her once-beautiful sister reduced to a body on a slab, the pale skin drained of all life, her lips edged with frozen blue. She had read enough to know that a heroin overdose brought no pain, just a kind of instant, weightless bliss, but that did not stop her imagining the fear that must have gripped her hopeful younger sister as she understood that she was entering her final moments.

But had Abigail understood that? *Nothing that suggested a struggle.* Maddy recalled the words and, above all, the expression on the detective's face as she had said them. How dared she imply that Abigail had been some kind of willing participant in her own death? Of course it was murder, of course it was. Madison just had to get the police to realize it. And soon: she had covered enough homicide cases to know that speed was critical. They always talked about that 'golden hour', the period immediately after a homicide has been discovered when detectives are able to gather the most, and the best, forensic evidence from a crime scene. Maddy feared that time had been and gone. That while they played around with their absurd sex-game theory, valuable evidence might be vanishing.

But she could not quite shake off Quincy's words. *You don't always know everything.* Quincy had insisted that Abigail did not do anything so 'urban' as drugs, but that did not exclude the possibility that she was daring in other ways. Did Abigail have a dark side hidden only from her, but known to the others? Maddy had always imagined it was only she who had sexual secrets, who had made countless bad choices. She had always assumed that Abigail was as wholesome as Quincy was straitlaced. But maybe she was wrong. And how to explain the high-end clothing she had seen in the closet, each item far beyond the reach of an elementary school teacher's budget?

Her phone vibrated. She glanced down: Detective Jeff Howe again. High probability that he was merely 'checking in' – his phrase – making sure she was OK, even though next to no time had passed since he had last been here. But there was a chance he was calling for the reason she had asked: to convey information. She pressed the green button.

'Hi Madison. You OK?'

'Yes,' she replied, hoping her terseness sounded sad rather than impatient, even though the latter was the truth.

'I've seen the coroner's report.'

'Right. Can you—'

'Not the whole thing. Only a summary, by the looks of things. But I've got the concluding section.'

'And?'

'There were signs of pressure on the neck, suggestive of a chokehold. And indications that she was held, with some force, by her head, around the temples. Probably from behind.'

The thought of it, the *picture* of it that materialized instantly, made her unsteady. A kind of queasiness rose through her, as if she were dizzy. To visualize with great clarity her sister grabbed and held by a stranger, the fear that she knew would have consumed Abigail at that moment, the word *chokehold* – all of it made Madison nauseous. The sensation was physical.

But she forced the sickness away, as if she were pushing bile back down her throat. She would force herself to think, not to feel, to process what she had just heard the way she imagined Barbara Miller and Howe's fellow cops would: as information. As data: nothing more, nothing less. Judged like that, as the detectives would judge it, she told herself these latest findings were interesting and useful, but hardly destructive of the police's rough sex hypothesis. That Abigail had been nearly strangled did not mean she had been nearly strangled by a stranger. If anything, this evidence could be held to strengthen the LAPD's working theory of the case, confirming that the rough sex was really rough. Madison said nothing of this. Only, 'What else?'

'No needle retrieved from the scene.'

'Are there pictures?'

'None I've seen.'

'Jeff, don't spare me because you think I can't handle it. I can—'

'I'm not sparing you. I told you, I haven't seen the complete report.'

'All right, I'm sorry. Please. Go on.'

'No needle. And just one needle mark. No others.'

'Which confirms Abigail was no junkie,' Madison said, irritated by the betraying quaver of her voice.

'Actually,' Jeff replied, 'there's a note on that. Saying needle marks can often close up within weeks.'

'For God's sake, Jeff, Abigail was not a drug user.'

'I didn't write this report, Madison. I'm just the jerk risking his job to tell you what it says.'

'You're right. I'm sorry.' She swallowed, girding herself for the next and obvious question. 'Jeff, I have to ask.'

'Yes?' he said, though he knew.

She closed her eyes, bracing herself for what she would have to say as much as for what she might have to hear. She sought to smother her inquiry in the language of forensics, as if that might take the edge off. 'Was there any sign of sexual contact? Any . . . exchange of bodily fluids? Anything like that?' Her voice petered out.

The policeman answered quickly. 'No sign at all, Madison. None.'

Madison thanked Jeff again – aware of the obligation that was building between them – and hung up. Only then did she let out a long, deep exhalation, one she had not wanted him to hear. Thank God for that. For that small mercy at least, thank God. Whatever hell Abigail had endured, she had not been raped. In that instant when Jeff first told her Abigail had been found dead, that had been Madison's starting assumption.

But that only made the horror more baffling. At least a sex crime had an obvious, if grotesque, motive. But how was she to make sense of Abigail's death now? Perhaps the LAPD would cling to its sex-game theory all the same, but it struck Madison as a strange kind of sex that involved no contact. No, she was certain. This was no accident. It was murder. But the question remained, sharper now than ever: why would anyone want to kill her sister?

Chapter 7

The crowd was glowing in dawn sunshine, the faces turned upward. They were happy, some clutching flags bearing the stars and stripes. The faces at the centre made up the standard LA crowd: black woman, Hispanic man, Korean children, younger white woman and finally, because you had to have a white male somewhere, a white-haired, seventy-plus man, smiling a benign, grandfatherly smile. But dotted among them was a departure from the usual formula: a noticeable number of Chinese, including several young men. They were smiling too. Not wide grins, but gentle, summer-evening smiles – relaxed, content, as if marvelling at the good fortune of it all.

The music swelled, an informal, slightly ragged choir of voices that climaxed on the phrase, 'California, You're My Home'.

Leo Harris reached for the remote and watched it again, this time on half-speed. He wanted to examine the faces at the margins, those the viewer would not notice on the first or second airing but would process all the same, if only subliminally. He was glad to see a couple more Latinos and what he guessed was a Jewish man. An older white woman: good. More Chinese. Seated, he turned to the young woman standing by his right shoulder and said only: 'Blacks.'

'I'm sorry?'

'African-Americans. You've only got one.' He paused the video, frozen now on the image of a beautiful black woman, her long hair in tight spirals, clutching a miniature flag. 'She's great, but we need more. That's ten per cent of our vote, remember.'

'But I thought you said—'

'That's true. So use a child or an older man. No one's frightened of them. Doesn't have to be real old. Just not young. Bit of grey in the sideburns, that'll do it.'

He turned back to the screen, playing the rest at normal speed. He sang along to the line: 'California, You're My Home'. Then, as the last word faded, he intoned in a voice not quite his own, '"I'm Richard Berger – and I approved this message."'

He stood up. 'OK, where's Susan?'

A nervous flutter passed through the room as the heads of those people relieved not to be Susan turned and looked for her. She was at the back, her head down, every few seconds swiping the page on her tablet. Leo guessed she was absorbed in poll numbers.

'Hey, Susan. Can we talk slogan?'

She glanced up, then returned to the illuminated page before her. 'Sure.'

'Can you remind me what we agreed would be the theme of this spot?' He was speaking across the room.

'Unity, harmony, all that.' She didn't look up.

'Er, yeah. That's the theme of the campaign. I mean this particular spot.'

Now at last she lifted her head slowly, as if to say, *I am a senior figure in this operation. I will not jump at your command like the rest of these candy girls in their skinny jeans and fitted tops. I will take my time if I want to.* The words she spoke out loud were: 'We can all get along.'

'Correct. We can all get along. No matter who we are. But

with one group in mind especially.' Pausing for a response and not getting it, Leo gave what was meant as a prompt, watched by the rest of the room. There were about a dozen of them, almost all young, including those who were not interns, written off, in the brutal vernacular of the trade, as mere *muffins*: sugary snacks for the delectation of the older hands. Susan Patinkin, campaign veteran, was the only person present over the age of forty. 'The clue is on the screen.' He rewound, freezing on an image which included two Chinese men. Neither were in uniform, but both were of military age.

Susan looked, then sighed. 'Your point is?'

'My point is that, yes, this ad is saying we can all get along. Even those guys.' With his back to the screen, so that he could still face Susan, he gestured towards the Chinese faces. 'But what's wrong with this picture?'

No answer from Susan, so now he looked around. 'Anybody?'

A hand went up. Young guy in a T-shirt decorated by a chimp in headphones, doubtless involved with social media. Leo had no idea of his name. He pointed at him instead. 'You.'

'They're not singing?'

Leo hurled his pen at him, forcing him to duck. 'For fuck's sake! Am I really the only person who can see the problem here?' He turned back towards the screen, spooled to the final few seconds, halfway through the final refrain. The choir was in full voice.

'. . . *you're my home!*'

'OK.' It was Susan, sheepish at the back of the room.

'Thank you!' Leo said to the ceiling, his hands spread like a preacher at the pulpit. 'Yes, Governor Richard Berger will bring harmony to the state of California. Yes, he will ensure the people of this state will get along with each other and even with the garrison. Yes, there will be no riots on his watch. But that doesn't mean he wants these guys to stay *forever*. He doesn't want California to be their *home*.'

Susan had now abandoned the data logs on her tablet. 'California, We Love You.'

'Better.'

She had another go. 'California, Place of Harmony.'

'Too Chairman Mao.'

There was silence. Eventually Leo turned to the woman who had been at his shoulder, taking notes during the viewing, and who was, as it happened, wearing a tightly fitted top: knitted, cream-coloured and, Leo clocked, unable to hide a pair of very generously shaped breasts. 'Collect four suggestions for alternative tag lines to run on this spot. Then focus-group all five.'

He was already at the door, giving a curt nod to Susan as he passed her, when the assistant called out. 'Focus-group five? But you said we needed four. What's the fifth?'

'Richard Berger. Bringing California Together.'

There would be another year of this, Leo thought. All right, closer to ten months, but it would be like this every day. In fact, days like this would seem like a breeze come the fall. He remembered what Bill Doran used to say, his face cragged and scarred after more than thirty years on the road: 'Campaigns are never tiring – unless you lose. Then they hurt like hell.'

As Leo boarded the jet that would take him and Mayor Richard Berger to Sacramento – squaring the Democratic delegation in the state assembly, ensuring they endorsed early and often – he allowed three thoughts to circulate. First, he had no intention of losing. He would sweat from now till the first Tuesday after the first Monday in November to ensure his boss was installed in the Governor's Mansion. Second, he already regretted his own, populist suggestion that the mayor, as the Democratic candidate, should eschew the private jet offered to him by donors and fly commercial whenever possible. Make no mistake, come Memorial Day, if not earlier, Leo would be invoking that 'whenever possible' clause and the wiggle room it very deliberately allowed.

Third, he was thinking of Bill Doran. He knew that was bad form, or 'malpractice', to use Doran's preferred word. It was a violation of one of Bill's own commandments: never let them get inside your head. Normally, Leo observed that stricture without effort. But this time was different. His adversary, his opposite number on the rival campaign, was the very man who had taught him the fundamentals of political combat. If Leo were to win in November, he would have to turn his first boss and ongoing, if occasional, mentor into a loser.

That they would clash one day, he had always known. They were on opposite sides of the aisle. It was only through a freak accident that they had worked together in the first place. It was Leo's first campaign. He had signed up straight out of college as an unpaid volunteer for a millionaire Democrat-turned-independent, who had hired Bill Doran – the best known Republican consultant in the state – to underline his new, bipartisan credentials. It was a gimmick that had ended in disaster: the candidate was crushed, despite the expensive advice he had hired.

But it had been the best possible education for Leo. Doran spotted him early, deeming him 'the brightest of the bunch, no contest'. He let him sit in on strategy meetings way above his pay-grade, patched him into conference calls with the candidate, allowed him to hear Doran alternately soothe or rev up 'the talent' before the cue came to walk out on stage at a rally or fundraiser. 'You can do this. You're going to be the next senator from the great state of California.' All bullshit, but necessary.

Soon Doran was beckoning Leo to come forward and look over his shoulder when the data came in, the charts and spreadsheets filled with numbers gathered by pollsters crawling over every corner of California. Doran taught Leo to look first for Ventura County, specifically the 26th Congressional District. 'That's a toss-up seat, Leo. If you're ahead there, you're ahead.'

As for TV spots, Doran was the master. There was no one with a better grasp of the visual campaign. What looked right, what looked wrong. No detail escaped him. To this day, more than nine years later, Leo could not look at a TV ad for anything – from soda pop to Depends undergarments – without seeing it through the eyes of his former mentor. When they last met for a drink, after running into each other during a straw poll event in Bakersfield four months ago, he had sat back and listened, astonished to discover that Bill Doran's supply of political wisdom was still not exhausted. The man himself, however . . . well, that was a different story.

Leo buckled up. The boss was next to him, still on a call to a radio station in Oakland. 'I agree, Trisha. That's one reason why I'm running. I want to be able to look every Californian in the eye and . . .'

Leo made a mental note. Save the 'every Californian in the eye' for the tax pledge. Don't waste it on other stuff, blurs the message.

He gazed out of the window, the candidate having been placed in the aisle: 'No point flying commercial if people don't see you flying commercial.' Leo thought about the Mail Room last night, enjoying the images his memory reflexively served up for his perusal. He caught himself as he realized it was not Jade or her long neck and backless dress that he was picturing but the maddening, repeatedly insulting Maddy Webb. His reflection in the porthole told him he was smiling.

'Trisha, I'm glad you asked me that. I know in my own area . . .'

Good. Berger was learning. Leo had told him: fight the habit of the last years and stop mentioning Los Angeles by name. It only turns off voters upstate. Downstate too, for that matter. Anywhere but LA, in fact.

He could see the mayor was on his last question. Quick check of the phone before take-off. He scrolled through his messages. One from an old friend.

Just heard. Can't believe it.

Just heard what? He couldn't stand it when people played enigmatic. Total power trip, lording over you the fact they had caught some nugget of knowledge that you lacked. He would not succumb. He would not send the words his pal wanted to hear: 'Can't believe what?'

It was bound to be about the food export story. There were new figures showing Californians were exporting so many of their staples – oranges, strawberries and avocados among others – they were running short themselves. He checked his watch. Yep, this was about the time the numbers were due for release.

But he checked Weibo to be sure. He scrolled through, but stopped short.

Tragic news about @maddywebbnews's sister. Thoughts and prayers are with her family.

And then:

What a senseless waste of precious life. Hearts go out to @maddywebbnews #tragedy

That came with a link to an *LA Times* story:

Abigail Webb, 22, an elementary school teacher from North Hollywood, was found dead early Monday in what police now believe was a likely homicide. An LAPD spokesperson would give few details, but sources indicate the cause of death was a heroin overdose. Despite an initial examination of the dead woman's apartment which could find no confirmed signs of forced entry, detectives say a later probe of the scene found damage suggesting a break-in. Ms Webb is the younger sister of the award-winning LA Times *reporter, Madison Webb.*

Leo read the words several times over, believing it less and less each time. He and Madison had been together for just short of a year, but he had seen Abigail at least a dozen times. She was the first member of her family Madison had let him meet. He liked her: she had all the fizzing energy of Madison and none of the *taidu*, the attitude. Perhaps a bit too wide-eyed for his tastes, but her enthusiasm was contagious. He and Maddy had been to see a show at the Hollywood Bowl on a double date with Abigail and a short-lived boyfriend, dropped soon afterwards. But once those two were up and dancing, Maddy and even Leo – usually too shy and world-weary for such things – had felt compelled to follow.

Now he thought about it, Madison was different around Abigail. The cynicism receded; she was gentle. She smiled more. In their moments together, the older looking out for the younger, he realized he had caught a glimpse of the mother Maddy might one day be – a thought which he had never articulated at the time and whose tenderness shocked him.

He read the weibs again. He was scrolling further down, as if he might see a message voiding the others, announcing a mistake. He kept scrolling.

'Leo, you better shut that down. Take-off.'

He said nothing, but turned off the phone all the same and stared right ahead.

They were fully airborne, the plane straightened, before the mayor spoke. 'You mind telling me what this is about? You look like shit.' Getting no answer, he pushed on. 'You've seen some numbers and you don't know how to break it to me, is that it? This that Santa Ana focus group? I'm not worried. Wait till we're on the air in—'

'It's nothing to do with the campaign.'

60

'You don't care about anything but the campaign, so tell me: what's the problem?'

Leo turned his face to look at his boss for the first time. 'There's been a murder. Woman, early twenties, found dead in her apartment in North Hollywood. Suspected heroin overdose.'

Berger hesitated, letting his eye linger, as if he were assessing a job applicant rather than his most trusted advisor. 'OK.'

'We need to get out ahead of this one, Mr Mayor. We have to make sure that this is investigated with the utmost thoroughness.' His own voice sounded strange to him, too formal.

'We always do that, Leo.'

He tried to steady himself, took a sip from the water glass on the tray in front of him, which appeared to have arrived by magic: he had no memory of anyone giving it to him. He told himself to get a grip. *Focus.*

'LAPD are only calling it a "likely" homicide. Which means they've got some doubts. But the victim's sister's a journalist. She's going to be demanding answers. High-profile, award-winner, big following on Weibo. That means this case is going to be noticed. People are going to be watching the Department, the DA, to see how they handle it.'

'Sure.'

'And they'll be watching you. You don't want to be going into the summer with a big, unsolved murder on the books.'

'So what's your advice?'

'I think that when we land your first call should be to the Chief of Police, ensure this case is a priority.'

'As soon as we land, huh? That urgent.'

'I think so, yes.'

'Anything else you want to tell me?'

Leo turned back towards the window, the city below now little more than a blur. He pictured Abigail and then he pictured Madison. He shook his head.

'Anything else you *ought* to tell me, Leo?'

'No.' He paused. 'Like what?'

'You sure you don't have a conflict of interest here?'

Leo hesitated, so Berger spoke again. 'I know who the victim of this murder is, Leo. The police department of this city – sorry, of the *area* – do still talk to me. I know her sister is your ex, so there's no need to bullshit me, OK?' His gaze lingered into a stare until eventually he looked away, towards the window, watching the earth below swallowed up by clouds. When he turned back, he was wearing an expression Leo had not seen before, one that unnerved him. 'As it happens, I agree with your advice,' the mayor said. 'We need to get out in front on this one. In fact, I'd go further. You need to make this story go away. And, most important of all, you need to keep me out of it.'

Chapter 8

The phone had been buzzing all day and was buzzing again now, vibrating its way across her desk. Maddy glanced down at the screen and decided she would treat this the same way as the rest, that she would not pick up.

She had ignored Weibo altogether, or rather she had avoided the continuous flow of messages directed at her. She did not want to read words of condolence, no matter how touching or heartfelt. She had, however, taken a look at Abigail's timeline: so far it consisted of tributes and declarations of shock – many of them addressed to Abigail herself. She skimmed her sister's Facebook page too, filling up with messages in a similar vein. But for herself, she wanted none of it.

She had made two exceptions. The first was a call from Katharine, saying that Enrica was on her way over with a vat of soup and that she would not take no for an answer. At that moment, Enrica had grabbed the phone, proving she was not in fact on the way, and said, 'Darling, don't even talk to me. Just let me into the kitchen. I'll be silent, I'll be *invisible*. But you have to eat.' Maddy had conceded, but just hearing her bereaved friend's voice had apparently proved too much for Enrica. She sent something like a howl down the phone, which brought Katharine back on. 'She loves you so much, that's all.'

The second call was from Quincy. Maddy had stared at the phone for at least six rings before finally deciding to pick up.

She offered no pleasantries, but asked straightaway about the conversation between Quincy and their mother. 'How was it?'

'Well, it's done.'

'Did she understand?'

'I think so. She asked after you.'

'After me?'

'First thing she said. "Is Madison OK? She'll know what to do."'

'She doesn't know what she's saying.'

'I'm not so sure, you know. With her, I'm not so sure.'

'Do you think it was right to tell her? Maybe we should have spared her. Or maybe we should have asked Dr Glazer first.'

'If you felt that way, Maddy, you should have told me. Or come with me. Otherwise you don't get to have an opinion.'

'I'm not . . . I'm not arguing with you.' Madison sighed, turning her mouth away from the phone so that her sister would not hear her exhalation. 'I'm grateful you did it, Quincy. You're braver than me.' She said it and it sounded right, even though she knew it was partly a lie. And for a second she remembered the secret that, brutally, she now held alone, the event that existed in the memory of no one but her.

She felt a wave of tiredness, one of those that seemed to taunt her. She knew that if she did not surrender to it immediately, closing her eyes this instant, the moment would pass. Perhaps this was how surfers felt on the ocean, confronted by the rare perfect wave that seems to say, 'Ride me now or lose me forever'.

'Yes, well. It's done.'

'And she understood it was Abigail. Did you need to explain that?'

'I think she understood. I said it was peaceful, that it was an accident.'

'Maybe we should have said she'd gone travelling or something.'

'Don't be ridiculous, Madison. It's everywhere already. When I went to see Mom, they were showing a picture on the local news. That's why we had to tell her. Better coming from us, or rather better coming from me, than the TV.'

'What picture?'

'From the high school yearbook.'

'Jeez.' There was a silence down the line. 'Quincy, you still there?' Another pause and then her sister's voice.

'I think it's because of you.'

'What, the picture? I would never—'

'I don't mean you *gave* it to them. I mean this interest in Abigail. It's because of you.'

'I'm not sure that makes—'

'Of course it is. It's all over Weibo, tributes from journalists and news people. And on the *Times* website: "Abigail Webb, sister of the award-winning *LA Times* reporter."'

'Is that what it says? I had no hand in that, Quincy, I promise.'

'Well, the damage is done. You can't change your precious career, can you? That's why I'm going to the school now, to pick up the kids. I've got to get to them before Facebook does. Though I'm probably too late.'

But those were the only two calls she took. The rest, Maddy let pass. Once or twice, she checked her texts: messages of sympathy and shock from friends, colleagues, from Howard on the newsdesk, scolding her for filing in such circumstances (adding that they planned to run the piece tonight and she should call if she had any suggestions for accompanying graphics), even from Jane Goldstein herself. And a couple from Jeff Howe, unreturned because they were apparently offering no news. 'Just wanted to check in, see how you're doing. If there's anything . . .'

She thought about resting but was too agitated even to attempt it. She was aching all over, the bright, pulsating centre of the pain as always radiating out from, and homing in on, her lower back. All she could see was Abigail on that slab.

The pacing back and forth in front of the window was providing nothing except the illusion of respite. Maddy returned to the computer, to look again at the tabs she'd left open. One was on the pharmacology of a heroin overdose:

Heroin is an opiate, similar to morphine but more potent, quicker-acting and more addictive. It acts as both an analgesic (pain suppressor), and an anxiolytic (anxiety suppressor), as well as producing a feeling of euphoria.

There was information on the signs that any doctor would look for if presented with a person suspected of an overdose: *weak or no pulse, delirium, drowsiness or disorientation, low blood pressure, shallow, slow or laboured breathing, dry mouth, extremely constricted 'pinpoint' pupils, discoloured tongue, lips and fingernails turned blue, muscle and stomach spasms and constipation.*

Jessica had seen the strange colour of Abigail's tongue and had reported the blue of her lips – though, poor thing, she had assumed those were things that happened to every dead body. Abigail had been her first corpse.

It struck Madison that Abigail would have been just as clueless. Thank God, she had seen no such horrors in her short, bright life. That stuff had been left to Maddy, who had seen enough nastiness for both of them. She had done her best to spare her younger sister.

But she had not done enough.

The subject will typically pass out very rapidly in what may feel like a euphoric, rapturous rush. The breathing will slow, they will become cold and sweaty, the hair can become matted with sweat, excess saliva may exit the mouth, so that the subject can appear to be drooling, although the mouth will also be dry. Eventually, the breathing stops entirely and later the heart will follow.

None of that was any comfort now, but Maddy filed it away for later use: the meagre solace that her sister did not die in pain.

There was a bit more – about how heroin could elude an initial examination by a coroner because the key chemical agent disperses within the body after death – but none of it helped. She headed to the search window on the machine and typed the words 'heroin', 'death' and 'Los Angeles'.

A raft of news stories appeared. New figures released by the Health and Human Services Department, the opening of a rehab clinic in Burbank, academic research on methadone by UCLA. She refined the search adding the initials, 'LAPD'.

That turned up some brief stories from the Metro section of the *LA Weekly*:

A batch of heroin linked to a number of fatalities is believed to have claimed the life of a known drug user in South Central LA. The 33-year-old man died suddenly at a property on Normandie Avenue shortly after 5pm Wednesday. Police are not treating the death as suspicious and have referred it to the coroner for an inquest. 'The deceased was a known drug user and his death follows a number of other deaths of drug users in the region in recent weeks,' said a police spokesperson.

There was the story of a mother in Vermont Square who had narrowly escaped eviction after a court found that she had knowingly allowed her twenty-seven-year-old son to store heroin and crack cocaine in his bedroom. Another about an addict jailed for dealing drugs to a cop. And one more about a successful, undercover police operation that had 'smashed' a drugs ring operating out of Boyle Heights.

The problem was in that first story: *known drug user*. That there was a whole netherworld of dealers, addicts and corrupt cops, themselves addicts; of skeletal teenage girls selling their bodies to pay for the next fix; of men who would roam the city looking for coin boxes, on payphones or parking meters, to smash, hoping to disgorge enough quarters to pay for another bag of powder – that this Hades existed in the streets and alleys of this city, she already knew. It had been part of her beat. After child abuse stories, it was the area of crime reporting she hated most.

But that was not Abigail's world. No one could have been further from it. Quincy's words from early this morning – *You don't always know everything* – resurfaced once more, as they had all day. Whatever Quincy had meant by that, it surely didn't extend to Abigail sinking to the level of those lowlifes.

Madison stared at the screen, suddenly aware that she didn't even know what she was looking for. She sprang back up and paced again, her teeth crunching down on the top of the plastic pen she had been chewing for the last half-hour.

Drug addicts who'd died of drug overdoses were not going to help. She needed to find people like Abigail, those who were avowedly non-junkies who had nevertheless died that way.

But how? As she walked around the room, she thought of the story she would write reporting what had just happened to her sister. What would the headline say?

She rushed back to her seat and typed the words in the search window:

Mystery heroin death

A string of items appeared, one linking to a novel, another to a TV movie, a third to a story in London three years earlier. She added another word to her search. *California*.

Now the page filled with news stories, including several from the other end of the state and from two or three years earlier. She eliminated those, confining herself only to deaths that had taken place in the last year. Her first click was on the *San Diego Mercury Tribune*, from nine months ago.

The widow of a San Diego man has filed an unprecedented complaint against the state's drug rehabilitation program, alleging that he was given an incorrect and excessive dose of the transition drug methadone which led to his . . .

No. She tried another one. Once more, the problem was a tainted batch of heroin.

She clicked on a third, nearly a year earlier, in Orange County. This told of a grief-stricken father baffled by his daughter's apparent suicide by heroin overdose. '*I always thought she loved life too much to kill herself,*' he told reporters. But, in the sixth paragraph, he admitted his daughter had been depressed for several months. Not so baffling after all. She clicked on.

Finally she came across an item in her own paper, just a few paragraphs long, from two weeks earlier.

Padilla family threaten to sue coroner over woman's death

A Boyle Heights family is demanding the coroner's department reopen the case of Rosario Padilla, a 22-year-old woman registered as a suicide after she was found dead from a drugs overdose. Mr Mario Padilla, the dead woman's brother, refuses to accept that his sister took her own life, insisting that 'she never took drugs in her life, not one single time'.

In a statement, a spokesperson for the coroner's office said, 'We very much respect Mr Padilla's grief at this very difficult time. It is very common for close relatives of those who have died at their own hand to struggle to come to terms with the loss. Our thoughts and prayers are with the entire Padilla family.'

Madison could feel a throbbing in her brain. Not a headache, but rather the opposite. A surge of energy or whatever chemical it was that kept her awake even after days without sleep.

She opened a few more tabs, cross-checked the information she had, then sent it to her phone. She grabbed her keys and a coat and left the apartment as it was, not turning out so much as a single light. For the first time since her sister's death, Madison Webb had an idea.

Chapter 9

'This is all about the sister, right?'

'Give me a break, Barbara.' They were at police HQ, round the back by the fire escape – the only area now allowed to smokers, a category that included Barbara Miller, and reliably the best place to catch her.

'I don't mind, Jeff. Just admit it. You want me to give you details of a sensitive police investigation so that you can share them with the sister of the deceased who you just so happen to have a hard-on for.'

Detective Jeff Howe smiled in appalled disbelief. 'You're unbelievable, Barbara, you really are. Just help me out here. The family is distraught.'

'I don't blame them, honey. That's quite a scene they found in there.'

Jeff eyed her carefully. Though three years younger than him, she had always acted the older. An African-American who had come up the hard way, she spoke with a shrug in her voice as if she had seen it all before. No armed robbery, no drugs bust and only the rarest homicide ever struck her as a surprise. A father who stayed with his kids, a man who didn't whack his woman around the head when drunk or high, now *that* was a novelty.

'What's that supposed to mean, Barbara?

She let out a jet of smoke. 'Pretty girl on her back. Nothing taken, nothing broken. That's what I mean.'

'For Christ's sake, we're not back on this, are we? She had heavy bruises on her neck and on her temples. The lock was damaged because someone had forced their way in.'

'Because? *Because?* That new partner of yours rotting your brain, sweetheart? You need to go back to detective school, my friend, if you're coming out with that shit. We can say the lock was damaged. We can say that *suggests* someone forced their way in. We don't get to *because* just because we want to. No way.'

'All right. So why don't you tell me what explains those marks on the door frame?'

'Could be anything, you know that as well as I do. Could be a domestic. Could be an ex-boyfriend, trying to bust his way back in. Could even . . .' She didn't complete the sentence.

'Could even what, Barbara?'

'She could even have done it herself. On her way in.'

'What, Abigail?'

'Say she was wasted from wherever she'd just been, all right? Maybe she couldn't find her key, pushes at the door a little bit, gives it a shove.'

'You think she was high before she even got home?'

'Look, I don't know, Jefferson. That's my point. We don't know what happened here. You especially. Which is exactly how it should be. This is not your case, remember.'

'OK. Just tell me, do you accept this is a homicide?'

'Yes, I do.'

'OK. So why are you still hinting this is some kind of sex thing? We know for a fact there was no penetration, no sign of sexual contact at all.'

'OK. But that just makes the "forced entry" scenario a little harder to explain, don't you think? How many cases d'you know where a stranger busts into the apartment of some gorgeous girl and doesn't lay a finger on her? Not many, right? Look, all I'm saying is I'm not sure you know what some of these white girls get up to. I thought, since your divorce and all, you might be out there a bit more, if you know what I mean. But let me enlighten you. There's a whole scene, darling. What's that word for them everyone keeps using? *Baimufei*?'

'*Baifumei*. But Abigail wasn't like that. She wasn't some pampered rich girl. She taught elementary school. They grew up in Beverlywood.'

'Yeah and Zong Qinghou grew up on a salt farm.'

'Meaning?'

'Meaning, people change.'

Jeff kicked at a loose cigarette butt and then pulled himself up to full height, to signal a change in direction. 'All right. We're not going to agree. It doesn't matter what I say anyway, because, as you say, this is not my investigation.'

'See. It's not true we don't agree. We agree on *that*.'

'OK, OK. Forget me. Take me out of it. A young woman is dead here. She left a family behind who have no idea how it happened. We owe it to them to find out who did this.'

'That's my job, sweetheart. You don't need to tell me that. Besides, I'm getting all the pressure I need already.'

'How do you mean?'

'Sutcliffe says this is a "priority".'

'And where's he getting that from, do you think?'

'I don't need to think. I *know*. He told me.' She used the index finger of her smoking hand to point upward.

'The Chief of Police?'

'Uh-huh.' She took one last, extra-long drag on the cigarette.

'What'd he say?'

'Just that Jarrett wants results. Doesn't want to let this case fester.'

Jeff looked through the chicken-wire fence that cordoned off this unofficial yard. The question formulated itself in his

mind, though he did not say it aloud: *Why would he care?*
'So what have you got to go on?'

'Come now, Jefferson love. I told you: we can't talk about this one.'

'I know, I know. What I meant was – and then I'll leave you alone, I promise – perhaps I can help. Maybe there's some open cases I can look at, make a connection. Remember Menendez?'

'Oh no you don't, Jeff.' Her expression suddenly hardened. 'Don't you dare start doing that.'

'I just mean, there may be some useful—'

'I'm serious, Jeff. Don't go wading into what you don't understand. This case is being handled in a particular way which, trust me, you really don't want to mess up.'

He fixed his gaze on Barbara. 'What kind of "particular way"?'

'Don't try that. I've already said way too much. Especially to you.'

'Especially to me? Why would you not—'

'I'll give you a clue. Hard-on.'

'Madison?'

'Madison Webb of the *LA Times*. Yes.'

'She's the sister of the victim.'

'Who also happens to be a reporter and the object of the most notorious infatuation in the history of the LAPD. Everyone knows you want to get up close and personal with that girl, Jeff. The dogs on the street know that. So do me a favour. Butt out.' She forced her features to relax, to project nonchalance. 'Besides, we don't need your help, thank you very much. Steve and I can handle this one all by our pretty little selves. Don't think he doesn't want to kick your ass.'

'Who, Steve?'

'You're not the only one with ambition around here, honey.'

'Of course,' said Jeff, nodding his comprehension. The new man always needs to prove himself, to get a win.

'Gotta show that he's just as good as you. I want that too, I don't mind telling you. Don't want people thinking, she can't solve a case unless she got that skinny white boy with her.' She gave him a punch on the shoulder, her first friendly gesture.

'All right.' Jeff attempted a smile. But he could see that, for all the banter, the panic in his former partner's eyes had not gone. For the first time since he had known her, he knew Barbara Miller was hiding something.

Chapter 10

She was driving south on the 5 when she realized she didn't
know what day it was. She had been in such a blur since that
phone call, she had lost track of time. For most insomniacs
that sensation, at least, was not so unusual. When you have
no nights, it can be hard to keep a grip on the days.

But in LA, as she had learned through direct experience, it
could be costly. Get caught driving on, say, a Thursday in a
No Thursday vehicle and you'd get more than a lecture about
smog and pollution from the Highway Patrol. They could
revoke your licence on the spot. You had the right to appeal,
but while you did you were off the road. Appealing was all
but pointless anyway. There was no case you could make,
short of a life-and-death medical emergency – and even then
the court would ask why you didn't get a taxi or hitch a ride.
Keeping the smog out of southern California was a state
priority. Everyone mocked it, but the slogan that launched
the scheme was now engraved into the Californian collective
memory. School kids could sing the jingle even now: *Everyone
can drive sometime when no one drives always.*

She had to work her way back to getting kicked out of the
sweatshop, reconstructing the sequence event by dreadful
event, before she realized with relief that today was still

Monday. It was late afternoon and, as it happened, smoggy. The driving restrictions had succeeded in making people mad but not, it seemed, much else. For days on end, the city would still be wreathed in thick white cloud. At dawn, it could look like a morning mist. Except it would refuse to disperse or burn off as the sun came up. Instead it would linger, squatting there in the bowl of the city, refusing to budge, sometimes so dense you could stand on one side of the road unable to see what was on the other. Some blamed the slashing of the old clean air standards, shredded years ago in the name of maintaining America's competitiveness. The US authorities said the responsibility lay with 'Asia', insisting that the smog came in on springtime winds from the east. On the street, less fastidiously, people blamed China.

It didn't smell, but it played havoc on your lungs. These days even Maddy had a smog mask, though she kept it tucked away in the glove compartment.

The phone rang, its sound quickly transferred to the speakers. She glanced down to check the caller ID, but the phone was in her bag. She took a second, weighing the chance of dodging a call from a sympathetic friend against the risk of missing Jeff or one of his police colleagues bringing new information, before deciding the latter was too great. She pressed the button.

'Hi there, is that Madison?' The voice young, chirpy. Valley.

'Who's calling?' Maddy said, wary and driving slower now, peering through the oncoming smog, the headlights on even in the afternoon.

'Hi, I'm from the *Los Angeles Times*? We haven't met?'

'Hi.'

'I just want to say how sorry we all are about your loss? Everyone here sends condolences?'

'OK.'

'We're just trying to put together something about Abigail for Metro . . .'

A surge of irritation passed through Maddy, the first cause being that 'Abigail'. *Don't you dare speak about her as if you knew her, as if she were your friend.*

'. . . you know, just some details, maybe an anecdote about what she was like.'

It took a second or two for Maddy to process what she had just heard. Then she said, 'Are you seriously trying to interview me about my sister? Is that why you're calling?'

'Well, it's not . . . I wouldn't call it an interview, just maybe something you'd like to . . .' The reporter at the other end of the line suddenly sounded very young.

'Who put you up to this?'

'Put me up to . . . I'm sorry, I don't understand?'

'Who told you to call me?'

There was another pause and then: 'The news editor. Howard? He thought it'd be OK to call you? I'm really sorry, is this a bad time?'

'You're damn right it's a bad time. And you can tell Howard Burke that next time he wants to know about my family he can damn well have the balls to call me himself.'

'I'm sorry, I just . . .'

Maddy could hear the nervousness in the woman's voice. Suddenly she felt a jolt of familiarity. It used to be her on the end of that phone. She had done it a dozen or more times, especially when she first started out on the police beat. Calling the victim's family, perhaps the most gruesome part of the job, harder even than seeing the body – and Howard had made her do it. After the first or second time, he hadn't needed to ask. It became routine. She was more adept at it than this one; she knew not to sound perky, not to sound like a girl who had just spotted a bargain at the mall. She had a bereavement voice, which breathed sincerity. But now, sitting alone in her car, on a smog-bound, jammed freeway, she was not sure that put her on any kind of higher moral plane. In fact she knew it didn't. She was just better at it.

78

She apologized to the woman and promised to text her a line or two later.

Forty minutes later and she was at the house – or as near to it as she could get. There was no room to park: both sides of the road were filled. She checked the note she made, to be sure she was in the right place. But there was no mistake.

There was a small crowd by the front door which, as she got nearer, she could see was an overspill from inside. She slowed down, making an instant assessment of the people there: poor, but dressed in their most formal clothes. It was the mud she spotted on two pairs of dark leather shoes that settled it. Rosario Padilla had died nearly three weeks ago. In homicide cases it often took that long to release the body from the morgue and return it to the family. These people must have just come from the funeral.

She nudged and excused-me'd her way in, working herself up the steps onto the porch and through the screen-door into the house. Once in, she heard the hush. Someone was making a speech. She stood behind a knot of middle-aged Latinas, all nodding as they listened. Before them, next to a mantelpiece covered in family photographs, was a man she guessed was her own age. Dark and in a suit that seemed too small for him, he was speaking with great intensity.

'And her faith was important to her. My aunts will tell you, Rosario was the one who actually *wanted* to go to church.' The women in front of Maddy turned to smile at one another at that. 'I hope that faith is a comfort to her now. Because I'll be honest with you, and I didn't want to say this there, at the cemetery. But I'm finding it hard to believe right now.' His voice choked, a show of weakness that made him shake his head. An older man placed his hand on his shoulder.

Maddy had seen plenty of moments like this: a father comforting the brother of the deceased, the extended family wiping away their own tears. It was familiar to her, yet it struck her with new force. Soon she would not be watching this scene, from the back. She would be there, at the front: she, Quincy and her mother, the mourners. Quincy would doubtless demand one of them do what this man was doing right now: deliver a eulogy at the wake, offering a few words about the life of Abigail. She realized her eyes were stinging, but the tears did not come.

He stopped speaking now, held in a long, silent embrace by his father. The mother was hugging the aunts who were hugging her back. The rest were shuffling on the spot, uncertain where to put themselves, waiting for a moment to speak to the family.

Maddy held back, examining more of the photographs on the walls, trying to work out how each of those she could see here related to each other. Eventually she found herself next to the brother. She extended a hand.

He took it, showing her a puzzled brow. 'Are you one of Rosario's friends?'

'No, I'm not. Though I wish I was. She sounds like a great person.'

'She was.'

'I'm here because I lost my sister too.'

'OK. Um, I'm sorry.'

'It just happened actually. In quite similar circumstances to Rosar—' She stopped herself. 'To your sister. Is there somewhere we can talk?'

He led her first into the kitchen, but that was packed even more tightly than the living room. The hallways were jammed too. Finally, he ushered her out back, into a tiny concrete yard. There was no option but to stand close together, their faces near. He introduced himself as Mario Padilla. She said her name was Madison Webb.

'Hold on a second, I know that name.' He checked his phone, scrolling down, as if looking for something.

'Is there something wrong?'

80

'Here we are. I knew I'd seen that name. You're a reporter, right?'

Her answer sounded like an admission of guilt. 'Right.'

'You wrote that thing about the sweatshops. I saw that. That was good. Those guys need to be exposed.'

'Thank you.'

'But I'm confused. According to this,' he held up the phone, 'your sister died last night.'

'Yes.'

'And you're *here*? At *my* house? Shouldn't you be with your family or something?' Seeing Maddy's face fall, he rowed back. 'I'm sorry, I don't mean to judge you. But this is hard. You need to give yourself time.'

She wanted to say that there was no time, that the golden hour had already passed, that that had been his mistake: he had waited till it was too late and now he was hurtling down the dead-end of a lawsuit against the coroner. She even felt an unfamiliar urge to tell him that there was no family to speak of, just Quincy and a mother who . . . But she would say none of these things. Instead all she managed was, 'I know I do. But I also want to know what happened.'

'And you think talking to me might help?'

'It might. I know you think the coroner got it wrong, that your sister did not kill . . . did not die by accident.'

'There's no way. A heroin overdose? Rosie? That's just crazy.'

'How can you be so sure?'

'Because Rosie lived in this house, same as me. I saw her come home every evening and leave for work in the morning.'

'What work did she do?'

'Catering company. In accounts. Good job, but didn't pay so great. I told that to the police. Smack costs. It's expensive. If they think she was some kind of addict, how do they think she was paying for it?'

'What did they say?'

'They didn't give me a straight answer, because there is no straight answer except "We got it wrong, she wasn't on drugs." Tried to tell me addicts get very good at deceiving people, even their loved ones.'

'*Especially* their loved ones.'

'That's right! That's exactly what they said! They say that to you too?'

'Not this time. But I've heard it often.' When he gave her a quizzical look she explained as concisely as she could, as if it were a mere aside, that she used to cover crime. Then, 'And you don't buy it?'

'Course I don't. We know our own family, I bet you're the same as me. You can't keep nothing secret in a family.'

There was so much Maddy could say to that, but she wouldn't have known where to start. Instead she said, 'Was there anything else that didn't fit? In your lawsuit against the coroner, what's the case you're going to make?'

'We've got letters from doctors and all that, saying she was healthy. She'd had an exam like a month before: no sign of any of that shit. So we're going to say that. But the main thing is the arm.'

'The arm?'

'Rosario was found with a needle hole in her right arm.' He tapped the crook of his right elbow to show where. 'Now, I've never injected myself with anything. But I'm guessing this is how you do it, right?' He mimed the action of pushing the plunger of a syringe into his arm.

'Right,' Maddy said, with a glimmer of what was coming next.

'I'm using my left hand. That's the only way I can do it. I can't be doing this,' and now he mimed administering an injection into his right arm with his right hand, his wrist forced into an impossible contortion. 'If the hole is in the right arm, then it has to be done with the left hand. Ain't no other way.'

'OK.'

'But why would you do that? It's much easier for me to inject into my left arm.' He mimed that, to show her how much easier. 'That's what anybody would do.'

'Unless they were left-handed.'

'Exactly. Unless they were left-handed. Which Rosario was not. Same as me, same as everyone except my dad. We're all right-handed.'

'And you said this to the police?'

'Course. But they gave me the same bullshit. "Addicts will inject wherever they can inject."'

Maddy nodded, taking in what she had heard. 'So a healthy woman, with no history of drug use, is found dead with a single needle mark in her right arm and a massive dose of heroin in her system.'

'That's it.' He looked back into the house, at the crowd filling the corridor. 'Same with you?'

'Same with me. Although, as it happens, my sister was left-handed. So theoretically . . .'

'And is that what the police are saying to you? They saying she did that to herself?'

'Not quite. And where was your sister found?' This was the more polite version of the question she really wanted to ask: *in what state* was your sister found?

'That's what's so crazy about this. She was *in the hallway*. Just there.' He pointed towards the front door. 'Just kind of stretched out. On her back. Arms at her side.'

'And this was late at night?'

'Nearly one in the morning. More than two weeks ago. She'd been out.' Madison remembered the police estimate of Abigail's time of death: shortly after one am. Abigail too had been out.

'And do you have any idea why she would be in the hall?'

'No I don't. Even if you think my sister was some kind of junkie, which she was not, she's waited this whole time to get home. Why wouldn't she wait the extra two or three seconds it would take to get to her room? Or even the bathroom? The only reason it'd be out here, is someone followed her home, followed her into the house, did this thing *to* her – and that someone didn't want to get caught.'

Maddy paused, looked back towards the front door, as if taking in what Mario had just said. 'And did she look as if she had been . . . hurt in any way?'

'That's it, you see. Police said there was "no sign of a struggle". Couple of scratches here and there, but they said she could have got those anywhere.'

Maddy girded herself for what she was about to ask. 'Did the police suspect anything else had happened to your sister?' She let the question hang in the air, the weight on the words 'anything else'.

His head sunk onto his chest. 'No. I'm grateful for that. No.' He looked up, his eyes conveying a question.

'No,' Maddy replied. 'Nothing like that either . . . All right,' she said finally. 'Thank you for telling me all this. It sounds like we've suffered something very similar.'

'Tell me, Miss Webb. Do you think the person who killed Rosario killed your sister? Is that what you're saying?'

'I don't know.' He looked at her with great need, an expression she recognized. It was the face she had seen in the mirror a matter of hours ago, her own need for answers reflected back at her.

He showed her out, leading her to the front door. 'You should have a mask on,' he said.

She wheeled around, feeling very suddenly exposed. Had her emotions been that obvious, written all over her face?

'For the smog. I told Rosario that all the time. "You gotta wear a mask when it's like this."' He paused, staring into the street, ignoring the couple touching him on the shoulder by way of a goodbye as they left the wake. 'I was worried about her.'

And then, as if remembering himself, he reached into his

pocket for his phone. 'I just realized, I never showed you a picture.'

'Oh, I'd love that.' This too was a familiar ritual. Every homicide Maddy had ever covered, the family always wanted to tell you stories or show you photos, to make sure you understood what they had lost. He swiped a few images, then settled on one he liked, turning the screen towards Maddy, angling it in the light.

'See,' he said. 'She was a beautiful girl.'

Filling the frame was a standard, college graduation photograph, a smiling young woman in mortarboard and gown. Maddy nodded her agreement that she was indeed lovely looking. But that was not what struck her with great force, settling at last the question that had nagged at her since she had embarked on that computer search nearly three hours ago. She had seen this picture online, but had assumed it was some kind of mistake. Because the woman before her, beaming from the screen of her grieving brother's phone, was not what she had expected. In striking contrast with her brother and her aunts, Rosario Padilla had long blonde hair and skin as fine and pale as alabaster.

Chapter 11

Who would dominate? If you had to bet, you'd say it was the guy in the Dead T-shirt, longish hair. If they were testing ketchup or soda, he'd be the alpha dog, no doubt about it. But for this? Not so sure. Maybe the woman, overweight, polyester pants; you'd bet on her having strong views. Or the older man, retired accountant maybe. Or a dentist. If this were a jury, he'd be the foreman: prissy, stickler for the rules, president of his condo residents' association. You'd stake your wages on it. But this was not a jury. Way more unpredictable.

The man at his side leaned in to whisper. 'We'll do a dummy first,' he said before straightening up again. They were both standing, gazing through a large, rectangular window, like engineers behind the glass in a recording studio. Except no one was making music on the other side. Instead, this scientifically selected sample of the California electorate were being paid 'expenses' to give up an hour of their early evening to sit in a semi-circle of hard chairs in a specially equipped room in a hotel off the 605 near Anaheim. They had come on the promise of 'an exciting opportunity to be involved in the early stages of marketing a brand-new product!' As always, no one had warned the members of this particular focus group that the product in question was a new political message.

Bill Doran remembered the days when these were a novelty. The first one he witnessed seemed to him a revelation, the tool that would transform the trade plied by him and his fellow political consultants, that travelling band of mercenaries who rented out their smarts and experience to the parade of shallow, shiny inadequates and deviants who hankered after public office in the United States. Now focus groups were part of the established order. If anything they were under threat, dismissed as old school by the kids who seemed to base every judgement on the latest meme coursing through Weibo.

Bald, barrel-chested and thick-necked and, as such, a long-time standout among the bespectacled, chess-club dweebs of the political consultant community, Doran checked his phone while the dummy was underway, a question about the pizza that had been offered and chowed down by the group. 'I knew it,' said the Deadhead. 'I told my pal, Joe, I said to him, "I bet it's pizza". And boom! It's pizza.' The man chuckled to himself and Doran adjusted his expectations, predicting that this was not a man his fellow focus-groupers were likely to follow.

'All right, thanks everyone,' the facilitator was saying, a studiedly informal man in dark jeans and a pressed white shirt. 'Moving on. First of all I want to show you a very short film. Then I'm going to be asking for your responses to a few statements. I'll read them out and you just tell me what you think, OK? Just like we did with the pizza, all right? Everyone happy?' There was nodding around the semi-circle, except from the Deadhead as he slowly realized he had, in fact, lost his bet with Joe.

Doran watched as the film played on the other side of the glass, a short video primer explaining the Chinese presence on US soil. Apparently aimed at twelve year olds – *The story starts on Capitol Hill . . .* – it was ideal for this audience. Not that Doran was looking at the screen. His focus remained fixed on the faces in front of him.

Less than three minutes later, the focus group facilitator was rising from his chair. 'Thank you, folks. Now, as prom- ised, I'm going to read you a series of statements and I want to get your reaction. OK, here's the first one. "The only troops on California soil should be American troops." Anyone want me to read that again? OK, here goes. "The only troops on California soil should be American troops."'

There was some spirited nodding and a rambling few sentences of assent from both the polyester trousers and the Deadhead. But then the dentist (or accountant) said, 'We all agree with that, sure. In an ideal world, we'd only have American troops here. We all want that. But it's not going to happen. The Treaty's the Treaty. It's signed, sealed and deliv- ered. Nothing we can do about it.'

'It's too late,' nodded a woman who, Doran guessed, had been recruited to represent the suburban married female demo- graphic, the one they had called 'soccer moms' back when he was starting out in this business. Quaint, that phrase seemed now.

Doran checked his watch. Precisely twenty-three seconds after the idea had been floated the obvious rebuttal had followed: nice idea, but impossible. He watched as the rest of the group fell into line behind the accountant. The Deadhead attempted a rallying speech: 'But we don't have to accept that! Washington and Lincoln didn't just accept the British being here, did they? They fought back!' But, though no one corrected him on his history, his argument found no takers. Brief as it was, this little episode would be useful ammunition next time he got pressure from Ted Norman and his band of ultras in the state party, demanding the candidate adopt a more muscular nationalist position. He could tell them, 'That'll work – for precisely twenty-three seconds.'

'All righty,' cooed the facilitator, scribbling a note. 'How about this one? "This is our country. We've accepted the

Chinese presence here, but it's got to be on our terms." Shall I repeat that? Here goes . . .'

Much more support for that. It took a full minute and a half before anyone asked what, exactly, 'our terms' meant. Doran and the pollster looked at each other. Suitably vague, instantly consensual, apparently commonsensical: you couldn't ask much more from a campaign message.

'Let's do a couple more. OK, this one's a little longer. "The Chinese are here now, but that doesn't mean they should be here forever. The new Governor of California should try to renegotiate the Treaty."' Lots of enthusiasm for the first sentence, Doran noted, but confusion on the second. The word *renegotiate* needed some work. That would never fly in a thirty-second TV spot. He heard his own voice, nearly a decade ago, tutoring the young Leo Harris: 'Avoid Latinate words wherever possible, go Anglo-Saxon every time. No one wants to have *intercourse*. They want to *fuck*. Same with politics. It's not *financial institutions*. It's *banks*.' Harris was such a good pupil, he had remembered it all. Motherfucker.

'And here's our last one. "The Chinese army are here. But they don't have a blank cheque. They can't do what they like. They need to follow our rules and obey our laws."'

Every head nodding.

Doran felt his phone buzzing. Cupping his hand over the mouthpiece, he turned his back to the two-way mirror, making sure the pollster – whom he had long suspected was leaking to the *LA Times* – could not hear the conversation.

'What can I do for you, Elena?' It was the candidate, the underdog challenger for the governorship of the great state of California. Though the voice was not the one known to millions of viewers of Fox News, where she had become a favourite. There she was sharper, more acidic, obligingly playing to her network billing as 'the tough-as-nails former prosecutor'. In person and now on the phone, her voice was smoother and calmer. (One of the tasks Bill had set himself was to encourage Elena Sigurdsson to behave on camera the way she did in person. That was always harder than it sounded, but in Sigurdsson's case there was an extra difficulty: the Republican base, including the Ted Norman crowd who'd made sure she bagged the nomination, liked the persona of the ball-breaking former DA of LA County and she was reluctant to let it go.)

'I won't have any numbers from here for a while. But I can give you a readout based—'

'No,' Sigurdsson said. '*I* have some news for *you*.'

'OK.' This was worrying. You never wanted candidates to have their own information stream. Ideally you'd remove their smartphones altogether, citing security reasons. 'How intriguing! Fire away.'

'You know about this murder story, the sister of the journalist?'

Doran had seen a single weib mentioning it, which he had glided over and failed to absorb. 'Sure.'

'I'm hearing Berger's nervy about it.'

'Really? Why would he care?'

'Not sure. Seems he's putting the squeeze on the Chief of Police. Wants to get this done.'

'"Seems"?'

'The Chief of Police has declared it a priority. Putting pressure on his team.'

'And he's said this publicly, the Chief of Police?'

'No, but that's what I'm hearing. From my people at LAPD. They reckon it must mean he's getting heat from the mayor. For Christ's sake, Bill, is there a problem here?'

He was, he realized, challenging her. Some candidates liked that, but they were a minority. Even the ones who told interviewers the last thing they wanted was to be surrounded by yes men wanted to be surrounded by yes men. They needed the reassurance. He had given Sigurdsson more credit than that, but perhaps she was the same as the rest.

An awkward thought eeled its way into his mind. Was he showing her less respect because she was a woman? She had brought political information to him and he hadn't simply accepted it but had doubted her. Would he have done the same with a man?

Who the hell cared? He had been right to doubt her, hadn't he? She had jumped to conclusions – that Berger was nervy – on the basis of nothing her opponent had actually said or done, nothing even that the Chief of Police had said or done but just some watercooler talk she'd picked up from her cop friends. Not good enough. He had been right to push her. Worrying about sexism was Leo Harris, Democrat, political correctness bullshit. He scolded himself for breaking one of his own rules: *never let them get inside your head*.

'I'll look into it. That could be very useful. Thank you, Elena.'

'If Berger's sweating, that's an opening. You said it yourself, he hasn't shown us many weaknesses.'

Doran hung up, dissatisfied with both himself and his candidate. His assumption was that she was wrong. There was no reason for a mayor to worry about a single death in his city. That the victim's sister was a journalist certainly raised a flag: the police would need to do their job properly, otherwise she could make some noise. But that was a long way off.

Still, Sigurdsson wouldn't have got everything wrong. If the cops were telling her they were feeling some pressure, they probably were. Such pressure could originate in a dozen places. Could be Berger, over-anxious about his campaign, could be the Chief of Police himself. Or someone neither of them had even thought of.

Chapter 12

The Great Hall of the People was a landmark. The building itself was nothing special – an entrance on South Wall Street next to a vintage clothes store – but everyone knew it, thanks to the green-uniformed sentries who guarded the door, alongside two outdoor flame-heaters, in oversized peaked caps and retro People's Liberation Army fatigues.

Maddy had only been once, but she remembered it. Beijing kitsch was the theme: heroic posters of Mao, waiters in workers' caps, and on one wall a giant TV screen, the pixels usually flooding red, projecting patriotic slogans. Even from her vantage point in the car parked on the other side of the street, she could see the words 'Innovation, Inclusiveness, Virtue' in bold yellow and in English, against the rippling flag of the People's Republic.

She guessed the place was heaving now, the long, long tables – styled after the dining hall of a Mao-era peasant farm – packed and spilling over. The Great Hall filled up early every night, serving Chinese fusion – dim sum with Waldorf salad, roast duck served with fries – to couples and irony-chasing twentysomethings before nine, then giving way to business types grabbing a midnight bite after their morning calls to Beijing and Shanghai. The food was surprisingly good for what was essentially a theme bar, good enough that even Chinese expats were known to eat here, though maybe they came for the irony too.

She stayed low in the driver's seat, eyeing Barbara's car, the same one the detective had once shared with Jeff Howe.

Jeff. Even the name induced a pang of guilt. The very worst thing you can do, she knew, with a man like that was to offer false hope. In fact, that was not the very worst thing. The very worst thing was to give him false hope *and* somehow become obligated towards him. She had managed to do both.

She had been driving back from the Padilla house, still reeling from the discovery that Rosario belonged in that category the California bureaucrats called 'white Hispanic' – that she, like Abigail, was a blonde. It was hardly conclusive but, coupled with the fact that Rosario, like Abigail, had no history of intravenous drug use, it should at least be of interest to the police. It might be a lead. Maddy had covered enough homicides to know that the mere possibility that they were looking for a man who had killed a similar-looking woman in a similar way would be worth checking. At the very least she should telephone Detective Barbara Miller, pass on this nugget of information – which might or might not be of relevance – and then she could leave it to them. Only then did Maddy spell out to herself what that would mean: that her beloved baby sister was the victim of a serial killer.

She had pulled over at the next rest-stop, then dug into the pocket of her jeans to extract the already crumpled business card Miller had given her when they met. The conversation had been short, the bare minimum, Maddy suspected, that would allow Miller to check the box marked 'family support'.

Shit.

The card was the standard one, giving the general number of the LAPD switchboard. But Miller had scribbled a number on the reverse. At the time, Maddy had assumed that this would be the detective's personal cellphone number. Except now she looked and could see that Miller had simply written on the back the same switchboard number that was printed on the front.

Maddy wondered if that was generic unhelpfulness, designed to keep any outsider at bay, or whether this was bespoke bullshit, tailormade for her. Perhaps Miller feared journalistic meddling in her investigation, but she was denying Maddy the treatment all other victims of such a serious crime would regard as their right.

Madison had let her head fall into her hands. She was so unbearably tired that the interior of the car was revolving around her. But she had to pass this information on.

The LAPD switchboard was the twenty-first-century labyrinth of the ancients: no one got out of there alive. If she was to make contact with Miller, she would need her cell.

She got out of the car, so that she could pace around it. There on the cracked asphalt, standing by a tall weed that had grown through a crack, was a trucker, baseball cap pulled low over his eyes, taking a break. He nodded in her direction. She turned away, aware that a return nod could well be interpreted as a friendliness she did not mean and that could only delay her.

She realized what it looked like. The windows of her car open, Maddy pacing around in her skinny jeans and tight sweater, albeit one with a hole below the armpit. That was the trouble with being a woman her age and not physically repulsive: you had actively to signal your lack of interest and non-availability. Otherwise any activity that for a man would be regarded as normal, human behaviour – including taking a break from driving to get a breath of fresh air – would be read as a come-on.

The trucker was still smiling, refusing to take the cue and look away. Had this man appeared before or after she got here? Was it possible he had turned off the freeway when she had? *Because* she had? Had he been there the last twenty minutes, watching her make her phone calls, waiting for her?

Suddenly she was seized by a feeling she had not known before, a kind of vicarious fear. She was imagining the terror that must have grasped her sister in her final moments, the fright that must have shaken her as she understood that she was about to die. Had Abigail too been pursued by a man like this? Had he followed her home, chased her up the stairs and, just when she thought she was safe and that she had eluded him, had he caught up with her, jamming his hand in the door just before it was slammed shut, shoving it open and forcing his way inside her apartment? And then . . .

Maddy realized she was breathing too heavily. Audibly. She looked over towards the baseball cap and, to her relief, saw that he was back in his cab, about to set off. Clasping the top of the car door, she allowed herself three more deep breaths and resolved to get a grip.

And that's when she turned to Jeff.

'I need Barbara Miller's cell,' she said, her voice tight and short. Striving to give him no more misplaced encouragement, she sounded terse and somehow entitled instead. She took the number and could almost visualize the debt that was mounting between them.

He told her that Miller was clamming up, that she was nervous about him leaking any information on the investigation to a journalist. Madison needed to be very careful with whatever he told her, otherwise he would be exposed and compromised. It had to stay private, just between them.

Then he asked her to hold, returning sixty seconds later. That same hint of eagerness – of a man handing over the *quid* in expectation of the *quo* – in his voice.

'I've just checked on the tracking system here. Barbara and Steve are at the Great Hall bar, downtown,' he said.

'I know that place. What are they doing there?'

'It seems a girl matching Abigail's description was seen there last night. With a young white male; possibly left with him.

There's a witness who says they heard an argument between them. There's CCTV footage apparently. Miller and Agar are looking at it right now.'

So here she was, waiting in her car across the street. She worked through her options. Dash in, wade through the throng and find the security room, interrupting Barbara and Steve while they viewed the CCTV pictures? Disaster. They'd have her down as a stalker, shadowing their investigation, making it impossible to do their jobs. She could write the official complaint they would make herself. Besides, she would glean no information that way. They, and whoever was showing them the footage, would immediately clam up, demanding she tell them why and how the hell she had tracked them down there. Jeff would be disciplined – and would never tell her anything again.

And yet whatever it was they had just found out, she needed to know.

Waiting. Never her first instinct, but the only viable course for now. She would watch and wait.

Ten minutes went by, then another five and finally she could see movement by the door that suggested people coming out rather than in. Steve emerged first, talking into his cellphone. Barbara followed. Maddy sunk still lower into her seat, regretting that she was not wearing a top with a hood.

She watched the pair of detectives drive away, their vehicle unmarked, save for a white-on-black 'W' on the licence plate: the symbol that connoted permission to drive every day of the week. Maddy counted to ten, pressed the three digits that would keep her hidden from caller ID software, then dialled the number she had already searched and loaded onto her phone.

Three rings, then: 'Great Hall of the People.' The accent American, the voice male, young, bored.

Involuntarily, she closed her eyes, less to steel herself for what she was about to do than to focus on it, to concentrate all her energies on the task at hand. She lowered the pitch of her voice and spoke.

'This is Detective Miller, my colleague and I were there just a moment ago. Sweetheart, could you put me through to the manager please?'

A short delay then a new voice, female and brisk. *Damn.* Women, Maddy had found, were less credulous than men. But there was no going back.

'Hello there. My colleague and I were with y'all a few moments ago, viewing the security footage?'

'Yes.'

'I think there's something we may need to review again. I wish I could come back myself, but we don't have much time. I'm sending over one of my junior colleagues to see you, her name is Madison Halliday. Is that OK, honey? Nothing complicated, just show her what you showed me.'

She held her breath, her eyes still closed. She was wincing. Eventually the manager spoke. 'Is there something wrong?'

'Nothing wrong, sweetheart. Just need a second look.'

Another delay and then, 'OK. How long will she be?'

'Not long at all. I've put Officer Halliday on it because she's in the area already. With you in the next few minutes. Thanks, honey.'

She had been nodded through, thanks to a glimpse of the LAPD badge she had never removed from her pocketbook, kept there well over a year since Katharine had knocked it up for her, reluctantly, using a 3D printer. Madison had solemnly promised that it was for one time only, that she had no other way of doing that story – on a sex trafficking ring operating out of Long Beach – and that she would destroy it as soon as the story was done. But a fake police ID belonging to a fictitious Officer Madison Halliday was too good an asset to throw away. Without telling Katharine, Madison had saved it for a rainy day. Like today.

So the woman she guessed she had spoken to earlier stayed with a phone cradled in her neck by the reservations lectern, serving as a traffic cop for a line of would-be diners, merely glanced up, clocked the badge, then mouthed and gestured her towards a downstairs room marked 'Private', next to the men's and women's bathrooms.

Inside was a bank of four television monitors, each one flicking at intervals between different angles and locations. She could see the long tables, the bar, the kitchen, a series of what looked like small lounges, bathed in the white light of karaoke screens, and the basin area of what she supposed was the women's bathroom. So, she noted, cameras even there.

In a chair, eating a salad out of a plastic box, was a young, white man whose scraggly beard could have denoted either hipster or loser, it was hard to tell. Maddy decided it was he who had first picked up the phone when 'Barbara' had called a few minutes ago. That suggested a general dogsbody rather than a 'head of security'. Whether that was good news or bad, it was too early to tell.

'Hi there,' she said, her voice self-consciously higher and lighter than normal, as if to stress that she was absolutely not the same person he had spoken to earlier. 'I'm here to review again the footage from last night?'

He munched on a fork loaded with spinach leaves, a cherry tomato squirting from the left side of his mouth and onto his shirt. He nodded, too full of food to speak, then keyed a few strokes at his computer. A second or two later, the central and largest monitor was showing a sequence on fast rewind, jerky figures moving off and on stools, taking glasses from their lips and putting them down on the counter.

'What are we looking at?' Maddy asked, doing her best to sound no more than professionally curious.

'This is the bar camera,' salad boy said, about to take another bite, nodding towards the screen for emphasis. He pressed another button, the picture now displaying the timecode and the rest of the on-screen data that had been missing until then: 12.13 am, today's date. 'This is what your . . . this is what those guys were looking at before.'

The camera was above the bar, mounted, judging from the angle, high up on the right-hand wall. It revealed the bar staff in full face, two of them, but she could see the customers in profile only. At this moment it showed five people sitting on stools, three men and two women. Laboriously, starting at the left and moving rightward, Maddy fixed on each one in turn. Middle-aged man, possibly white; middle-aged man, Asian, could be Japanese, Chinese, Korean; both turned on their stools to face a woman in a black mini-dress, sheer sleeves, hair fair, almost silver on the screen, though that could be the lights. The picture was not sharp enough to be sure, but to Maddy it looked like a classic late night scene: two businessmen hitting on an attractive single woman. The men at least were smiling; the woman had a glass in her hand.

Next to the female drinker, though visible only in profile, was a younger man: white, mid-thirties, hair brown and cut short, well-built. He was talking to the last figure on the screen who, because she was seated at the curve of the bar, had her back to the camera. Distracted by the little *ménage á trois* at the other end, Maddy had not noticed her at all till now.

'Can you freeze the picture? Just here.'

Maddy looked hard. The young woman was dressed in a fitted, sparkling top. Yesterday she'd have said that was not Abigail's style at all. But a few hours ago she had seen items in Abigail's closet that were just like it. The hair was the right colour, blonde, though you couldn't tell if it was Abigail-blonde, full of sun and fresh air, or the bottled variety. It was definitely the right length though. Still, the similarity ended there. This woman's hair was dead straight, falling in a sheet, as if it had been ironed flat. Abigail never wore her hair like that.

'The other guys looked at this too. It's Abigail.'

The name, spoken by a stranger, broke Maddy out of her trance of concentration. She turned to the technician, still gesturing with his fork at the frozen image. She was about to snap at him, when she remembered who she was supposed to be. She was Madison Halliday, junior police officer on an errand. She was not Maddy Webb, sister. She looked back at the screen, telling herself that this was what happened in murder cases. The victim became public property, often referred to simply by their first name – especially, it had to be said, when the victim was young and female. She could picture the headlines and TV captions she had seen over the years. *The search for Tanya's killer. Will we ever know who killed Amanda?* It was a journalistic tic, and she was no less guilty of it than the rest of them.

'Is that what, um, my colleagues said too? That that's Abigail?'

'Yep.' He took another bite. 'And me too.'

Maddy stiffened. 'You? What do you mean?'

'Well, I'm not here all the time. But she's one of the regulars. I mean, *was* one of the regulars. Sorry. It's just so weird.'

'I don't follow.'

'Someone being here and then the next day, they're gone. I know they say death is part of life, but—'

'No, I mean I don't follow about her being *one of the regulars*.'

'I explained it to your friends before. She was a regular here. In the KTV area, in the bar. Couple of nights a week, at least. Anyway, look. This is the bit I think you're meant to look at.'

Maddy could hardly take in what she was hearing, his words ricocheting around her head, rebounding against the echo of Quincy all those hours ago. *You don't always know everything, Maddy. Not even about Abigail.*

But now the monitor was showing her younger sister at a

100

slightly clearer angle, because Abigail had turned a few degrees to speak to this man whom Maddy had branded a soldier of some kind. He was smiling, then giving a large nod. From the way Abigail's back was moving, she would guess they were having an amicable conversation. Maybe flirting.

But then his posture stiffened. He leaned forward, said something that prompted Abigail to stand up and walk away. She disappeared out of shot on her right, then briefly appeared a half-second later in the far left of the screen, as if she had walked round the bar, past the soldier, though without looking at him, and out. The man downed his drink, scoped the room, once to his right, then to his left – where the middle-aged trio were still making each other smile – once more to his right, before placing a dollar bill on the counter and leaving too. According to the CCTV timecode that did not stop ticking, he followed Abigail out of the bar less than thirty seconds later. Out of the bar, out into the cold, LA night – and out, it seemed, to pursue Abigail.

Chapter 13

Leo Harris had sent texts, several direct messages via Weibo and, heaven help him, an email. Short of sending smoke signals from the Hollywood Hills, he didn't know what more he could do. But Maddy had ignored them all.

It was, he reflected now – still wearing his suit, his feet up on the coffee table, his back slumped into the couch – not just sympathy for an ex-girlfriend in mourning. The term stopped him. Was she even an ex? Was that the right word, given what had happened to them? They had never had the break-up conversation; they had never really broken up. They had tried to 'take things to the next level' – they had moved in together – but that had not worked out and suddenly they were no longer together at all.

He never understood that dynamic, though he knew it was real. It was the same in politics. Pundits were always saying of this or that initiative that it was high risk because, if it failed, there was no going back to the status quo ante. He would nod along, but truth was, he never completely got it. Why couldn't they go back? OK, so they tried something else, it didn't work out, back to square one. But no, square one would be blocked off, suddenly deemed inaccessible. The conventional wisdom was adamant on this point: advance and fail and there was no going back. In an election campaign and in romance, the same stubborn rule held. But he couldn't tell you why.

Nor could he give a precise answer to the specific question of why living together had failed. He had been the one to push for it and while Maddy never quite said no, she did not quite say yes either. He had turned up at her apartment one Sunday morning with two lattes and thirty flat, self-assembly cardboard storage boxes: no more talking, let's just get you packed up. He figured he would learn the lesson of their first night together. He had not asked her out on a date: if he had, she would only have said no. Instead, after some City Hall event, he had simply leaned in and kissed her. That's how they had started: no process of deliberation, just action.

But it had not been easy: even staying the night was tricky with a woman who didn't know how to sleep. For all that, he never lost his conviction that they would find their rhythm eventually. He had imagined coming home to Madison, turning the key in the lock and finding another person already there, the apartment already warm. He had even, God help him, imagined a child – a miniature bundle of their combined energy, talent and neuroses. A little girl probably, gorgeous but crazy.

Yet now he and Madison were barely in touch. Even at this moment, as she was reeling from the most unspeakable blow, he found himself unable to find the right words. *No one should lose a loved one that young*, was what he had left on her voicemail. *Her laughter will live on. You'll always hear it*. That's what he had texted. Trouble was, everything sounded like a presidential address following a natural disaster. He might have been in *Vanity Fair*'s list of Hottest Politicos Under Thirty-Five, but he already felt as if he'd been doing this too long.

Anyway, it wasn't just sympathy for Madison that had lodged inside him. Guilt was gnawing at him too. Leo had

103

seen the reported time of death and he had worked out, just as he felt sure Maddy had worked out, that at or very close to the moment when the beautiful life force that was Abigail Webb was being snuffed out, he and Maddy had been engaged in their usual dance: two parts combat to one part flirtation.

He had seen the way Maddy looked when she spotted him in the Mail Room. It was clear she'd have preferred he hadn't been there. She had rebuffed his offer of unlimited access to Berger and had told him she didn't want to be anywhere near him (or his balls, to be precise). After she had been forcibly introduced to the girl in the backless dress. Amber, wasn't it?

He could survive banter like that; it was easier for him. He had stood there with . . . He closed his eyes. *Jade.* That was it. He had stood there with Jade while Maddy had been on her own. And gone home alone, back to that tiny one-room apartment they had briefly shared and which she had insisted on keeping, even when his own place had ample room for both of them. Now all she would remember was that, at the moment her sister was murdered, Leo Harris had not been kind or generous or a true comrade, there for her no matter what, but a bona fide asshole.

The eleven o'clock news was starting. He reached for the remote control. First story: budget crisis in Sacramento. Second story: big movie star divorce. Third: Abigail.

He cranked up the volume, far louder than he needed it.

A major development in the hunt for the killer of twenty-two-year-old Abigail Webb tonight. KTLA News correspondent Ryan Christie has that story. Ryan?

'Thanks, Jacqui. LAPD sources tonight telling us of a potential breakthrough *in their inquiry into the death of the young woman who, as we've been reporting throughout the day here on KTLA, was found dead from a massive suspected overdose of the drug heroin in the early hours of this morning, an overdose police believe was* forced *on her. Sources now telling KTLA News they believe Abigail could have been the victim*

of a sexual *encounter that went tragically wrong. One official hinting that Abigail Webb may have* known *her killer and have been with him consensually when events took their fatal turn. Jacqui?'*

And, Ryan, any word from the police about a possible suspect?

'Jacqui, police are telling KTLA News tonight that they are increasingly confident that they now know who they're looking for and that, to quote one official, they could be "closing in" very soon.'

Thanks, Ryan. For KTLA News, Ryan Christie reporting there. Coming up after the break, why those lanterns for Chinese New Year could soon be—

Leo hit the mute button and stared straight ahead. He knew some of the effect this would have on Maddy. She'd be distraught at her sister being discussed this way in public, of course. But would it make it worse, to know that Abigail might have trusted the man who killed her, that she might even have made herself vulnerable to him sexually? Was that more or less terrible than the thought that she had been murdered by a complete stranger? Maybe it made no difference. Abigail was gone.

But surely there would be comfort in hearing that the police would soon be closing in on the guilty man. They clearly had someone in mind. There was no way they'd have briefed that otherwise. Perhaps it would be a cause of relief for Maddy and the rest of the Webb family that justice would soon be done.

He reached for his phone, to try her one more time. She surely knew about this development already. The police were bound to have notified the family before going public with such news. Although where the LAPD were concerned, you could never take anything for granted.

He looked over towards the window, remembering his conversation with the mayor en route to Sacramento. Leo had tried to argue that there were political risks in a murder inquiry with a young, attractive victim whose sister was in a position to make a lot of noise. He half-believed it too, even if Berger had seen through him pretty fast. Still, there was no doubt it was better for the campaign if the hunt was over. One less thing to worry about. He hit 'M' on his keypad. Berger answered after a half-ring.

'Just seen the eleven,' Leo began. 'That's pretty good for us.'

'Yep. I saw it too. It's excellent. Like I always say, Leo. Bowling ball.'

Leo shook his head with an exasperated smile and repeated with faux-weariness, 'You think it's coming at you, but nine times out of ten it rolls into the gutter.'

'That's it. Nine times out of ten.' The mayor sounded as if he was stretching, arms aloft, ahead of a big yawn. The voice of contentment and relief. Leo wondered if he was at home or . . . somewhere else.

'And the police say they could be "closing in".'

'Yep. With the CCTV pictures, I don't think it'll be long. Your friend can sleep a bit easier. Get some rest, Leo. Big day tomorrow.'

Leo hung up, allowing himself to feel some of his boss's pleasure. He was right about the bowling ball. So often you'd fret and angst over a problem that, in the end, just rolled out of your path altogether. The hard part was knowing which ball was the tenth.

He went to the kitchen, plucking a beer from the only inhabited shelf of his fridge. As he cracked it open, he returned to the living room, standing by the window with its shimmering view of the Hollywood lights. He took a glug and as the alcohol made contact with his brain cells, he could feel his brow furrowing.

With the CCTV pictures, I don't think it'll be long.

He picked up the TV remote and jabbed at the rewind

button, stopping at the smooth, tanned face of Ryan Christie, standing outside the LAPD headquarters. He listened closely to every word. As he thought, no mention of CCTV pictures.

He knocked back another slug of beer. That the mayor was privy to more information than a KTLA News reporter was no surprise. That the LAPD would keep him informed during a high-profile investigation was no scandal.

No, what worried Leo Harris, the mayor's closest and most senior aide, was that the mayor had kept this information to himself. He had rarely, in fact never, done that before; not once that Leo could think of. So why would he do it now, over the murder of Abigail Webb? What secret was Richard Berger hiding?

Chapter 14

The night had brought no calm. Earlier, Maddy had entertained the perverse thought that the night after the death of her sister might at last bring sleep. If she was sleepless when she had nothing to worry about, then perhaps the reverse might be true, a great trauma inducing slumber? She didn't expect it to be peaceful or serene, of course not. But some kind of neurological shutdown associated with grief, an anaesthetized unconsciousness – she'd have accepted that.

She had done everything to prepare for such an unfamiliar visitor. The blackout curtains which had been a gift from Quincy were drawn. She'd turned off the computer an hour before bedtime, like the books say. (In truth, if you counted her repeated returns to the machine, checking the KTLA and *LA Times* websites one last time and then one more last time, it was closer to thirty-five minutes.) She even found the device that played gentle, soothing sounds – ocean breezes, water lapping against the shore – that had been a gift from Abigail.

But her mind refused to switch off, its internal screen, like that of her computer, sparking to full brightness at the slightest movement.

Instead she spent a long half-hour, or maybe it was an hour, holding that photograph, staring by turns at her beautiful mother and her two sisters, the youngest just six years old, apparently brimming with happiness, her life stretching ahead of her. She could hear Abigail's voice, sometimes adult, sometimes infant. For one pleasingly familiar moment, the voice spoke to her in the plaintive whine of a teenager. 'Madd-eeee, when are we going out?'

But then she heard the sound she couldn't bear, the one she had fought so hard to lock away: the childish howl of the six-year-old Abigail, aghast at what she had witnessed her fourteen-year-old sister do. Madison could hear it now, loudly, tearing through the room. The pain of that little girl, pain that Madison knew she had caused.

And suddenly the pitch deepened. The sound she could hear was the scream of an adult. It took Maddy a moment to realize what her imagination was inflicting on her: the sound Abigail unleashed when she realized she was about to die.

Madison closed her eyes. Or perhaps opened them. In this light, and in this state, it was hard to tell. Her exhaustion was total. She felt as if someone had opened a tap and let out all her blood, all her energy. She was empty. There was nothing left.

Only adrenalin, which continued to course through her system even when all else was gone. Still, as depleted as she was, the fever in her mind would not cool. After three or four hours spent in bed, perhaps fitfully dozing for a few minutes – or seconds, she could never be sure – here and there, she surrendered just after four thirty am.

She went first to the laptop, to visit Abigail's Facebook page. Again. It was the third time she had looked, though earlier she had done only a quick scan, scrolling through for anything that stood out. This time she would look more carefully.

She started with the profile photograph. Abigail was heavily made-up, wearing a very obvious dark wig and, though only the distinctive collar was visible, what appeared to be a *cheongsam* in gorgeous red silk. Maddy guessed this was for a New Year party, though these days that look had become fashionable all year round. She clicked on the photo and saw the date. She was right: Abigail had changed over to this picture only a week earlier.

The page was full of tribute messages, scores of them – some from friends, some from members of the public, and lots from pupils and parents.

> *You lit up our school. You have left a big hole in our hearts.*

> *When I heard about it, I was so sad, love from Kayleigh.*

> *Abigail, you were the best friend a girl could have. Always there for me, never thinking of yourself. Heaven just got itself a new angel.*

> *I hope you are now at peace. No one deserved that.*

They kept on in that vein, though Maddy couldn't read them for long. She didn't know why. Perhaps the mawkishness. Maybe she didn't like sharing her sister with strangers. Or perhaps it was the way these messages reinforced the irrevocable deadness of Abigail, hammering the same dread truth again and again. She clicked on Abigail's housemate, Jessica, and sent her a message in addition to the two texts she had already fired off during the day. *Please get in touch when you can. I'd really like to talk.*

She hit the machine's 'Sleep' button, wishing enviously that she had a similar feature. She wondered how long she would have to wait before calling Barbara Miller or, failing that, Jeff Howe. She was torn. As a bereaved sister, she wanted to unleash on the LAPD, slamming them for what they had told the TV news last night. For once she agreed entirely with Quincy, who had phoned her minutes after the broadcast was off the air. Her sister had been in tears, her voice hoarse. Maddy guessed Quincy had been crying all day – a contrast with herself that she chose not to think about.

'I can't believe they would be saying those things about Abigail. *Sexual encounter.* Where do they get off talking like that? As if she was some kind of . . . I mean, heroin? And sex? Who do they think they're talking about here? This is *Abigail.*'

'I know. It's terrible. I had no idea they were—'

'That's just it. Aren't they supposed to talk to us, keep us informed? I mean, you know them all, don't you? You're always saying you've got such good "sources" and all that. Well, why didn't they tell you they were going to be saying such *horrible* things on the TV? And why didn't you stop them? What about that man Abigail told me about? Jeff. She said he liked you. Why don't . . .'

Quincy's voice trailed off. Perhaps even she couldn't quite go through with blaming the latest layer of this family tragedy on Maddy's uselessness with men. But it was clear what she was thinking. *If only you weren't such a mess, if only you didn't always go with the wrong ones and reject the right ones, you and your weird, borderline-disgusting career might actually have been useful for once.*

'Has anyone been to see you?'

'Yes.' Quincy blew her nose, noisily. 'This afternoon. A victim support officer, I think they were called. Or maybe family liaison, I'm not sure.'

'Did they say anything?'

'They wanted to know about Mom. Anything they could do. Whether she would want a visit.'

'You said no, I suppose?' Maddy asked, though what she was thinking was, *Why is Quincy getting this treatment? Do they think single people don't need a family liaison officer?*

111

Do we not count as family, even when our sisters are tied up and murdered, put to sleep with a needle like a household pet?

She replayed that conversation and several others as she paced around the apartment in the early hours, her conscious brain performing the task of processing the previous day that normal people experienced while fast asleep. She peered behind her window blind at the Korean store opposite, its lights still on. She wondered who was on duty tonight. Maybe the son. He was living and working at home, but was probably her age. She half-considered getting dressed, crossing the street and picking up something: cookies or a tub of ice cream. Just for something to do. But the chances were the Korean guy would recognize her and offer condolences and ask how she was doing and she couldn't face any of that.

She lay back on the bed, not asking her body to go to sleep, letting it off for the night. Again she asked herself, how early could she call Barbara Miller? When was the acceptable start of the day for normal people? Leo used to take calls from six in the morning, but politics was different. They worked late *and* early. It was an insomniac's business.

The clock was crawling; still not five thirty. She rehearsed what she would say to Miller, the lines restated in her head. Repeatedly, she would stop herself mid-flow, make a slight amendment and go back to the beginning:

It's outrageous that I had to find out about my sister from the TV news. I know the procedure: the family is meant to be kept informed of any major developments in a homicide inquiry. You owed it to us to let us know what you were thinking – not to accuse her like that in public. You just smeared the reputation of a dead woman. This whole sex-game theory is bullshit, you, you . . .

She would run out of road at that point, pausing to wonder how certain she could be. The meagre evidence of the use of

112

force, the CCTV footage of Abigail at the bar earlier, perhaps picking up that guy. Maybe.

Occasionally, she would hear Abigail's voice again. Her younger sister was not speaking to her exactly. But Maddy would hear fragments of her all the same. Some she thought were memories, the rest were a combination of recollection and imagination.

E is for England, that's right. Who can tell me another E word? E is for Everything. That's very good, Georgia. Who has another E word?

Maddy liked listening in, closing her eyes and hearing Abigail. She wondered if she might drift off to sleep to the sound of her sister. And then she heard her again, in a voice that was louder and firmer. *Call Barbara at seven thirty.*

Maddy's decision was made: at seven o'clock, she went to the kitchen to make coffee.

While she waited, she forced herself to undertake a task she had been putting off, perhaps, she imagined, forever. She fired up her own Weibo account and went to her 'mentions', to see what people had been saying about and to her in the aftermath of Abigail's death. The first shock came the instant she hit the 'Connect' button. There were close to a thousand such messages.

She loaded them all up, planning on reading them in something like chronological order, the first ones first. There, dozens of screens down, were lines that might as well have been artefacts from a different age: plaudits to her for her piece about the sweatshop, others linking to it and branding it a 'must-read'. A few dissenting voices too:

Just read knife-job by @maddywebbnews. One more tired rant against Chinese. When will we realize we had our chance as No 1 and we blew it!!

113

She waded through those and then saw the first references to Abigail.

Just heard terrible news about @maddywebbnews's sister #sosad

What a senseless waste of precious life. Hearts go out to @maddywebbnews #tragedy

Then one she had to read a few times to understand:

Hmm. @maddywebbnews writes a story exposing sweatshop conditions, then her sister ends up dead #coincidenceidontthinkso

It struck Maddy as absurd, but that didn't stop her doing the math. Her piece on the factory had gone live at midnight; Abigail's estimated time of death was shortly after one am. One hour for the angry owners of that hellhole to decide to get their revenge not by killing her but by finding and following her sister? Ridiculous.

Her eye skimmed over the rolling wave of condolences and sympathies from strangers, including readers who said how much they had appreciated Madison's journalism, 'exposing wrongdoing in their midst', as one put it. Messages from other journalists leapt out at her, as did one from the mayor.

The people of California will have the Webb family in its prayers today. My heartfelt condolences to @maddywebbnews

She could picture Leo hammering out that one. 'People of California' indeed. Positioning himself for the election, even in a message of condolence.

There were some old friends there too. Donna, one-time

114

college room-mate, now with glamorous job and rich husband in Shanghai, said how sorry she was and asked if there was anything she could do. Several more in that vein, too, most of them hedged with embarrassment at saying something so personal over Weibo, with its tacit admission that the sender had no other way to make contact, that in fact they had lost touch.

And then there was this, though Maddy missed it in her first roll through the feed, spotting it only when she made a second round, this time looking for those of particular sentimental value she ought to save and take to Quincy and her mother:

> @maddywebbnews heard your sister killed through drug overdose. Think same may have happened to friend of mine. Follow me pls: can explain.

Chapter 15

Maddy had hesitated at that, reading it two or three times to be sure there were no hidden traps. The user's name was Amy Alice. The alliteration troubled Maddy; it sounded fake. But then the user profile identified Amy Alice as an actress. A link took her through to a basic, homemade website, consisting mostly of portrait photographs. Maddy reckoned she was in her mid- to late-twenties, though there was no date of birth. Not unusual in that business or in this town. She was pretty, her skin a shade of mocha, though whether that meant she was black, Latina or of mixed race Maddy would not have hazarded a guess. As Rosario Padilla had proven, ethnic profiling in the LA of the twenty-first century was a fool's game. In one photo her dark hair was braided, in another it was worn long and, apparently, straightened. Maddy scanned the list of acting credits: a couple of musicals in the suburbs and a reference to 'theatre in education', which meant performances for schools. If Amy Alice was going to get a break in show business, she had clearly not got it yet.

Maddy did as she had been asked and hit the 'Follow' button. Now they would be able to communicate privately by direct message. Maddy's first approach was brief but Alice replied quickly, her tone suggesting an eagerness to talk.

Maddy glanced at her watch. It was now seven twenty. Was it odd for a struggling actress to be up and online at such an hour?

Ordinarily Maddy would have asked for a phone number. After all, any middle-aged sleazeball scratching his nuts in front of a computer screen could rip a few pictures off the internet and give himself a sweet, girlie name like Amy Alice. Covering some of the state's most appalling crime stories over the last few years had taught her that there was no shortage of sickos aroused by making some connection, however vicarious or indirect, with a murder. She had interviewed the women who had befriended – seduced, in one case – men jailed for the foulest acts, visiting them in jail, writing daily letters, somehow turned on by the proximity to evil. Contacting the sister of a victim for kicks, and posing as a woman to do it, would be novel but different only by degree.

Still, Maddy was reluctant to talk on the phone about this. She told herself it was too sensitive; it needed to be done in person. Nevertheless, in the back of her sleep-deprived mind there was a nagging sensation that she was not telling herself the whole truth, a suspicion she was not bringing to the surface. She left it there, unarticulated, and restated to herself that on any story that counted the key information was always garnered face to face.

They agreed to meet later that morning, at the Coffee Bean and Tea Leaf, on the corner of Sunset and Fairfax. She tried to make it earlier, but that was the earliest Amy could get out of work. Which meant at least four hours of inactivity, a prospect Maddy could not countenance. She paced some more, trawled through her weibs to see if there were any more leads she might have missed, checked her email for the same reason – but there was nothing.

It was past seven thirty, past time to call Detective Miller. But now the urgency had cooled. Maddy returned instead to the search window of her computer. She knew she was

117

retreading old ground but she also knew that the first time she had done this she had been numb with immediate grief. Maybe she had missed something. She typed: *heroin, victim, overdose, suspicious.*

Most of the stories that came up were ones she had already read. The rest were scientific entries, detailing or debating the chemistry of excessive opium intake. Not relevant. There was one that gave her pause, from a blog – Pleasure Dome – apparently written by a heroin user, who posted only as 'Coleridge'. There were dozens of posts, but the one that had come up was called 'On passive injection'.

I've been asked for my thoughts on the evergreen topic of passive injection. I discussed this earlier here and here but the focus this time will be on the erotic aspects of helping out a friend or being helped out, rather than simply shooting up for yourself by yourself.

As regular readers will know, I've long seen using as a very sexual act: after all, when it comes to bliss, orgasm is junk's only rival. So it's only natural that people would want to share the pleasure. When that involves a needle, well, it hardly needs spelling out, does it? It is an act of penetration, one person breaking through the outer layer of another, inserting themselves, then releasing their holy fluid into the person they love. It is a moment of total intimacy. The trust required to offer your naked skin to your lover, to allow them to pierce it, to fill you up with a serum that will bring life and ecstasy . . .

Maddy clicked away, repelled by the suggestion that the fate that had befallen her sister was somehow sexy. She only hoped that Barbara Miller hadn't found this same blog. If she had, she'd doubtless have tucked it away in the file as further reinforcement for her theory.

Then Maddy went back to the stories she'd already opened

once before, forcing herself to read more slowly this time. The incidents of tainted heroin she dismissed again. But she stopped at the report of a grief-stricken father, mystified by his daughter's apparent suicide by heroin overdose. There was a photo of the victim: the usual graduation shot, though it was hard to make out the colour of her hair since most of it seemed to be gathered under the mortarboard. The story was given extra play because the girl's father, Ted Norman of Orange County, was a worthy in state politics, recently elected as chairman of the Republican party in California.

'*I always thought she loved life too much to kill herself,*' was the key quote. But then came the sixth paragraph of the story, explaining that the man's daughter had been depressed for several months.

Madison clicked on the accompanying photo. It showed an earnest, scholarly young woman looking intently at the camera. She was attractive, her most striking feature her long, curled hair. As if to confirm that 'there's no story here', as Howard Burke might put it, the girl's hair was not blonde, but a warm, dark brown. Madison clicked out of the item. It was tragic, but not relevant.

She showered and set off to meet Amy Alice. The smog was heavy, but not unmanageable: she could at least see the cars in front. At intervals, her view was impeded by a convoy of military vehicles, supply trucks by the look of them, each branded with the yellow-and-red star of the People's Liberation Army. Odd; they were usually more discreet than that.

As it often did when she was driving, the first wave of tiredness from the wakeful night began to break over her. For a terrifying moment, she had the dizzying sensation that the cars ahead of her might be a mirage, a hallucination of sleeplessness. She gripped the wheel tighter, seeking the firm evidence of solid matter.

She dialled Barbara Miller's number: straight to voicemail. She gave it two minutes, then dialled it again with the same

119

result. Needing the stimulation of another voice, she tuned the car radio to KNX, where the news headlines at quarter past the hour recapped the overnight developments in 'the Abigail Webb case', referring to the CCTV pictures 'now being examined by LAPD detectives'. So that detail was now out. It was the fifth item and there was nothing else. After it came a report on the Winter Olympics, where the USA was struggling to hold third place in the medals table, behind Russia and, at the top, China. That led into the obligatory light item, about a hapless US bobsled rider who had crashed in each one of his heats – and who had prompted a debate about whether he should be allowed to represent the United States or should be immediately withdrawn and sent home. His defenders had turned him into an ironic hero, branding him 'Billy the Bullet'.

Perhaps ten minutes later Jeff Howe called again. Before Maddy even had the chance to ask, he spoke about the leak to KTLA. Or, as she swiftly corrected him, the 'briefing' to KTLA. It was far too detailed and solidly sourced to be anything but.

'I was as shocked as you were by that, Maddy. Truly. You know if this had been my investigation, it would have been air-locked. But Barbara runs her own show, that's—'

'Air-locked would have been nice. Saying *fucking nothing* would have been great. But I know how these things work, Jeff. No one ever stays quiet. Here's the thing though. If the LAPD's going to start shooting its mouth off about my sister, somebody could have told me in advance. A little heads up, before going to the media. I don't mean as—' She hesitated, not knowing the word for a woman who refuses to be a girlfriend. 'I don't mean as someone who knows you. I mean as family, Jeff. We had a right to know.'

Frustratingly, he didn't argue. He pleaded guilty on behalf of the department and promised to get answers. There was nowhere left to go.

'So what's happening now?' she asked, exploiting her advantage.

He told her the current focus was entirely on the footage from the Great Hall of the People. Detectives were speaking to everyone there that night, trying to build as complete a picture of the man seen speaking to Abigail at the bar as they could, working out whether they had been seen together earlier that evening and whether they had, in fact, left together.

'The trouble is, I hear the picture quality is pretty poor. Abigail's clear enough, apparently. But the image of the guy is very grainy. There's not much there to work with.'

Maddy fought the urge to speak, fearing what she might let slip. She pictured the man she had seen, his face visible only in profile, much of it whited out by the glare of the lights. What had struck her at the time was the short hair and the muscular bearing, but it was quite true: the rest was just whitish pixels. Abigail, in those few seconds after she turned, allowing her profile to come into view, had been sharper but he, in Maddy's memory at least, was much harder to make out.

And then she heard the voice of the technician, munching on his salad among the CCTV monitors at the Great Hall. *A couple of nights a week . . . she was a regular here.* For the hundredth time, Maddy pictured her sister, turning up at that place. What was she looking for that she couldn't find somewhere else? Abigail was gorgeous, she surely had no trouble finding a boyfriend. Why would she want to hang out there, perched at the bar, not once in a while but twice a week? What kick did she get out of it?

Jeff was still speaking. Maddy forced herself to retune to his voice, to come back to the conversation.

'Listen, Jeff. I can't reach Miller. Can I tell you what I've picked up and you pass it on to her?'

'I don't feel that comfortable acting as go-between on—'

'What can I do, she doesn't answer her phone? Listen, it's

just one thing. Two weeks ago a woman called Rosario Padilla – papa alpha delta india lima lima alpha – died of a heroin overdose which her family believe is suspicious. Check the file. She had no history of drug use, just like Abigail. Suspicious circumstances too.'

'Madison, I—'

'Just hear me out. It may be nothing, but she had blonde hair and very pale skin. Just like Abigail.'

'Maddy. You're in shock. Worse than shock. You've suffered a great loss. This is not what you should be doing right now, chasing wild—'

'I'm serious, Jeff. I think there could be a connection here. The man in the bar, the man we're looking for – what if he's done this before?'

'We shouldn't even be having this conversation. It's completely inappropriate.'

'Inappropriate? What the hell is that supposed to mean? Having your sister murdered and the TV news telling you she was getting high and it was all her fault. *That's* inappropriate.'

'Please, Maddy, that's not what I meant. I mean it's not right for *you*. To be doing this now. Besides, you don't need me to tell you: serial killers can be opportunists. There's often no strict pattern to the victims.'

'Often, yes. But—'

'There may be a broad category of victim, but they'll also grab an opportunity when they get one.'

'You don't think the blonde hair—'

'I'm not dismissing it, Maddy. But—'

'So do me a favour. At least mention it to Barbara. Tell her it's worth looking at previous cases. Also—'

'No, Madison.'

'I haven't even said what it is yet.'

'I don't need—'

'Photographs.'

'What?'

122

'Photographs from the crime scene. Crime *scenes*, plural. Get Barbara to compare them. How was Rosario Padilla's body found and is that similar to—'

'Madison, I cannot stress enough how wrong this is. This is a hundred shades of wrong.'

'Will you just mention it? Or take a look yourself. I know how that database works. Just take a look. If I'm wrong and there's no connection, then you get to say "I told you so."' She was trying to keep it light, even ever so slightly flirtatious. It was the tone, the manner, that got her into this mess with Jeff in the first place. She shook her head at her own folly.

But it worked. He promised he would do what he could. Still, there was something in his voice that she could not quite work out, a hesitation, a worry, she was not sure. She ended the call and spent the next twenty minutes staring straight ahead, summoning again and again those blurred images from the CCTV cameras, each time her mind's eye trying to get a closer look at the man, his face becoming more indistinct the closer she examined it.

The car had turned off the freeway and had made the series of turns and lights that led to Circle Park. She had pulled up and turned off the engine before she realized what had happened. The sudden quiet in the car broke the spell. She was a good twenty minutes away from the café, but she understood what had brought her here.

She looked around before getting out, checking the distances and line of sight. She was far enough away, especially on a smoggy morning like this one. Still, she clambered out of her seat slowly and closed the car door softly, to attract least attention.

The air was filled with the tinny sound of a loudspeaker mounted on a mast. Made of metal, it seemed to have rusted from the inside. But the sound it played was clear enough, a disco oldie: 'Staying Alive'.

And there on the asphalt square, where on the weekends you might see kids on skateboards or bikes, were eight lines of people, seven or eight in each row, moving in time to the music. Most were in tracksuits, a few of the women in leggings, perhaps the same outfits they had worn in aerobics classes in the 1980s. For the distinguishing feature of this group was that they were all old.

This was not the first time she had seen them and the same things struck her as always. The group, in which women dominated by a ratio of about two to one, did not smile or laugh, but wore expressions instead of grave concentration. Their movements were similarly restrained, unexpectedly graceful, their feet making delicate turns, the fingers on their hands outstretched as they moved both arms across their chests to point first to the right and then to the left.

The style was not the disco dancing Maddy had seen on those eighties nostalgia shows, arms propelled wildly, heads thrown back in simulated ecstasy. These movements were more careful, less frantic. And everyone danced the same precise steps. For an amateur group they were remarkably well co-ordinated. Only one man was out of time, turning one way when it should have been the other, showing his back when it should have been his front. But even he did not laugh at his error. He too was concentrating, trying to stay in harmony with the others.

As always, Maddy looked in vain for the leader but if he or she was there, it was not obvious. Instead they seemed to move under their own direction, focused on the collective goal of dancing well as a group. When the song finished and before the next one began there was no applause, even from the few dog-walkers and morning joggers who had stopped to look. This was not a performance.

As the next routine began – to the backing of 'Mo Li Hua', the traditional Chinese tune which had become a kitschy favourite – Maddy filtered out everyone else and looked only at one person, the same way she always did. This woman's movements were especially neat, her toes pointed outward just as any ballet teacher would demand. A good dancer since her girlhood, she was not content merely to extend her arms, but turned her wrists too, her fingers rigidly in position. She allowed her hips a little extra shimmy on the turns, a departure from the script which made Maddy smile. It was not hard to see who, thirty years ago, would have been the beauty of this, or any other, group. Only the eyes betrayed her. Even from this distance, Maddy could see they were far away.

Madison watched her mother do one more song, but didn't risk waiting till the end of the routine, in case it was the last. She slipped back into her car and headed to the appointment she had made, to discuss the death of the youngest daughter of the elegant woman in the second row who, as Maddy drove away, was still dancing, each step as neat and perfect as the one before.

There was a strange comfort in doing this again: on the road, an address punched into the GPS, notebook on the passenger seat. She knew how to be a reporter, if nothing else.

The Coffee Bean and Tea Leaf was almost empty, the way so many places were in late January, its blackboard list of special lattes and themed mochas looking distinctly half-hearted. America always used to feel like this in the last few days of November, as everyone headed somewhere else for Thanksgiving, and at the close of December too, but this January exodus still felt like a novelty.

Maddy was early but so was Amy Alice. She was at a corner table, by the window, her eyes fixed on a pad and, next to it, a volume that was slim but heavily bookmarked, its pages sprouting little periscopes of paper. She was, Maddy guessed, of mixed race, her dark hair pinned back, wearing glasses and no make-up, that look favoured by so many off-duty actresses, especially the pretty ones, a look designed to convey seriousness of purpose, confounding any expectations of airhead starlet.

Maddy sat down without introduction. She had an urge to come right out with it, to save them both the time: *So. This friend of yours. Was she blonde or not?* In her exhausted state, she thought she had earned the right to dispense with the pleasantries, the journalistic ruses required to soften up a source. As the sister of a murder victim, wasn't she allowed, just this once, not to be sensitive or emotionally intelligent but to get straight to the damned point? Because if this woman's friend turned out to be a junkie, she might as well know now. And if she wasn't fair-skinned and blonde she needed to know that too because, at this moment, that's all she had tying Abigail to Rosario Padilla. Without it, Abigail's death was random – just another hardluck LA homicide.

But Maddy had no chance to try a new, direct approach. Amy Alice was giving her a long look. She then shook her head in rueful reflection on the pity of it all, before making a gesture that caught Maddy by surprise. She reached across the table and took Maddy's hands in hers. 'Oh Madison,' she said. 'I'm so sorry.'

Maddy tried to reply but could only manage a resigned, that's-life smile.

'I know that face, though,' Amy Alice said. 'That's how I felt for days afterwards. And Eveline was only my friend. You've lost your sister.'

Maddy nodded and then got to her feet, needing the busyness of a task to dilute the moment. She took Amy's coffee order, bought a bottle of water for herself, took a long draught from it and girded herself. She needed to wrest back control of this encounter, before it turned into bereavement counselling.

'So tell me about your friend,' she said at last.

Amy Alice took a deep breath and then placed her palms

126

flat on the table. 'Eveline was an actress, like me. She was doing better than me, too. She'd done some TV. She'd done a music video. She'd done some modelling. She was *sexy*, if you know what I mean.'

Maddy nodded. The fact that Eveline had been cast in a music video suggested curves: the Asian market in particular looked to America to provide T&A.

'She was very different from me. I'm from Chicago, but she was from Iowa. You know, a farmer's daughter.'

'What kind of different?'

'Sort of innocent, I'd say. People would laugh, if you saw some of the things she did. Bumping and grinding, wearing not that much. But she was real innocent, believe me.'

'This is why you don't think she ever took drugs?'

'Exactly. She'd grown up with people smoking and drinking, for sure. But *heroin*, no way. Just the very last person who'd be into that.'

'But naïve people can be sucked into that kind of thing, they can—'

'I know what you're saying, Mad—' She paused. 'What do I call you? It said Madison in the article, but you're Maddy on—'

'Call me Maddy. You don't think your friend might have been so innocent, she just didn't realize—'

'No. And I tell you why. We were very different, Eveline and me. We really were. I like all this stuff,' she gestured at the book on the table, a text of *Long Day's Journey into Night*. 'And Eveline wanted nothing more than to get a part in a soap. That was really her ambition. But we were both new here and we just hung out together.'

Maddy raised her eyebrows.

'As in, all the time. We shared the apartment; if we went out in the evening, we usually went together. We worked together a lot. If anything had been happening, I'd have known about it.'

'And you said all this to the police?'

Amy Alice nodded. 'But they weren't interested. I think it was because of some of the stuff Eveline had done. You know, the filming.'

'Music videos?'

'Yeah and maybe some other stuff. Before I met her.'

Maddy got the idea. 'So given her résumé, the police thought smack in the bloodstream was not shocking enough to merit any questions?'

'They took a statement from me. Since I was the one that found her.' Amy went on to describe the moment, in the early evening. How she had put the key in her front door, called out as usual. She had bought Chinese food for the two of them to share, partly as a thank you to Eveline. But there was no sound. Once she was in the shared living room, she saw her friend stretched out on the floor, arms at her side, her right sleeve rolled up, her lips blue. She thought she felt the faintest trace of a pulse. She had tried CPR, she tried breathing into Eveline's cold mouth, her hands touching her matted hair, her own blood draining from her face as she realized what was happening. She had called 911, but you know how it is these days: they took nearly twenty minutes to come. 'By then, she was dead.' As she spoke, Amy Alice's eyes began to glitter, but no more.

'Did you know she'd OD'd, as soon as you saw her?'

'I had a pretty good idea.' She made a slight upward roll of the eyes, a sign of too much experience. 'I'm from Chicago.'

'And was there any suggestion . . .' Maddy hesitated. 'Did it look as if anything else had happened to Eveline?' When she saw Amy Alice's look of incomprehension, she forced herself to be more explicit. 'Do you think she had been raped?'

The woman shook her head quickly. 'No. The police never mentioned anything about that.'

Madison added a sentence to her notebook and underlined it. She remembered what she had heard from Rosario Padilla's brother and Jeff Howe's account of the pathologist's report on Abigail. No sign of sexual contact, he had said. *No sign at all, Madison. None.* It was a relief, but also a puzzle. Back when she was on the crime beat, she had covered several multiple homicide cases involving female victims: she could not think of one that did not involve sexual violence.

She looked out the café window, at the cheap red lantern dangling from the awning of the store across the street and the notice in the window promising roast duck in a bag, special for the season, at half price.

'"Partly as a thank you",' Maddy began quietly. 'What were you thanking Eveline for?'

At that Alice's eyes darkened. She swallowed. 'Remember I said that we sometimes worked together?'

Maddy nodded. 'Yes. I suppose that was unusual, right? Getting parts in the same shows?'

Amy Alice smiled. 'That tells me you're not an actor.' She leaned forward, as if letting Maddy in on a trade secret. 'Most of the work you do as an actor is . . . not acting. You gotta pay the rent.'

'Of course. And how did you pay the rent?'

Amy Alice looked straight at her, an expression that contained a hint of defiance. 'Cleaning. That's where I've come from right now. I called you just before my shift.'

So that was why Amy Alice was working early but free by noon. 'You clean houses?'

'Don't look so surprised. There are lots of us doing it.'

'Of course. Sure.'

'It pays OK. And it's flexible.'

Maddy worried what her face was saying. One of the risks of sheer exhaustion: your face could have a mind of its own. 'And you both did it, you and Eveline?'

'That's right.'

'Where? In this neighbourhood?'

'All over. In private houses, offices. Wherever the agency sends us. Sometimes you don't know till you show up. Today was a daycare centre. And they don't care which one of you does the shift, as long as somebody does it.'

'And this had something to do with thanking Eveline?'

'I was booked to do a shift with the agency that day. And then this audition came up, the night before. An all-black production of *The Cherry Orchard*, out in Ventura. Eveline was so sweet about it. She was like, "You have to do it, Amy. This is for you." And I was like, "Really? Are you sure?" But we did that for one another. If you really couldn't make it, the other one would cover for you.'

'So that's what happened? Eveline did your shift?'

Alice nodded, mutely. Her guilt was solid, a presence in the room, so palpable Maddy knew the answer to her next question. 'And after the shift, that's how you found her? On the floor?'

She nodded again, the edges of her nostrils twitching as she held back tears. There are some women who cry readily. Maddy was not one of them and nor, she could see, was Amy Alice. Maddy extended her hand, to touch hers.

'That was meant to be my shift, you know?' Alice said. 'Eveline took my place and she . . . and she . . .'

'I know,' Maddy said uselessly, 'I know.'

She wished she could say something that would comfort this woman, who was clearly anguished. Bereavement was bad enough, Maddy reflected. To blame yourself must be a double burden. There was no escaping it though. She had to ask.

'Do you have a picture of your friend? Of Eveline?'

At that, Amy Alice turned to her phone and began pressing buttons and swiping images until she had one that she decided merited expansion, using her thumb and forefinger. 'Here,' she said. 'Eveline was so proud of this one. She looks lovely, don't you think?'

The sight of it came as a terrible, and wholly unexpected, disappointment.

Chapter 16

The woman in the picture had the looks of a glamour model. Her lips were full, whether through the kindness of mother nature or the generosity of a doctor's syringe, Maddy couldn't tell. The nose was short and pert as a button, the way they liked them on TV. Her skin was pale.

But her hair was the wrong colour.

This woman had dark hair, tumbling down to her shoulders. Instantly, Maddy felt a curious sensation of embarrassment. She had spun her theory to Jeff Howe, insisting he pass it on to the detectives handling her sister's case, that they could well be confronting a serial murderer with a fetish for blondes – a strange kind of pervert, admittedly, one who did not seek direct sexual contact with his victims. Her evidence had been Rosario Padilla and her own sister. But she had gone too early. She knew the rule, drilled into her by Howard and known to everyone in her line of work: you have to have three. Two is just a coincidence. And now two was all she had.

More immediately, she could see the look of expectation on Amy Alice's face. The actress had intuited, correctly, that Maddy had asked to see Eveline's picture for a reason. She had assumed it was because Madison was preparing to say something that might reassure the friend she had left behind, offering some words that might lighten the weight of guilt she had carried since that evening. And now she wanted to hear them.

'I'm sorry,' was the best Maddy could manage, her head beginning to swim, the room beginning to revolve. 'I was expecting . . . I thought . . . I thought she would look different.'

Alice was forlorn. 'Eveline liked this picture so much. She thought she looked, you know, classy. This was how she wanted to be seen, I think.'

Maddy looked at it again. She saw the eyes, needy and eager. She wondered if they had come on to that same brute at the bar, whose blurred face had been caught so close to Abigail's on the CCTV footage. Had Abigail too shown him imploring eyes, craving affection?

But it was useless. She was trying to construct a pattern and this woman did not fit. A tumbling wave of exhaustion rolled through Madison, starting somewhere in her gut and reaching her brain. She had wasted enough time here already.

As she said her goodbyes to Amy Alice, doing her best to repress her own irritation, to sound caring rather than terse, she realized that her entire morning had been wasted. Perhaps Jeff was right. Perhaps, God forbid, Quincy was right. Maybe it was crazy to be doing this. She needed to sit in a room, with pictures of her sister and mourn her. For days or weeks or months or simply let time stand still. To turn off her phone and Weibo and just stare at the ceiling. For a second, she heard her younger sister's voice. *Fresh air is what you need, Maddy. When was the last time you went for a run? Was it, like, even this decade?*

'Sorry not to be of more help,' Maddy said finally, as she shook the actress's hand, doing her best to limit her exposure to the woman's gaze, which radiated disappointment. She went through the motions of taking a few final details, dutifully writing down the deceased's full name: Eveline Linda Plaats. 'I've got your number, you've got mine. Call me if anything occurs to you. Anything at all.'

Back in the car, heading west on Sunset, she realized that she would only have to turn right on Kenter and she could soon be at Quincy's house. She could let go of this fruitless, draining task and rest. Quincy, she reckoned, would let her do that. She would tuck her up in one of their many spare bedrooms, with freshly laundered towels and an unlit scented candle on the bedside table, and look after her, providing her with home-cooked food – or at least food that had been cooked in her home by Juanita – and a constant supply of hot tea. There would only be one condition: Madison would have to admit that she had been wrong and that Quincy had been right – about Abigail, about the appropriate way to mourn, about their mother, about everything. Madison's foot pressed harder on the gas pedal and she drove straight on.

The traffic was heavy, giving her time to stare out of the window. The smog meant there was not much to look at – she could barely make out the giant 'Visit China' electronic billboard, projecting a field of scarlet poppies swaying in the pixelated breeze – but that suited her. It gave her time to think.

Mainly she relived the conversation with Amy Alice, kicking herself for not making the obvious move earlier. *Before we start, show me a photograph so I can decide if this is worth my while.* But you never could talk like that, could you? Not if you wanted to win someone's trust. You had to be gentle, take your time. Not because you were a good person, but because those were smart tactics. You were reeling in a fish and you couldn't rush. If you did, you'd only spook them.

She listened to herself. She could teach one of those J-school courses, offered to wannabe journalists by never-were journalists.

Maybe that's how she'd end up, one of those sad sacks recounting old war stories and telling the students how great she used to be. She'd run a special module on how to entrap the newly bereaved. 'I was really good at that,' she'd say. The premonition of it produced a shiver of disgust, the colder for being directed at herself.

Was she making too much of the blonde hair? Just because Abigail and Rosario were blondes did not mean that all the victims had to be, did it? Maybe the killer couldn't care less about colouring; perhaps the fact that her sister and Rosie were fair was mere coincidence.

And yet what did she have without it? Just that several women had recently died through a drug overdose which none of their families could accept. It wasn't enough. It didn't feel like enough. Her instinct – the inner voice that sometimes had to shout to get heard above all the others, but which belonged only to her – kept returning to the hair, the hair, the hair. It was Abigail's signature feature; it was what made Rosario Padilla striking. Her professional instinct told her it mattered. And it had rarely been wrong.

She played back the words Amy Alice had spoken, examining them for any unseen opening. None of it yielded much. Slowing down in the traffic, she caught herself staring at the woman in the car next to hers, only looking away when she realized the eyes above the smog mask were glaring.

Eveline liked this picture so much. She thought she looked, you know, classy. This was how she wanted to be seen, I think.

That last line of Amy Alice's had repeated itself several times on Madison's internal recording system. She didn't know why. Now stationary, she reached for her phone and Googled the name: *Eveline Plaats*. Only one image came on the first page, the same head and shoulders shot Maddy had already seen. She sighed and drove a few more yards till the traffic halted her again.

She went back to the phone and that photograph. A click revealed that it came from the *LA Times*, not a full-length story so much as an extended photo-caption in that part of the TV section that served up nuggets of industry buzz.

> *Eveline Plaats wins brief role in long-running soap,* The Bold and the Beautiful. *She will make her TV debut in the fall . . .*

Madison clicked further and found several more pictures of Eveline: one giving a come-hither look, another posing with a group of interchangeably attractive starlets. In each one, her hair was perfectly styled: long, thick curls of brown, like an English princess.

She thought she looked, you know, classy.

Now, as Madison moved the car a few inches further, her mind was revving. *Classy.* She knew the type of woman who believed brown hair made you look classy. She touched and swiped away at the screen on her lap, even as she controlled the steering wheel with her knees. Eventually she found a cluster of older photos of Eveline Plaats, enough of them to fill the little screen.

Maddy found Amy Alice's number and redialled it.

Without introduction, she said, 'You said Eveline liked the way she looked in that photo you showed me.'

'Yes.' Amy was hesitant, as if she was about to be confused.

'What did she like about it? Why did she think it made her look "classy"? That was your word. Why did she think that?'

'Because . . . I don't know exactly. Maybe it had something to do with the way she saw herself. And, you know, her low self-esteem and—'

'No, no. I don't mean that. Listen to me.' She could hear the edge in her own voice. 'What was *different* about that picture? Physically.'

'Oh I see. Well, I suppose the main thing—'

'Come on, Amy. Please.'

'Her hair was different.'

'Yes.'

'Normally she cut it shorter.'

'Is that it? Just the length?'

'No, no. Of course not. Sorry. She dyed it for the part.'

'She dyed it? So what was her regular hair colour, Amy?'

'Didn't I say? I thought I said. I'm so sorry, this whole thing's got me so . . . She was blonde. Like a gorgeous, kind of Swedish blonde. But she thought it made her look cheap. Like it was out of a bottle or something. But actually—'

'And was she blonde, you know, recently . . .' Madison let her voice trail off.

'Yes. Yes she was. The part in the soap didn't really pan out. They cut most of it. Kept like two lines. We recorded it, though. She must have rewound it, like, a hundred times. Her agent told her she should go back to being blonde. It was her USP, he said.'

'And could you send me a picture of how she looked with her natural colouring?'

'Well, I have one from a few months ago but that's how she looked.'

'Even at the end?'

'Yes,' her friend replied quietly.

Madison waited no more than thirty seconds before her phone chimed the arrival of a message. She clicked open the photograph that had just landed.

And there they were, a cliché as old as Los Angeles: two pretty girls, looking for their break in Tinseltown. On the left, grinning for the camera, her hair in cornrows, Amy Alice. And on the right, her best pal, doubtless looking as fresh and unadorned as the day she left behind the prairies and hogfarms of her home state – her skin fair, her hair as blonde as a bale of Iowa hay.

To Madison it was confirmation. Her sister Abigail had not

been the first woman to die this way. She had not even been the second. If Maddy was right, Rosario Padilla and Eveline Plaats had been victims one and two. Abigail was the third: the third victim of a brutal serial killer.

Maddy pulled over and asked Amy to find somewhere quiet where she could talk. As it happened, she had stayed at the café. The actor's life: there was nowhere else she had to be.

Maddy began by saying, 'I need you to tell me everything you can about Eveline's last day.' With a pen in her hand, her phone on speaker and a notebook on her knee, Maddy scribbled as she pressed Amy Alice on every last detail of the twenty-four hours that preceded the moment she found her friend cold and dying on the floor. She interrogated her over every memory, every phone call she overheard, every gesture Eveline made, forcing her to go back over the same ground twice or three times.

By the end they had assembled a fairly full account of the final movements of Eveline Plaats – but for one glaring gap.

'And you worked a cleaning shift just this morning, you say?'

Amy Alice hesitated, unhappily aware of where such a question was leading. 'Yes.'

'And how well do you get on with your supervisor or whoever it is that hands out the work?'

'Him? You don't want to get on with him. You don't want to make *eye contact* with him. Not unless you want a pair of sweaty hands on your ass.'

'Oh, a charmer.'

'Besides, he won't tell me.'

'How do you know?'

'Can't you just ask the police? He must have had to tell them about this.'

'Sure. If they asked. But, like you said, we're not so sure they were that bothered about a girl who'd been . . . a glamour model. Anyway, we're the ones who need to know. We're the ones who care, Amy. You and me. So how do you know he won't tell you?'

'Because I already asked.'

'You did?'

'Of course, I did. It was, like, the first thing I asked. "Where did Eveline work yesterday?" To his face. Can you believe they made me work the very next day?'

'And what'd he say?'

'He got very weird.' She dropped her voice an octave till she sounded like a meatpacker from Queens. '"None of your business, OK? You clean the houses, I'll clean up this shit."'

'Was there anyone else you could ask?'

'There's a sweet woman who answers the phone sometimes. She just shook her head when I asked, like she was terrified of the question.'

'Jesus.'

'They all said the same thing, Maddy. They told me to mind my own business. Sort out the funeral, contact Eveline's family, but leave the rest to them.'

Maddy bit down hard on her pen. 'Why don't you call them again now? Say you think she might have left something behind, you've been looking for it everywhere. The family want it. A necklace, a bracelet or something? I can patch you through from this phone. I'll be listening in the whole time.'

'It won't work.'

'I know. But you're an actress. Just say the lines. Let's see what they say.' Maddy smiled an unseen, plaintive smile.

After a delay and some false starts getting the phone into 'conference call' mode, Maddy sat in her car hearing Amy Alice's breathing as she waited for the manager of the CleanBreak Company to pick up. With her own phone on mute, she was able to eavesdrop unheard.

Amy began with an enthusiasm bordering on the flirtatious, as she chatted to the sleazeball at the other end. Maddy could tell he was confused, clearly used to the ice treatment from this particular member of his workforce. Maddy willed the actress to dial it down a little. But then came the request. *I've had Eveline's parents on . . . They say it's a family heirloom . . . I've looked everywhere for it . . . The only place it could be is the place where she worked that day. It must have fallen off . . . Let me save you the hassle, let me make the call. Why don't I come over there now? And afterwards maybe we can go get some—*

If Maddy hadn't heard the response herself she might not have believed it. Even when on the receiving end of a full blast of womanly charm from the beautiful Amy Alice, signalling interest and availability, the dispatcher from the cleaning firm could not have been clearer.

'The answer's no,' he said, his words followed by the stubborn, sustained tone of a phone that had been hung up.

Maddy exhaled and ended the call, then called Amy Alice back to thank her and ask for her confidentiality: for now this had to stay between them.

As she started the car, she felt that familiar pulse of adrenalin: the moment you realize you're working on a story someone, somewhere, doesn't want published. It felt like progress. Clearly the location of Eveline Plaats's last place of work was a secret, one sensitive enough to make a slimeball groper pass up the prospect of live flesh rather than betray it. There was only one person Maddy knew with even a remote chance of unlocking it.

Chapter 17

'You gotta be fucking joking.'

That Katharine Hu responded this way even before Maddy had made her main request was not encouraging. All she had done was to call her friend at work, asking if she could spare no more than an hour to meet somewhere outside the office – and to bring her laptop with her.

'You gotta be fucking joking.'

'What? It will only take an hour, I promise.'

'I mean, you gotta be joking that this is what you're doing. For Christ's sake, Maddy, didn't we talk about this? You're in *mourning*. And that's not a twenty-four-hour deal. You gotta give yourself *time*.'

'I can explain,' she replied lamely, though how she was not quite sure. She decided on a change of tack. 'I need you, K. That's the bottom line. There's no one else I can turn to.'

'Is this, "K, I need you because you're a great friend" or is this, "K, I need you because you're a computer genius". Because, I gotta tell you, 'bring your laptop' sounds a lot like the second.'

'Both.'

'If I do this—'

'Oh, K, thanks so much, I knew—'

'Whoa, I said *if*. If I do this, there's a price.'

'OK, what's the price?'

'You have to listen to me give you a stern fucking talking-to afterwards.'

'Done.'

'I mean it, Maddy. You gotta listen to me. You're not doing this right.'

'I will, I promise. I'm three blocks away. Soon as you can.'

Six minutes later, Maddy saw the figure of Katharine Hu, in her professional woman's uniform of a black pant-suit, stride into the café. Katharine's brown hair, barely styled at the best of times, was long and lank. Her eyes – perhaps because they were too raw for her usual contact lenses – were behind glasses that, Madison noticed, carried an oily film. Most of the time, Maddy forgot the decade-wide age gap between them. But at this moment, her best friend and closest colleague looked like a woman who had lived through forty hard years – at the very least. Still, Madison was relieved to have her there: she felt as if she'd been fighting a fire alone and at last had someone at her side.

'It's possible that this woman Eveline Plaats and Abigail were killed in the same way,' Maddy began. 'Trouble is, we don't know enough about Eveline's very last movements. Specifically, we don't know where she worked that day. But someone knows.'

'Who?'

'CleanBreak. It's a "domestic services" agency. They send cleaners out on jobs; they probably have records of who worked where. You know, on their system. But they won't tell us anything.'

'Oh no.'

'Come on, K.'

'Do you have any idea how illegal that is? People have been *jailed* for this sort of thing, Maddy.'

'I know, but that was for, like, hacking the Pentagon. This is—'

'*I* was nearly jailed, Maddy. As you well know.'

Madison replied with a moment of respectful silence. If ever Maddy had to explain who her friend and colleague really was and what she really did, she usually went for the news-in-brief version, explaining that Katharine was once part of 'the hacking community', a phrase whose absurdity Maddy would acknowledge with an attempt at a smile. Katharine had found her way to the *LA Times* after she had broken into the system of a major food company, revealing internal correspondence that showed the company had knowingly labelled their own products falsely. Or, as Katharine would helpfully chip in, 'They were selling shit and they knew it.' She handed the information over to the *Times* who then came under pressure to reveal their source. They refused. Katharine lay low for the best part of a year but once the pressure had eased, and several executives of the food company had been indicted, she was quietly hired. Initially in 'systems support', she had gone on to become a crucial part of the newsroom, deploying her intimacy with all things computer to ferret out data others wanted hidden. Nearly ten years older than Maddy, she remained as tech savvy as a teenager.

'The answer's still no,' Katharine said gently, leaning forward to touch Maddy's hand, a sign she had not abandoned the effort to persuade her friend to stop this craziness and grieve.

'Will you at least let me explain?' Maddy implored. She told Katharine everything she had so far: the unexplained and improbable deaths by heroin overdose of three women who had no history of using drugs, each woman of a similar age and appearance. 'The police won't even accept these other two were murdered at all. They're giving the same bullshit they tried with Abigail. You know, "Maybe there was a drug habit." Or sex, or whatever. But I'm convinced – no, I'm not convinced but I think it's at least *possible* – that these things

143

are connected. I don't know how, I don't know who. But it's got to be worth looking at.'

'So let the police do it, Maddy. That's their job.'

'It *should* be their job, I agree with you. Hundred per cent. But they're not doing it, K. Don't you see? It may be nothing. But I have to at least look. If there's even a chance this could lead to the person who killed Abigail, I have to look, don't I?' She could feel her throat drying. 'And the truth is, I don't think I can begin to mourn until I know who did this.' It was a statement Maddy had not yet made to herself. She was almost surprised to hear the clarity of it.

Katharine looked down and shook her head. She did not speak for a long while, Maddy allowing her the silence. Eventually, she raised her face. 'I'm doing this because I know you loved your sister. And because I would want my sister to do this for me.'

Maddy nodded, letting the silence between them acknowledge the fact that she had seen the tears in her friend's eyes. Katharine, no more able to speak than Maddy, squeezed her hand, before finally surrendering to a release of laughter. 'Look at me,' she said, wiping away the moisture from her cheek. 'And I'm meant to be the butch one.'

She pulled the laptop towards her, flipped up the lid and got to work.

'OK, let's start at the beginning.' First she went to a domain Madison dimly recalled from the last time they mounted an operation like this: windowssecurityfix.com. It sounded global and mighty. In fact it was a homemade little site of Katharine's own. She tinkered away for a few seconds, muttered something about updating for the latest version of Windows and then opened a new tab.

There she searched for CleanBreak, found it, clicked on it and inspected their website. 'I can't be certain, but I'd guess that this is a small- to medium-size business, with fifteen to twenty employees.' That had been Amy Alice's rough estimate too, safely recorded in Maddy's notebook. 'There's a chance they have an in-house mail server. I might be wrong, but let's start with that and see where we get to.'

She went to the Contact Us page and noted the email address: info@cleanbreakcleaning.com. A second later, she opened up another tab where she logged onto an email account. Not, noted Maddy – who had seen this trick before – in Katharine's own name, but one of her multiple aliases.

Katharine set about composing an email to an imaginary employee she knew would not exist, christening him with the least likely name she could dream up: tarquin@cleanbreak-cleaning.com, writing the single word *Contact* into the subject field and then this brief message:

Can you send me your rates, please?

She pressed 'Send'. A few seconds later, she murmured, 'Thank you very much, that'll do nicely.' The message had just bounced back, an auto-response which apparently informed her that her message to tarquin@cleanbreakcleaning.com had been undeliverable but which, to Katharine's trained eye, revealed so much more. A quick look at the headers exposed a long string of gobbledegook – or at least that was how it seemed to Maddy. But for Katharine it was a pane of glass, entirely clear. It told her that CleanBreak used a Windows server for its email and, therefore, almost certainly used Windows for everything else. Above all, it revealed what she was looking for, the name of the cleaning company's internet service provider: Unicom, Chinese-owned and the biggest ISP in the country.

Thinking out loud, she weighed up the probabilities that a company of that size and type would have its own dedicated IT person. She guessed they wouldn't, that at most they would have an administrator whose multiple duties included keeping the computers ticking over and calling for help when things went wrong. She looked up from her screen. 'Cellphone at the ready please, Maddy. OK. You know what to do. And remember: *slowly.*'

Maddy took the phone and dialled the number for CleanBreak, asking to be put through to the person in charge of IT. A short delay and then she began, expertly adopting the voice of a middle-aged, suburban woman. She spoke slowly, and got slower.

'Hello there, dear. I'm calling from the administration department of Ventura High School and, well, I don't know where to start. Some of our students have been receiving the most awful email messages today . . . Hold on, I'll explain what it has to do with your company. What was I saying? Oh yes, awful messages. And what's that? Well, that's just it, dear. We've traced them to a company called, hold on a moment, that's it, CleanBreak Cleaning. Exactly. Yes, I know . . . But they say it very clearly. Info at Clean Break cleaning dot com. That's the address. Now, some of them have pictures. Well, photographs . . .'

On she went, receiving an enthusiastic thumbs-up from Katharine.

Now, using a program on the laptop and with headphones firmly on, Katharine dialled CleanBreak for herself, reassured that the administrator at the other end was suitably tied up. She cleared her throat as she waited for the call to be answered. Once it was, she sat up straight and – a bit too loudly for a corner table in a café – asked to be put through to the person in charge of computer systems.

'Hello, this is Unicom calling with an urgent issue. Am I speaking to someone at Clean Break cleaning dot com? OK, I need to notify you that your network is being actively used to spread a piece of malware and we need to take . . . What's that? OK, let me back up and put it real simple. The network you guys use has been infected with a "zero day" virus, that is a "zero day" virus. We have a fix for it, but we need to act very swiftly . . . No, I'm afraid we don't have time for that process, sir . . . Well, I'm happy for you to do that, sir, of course that's your right, but that will entail termination of your service within the next three to four minutes . . . That's right, we'll have to cut you off the internet . . . I see that, sir, but we have a duty of care to our customers . . .'

Maddy was waving her hands, signalling that she couldn't keep up her end much longer. 'Let me just get a pen, dear,' she was saying, but it was clear she was struggling: whoever it was at the other end had lost patience and would soon surely be slamming the phone down. Katharine stepped up the pace.

'All right, sir. This virus is spreading and Unicom's policy is very clear. We have to cap off the source and that source is you . . . Good, OK. So here's what I need you to do. Yes, that's the good news. There is a fix for this. No, you don't need your manager to help you. It's real simple.'

Maddy was holding up her phone. Her decoy efforts were exhausted.

Katharine, however, was in full flow. 'Believe me, you don't want to see his face when you're the guy who got the whole office cut off. Sudden termination can often trigger loss of all data. Yes, exactly. So let's do this. Go to windows security fix dot com . . . Yep, two "s"s. No spaces, no dots . . . You got that? Excellent. Now see that little icon there, on the top right? That's the one. It says "security dot exe". Yep, that's it. Just click on that for me. Uh-huh. Just wait for it to roll through. OK, what's it saying now? "Security patch applied, your system is now secure." You've got those words on your screen? Excellent. Now tell me, have you got a little . . . That's it, the little smiley face! Good, that means we're done. Yep, all done. That's right, there'll be no termination of your supply. Let's just hope we've stopped that "zero day" in its tracks. They can be real evil, those viruses, believe me. All right now, sir, you have a good day now. No, thank *you*.'

Maddy and Katharine exchanged a mute high-five,

dampening both sound and gesture in deference to the fact that they were in a public place. Then Katharine entered a few keystrokes and was suddenly looking at the internal system of the CleanBreak cleaning company – fully exposed to her gaze the instant the hapless junior on the end of the phone had allowed himself to be bullied into downloading and installing a piece of software that acted as an electronic traitor, granting remote access to the person who controlled both it and the bogus windowssecurityfix.com website where he had found it. And that person was Katharine.

She turned the screen around for Maddy to see. With no graphics, this was plainly the back end of the CleanBreak system. Visible was a kind of menu:

SHOW TABLES;

PAYROLL

PREMISES

TAX

ROSTER

Maddy pointed at the last of those and Katharine took back the machine. She typed in answers to the questions that appeared, in single, blinking lines of text.

DESCRIBE ROSTER

Date

Client

Employee

'What date are we talking about?' Katharine asked.

'January ninth.'

'OK.' A few more keystrokes and then, 'Spell the name we're looking for. Real slowly.'

'Papa, lima—'

'You know I can never do that shit. Just spell it like a normal person. Slowly.'

'P. L. A. A. T. S. First name Eveline.'

A frown appeared on Katharine's face. 'No one of that name on that day. Could you have got the date wrong? Are you sure—'

'One hundred per cent sure,' Madison replied. 'Can you look again?'

Still nothing.

Of course. Maddy leaned forward and said quietly, 'Search for *Alice. Amy Alice.*' It was she who had been due to work that day. It was Amy Alice's shift Eveline had done.

A few more keystrokes, the briefest smile of satisfaction and then Katharine's face darkened, as if a shadow had passed over it. She turned the screen for Maddy to read for herself.

Next to Amy Alice's name was a simple description. The words were plain enough, but still Maddy had to read them and read them again to be sure. But even after she had looked away, catching Katharine's aghast expression, they were still there, carrying the same message in glowing light.

Amy Alice: Accommodation Units 88 to 101, S48 Division, Garrison of the People's Liberation Army, Port of Los Angeles.

Chapter 18

How many times had he done a wardrobe session, a dozen? Maybe two? The first candidates Bill Doran worked for would spend a maximum of two minutes on this exercise, usually delegating it to their wives. That changed as the industry got slicker, as more PR consultants were hired and experts popped up spouting seven jars of hooey about earth tones and 'giving off a beta male aura' and bullshit of a similar stripe. Now he was expected to pay attention to whether the candidate wore a red or blue tie or, more commonly, went open-necked and rugged.

He had gotten used to that, even become quite good at it. But now, he understood, he had to take it to a whole other level. He was working for a woman now; different rules applied. Like it or not, choosing the main campaign photograph – the one that would appear on the website and on lawn signs, on lapel buttons and as the final still image on the TV spots – was serious business.

Some wanted her in vivid red or canary yellow, conveying, it was said, strength and confidence. Others wanted something softer: 'Everyone already knows Elena Sigurdsson is tough enough to put Berger's balls in the blender. We need to show she can also be kinder. And gentler.'

'Sure, if this was *Leonard* Sigurdsson we were selling.' It was Ted Norman, mid-fifties, ruddy-faced chair of the state party. Hawkish on every issue even, it seemed, clothing. He was dressed like a Florida retiree: slacks, short-sleeved navy shirt. This man was, Doran concluded to his own amusement, the very personification of the Republican party activist: white, male, affluent and angry. The very rims of his eyes seemed aflame, with something that was either rage or melancholy or perhaps both. Doran could have sketched a profile of him then and there: watches Fox, likes no music recorded since 1978 and never vacations abroad. And, if he had to bet, suffers from high cholesterol.

'You do "kinder, gentler" with a woman and she's weak,' Norman was saying. 'You might as well show her tearing up. If there's a nuclear accident on the San Andreas fault at three o'clock in the morning, people don't want the governor to give them a hug. They want to know she'll take charge. And anyone who doesn't like it better get the hell out of the way.'

A few of the kids in the room stared at their feet, doubtless embarrassed by the lack of sophistication. But Doran knew better: Norman was the authentic voice of the activists. They might not know how to win an election – in fact, if you let them get their way, they'd lose you an election every time. But you had to show respect. They were your base. Without them you were nothing.

As the conversation entered its thirtieth minute, Doran watched and listened, aware that he had not spoken yet. That was no bad thing. It preserved his authority, set him above the fray, the adult in the room who would settle the squabble among the (mostly) kids. But in this instance, his silence sprang from a different source.

With each argument made by Sigurdsson's conflicting advisors – each of them speaking about her in the third person, as if she were not in the room – a hole was opening up before his eyes. The hole was at the heart of this campaign. They

151

couldn't decide how the candidate should look because they couldn't decide what the candidate should *be*. They had not yet agreed her core message. Sure, they had come up with plenty of slogans, several of them now focus-grouped, shrink-wrapped and ready to roll into production. But that was not the same thing. What they lacked was a mission, the *raison d'etre* of the campaign. It was the question that had undone candidates stronger, more experienced and better placed than Elena Sigurdsson: why are you running? And, as he listened to the debate over earrings or no earrings, he realized that Sigurdsson could not yet give a decent answer.

'What if,' the candidate said finally, 'we don't have a single image at all? What if we have different photographs for different contexts? So when I'm talking crime, we go with the pant-suit and jacket. When it's education, we go with that one.' She pointed at a picture of herself in weekend wear, a sweater draped over her shoulders and gently tied, with a backdrop of California countryside. To Bill Doran's eye, she looked like a woman in one of those five pm ads for Depends or Tylenol, generic and middle-aged, but he got the idea. And, as the competing factions in the room warmed to her approach, agreeing that it made a sensible compromise, offering the best of both worlds and all the rest of that baloney, he had the sinking feeling that his gloomiest analysis had just been borne out, indeed vividly demonstrated before his very eyes.

'Now,' Sigurdsson said, clearly relieved to have moved away from a debate about her appearance. 'I've been thinking about our security message. I like what we have so far, guys, but I'm thinking how we can sharpen it up a little.'

Hold on, what was this?

'I want to play to my strengths, run on my experience. As a prosecutor.'

Doran suspected he knew where this was going – and he quite liked it. 'You mean, whack Berger on all the crimes he hasn't solved, all the bad guys he hasn't put away?' he asked. Ted Norman was nodding enthusiastically.

Sigurdsson nodded too, but her gaze was focused on Doran alone. She gave him a look that said, 'Bill, you and I understand what all these over-educated kids don't understand. Which is that, in the end, this stuff is pretty simple.'

He leaned forward, warming to this new line of thinking. 'Do you have any particular variety of bad guys in mind?'

She smiled. 'What would you suggest, Bill?'

They both knew the answer to that, but he could see that she wanted him to spell it out – perhaps in order to enlighten some of the younger members of the team who, unlike both Doran and Sigurdsson, had not yet built a career, or at least not given it a boost at several critical junctures, by milking one kind of crime in particular.

'Well, the most obvious category is anything to do with kids. You prove your opponent failed to do enough to prevent or prosecute the killing of a child, you're home. But it can be tricky: families don't always like it, media accuse you of exploitation. Gets messy.'

'So therefore?' The candidate was smiling, the straight guy feeding the comic his cue.

'So therefore,' Bill went on, 'I'd suggest we focus on crimes with adult, female victims. Women identify with such cases, obviously. That's a given. But, if you pick the right victim – ideally one that stirs the same kind of outrage as the death of a child – then male voters get mobilized too. The polling is very consistent on this, has been for years.'

'How do you mean, "the right victim"?' It was the woman, Head of Media, who didn't want Sigurdsson wearing red or canary yellow. Probable feminist. Bill would have to word this carefully.

'I mean, it helps if the female victim is young and, so to speak, blameless.'

'Blameless?'

He could sense his questioner bristling. Get this wrong, and his misstep would be on Weibo before the meeting was over. He paused, trying to find the right form of words. Into the gap stepped Sigurdsson herself.

'Yes, blameless. I learned the same lesson myself. If you're prosecuting a man for the rape or murder of a woman, you need to know there are no flies on her. Not one. OK, these days not many people will actually come out and say, "Wearing that skirt? She was asking for trouble."'

'And those that would are members of the Republican congressional caucus.' Bill's joke lowered the temperature, not least because it was at his own expense: famously he had been the campaign manager for a Republican senate candidate who lost a highly winnable seat by suggesting certain types of rape were approved by the Bible.

Once the laughter had faded, the candidate resumed. 'OK. So not *many* will say that out loud, but on a jury there'll be three or four thinking it. And not just men. You need there to be not so much as a shred of blame attached to the victim. But if you're lucky enough to get that – to get a woman beyond criticism as your victim – well, that's the jackpot.'

'In the courtroom and at the ballot box,' Doran added. 'Both.' He watched the staff take notes, keying the main points into their sleek, Lenovo tablets and phones. Norman was still nodding. 'Then all you have to do is remind the voters who was the public official who dropped the ball. The politician who failed to find the villain. Not because the villain was hard to find. But because the establishment, politics-as-usual insider was weak—'

'—and soft on crime,' said Sigurdsson, completing his sentence.

As the meeting broke up, Doran felt better than he had in weeks. The double act he had just staged with the candidate had not only shored up his position against the Stanford twentysomethings – proving that he was not a dinosaur just because his career spanned the age of the fax machine – it had also injected him with confidence that he and Sigurdsson would work well together after all. He listened happily as the staffers set to work on how best to saddle Richard Berger with an emotive and unsolved murder case, the tactic tacitly approved by Ted Norman, general of the army of footsoldier volunteers.

In the post-meeting chatter, Doran was about to mention Abigail Webb by name but, better still, Sigurdsson got there first, repeating to members of the team the same instruction she had given him earlier: find out what they could, be sure the sex-game theory had been eliminated entirely, then begin discreet focus-grouping.

And yet, while he started shutting files on his screen and packing up, two thoughts nagged. The first was a matter of tradecraft. Although he was glad they at least had a plan of sorts, his gut knew it was not enough. California was a Democratic state. A few ads smearing Berger were better than nothing, but they wouldn't truly move the needle. For that, they still needed something larger, a *cause*. If they still had not divined such a driving purpose by now, one that might rally the people of the state to their flag, where on earth were they likely to get one?

The second was guilt. Politics was a rough old trade, he knew that. Still, there were rules. Call him old-fashioned, but he happened to believe that dog doesn't eat dog. The candidates were fair game: you'd say and do whatever it took to destroy them. But you never went after your fellow professional. And Leo Harris, he knew, had a connection with this Webb girl, via her sister. If they used the case, was that crossing the line? He wasn't sure. But the fact that he even had to ask himself the question made him uncomfortable.

Another question intruded, unbidden, related to what they

had heard about Berger's pressuring the LAPD. Was this all about Leo and his ex – or was there some other reason why the mayor was taking such a close interest in the case of Abigail Webb?

Chapter 19

Jeff Howe looked at his phone again. Nothing from Madison, nothing from Barbara. He knew what he wanted from one, but not from the other. From his fellow detective, he was hungry for whatever crumb of information she could supply him with. He wanted it so that he could, in turn, feed it to Maddy.

He understood Maddy's craving for knowledge, he had seen it in so many loved ones of the murdered. But he also knew that whatever appetite those other bereaved had had, Madison Webb's would dwarf it. Howe had known journalists before. As a detective of his rank, he'd dealt with crime reporters often. But Maddy was different from the rest. In a different league professionally, no doubt about it. But different in her motivation. Sure, she was ambitious. But it was more than that. She seemed to burn with curiosity. She would not rest until she knew *everything*. Until you had told her everything. That hunger was one of the things about her he found hard to resist.

So he was eager to feed her, to give her what he knew she craved. Anything he could get from Barbara, any update would do. Was that desire entirely for the enhanced wellbeing of Madison Webb? No. He wanted her to think well of the department. Not to think they were jerking around, but to think they were doing their jobs and doing their best. More to the point, he wanted Maddy to think well of him. To be grateful to him.

Jeff Howe was not used to rejection. The legal documents said he and his ex-wife had parted amicably, but they both knew it was his decision. Even in high school, the only time he ever said goodbye was when he chose to. People did not spurn the captain of the football team. Not at college either. But Maddy had ended that run. The novelty of it did not appeal to him. It confused him. He did not understand why she kept rebuffing him. So, yes, that was also on his mind. He wanted to give her reasons to think she was making a mistake. Because she was.

His own work was finished for the night. He had been assigned a gang killing that – and it surely offended no one to say this – was not exactly urgent. Young hoods in South Central, fighting over turf. Started with a knife, graduated to a gun. Same old, same old.

His partner, a decent enough cop, had gone. For him, there was no one to go home to. He had time to kill.

He glanced back at the phone. It was Maddy he wanted to hear from. A reply to the several messages he had sent, asking how she was doing. Anything which would acknowledge his concern for her. Even an update of her own investigative efforts would be welcome. She hadn't told him what she was doing – but he had no doubt she was doing something.

Idly, he moved his chair closer to the computer, logged in and entered the sealed area open only to the homicide department. He found the search menu, choosing 'overdose' as his key word.

The page filled with file names, ordered by victim. He narrowed the dates, asking to be shown only homicides of the last year. Now the page filled again. He paused, knowing the computer would record this little unauthorized expedition and betray him without hesitation. His electronic fingerprints would be all over it. He would have to explain why he was pursuing a case that was not his, that had not been assigned to him, possibly for the good reason that someone had decided he had an emotional attachment – or desired attachment – to a member of the victim's immediate family. What would he say? That these were his off-duty hours and he was just trying to help in a case everyone knew was now a must-solve for the entire department. It wasn't much, but he could say it if he had to – and say it with conviction.

Abigail's file was there but he avoided it, clicking instead on the most recent of the earlier cases, a death that had taken place nearly three weeks ago. The page that resulted was one he had not seen before on the LAPD system.

File not found.

He clicked on the file below, recording a homicide dated from the previous month.

File not found

Now he buckled, knowing that his next move would increase the risk he was taking: he checked Abigail's file. And saw the same message.

But when he took his cursor further down, to a fatal over-dose a full year earlier, the file opened immediately, yielding a full set of police papers, including the initial report from the officer who had found the body, photographs from the scene, the coroner's findings, witness statements, memos from the Assistant DA; everything, in fact, that he would have expected to be there. It meant the system worked. There had been no general malfunction. The problem was very specific. Only those overdose cases from the most recent period were unavailable.

Jeff Howe tried to open them one last time, just to be sure. But he was not wrong. Only one conclusion was possible. Those files which simple logic suggested were at least of potential relevance to the case of Abigail Webb were missing, and not through a technical failure, either. Someone had removed them.

He logged out and checked his phone once more. Still nothing. He thought back to his conversation with Barbara Miller, outside in the yard. She had told him about instructions from above, her finger pointing skyward. That suggested she was referring to orders from the Chief of Police himself. *This case is being handled in a particular way.*

At the time, Jeff had understood that to be a statement of priorities. The Webb death was to be the homicide department's number one case. He got that. The politics of it were obvious. A young, pretty schoolteacher, the very picture of innocence; sister in the media, with something of a following. Election year. It made sense to get a result and fast.

But now he heard the words, relayed by Miller, differently. *A particular way.* If Jeff was not mistaken, this was not an edict about what needed to be investigated hard but its very opposite. What he had seen on the computer was the proof. Someone very high up, perhaps at the very top, was not prepared to leave this as a matter of guidance. A string of cases had not merely been stamped with a 'No Entry' sign. They had been hidden from view, to shut out those who might discover their secrets.

Chapter 20

Instinct told Maddy to keep what she knew to herself. As she drove, she listened, rather than spoke, the car filling up with the sound of Barbara Miller on the speaker, giving what purported to be an update on the police investigation into the murder of Abigail Webb.

'It's all about the CCTV footage just now, sweetheart. I know how frustrating this is for the family, but—'

'Do you?'

'Excuse me?'

'You said you know how frustrating this is for my family. Do you really?'

There was a silence, a pause in which, Maddy suspected, the detective collected herself, bit her lip and suppressed the urge to tell Maddy where to get off. 'All right, no, I don't *know*, Madison. You're right. I've never been in your position. But I have investigated a lot of homicides. I think you know that.'

Maddy said nothing, waiting for Barbara to come up with more.

'And I know that these delays can happen. Investigating a crime like this is long, hard work.'

'I know.'

'I know you know. Outside the police department, probably no one knows that better than you. And I gotta tell you, Madison – it's still not even been two days. Remember, this crime is logged as having occurred yesterday.'

Yesterday. What garbage. What was this woman talking about? Yesterday! No wonder she wasn't making progress if she didn't even have a grip on the basic chronol—

But then Maddy glanced at her phone, lying face up on the passenger seat, confirming that the official day on the human calendar was indeed Tuesday, no matter what the clock inside her head was telling her. She should have learned by now that her internal clock was the most unreliable timepiece in America. Deprived of sleep, it lost track of day and night, turning time into a continuous, undifferentiated mass, not so much a permanent day or a permanent night as a never-ending now. The day before yesterday, the day before Abigail was gone, could have been twenty years ago or it could have been . . . now. Without the punctuation of sleep, time lost itself.

'I understand. I'm trying to be patient,' Maddy said now, her fire temporarily doused. 'Can you at least tell me what's taking so long?'

'We need to get a positive ID on those pictures from the Great Hall. We very much want to talk to the man seen speaking with your sister.'

'How hard can it be to do that? Why's it taking so long?'

'If you saw the footage yourself, I think you'd understand, Madison. It's not a clear image. We're interviewing everyone we can, taking statements from everyone there. Customers, other staff, everyone. But the bar was very crowded that night. It's not easy.'

Maddy gripped the steering wheel, a physical reminder to herself not to blab, not to let on what she had seen and what she knew. *Just listen.*

'What about past cases? Other deaths in similar circumstances.'

'Sweetheart, believe me. You don't want us diluting our energies, you know what I'm saying? You want us completely focused, one hundred per cent, on Abigail. That's what we're doing. You start running through old files, you're gonna lose track, waste resources, lose *focus*. I've been doing this a long time, Madison.'

'I know.'

'I want that to be reassuring for you. And your family. We're on it, Madison. OK? We're on it. Now why don't you take care of your mother and your sister: they need you right now. I mean that. You leave this shit, pardon me, to those of us paid to wade through it. You focus on Abigail and your family now, you hear?'

Maddy drove on, too fast, she knew, for the smog which had thickened through the day, settling in the bowl of Los Angeles, growing stagnant and somehow greasier as the hours passed. She was driving towards the Padilla house but, checking the time, she became agitated. What were the chances she'd find Mario there? Of course, ideally, they would have this conversation in person. But, judging by the traffic, that could cost her an hour or two, maybe more. She needed to get on. Her finger hovered over the keypad for a minute, then another until, her patience exhausted, she dialled his number. Relieved to hear him pick up, she got straight to it.

'Mario, there's something I should have asked about your sister. You never told me about her work.'

'Imm thimm smmthimm to dmm wimm whttt—'

'Mario?'

'Ymmm?'

'Have you got your mask on? I can't hear a word you're saying.'

There was a rustle by the mouthpiece and then, 'How about this? Can you hear me now?'

'Loud and clear.' This was happening more often. It used to be just the soya latte drinkers and the joggers who covered up against the smog, along with mothers like Quincy who didn't let their children set foot outside without wearing what amounted to an astronaut's helmet. But now even regular people like Mario were wearing the mask, even inside their own cars. Maddy's devil-may-care disregard for the toxic air was becoming ever rarer, an unusual vice, like smoking. She looked guiltily towards the glove compartment which somewhere contained her own face mask, buried and unused.

'So,' Mario began again. 'Is this to do with what we talked about? About proving that—'

'Yes,' she said, cutting him off before he had a chance to go further. No benefit saying anything too direct on the phone. 'That's right.' She should have waited and done this face to face. Most people weren't as careful as she was; or, as Abigail would have put it, most were not as paranoid. 'Can you tell me where she worked?'

'In accounts.'

'Rosario was an accountant?'

'Yep. Well, a *trainee* accountant actually. She was learning, doing the books, all that. She worked for a catering company, based in Park La Brea.'

'And two and a half weeks ago? The police estimated the time of death was around ten o'clock, is that right?'

'That's what they said.'

'And do you know what she had been doing that evening?'

'She'd gone out with some friends from work.'

'OK.' Maddy had the sensation of lowering a bucket into a well that had run dry. She did not quite know what to ask next. 'Do you know where they went?'

'A restaurant, Amici. It was near.'

'Near to the office?'

'No, sorry. Near to the job her friends had been doing.'

'I don't—'

'The catering job that night. Her friends were running it, you know, organizing the waiters, all that stuff.'

'Oh I see.' She paused, trying to piece together a picture. 'So she met up with them afterwards?'

'Yeah, she did that sometimes. She might meet them there, after the job. Or she'd tag along for the whole evening, see how it was done. Thing you gotta know about Rosario, she was ambitious.' His voice contained a chuckle. 'Real ambitious. She said that maybe she'd open up a restaurant of her own one day. She wanted to see how it worked.'

'And she did that that night?'

'Remember, I only got this second hand. But I think what happened, what her friends told the police, is that she worked in the office till late, finishing off the books. Then she headed out to meet them.'

'At the restaurant?'

'At the job. She wanted to meet them there. But she couldn't get in. Had to hang around outside.'

Maddy could imagine that easily enough. Upscale functions in LA were always like that – a movie premiere after-party or a museum opening. When she was starting, she had done her share of standing outside those events, notebook in hand, on the wrong side of the rope line, hoping some bouncer would take a shine to her and let her sneak in. Back then she had a dress she used especially for those assignments, the only one she owned that was fancy enough.

'So she met up with them outside the house or hotel or whatever it was. And then they went out?'

'Yeah, for something to eat.'

'I don't know Amici. What kind of place is that?'

'Nothing special. Pretty basic, kind of family, Italian place. Ideal for Rosie. She didn't like to drink, didn't like bars. The others did, especially the waitresses. But not Rosie. I'm guessing they only went there because everything else was full. You know how it gets round there.'

'Round where?'

'Down there, by the port. Terminal Island. That's where

the job was, the drinks reception. At the garrison. Brief thing, over by eight. But a big hassle getting in and out. Security and all that.'

'The event was at the garrison?'

'Yeah. Didn't I say that? Annual thing they do, thanking the staff and all that. A gesture for the Chinese New Year.'

Chapter 21

Leo closed his office door, something he did only rarely. It wasn't that he didn't *like* having the door closed. In an ideal world, it would be closed all the time, allowing him to get on with his day in private. But, to his great regret, that was not the world of this campaign. As mayor of LA, Richard – sometimes Rick, never Dick – Berger had been a great advocate of the open-plan office. Yes, of course, he had his own separate quarters at City Hall on the third floor but, as an obliging *LA Times* headline had it, 'My door is always open.' The accompanying picture of him at his desk was taken through . . . an open door. As a former reporter, Leo knew that journalism could be a very literal business.

Most of the time, he didn't mind obeying the Berger principles at campaign HQ. He understood the PR hit they'd take if someone weibed a snap of his door firmly shut. Besides, he didn't think it hurt if the candy girls occasionally overheard him carpeting, menacing, cajoling and otherwise handling the California press corps. It would serve a double purpose: educating the younger cadres in the ways of the world and boosting his hard-won reputation as a player of political hardball.

The drawback came at moments like this, when he needed

to have a discreet conversation on the telephone. It was now impossible to do that without announcing it first with a visible or audible click of the door. He might as well put out a sign.

He swivelled his chair so that he faced away from the door, in what he imagined was an extra precaution, adding a layer of soundproofing between himself and the outer office. He glanced down at his desk, spotting a Post-it he had missed: calls from reporters at *Politico*, Buzzfeed and the *Sacramento Bee*; one from his one-time mentor, Bill Doran, suggesting a drink 'for old times' sake'; another from the chair of the state Democratic party, saying he'd been approached by Ted Norman, his Republican opposite number, with a 'proposal', please call back. Nothing from Madison Webb.

Leo pushed the Post-it to one side, looked again at his phone and brought up the name of his contact at the LAPD. He stared at it a while, wondered about leaving it for another hour. Then pressed the button.

'Long time no speak.' In other contexts, a friendly enough opening. In this context, from Leo Harris, it was a declaration of disappointment likely to lead to further hostility.

'Yeah, it's been, like, at least two hours. I missed ya.' *Ya.* You can take the cop out of New York . . .

'Any news?'

'What, since we spoke, like, a hundred minutes ago? Look, Leo. This is not easy, this case. The way—'

'If we wanted *easy*, we'd never have gone into this line of work, now would we?' offered Leo, giving no quarter. 'We just want to know what's up. Did we ask for anything more than that?'

'It's the same, Leo. We've got people working over that bar, studying the pictures, talking to everyone there: staff, johns, everyone. It takes time.'

'I appreciate that. But what I—'

'I tell ya what, though. We are *definitively* talking about a murder, that's for sure.'

'I don't think that's news, is it? We knew that, right?'

'Sure, sure, Leo. Sure. But there were some, you know, *doubters*, put it like that.'

Leo leaned back, recalling the fragment of intel he'd picked up about the detective in charge, Barbara something. 'So what's made it definitive?'

'Well, I hear we've checked out the pictures from the apartment building. You know, the girl's.'

'You mean, the *victim's*? The apartment belonging to Ms Abigail Webb?' Jeez, these people.

'Yeah, exactly. We had an officer on it, came back with nothing. Rewound the tape, back and forth and could see nothing, no sign of the, uh, victim arriving home.'

'OK.'

'So Miller goes over there, sits down with the tape and goes over the same time. Also sees nothing. It's just dark. There's no light by the entrance to the apartment building, just one of those security lights, you know, motion sensitive or whatever?' *Whatevuh.* 'But Miller slows it down and notices something.'

'Yes.' Leo was becoming exasperated. The voice on the other end of the phone was enjoying this too much.

'Get this. She sees that it's *a different kind of dark*.'

'What the hell's that mean?'

'There's a change in the picture. Real subtle. But she watches it again and can see that, for eighteen and a half minutes, from 11:50 to 12:08 and thirty seconds, the picture is showing a pure black. The rest of the time, it's like a very dark grey.'

'Someone had cut the camera.'

'Yes! How'd you know that? Someone tell you this already?'

'I took a wild guess.'

'Well. That's exactly what happened.' The air was seeping from the policeman's balloon. But he soldiered on. 'The camera had been cut. Miller goes over there, to the entrance. Gets the super to bring a step-ladder, 'cause she's not tall, and right there, she starts inspecting the camera. She's expecting the glass to be shattered, but it's much better than that.'

'Better?'

'Neater. The lens and all that is OK, intact. But she feels around the back and she sees the wires had been cut. Real precise, like a real classy job. And taped up afterwards. You know, with black duct tape?'

'So the feed started up again?'

'You bet. Straight afterwards. So later on, through the night, anyone looked at those pictures, it was all back to normal. Saw people coming in and out. No one realized the camera had been fucked up till today.'

'And that settles it?'

'I'd say so, wouldn't you? Camera was taken out at the exact time of death. That ain't a coincidence in anyone's book.'

'OK,' said Leo, now biting on a thumbnail.

'And it means we're dealing with someone skilful. Methodical.'

'All right,' said Leo, keen to end the call so that he could think about it, uninterrupted.

'So you see. We've not been sitting around, picking our asses.'

'I see that. We're very grateful. Thanks.'

'Oh, Leo? Before you go. When you say "we're very grateful" and "we just want to know what's up" and all that?'

'Yes.'

'Can I ask, who exactly *we* are? Is "we" you and the mayor's office – or is we just you? Because it has been noticed downtown. Your interest in this case, I mean. Your *intense* interest, you might call it. Always wanting to know exactly what we're doing, how close we're getting to the killer. Is there something we should know, Leo? Is there something – somebody – you're worried about here, somebody we should know about? And by we, I don't mean me personally. I mean the homicide squad of the Los Angeles Police Department.'

Chapter 22

The explosions were going off at regular intervals now, flashes of light like white phosphorus bursting every few seconds, filling the sky. She knew it was not safe to drive in this situation, when the view was obscured, when the light was so bright. Experience taught her long ago that when a migraine was rolling in, like a storm thundering your way, the only safe option was to find somewhere dark and hide.

She found a turning near Olympic and pulled over, letting her head fall onto the steering wheel. Her brain was throbbing, rhythmically pushing itself against her skull. Was that the migraine or the thought now chasing its way around her neural system, gaining strength and force with each circuit?

Two's a coincidence, two's a coincidence. But she couldn't dismiss it. Both Eveline and Rosario had spent their last hours close to the Chinese garrison. It probably meant nothing. Rosario hadn't even been inside the base and had gone on somewhere else afterwards. Eveline too might have met her fate elsewhere, hours after she'd done her cleaning shift. And none of it had anything to do with Abigail. Yet still the thought wouldn't leave her.

Another explosion, white and glowing. She wound down

the window, noticing the glances of the few people walking along this side street, where the main attraction appeared to be a liquor store with an unlit neon sign and a torn awning. She took in deep gulps of air, hoping they would chase away the firestorm in her head.

Instead they seemed to make it worse, the oxygen feeding the flames. Now there was a loud, insistent clanging sound. She lifted her eyes, wondering if a fire truck had screamed its way into the street. But there was no sign of it. No police cars with sirens wailing either.

From the corner of her eye, she identified the source of the din. The screen on her phone was lit up, flashing a name. That infernal klaxon was no more than the sound of an incoming call.

She squinted to see a single word. *Quincy.*

There was no way she could pick up, not now. She watched it ring and ring, then divert to voicemail. Thirty seconds, then a minute passed before the device shook with the arrival of a message. That meant it was a long one. She could hardly face it.

She took more air, then finally pressed the button. Too soon, her older sister's voice was filling the car, sending Maddy's fingers straight to the volume button to turn it down. But she had caught enough to know the gist. *I can't believe you still haven't seen or spoken to Mom. I despair of you, Maddy, I really do.*

Maddy tried to look out of the window, needing the safety of middle distance. But the whiteness, the brightness was still overwhelming. And now the sickness was coming, the nausea rising in her throat.

She knew Quincy was right, but that didn't help. It made it worse. She reached for the phone, determined to tell Quincy that she could go to hell. She pressed the button, her nerve endings standing stiff and ready as she heard the ringing sound, the white explosions still there but no disturbance now.

If anything they added to her energy; they could serve as the soundtrack for the bombardment she was about to unload on her older sister.

Another ring and then another. Maddy cleared her throat and sat up straight, flicking the hair out of her eyes so that she could stare straight ahead. She was primed, an explosive device ready to go off.

And then the sound of voicemail, her older sister's voice taut and, it struck Maddy now, full of false, tense jollity, the neurotic suburban woman desperate to convey domestic perfection: *Hi there! I wish I could be there to take your call, but darn it, I can't get to . . .*

Maddy didn't hear the rest because she had hurled the phone at full force across the car. It bounced off the vinyl surround and onto the floor, landing among the detritus of discarded soda cans, chewed pen tops and once-crucial notebooks.

She checked her watch and began to drive, cursing the futility of the gesture she had just made, not least because she needed to call Jessica, Abigail's friend, if only to leave yet another message. As she pulled out onto the road, she told herself that her destination owed nothing to Quincy's message and everything to the riddle left for her by the last movements of Eveline Plaats and Rosario Padilla, two women who had no connection with her family and whom she had never met.

To her enormous relief, there was no car parked outside. It would be just her and her mother. And Paola, the Mexican carer Quincy had hired four or five months ago. Maddy used her own key to let herself in, calling out softly as she eased the door open. 'Mom? It's me. Maddy.'

Paola called out, ''Allo. We in here.'

It sounded like dinner time. *Four forty-five pm.* Why on earth did her mother have to eat as if she were a child? The

173

more they treated her this way, the more she would regress, Maddy was convinced of it. She felt a surge of resentment towards Quincy, pushing her mother ever further and faster down the slope of decline. But she could hear her sister's inevitable reply: *If you think I'm doing this so badly, then why don't you take over and do it better. Be my guest.*

Maddy advanced gingerly, not wanting to give her mother any surprises. In truth, she also needed the time to adjust to the sight of the faded, frail woman who had replaced her once-vibrant mother. At last she had come far enough to see her there, in her favourite armchair, a tray on her lap, Paola hovering close by. Thank God: she was holding a fork. Madison feared deeply the day she would walk in here and see her mother being fed like a child. It was one of the reasons she hated visiting, at least one of those she could admit to herself.

Maddy leaned in, gradually entering her mother's field of vision: no sudden shocks. The older woman looked up slowly, her eyes taking in the visitor, assessing her clothes, her limbs, her face. The two of them shared a long moment of mutual panic, the mother fretting as she tried to place the child born to her some three decades earlier – and the daughter fearing that, this time, the task would prove beyond her.

'Madison!' she said at last, her face brightening as a wide, childlike smile spread. She was still lovely to look at, even now, dressed in her old-lady cardigan. Her skin was soft, her features elegant, her hair a well-maintained blend of ash, silver and blondes – credit to Quincy for that. Was that smile born of pleasure at seeing her or relief that she'd been able to place the name? Maddy could not be certain, but the smile warmed her all the same.

'Hello, Mom,' she said, bending down to kiss her cheek. It was soft, though missing the fragrance Maddy had expected and, frankly, wanted. If her mother couldn't be the way she used to be, at least she might smell the same. She would have a word with Paola.

'You want private time?'

Paola moved a chair, gestured for Maddy to take off her coat, to sit a while. 'You have private time.'

Madison did as she was told, watching as Paola made herself busy elsewhere, wielding a cloth, popping in and out.

'So how are you, Mom?' She realized she had no idea what to say or what tone to strike. How aware was her mother of Abigail's death? 'You look good.'

'You don't,' her mother replied, not unkindly. It was a statement of fact. The doctors had warned her about this. *We find disinhibition is one of the most common signs . . .* 'You look tired.'

'I am tired, Mom. I'm real tired.'

'You should sleep more.'

'I know. But it's hard. Especially now.'

Her mother let her fork idle on the plate. 'It's hard. Hard for you.'

'Why is it hard for me, Mom?' A small grenade of white light exploded in the rear of her brain, somewhere behind her left ear.

Her mother took a while to answer, as if considering the question from all angles. Her eyes stayed fixed on the plate, the fork skating around, gliding through the gravy, leaving a trail that vanished almost immediately. 'Because . . . you know,' she said eventually.

Another explosion of phosphorus. 'Harder for you, Mom. All of it.'

'No,' her mother said, looking up at last. 'Harder for you.'

Maddy met her mother's gaze, unsure what to say. The three words lingered in the air, like a trace of old perfume. Was her mom just echoing back what Maddy had said, making the sounds without understanding their meaning? The doctors said that could happen. Or had her mother dredged up a memory, pulling it out of the swamp of her dementia, a rare moment of clarity induced – who knows – by the shock of losing her youngest daughter? And if it was a memory, was she referring to something specific? If so, was it the obvious? *Because . . . you know.*

Her mother spoke again, with a sentence that seemed to break through Maddy's hide, the thick layer of exhaustion and experience that had accreted over the years, and pierce her heart. 'You're the best of them,' she said plainly, as if it were a simple statement of fact. 'You're the best. You're the strongest. You always were.'

At that, perhaps the most coherent sentence her mother had managed in months, Maddy felt a pricking behind her eyes. An instant later, she realized her cheeks were wet and her nose was running. She was finding it hard to see, her eyes blurred by tears, like a camera lens in the rain.

Her mother spoke again. Or rather she made to speak, readying her mouth for words, but then stopped herself. She placed a single finger over her lips. 'Shhhh.' She smiled and repeated the action. 'Shhhh.' Another smile. 'You see, "Never tell a secret."'

'What secret, Mama?' Maddy asked, her voice tremulous.

Her mother hushed herself once more. 'Shhhh.'

'That's good,' Maddy said. 'We'll never tell, will we?' With Abigail gone, the question had gained a new intensity.

Her mother repeated the sound. 'Shhhh.'

Maddy wanted to say more, but she couldn't. Her voice wouldn't let her; her shoulders were shaking. So she reached for her mother's free hand and held it. It was warm and soft, the skin thinner than she remembered, but still so familiar.

Her mother looked up, registering not surprise but almost its opposite. She enclosed Maddy's hand in hers, giving it a strong squeeze. And suddenly Madison was five years old, crossing the road with her beautiful mother, hand in trusting hand.

She reached for a tissue and attempted to blow her nose.

The sound meant she almost missed what her mother said. But she just caught the words: 'Don't listen to what she says.'

Maddy wanted to ask who 'she' was, but she knew she didn't need to. She was thinking of a response that would signal her understanding but she could see it was too late. Whatever thought had been in her mother's mind had disappeared. The woman facing her had wandered elsewhere.

Maddy blew her nose once more and decided to start again. She let go of her mother's hand and said, 'Mom, I wanted to talk about Abigail.'

Her mother's face darkened at that, though it recovered with surprising speed. One of the doctors had spoken of that too. He had a name for it, if not *avoidance* then something similar. *We find that, with this condition, the brain finds ways to shut out that which is too difficult to process.*

Her mother reached for her book of Sudoku puzzles. Initially a doctor's suggestion – *Even when the brain loses its hold on words, it can retain its grip of numbers, but that muscle needs regular exercise* – it had become a near-addiction.

Madison tried a different route. 'You know Abigail's job, Mom?'

'She's a good girl.' She had her pencil in her hand, hovering over the grid of digits.

'She is, she's great. They like her, don't they?'

'Well, the children do.'

That was a good sign, one Maddy could not help but seize on as a point scored against Quincy. 'The children?' she asked, seeking confirmation.

'The other children at the school.'

That 'other' landed with a thud. She was imagining Abigail as a child.

'Abigail is a teacher, Mom. And she's good at it.'

But her mother was too focused on adding up, using her

fingers. As she pencilled in her findings, Maddy repeated herself and this time got an answer. 'They offered her another job.'

That was news to Maddy. Could it be true? Had Abigail started working somewhere else, somewhere perhaps where she might have had a connection with the garrison?

She was getting ahead of herself. Her mother was hardly a reliable source and Maddy had spoken to Abigail about work and careers not that long ago. She surely would have told her if there had been any change.

'What kind of job, Mom?'

Her mother suddenly brightened, her face a picture of light. She looked down at the puzzle book, hurriedly filling in several numbers at once. 'There,' she said proudly. But then she checked her work and a shadow fell. 'Too good to be true,' she said. Her catchphrase.

'What kind of job, Mom?'

Her mother paused from rubbing out the ill-fated numbers and looked up blankly.

'You said they offered Abigail a job? What kind of job?'

'Same job.'

'Oh.'

'But better.'

'At the same school?'

Her mother moved her head in what Madison wanted to see as a nod. But it wasn't obvious. It might have been nothing, some mental flotsam that had wafted into her mother's mind and then out again. Even if her mother had been making sense, it was simply letting her know about a promotion: it didn't make much difference. 'What about anywhere else? Did Abigail ever mention anything?'

'Why would she?' Whether this was *Why would she look for a job somewhere else?* or *Why would she mention it?* was not obvious. Truth was, it was quite possible that the words her mother had spoken bore no relation to the question she had asked at all. *Why would she?* could refer to anything and everything.

Maddy leaned forward to take her mother's hand once more. She held it for a second, her mother gazing at her with that same eager blankness. 'Mom, is there anything else Abigail might have mentioned, even something that didn't seem important at the time? Try to remember, Mom. I know it's hard. But I think you can remember more than—'

A voice rang out, simultaneous with a change in the light from the hallway. 'Hello! It's me!'

Quincy.

Instinct made Maddy withdraw, pulling back from her mother, letting go of the comfortable cave the two had made of their hands. At the same moment, Paola emerged from the kitchen, with a speed that suggested she had been hovering by the door.

'Maddy! This is a surprise,' her sister said brightly, her cheeks flushed with fresh winter air. She was carrying two – no, three – shopping bags, overflowing with groceries. In that instant, and not before, Maddy realized that she had announced her own visit by bringing precisely nothing. 'How long have you been here?'

'Actually, I was about to leave.'

'Oh, don't go so quickly. I'm sure Mom's enjoying having a chat.'

Paola stepped in to remove the plate, where the rink of gravy had now congealed. 'You tired now, yes?' she said gently. 'Tiring answer all those questions.'

Maddy could feel the temperature drop and stiffened herself for the inevitable.

'Questions?' asked Quincy, the brightness in her voice becoming strained. 'What questions?'

'We were just having a chat,' Maddy replied, the words sounding feeble in her mouth. 'Weren't we, Mom?'

The older woman herself now spoke, her expression

suggesting that she wanted to help Maddy out. 'Abigail's happy where she is,' she said, her face filled with that same, innocent smile.

Quincy said nothing, but the urgency with which she moved to dump the bags in the kitchen signalled that she was far from done with this topic. Maddy watched the way she handed the third bag to Paola, no words necessary, hinting at a complicity between the two women which rather explained the latter's minor act of intelligence gathering.

'Maddy, why don't you help me get some of these things out of the car?'

She did as she was told, even though she knew what was coming.

Once outside, by the empty trunk of her oversized SUV, Quincy launched right in. 'This is not a "story", Maddy, do you hear me? This is real life.' The telltale redness was spreading up Quincy's neck. 'That's your mother in there, who's just lost a child. You have to . . .' She stopped, as if she could not find words potent enough to convey her anger. 'Why not talk to us for once, Maddy. Not interview us, but *talk* to us. Just once.' She let out a noise – part growl, part grinding of teeth – an animal expression of sibling fury.

Maddy wondered about saying nothing, a technique from childhood which, when she had the self-discipline to deploy it, usually delivered great results, maddening an already-mad Quincy still further. But that required a self-restraint she didn't have. Not today, not any more.

'You know, Quincy, just because you're the older sister does not give you the right to tell me how to behave. It didn't then and it doesn't now, OK?'

'But I wouldn't have to tell you if you only—'

'And it's about fucking time you stopped doing it, Quincy. I mean it. In fact, it's way *past* time. We're adults now, Quincy. *Adults.* And I don't need you acting like—'

'Adults? You! You've got to be kidding. You don't know the first thing about adult responsibility.' She gestured towards the house, whose front door was still open. 'Who do you think makes—'

'I don't care, Quincy.'

'Oh, I know you don't care. That's completely obvious, Madison. One hundred per cent *obvious*. You don't care about anyone but . . . in fact, I'm not sure *who* you care about. It's certainly not us. But do you even care about yourself? I mean, look at the state of you. You're a—'

'Why don't you just shut the fuck up, Quincy? Just shut the fuck up. You don't know the first thing about me. And not just me. Abby and I talked about this hundreds of times. About how you act like you're the mother—'

'But—'

'And don't think that's just 'cause of what's going on now. You've always been doing it, long before Mom got . . . sick. Abby agreed. You've been a bossy bitch since we were kids and you know what, Abby couldn't stand it and nor can I.'

At that, Maddy felt the hot, sharp sting of a slap across her cheek from her older sister, her arm, muscled and toned through a thousand sessions with a personal trainer, able to deliver quite a blow.

Inside, Maddy dabbed at the burning flesh of her face, but she did not cry. On the contrary, she almost welcomed the blow. It had ended the argument between them just now. But, even in this first instant, she suspected it had done something more. She had felt the bolt of lightning that ends a close, humid day.

Their mother was asleep as they sat chatting in the kitchen, Paola a safe distance away washing sheets. Maddy nursed a cup of hot jasmine tea, prepared for her by her oldest sister.

'All I know is,' Quincy was saying, 'Abby was proud.

181

Certainly too proud to ask Mark and me for help. And too proud to ask Mom.'

'Or me.'

'Or you. That's right. So she took on extra work.'

'What kind of work?' Maddy asked, desperate to adopt a tone that was talk rather than interview.

'Extra teaching.'

'Where, at the school?' Maddy took another sip of tea, to maintain the grammar of a chat.

'She was hired by some parents at the school, to tutor kids who needed extra back-up.'

'What kind of parents?'

Quincy flashed her a warning look, as if she was approaching but had not yet crossed the red line that separated journalism from family. 'Do you want to tell me what this is about, Madison?'

Maddy hesitated. 'I'm not sure yet. It may be nothing. But there may be a . . . pattern.'

'A pattern?'

'Other women. Killed the same way.'

'Jesus.'

'So what kind of parents?'

'Around there? Fairly affluent, I guess. Comfortable without being tony.'

'Any Chinese expats?'

'Chinese? Seriously?'

'Maybe. Everything's a maybe at this stage, Quince.'

'Do the police know about this?'

Maddy looked down, staring into the ripples her spoon was making in the tea.

'Maddy?'

'I don't know. Put it this way, I don't think they care as much about Abby as we do. So, that school. Any Chinese expats?'

Quincy barely paused. 'No. I'd be amazed if there were any. Not there.'

Maddy did her best not to show any disappointment. Not to feel any was harder. But she let the conversation with her sister run on, only clamming up when the subject of Abby's funeral surfaced. She said there would be issues with the coroner's office, that the autopsy process for a homicide could take weeks, that it was not in their interest to rush things. But she knew she was not telling the whole truth, even to herself.

After she had gone into her mother's bedroom to say good-night – planting a kiss on her forehead, tasting the cold fragrance of her night cream – she found herself, once again, outside and by Quincy's car, preparing to say goodbye.

'I'm sorry about what I said before,' Quincy began. 'About how you looked.'

Maddy gave a wan smile, the humour of it not eluding her. Two sisters can say the most vicious things about the very core of each other's character, that's natural. But to criticise the other's appearance, now that's crossing the line.

Quincy saw the joke, allowing a smile of her own to escape. She shook her head, repeated her apology for pointing out how exhausted Maddy seemed then said, as if to herself, 'What is it with both my sisters? Gorgeous girls, if only they got more sleep.'

Maddy laughed along but then stopped herself. 'What was that?'

'You and Abby. The beauties of the family. You always were.'

'No. About sleep.'

'Oh, it was nothing. I didn't mean anything by—'

'You said *both* of us got no sleep. Did Abby have . . .' She hesitated, as always, over the word *insomnia*. She hated having a label, a disease with a name. Besides, she resented the idea of so stubbornly large and complex a part of her life being reduced to a single word. If it was simple enough to say in eight letters, why could it not be solved just as simply? To her mind, it belittled a foe that was too mighty, too greedy to be captured in so short a space.

'No,' said Quincy, kind enough to pick up the cue without needing the actual word. 'No, it was nothing like that. I just think Abby was worrying some – about the extra work she had taken on.'

'What kind of worrying?'

'That it was interfering with her regular work, at the school. "Too many late nights," something like that.'

'She said that?'

'Yes!' Quincy replied, the edge returning once more. 'But don't start quoting me. Remember what I said, Maddy.'

'Sure,' she replied. 'You're right. I remember.'

They gave each other a brief embrace, awkward, the arms and hands not quite in the right places. They promised to speak soon, about Mom, about logistics. Maddy did her best to say goodbye the way a loving sister would leave a house of mourning. But the only thought in her mind as she reversed the car and pulled away was the one that had just been planted.

Too many late nights.

Chapter 23

Despite everything they had said to each other at their mother's house, it was Quincy's earlier barb that kept returning to Madison. *You don't know everything.* She could not deny its truth in the area where it should have been least applicable and which mattered most: her knowledge of her younger sister. There was so much she didn't know.

The expensive clothes in the closet, the nights glued to the bar at the Great Hall had no place in the portrait of Abigail that Madison had carried around all these years. Perhaps, she now wondered, she had barely updated it since Abigail was a child, tumbling and rolling around with their dog, Chilli. Perhaps she had never really known the adult Abigail at all.

As she contemplated the computer screen – emptied now after a Skype call with Jessica, in which the housemate had detailed a dramatic increase in Abigail's spending power to match the striking change in wardrobe, but could not explain either – the pain of it entered her. She would now have to *research* her own sister. The chance to talk, to find out and explore, that chance had been available to her every day for years and years. Unlike most families she knew, they all lived in the same city. Abigail had been within easy reach. But now it was too late.

After a futile glide through Google, she went back for the fifth or perhaps sixth time to the Facebook page. The messages from friends now fought for space with countless statements from strangers.

This tragedy shows how much we have forgotten what it means to be an American!!!

Words cannot say, how much pain is in my heart. You're in a better place now, even though we are apart.

She kept scrolling, but there was page after page of them. Weeding out the rubberneckers, gathering on this page the way they might at the scene of a car crash, focusing only on those who knew Abigail, whether as a teacher or a friend, this was unarguable evidence that Abigail was deeply and widely loved.

She was skimming over them now, taking in their shape and flavour rather than reading each word, when she stopped suddenly. She took her finger off the downward arrow and went back.

I loved to watch you dance. You weren't just hot like the others. You had real beauty. RIP.

She read it three times, lingering in a different place each time. 'Hot' caught her, as did 'the others'. She had a rising sense that she understood what she was looking at, and as that grew a creeping nausea grew with it. She clicked immediately on the username, Greg Stanhouse, to see a generic silhouette where the profile photograph should have been.

Surely Barbara Miller and the homicide department had seen this? She should call, if not Miller then at least Jeff. This had to be of paramount relevance. She was furious with herself for not spotting it earlier.

The nausea had reached her throat. She pushed back in her

186

chair, tilting her neck in the same direction, as if on the receiving end of an unseen but almighty upper cut. The desire for sleep was so powerful and, in this moment of shock, the prospect of it seemed plausible. She closed her eyes.

Her head filled with a swirl of colours, dulled but insistent. What she saw behind her eyes resembled a thermal imaging map, the shape of it shifting. There was a sound to it, throbbing and arrhythmic, like shellfire in a war zone. Her body was crying out for it to stop, desperate for the quiet, or at least constant, steady noise that might bring rest.

But the explosions would not let up and nor would the voice inside, rattling through the facts and what they might mean, a running commentary that was telling her that the author of that one-line Facebook message might well be the man who murdered Abigail and maybe even 'the others'.

She should call the police, this was too serious to handle alone. But she could foresee with great clarity the consequences. In less than a second, her mind displayed for her in telescoped form the scenes that would follow: the struggle to reach Miller, the messages left and ignored; the eventual, reluctant call to Jeff, in which he would try to soothe her, urging her to get some rest, as if it were that easy, and to leave the police work to the police; the frustration and delay; the low-level detective assigned the task of checking out one among hundreds of leads, doubtless treating Maddy's discovery as if it were no better than any of the random tips such a case brought in from the public . . .

No. There was no time for any of that. She would do this herself. Avoiding delay was the official reason, the one she told herself as she forced herself to sit back up, then stood, walking in stiff, upright steps, like the undead in a silent horror movie, over to the bathroom, splashing her face with water then recoiling as she sniffed the old, unwashed towel. She told herself that doing this alone was about saving time, but even she was not entirely fooled by that story.

187

She reached for the phone and called Katharine, briefing her rapidly. They had done this before, cracking the identity of a Facebook user hiding behind a pseudonym. Besides, once she had heard the message addressed to Abigail, repeated by Maddy as coolly and dispassionately as she could manage, her friend did not need to be persuaded.

In the interim, Maddy paced. She made a brief stop in her bedroom where, still thinking, she perched on the end of her bed.

What felt like an instant later, she felt her hand vibrating, the sound of it reaching her brain only much later. She put the device to her ear, hearing her own voice, thicker than usual. 'Hello?'

'I've got something.' Katharine.

'That was quick.'

'Actually, it wasn't so quick. That took me forty minutes.'

Maddy pulled the phone from her ear to look at its clock. Her friend was right: without realizing how it had begun, with no idea that it had happened at all, she had fallen asleep, her hand coiled tightly around her phone.

She grabbed some clothes, the top chosen simply for being the only one in the closet guaranteed to be clean. She caught a fleeting look at herself in the mirror. Somehow, despite the permanent lack of sleep, her body was refusing to give the game away entirely. Yes, there were dark circles under her eyes, but they gave her an oddly sultry look. The phrase 'come to bed eyes' slipped into her head. She gave a bitter laugh: it had been a while.

She had the sense that her exterior appearance concealed a full-scale disintegration beneath – that one day, as in a fairytale, the pleasant, youthful-looking mask would fracture, the splinters falling away to reveal her true face: that of a haggard old crone.

She reached for the car keys, took the elevator and was soon in her car, on her way to the address she had been given.

She rushed, not because Katharine had told her there was any great urgency – on the contrary, her friend had warned her to take great care – but because she did not want to create a pause in which hesitation might grow. Neither of them had said it explicitly, but there was no doubting what they both thought: that Maddy might be on her way to confront her sister's killer.

Katharine had established with near-complete certainty that 'Greg Stanhouse', the author of the message to Abigail, was in fact Denis Parker, male and in his fifties, resident of San Pedro and Second downtown: Skid Row. As she got closer, Maddy remembered she had been in precisely this area on a story about five years earlier, investigating a drugs ring, but she had not been back much since. It had been seedy then. It was worse now, one boarded-up storefront after another, the only economic sign of life coming from the occasional neon flash of a liquor store.

She parked up, around the corner from the address. She glanced at the glove compartment in front of the passenger seat. Not for the first time, she regretted that it contained no gun. But it was a shared view in the crime reporters' fraternity, reached by the older hands the hard way, that journalists needed to be unarmed if they were to do their job: carry a weapon and they'd be seen as just another arm of 'the Feds'. Most of the time, Maddy believed it made her safer too. Trouble was less likely to escalate. But she did not feel that way tonight.

She was careful how she walked. In an area like this you had to be. Too slow and you're a tourist. Too brisk and you're the authorities. But she was not kidding herself. She was young and female and from the other side of the tracks. She stood out no matter how she walked.

She was there at the door, sandwiched between two stores. There were vertical bars to protect the glass, their once cream-coloured paint peeling. At the right side, caked in dust and painted over, was what had once been a doorbell. She pressed it. The button responded to her touch but she could hear no sound from the other side of the door. She tried it again. Still nothing.

There was a whisper of noise behind her. She wheeled around to see a homeless man shuffling past. He gave her a sideways glance from a bloodshot eye and moved on.

She ran her finger around the door frame, lingering by the single lock. She pushed at the wood, confirming what she had suspected, that the timber was soft and rotten. With no fore-thought, she turned sideways and gave the door a single, firm shove with her shoulder. It offered the scantest resistance and was open.

In front of her was a staircase, covered in a carpet so thin and moth-eaten it barely merited the name. She looked down at her feet, using the small flashlight she kept in her bag to reveal a half dozen fliers and junk circulars. She saw one addressed to a Mr D Parker. She started climbing the stairs, her tread gentle and noiseless.

She came up into a landing that was bare, leading off to three doors. There were no pictures on the walls, nothing by which she could orientate herself or about which she could make any kind of guess. She could feel her heart, the pulse from her neck accelerating.

With her foot, she pushed at one door to reveal a tiny kitchen. The torch picked out a table, a sink full of dishes, a rear door leading to a fire escape. There was a smell of old garbage.

She was about to choose between the other two doors – one surely a bathroom, the other a bedroom – when she saw a sickly line of greenish light escaping from underneath the nearer of the two. She could hear voices too, muffled and distant. Her heart was pressing against her ribs, loud and insistent.

She caught a scent and with it an elusive, yet definite

memory. It took her a second or two to grasp hold of it, to catch the source of its familiarity. It was from a long time ago, but the memory was sharp, one that she had never been allowed to forget, one that stayed with her every day and especially at night. Strange, she had never associated that event with an aroma until this moment. But there was no doubting the connection. Filling her nostrils, now as it had that night when she was fourteen years old, was the smell of fear.

Any longer and she knew it would overwhelm her; her courage had limited patience. Before she had even formed the thought, she stepped forward and, in a single motion, turned the handle and flung open the door.

What she saw first was the bareness. The room was almost empty, the floorboards uncovered, the walls naked, not a shelf or closet to be found. Only at the back, visible in mere outline, was a single bed. It was less a bedroom than a monastic cell.

In the centre was a plain, wooden table. On it seemed to rest nothing but a computer screen, its back facing her, sending out a fan of unnatural blue-green light. And then – seen by Maddy first, yet understood last – a man, hunched over the machine and masturbating furiously.

'Stop. Police,' Maddy called out, in a voice that was not her own. She thrust both hands forward, one gripping the flashlight, the other displaying the badge of Detective Madison Halliday.

The man sprang up and backward instantly. He put his hands in the air, a motion which saw his pants and underwear slip to his ankles. He stood before her in a loose, night-time T-shirt, which struggled to cover a hairy, pregnant belly and which did nothing to conceal his erection, nor the dark forest from which it sprang. His face was unshaven and exhausted, the face life gives you after years of hard work and no money. His eyes conveyed terror rather than anger, an impression confirmed as the exposed part of him shrank and shrivelled before her eyes.

'Step back from the desk,' she commanded, wielding the flashlight as if it were a weapon, aiming its beam directly into his eyes. Her hope was that the combination of the light, which had blinded him since she burst in, and the badge would lead him to assume she was armed.

He did as he was told, giving her a chance to glance down and check the table to be sure there was nothing there he might try to deploy as a weapon. She could see nothing that represented any threat but she bent slightly, extending her left forearm out to her side – her eyes remaining fixed on her captive – while she made a single, clean sweep across the surface of the desk just in case, bringing a mouse, a couple of pens and a phone to the floor.

For the first time she registered the noise leaking from the computer, tinny and at low volume. Intermittent moans and yelps of pain, set against a repetitive and lazy soundtrack. The sound of porn. Maybe that was why Abigail and the other women had shown no sign of physical contact. This man didn't want to touch. He liked to look.

Now she ordered him to crouch low and empty out his pants pockets. Only once she had seen him produce a couple of quarters and a yellow-stained, balled-up tissue, and then tug both pockets inside out to confirm their emptiness, did she allow him to pull up his pants. The rest of the time his hands had to stay in the air – and the light remained in his face.

'You gonna tell me what this is about?' he said finally, his voice working-class New York. From his complexion, she'd guess Italian-American, maybe Greek.

'It's about you, Denis Parker.' The voice was louder, more strident than her own. But she was glad of it. It almost concealed the tremor that wavered beneath.

'What do you want? I ain't done—'

192

'Hey, keep your hands in the air! I want to know about the message you wrote Abigail Webb after her murder on Sunday night. Very soon after.'

'I don't know what you're talking about.'

'On Facebook. Under the name Greg Stanhouse.'

He paused, long enough to confirm that Katharine had indeed identified him correctly, not that Maddy ever doubted it.

'There's no proof—'

'Don't even bother. You'll only be in deeper shit than you're in already. Tell me how you knew the deceased.' She hadn't planned to use this technique, though it had always served her well, even without the badge. For the right kind of interviewee, cop language triggered the right kind of response. It was almost instinctive. Maybe because they'd seen it on TV, or perhaps because people automatically reacted that way to the vocabulary of authority. But she had got results from it dozens of times, asking 'When did you enter the vicinity?' or 'Did you approach the suspect?' or now 'Tell me how you knew the deceased.' If you talked like you were the police, they'd answer like they were a witness.

'I saw her, two, maybe three times. Nothing happened, I swear.'

'Saw her where?'

'At the club.' The beam of light picked out the spheres of sweat forming on his upper lip.

'What club?'

'You know, where she worked.'

'I want you to tell me.'

'The club. You know the club, don't you?'

Maddy understood what was at stake here, the small loss of credibility that would ensue if this man believed his sudden inquisitor was not in full possession of the facts. It struck her as a much more severe blow than if he discovered she carried no firearm.

'We know everything, Parker. Just like we know your name and what you do online and what you jerk off to at night. But I want to hear it from you. So tell me again, how did you know the deceased? No questions, just answers – and keep your hands in the FUCKING AIR.'

'All right, all right.' He cleared his throat, which she took as a sign of acquiescence. In the momentary pause, she could hear that the exclamations coming from the computer had turned into cries of agonized anguish. God only knew what filth he was watching. But she was not going to move forward far enough to find out. She needed to maintain her distance. She advanced sufficiently to reach the power cable at the back of the machine and, with one firm tug, yanked it out of the socket. Instantly the noise and the electronic glow were gone.

Now there was only the white beam of her torch on his face, as if he were under military interrogation. She saw him swallow. 'I saw her dance at the opium den. Maybe three times. Four, max.'

The opium den. A shiver passed through Maddy, one consisting not of fear but of a chemical agent far more corrosive. Had she been wrong after all about Abigail and drugs? Was her sister in fact a drug user? And, if she was, did that mean that everything else Maddy had assumed – culminating in her belief that Abigail had been murdered rather than dying from a self-administered overdose – had been wrong too?

'Tell me about this opium den.'

'It opened a year ago, maybe eighteen months. It's upstairs at the Great Hall of China. Very exclusive.'

It took another second for Maddy to understand what she was being told. But 'opened' helped her. He was not speaking about an opium den, but *the* Opium Den, a private members' club. She had had no idea of its existence until this moment.

'And you saw Abigail Webb there?'

'I didn't know her name then, but yeah. She was a table dancer. I saw her, like, three times.'

Maddy's head was flooding. She closed her eyes briefly, as if that might somehow enable her to process the information she was taking in. But it didn't work. She pictured the multi-coloured, spinning wheel her computer displayed when it could not cope, as if putting its hands up in surrender.

So her sister performed for men like this one. She pictured Abigail in the CCTV footage, her usually free, wavy blonde hair straightened so it fell like a curtain: that must have been her stage look. And she was a regular at the Great Hall bar because she worked just upstairs. Maybe she went there to wind down after a shift. Or perhaps being there – at the bar, looking hot – was part of the job.

Perhaps this was what her mother had been referring to when she said Abigail had been offered 'another job'. But it hardly dispelled the mystery. Her own sister had been a stranger. She hardly knew her.

'Did you ever talk to her?'

'No. Maybe, you know, like "Hi" or something.'

The next question had to be forced out of her throat. 'Did you ever leave the club with her?'

'Christ no, you kidding? Me? You gotta be joking.' His laughter made him even more repulsive. 'I don't have that kind of dough.'

'You said the club was – keep your hands where I can see them! You said it was very exclusive.'

'Oh it is.'

'So how come you . . .'

'What, you think I was a guest there?' He was smiling at the absurdity of it. 'Do you have any idea what that place costs?' He shook his head in disbelief and, Maddy detected, relief. As if her misunderstanding meant he was off the hook. 'I *work* there. I'm on security. That's how I came to see April.'

'April?'

'That was the name she used, the dead girl. They all have phoney names there. I didn't know her real name till it was on the TV. Jeez, she was gorgeous though.'

Maddy pushed herself to go on. 'And you would watch? While she danced for someone who could afford to pay?'

'Yes. Last time I looked that wasn't a crime in the state of California. Hey, don't LAPD always send people in pairs? How come you're on your own?'

She swallowed hard. She had to wrap this up and get out soon. 'What kind of people did she dance for?'

'The usual. Rich guys, young guys, the ones who arrive in the big cars. The Opium Den's become real popular among high rollers, you know? Big with the Chinese, they love it there. Maybe they think it's funny, you know, 'cause of the name and all. Especially the boys from the garrison. They're there all the time. And boy, do they love the American girls. Pale skin, blonde hair – they can't get enough of it.'

Chapter 24

The room was cold, but Madison barely noticed. She had built a fortress around herself, tottering piles of paper along with the detritus of an earlier attempt at dinner. The computer was on, but she wasn't looking at it. She was hunched instead over a yellow legal pad, pen in hand, scribbling page after page, filling each one with lines and words, sometimes arranged in the form of diagrams, arrows linking one fact or thought with another.

She was doing it at feverish speed, her breathing hard and heavy. She would follow one path of reasoning – tracing, say, the common elements in the deaths of Rosario Padilla, Eveline Plaats and her younger sister – only then to hit a dead-end or to see a new connection that had earlier eluded her. She'd rip the paper from the pad, enjoy scrunching it into a ball, taking pleasure in the concrete physicality of the act, in hurling it away – only to start on a fresh sheet, certain that this page, this version, would be the definitive account that would, in a series of neat, logical moves, explain the fate of her sister.

More than an hour passed like that, writing furiously as well as reading thousands upon thousands of words – every scrap she could find on life in the People's Liberation Army garrison that had arisen on the ruins of the old Long Beach

Naval Base on Terminal Island, that vast stretch of docks, piers and warehouses by the Port of Los Angeles that had been all but abandoned once the US Navy pulled out at the end of the last century. Eventually a wave rolled through her, heat that seemed to start at her toes and work upward. The first time she had felt it, years ago now, she had been frightened. But these days she knew she just had to wait it out. She folded her arms on the table and rested her head there, closing her eyes as she let the storm pass. For a few minutes she would sleep, the body taking by force what it needed and what it had been denied.

When she awoke, she was newly energized. Of course it was false and fleeting, like a junkie's high after a fresh fix. But it gave her what she needed. Still surrounded by papers, some balled-up around her ankles, others still intact and spread out over her desk, she turned to the keyboard. She had no plan beyond continuing with the keyboard what she had already started with the pen. She would arrange what she knew, the only way she knew how: by writing it.

The minutes rushed past her, too fast for her to see them. The adrenalin carried her; she surfed it, letting its speed take her. This feeling too was not novel. Writing could do this to her, holding her in a trance, unaware of anything but the sentences flowing out of her fingertips, her concentration total, the sound of the keys, hammering and thudding to her will, a kind of music.

Less than an hour later, it was finished. She read it over, only then fully comprehending what she had done. This was no memo to herself, no plain catalogue of the facts for use as a guide to her own investigation. What she had written, without planning to, was a news story for the LA Times.

Three women murdered in the Los Angeles area could be the victims of a serial killer, with suspicion centring on Garrison 41, the People's Liberation Army base in the city, according to the families of the dead.

The LA Times *has learned that Abigail Webb, who was found dead this week in North Hollywood, Rosario Padilla and Eveline Plaats all died the same way – of an unexplained drug overdose, described in each case as utterly out of character for the women involved – and all had close links with the garrison. A spokesperson for the Webb family insisted the similarities amounted to a distinct pattern. 'We demand that the Los Angeles Police Department now pursue this lead. The evidence is too clear to be ignored.'*

While Webb had worked as a dancer at the Opium Den nightspot, a favourite nightspot of young Chinese officers from the base, Padilla's last known . . .

She read the story one more time, making the occasional tweak. She did not want to give herself any time to change her mind. She tapped out Howard's email address – and pressed 'Send'.

They were in a rowing boat on a bright summer's day. Abigail was turning her face towards the sun, trailing her fingers in the water. Quincy was rowing, while their mother was at the other end, fussing over a bag, producing an endless supply of sandwiches. Maddy was sitting on the cross-bench in the middle, facing towards Abigail and her mom, her back to her older sister. She was enjoying the weather too, until she became aware that her ankles were becoming wet. She looked down to see water coming through. At first she thought it was a puddle, but now she understood that there was a hole in the boat. It was getting wider and wider, so wide she could see the ocean. The water had reached her knees and was getting higher. And now there was a knocking sound, as if a paddle were banging against the side of the boat. *Knock, knock,*

knock. Knock, knock, knock . . .

She woke with a jolt, lifting her head from the desk. It was dark but the clock in front of her said it was five forty am. Was that right? She had no recollection of the night or of when she fell asleep. And there it was again. *Knock, knock, knock.*

It was coming from close by. And now there was a voice, an urgent stage whisper. 'Maddy, open this door now. *This minute.*'

She recognized it, though it took several long, slow seconds to process this information, to understand what she had heard and what it meant. The voice belonged to Howard Burke, news editor of the *LA Times*. He had never, ever come anywhere near her home. It surprised her that he even knew where she lived. And it was not yet six in the morning. In journalist terms, it was the middle of the night. What the hell was he doing here?

She looked down at her feet, expecting to see her jeans soaked from the water in the boat. It took another second to compute that this was not a dream, but she was now awake. The way her clothes felt on her skin, her temperature, made her suspect she had not been asleep all that long. But she had gone down very deep. And now she was coming back to the surface too fast.

'Maddy. You *must* open the door.' The phone on the desk was vibrating, the name 'Howard' flashing across its screen. His urgency scared her.

She looked at her computer screen and her desk, scanning for anything she might not want to be seen. The rest of the room was a mess, but there was nothing she could do about that. She scooped up a pile of discarded clothes, including underwear, and shoved it into the nearest available space which at this moment turned out to be the oven. She called out, hearing the croak of just-interrupted sleep in her voice: 'Coming.'

She turned the latch and Howard surged in, as if the door had been holding back a tidal wave of water. The language of his body, tense and coiled, was anger. But his face, grey with tiredness and too much computer light, revealed desperation. And, she decided on an instinct, fear.

He didn't wait to sit down or be asked to sit down or even to adjust to being in the room. He spoke as if he were continuing a conversation that had been unspooling in his own head for a while. 'Maddy, there is no way in the world we can publish this.' He was pointing at his phone, breathless, as if he had run up the stairs to get here. Perhaps he had. 'I don't know what the hell you were thinking but *this* . . .' He tapped the phone again, to indicate its contents. 'There's no way. No way.'

Now it came into sharper focus, Maddy's last move before she had finally faded – what, an hour or two ago? She remembered writing the story but until now had been hazy about what she had done next.

Howard took her silence to be resistance. Now his voice rose. 'Every word of it is speculation. There's no evidence at all. Just blogosphere, conspiracy wingnut speculation. OK, a few crumbs – but they're all circumstantial. In other words, bullshit.' He leaned in closer, so his face was just inches from hers. 'Bullshit, Maddy.'

She noticed that Burke, usually clean-shaven, had stubble – a few white whiskers which belied the dark, reddish hair on top. He smelled of toothpaste, a scent struggling to cover the fact that he had obviously had no breakfast. Maddy felt an unexpected sympathy for her boss. She was used to being awake at ungodly hours at both ends of the day. This man clearly was not.

He turned his back to her, as if he needed to regroup. He walked a few paces across the studio apartment, the strangeness of seeing him here, by her couch, inches from her bed, close to her kitchen, struck her again. This was her sanctuary and he had intruded upon it.

'Listen, Howard. Just think about the facts for a second.'

'Facts! What facts? There's not a hard fact in there.'

'One, three women who have never injected drugs in their lives suddenly OD. Think about that. Not one of them was a drug user. Second, all three women have a direct connection with the garrison.'

'Oh no they don't, Maddy. That was you having two and then another two and making six. One of the women went to meet friends who were working at Terminal Island. Big deal. She then went to an Italian restaurant. What, we gonna say there's an Italian serial killer on the loose? The spaghetti strangler?'

'Don't joke about this, Howard.' She spoke quietly, but his anger was unleashed now. It had its own momentum.

'And the other one, the cleaner? OK, her last job was at the garrison but where did she go after that?'

'That's the last place she was seen alive.'

'That's the last place you *know* about, you mean. Come on, Maddy. This is beneath—'

'And my sister. What about my sister?'

That slowed him down, but it did not stop him. He replied, his voice deeper than before, the volume dropped a notch. 'She danced at a nightclub that was popular with Chinese people. That's it. That's what you've got. Can you imagine what you'd say if this was any other story? You'd laugh in my face. If you saw that in the *Times*, you'd march over to my desk, tell me I'm a pussy and threaten your resignation for the fiftieth time this year. On principle.'

He was trying to lighten the mood, but she didn't feel like lightening it. 'What do you mean "any other story"?'

'Come on, Maddy. Don't make me say it. Everyone is in pieces over what happened to your sister. It's just horrible. But . . .'

She felt her teeth clench. 'And when you say "what happened to your sister" so confidently like that, perhaps you can tell me: what did happen to my sister? I mean, you seem to know. So tell me. What happened to her? *Exactly?*'

He shook his head. 'I don't know, Maddy.' He sighed, allowing a gentleness into his tone. 'I wish I knew. That's what the police are doing—'

'The police? Are you kidding?' Now it was her turn to get angry, as if the energy that had drained away from him had flowed into her. 'The police are doing jack shit, Howard. They are *miles* behind me. They haven't even *begun* to look at past cases, they haven't seen the *pattern*. There's a pattern here, Howard. Three deaths, almost identical.'

'Almost? Since when is "almost" good enough, Madison?'

'Look,' she said, stepping closer towards him so that she was intruding directly on his space. '"There's no such thing as a triple coincidence." Remember that? You should. Because that's one of yours. "Two can be a coincidence, three's a trend." That's another. There are three women who *never* do drugs who are found with a vat of heroin in their veins. They're all pale-skinned, pretty and blonde. Which just happens to be the look of choice for the boys over there in Garrison 41. In my book, that's a story. Maybe I'd have called it a fluke when it was just the first two. No one else noticed it then, did they? No one wrote a word about Eveline or Rosario. But the third one made all the difference. Especially to me.'

Burke walked the two paces to the couch and slumped into it, letting his elbows rest on his knees. A middle-aged paunch spilled over his belt. He exhaled and then spoke quietly, barely above a whisper. 'This makes no sense, Maddy. No sense at all. We can't edit this like it's a regular story. It isn't. This is your *sister*. A death in the family.'

She turned away from him, heading to the kitchen to get a glass of water. And then, as an afterthought, another one for her guest. She could hear him throughout.

'You shouldn't be writing, Maddy. Not about this, not about anything. Of course you can't think straight, you—'

'How dare—'

'Sorry, sorry. That came out wrong. What I mean is, no one can work after a shock like this. No one could do it. And you shouldn't even try.'

'What would you have me do then, Howard?'

He smiled a weary smile. 'You're asking for life advice from a guy who's this close to his second divorce and who sees the security guy at the office more than he sees his own kids. What do I know, Maddy? You're in grief. So grieve.'

There was plenty she could say to that. The sentences formed in her head. *I would grieve if I could but I don't know how.* Or, *But if I start that, then who knows where it'd end?* She thought of telling him what she had told herself: *Once I know what happened, and who did this to Abigail, then I'll start mourning. But not before.*

Instead she gave a little shrug and said nothing. It was weird enough having the news editor in her house without attempting some intimate chat unlike any they had had before. She wanted this conversation over.

He picked up her cue and stretched himself out of the couch, his knees creaking as he got up. She hovered by the front door, just so there could be no doubt that she was concluding proceedings. As he shook her hand, as awkward as ever in dealing with a young woman, she asked the question that, had she been more awake at the start, she would have asked then.

'Howard. You came here at quarter of six in the morning. You didn't need to do that.'

'Don't mention it, Maddy. We may have had our differences, but I care about all our—'

'No. Don't get me wrong. I'm not thanking you. I mean it literally. You didn't need to come here. You could have called. You could have replied to my email. You could have told me to come into the office – you know, summoning me to . . . what do you call it when you're mad at a reporter? "A chat without coffee." But you came all the way here. All but banging on the door.'

'I didn't bang on the door.'

'*All but*, I said. I caveated the statement – just like you taught me to.'

'I wanted to do this in person. Given the context.'

'What context?'

'You. Grieving. Thought it better to do it face to face.'

'All right, Howard. "I hear you."' She smiled. 'Thanks for coming over.'

She watched him head for the staircase – impressed that he would be considerate enough to avoid a noisy elevator while the neighbours were asleep – and closed the door behind him. He was a decent enough man, she reflected. Thorough, rigorous and protective of his reporters. But on this particular matter, she concluded, he was full of shit.

If he cared so much for her wellbeing, he'd have come over yesterday. And no one makes a condolence call at five forty am. Nor do they bang on the door and call you on your cell at the same time, bursting into the room with a desperate look in their eyes. If he wanted to talk her off the story he could do that the way he'd done it a thousand times: on the phone, by text or email. No, he had been in a hurry to see her because he was worried. The story she had written had scared him rigid.

They both knew why. It was an insult to her intelligence to pretend otherwise, as he had done at the door just now. The problem was that she had pointed the finger in her story and where she'd pointed it had terrified him.

If he had told the truth, she would have listened to him. Sure, she argued with him day and night in the office, often over the tiniest point (they once debated the placing of a comma for a full twenty minutes before Jane Goldstein promised to sack them both if they did not release the page). But that was a mark of respect on her part. If she did not admire his mind, she would never try to change it.

Instead he had spun her a bullshit yarn about bereavement and impaired judgement. Well, they would soon see about that.

She brought the screen back to life, the story she had written during the night – perhaps only a couple of hours ago – still up where she left it. She opened her browser and, with a few keystrokes, entered the back-end of the *Times* system, thanks to access privileges granted to all specialist correspondents back when Goldstein's predecessor was determined that all reporters cut, edit and post their own stories. Maddy was old school, knowing that she needed at least one pair of eyes to read whatever she had written before it was unleashed upon the world. Not least because sleeplessness often resulted in wild departures from accepted grammar. Maddy hardly ever used the codes she had just typed in. But she had not forgotten them.

She read the words one last time, attempting to address some of the points Howard had raised, making a tweak here and there. She knocked out a headline – *Victims' families fear an LA serial killer, with Garrison 41 in their sights* – let her finger hover for just a second or two and then pressed the button marked 'Publish'.

Chapter 25

Jeff was not too hot on social media – for a cop, it was tricky knowing what you could or couldn't say, so the whole thing was easiest avoided. That meant he missed Maddy's 6.13 am weib, which in a few, terse words announced her story:

Latest on murder of Abigail Webb, possible China connection?

Nor did he see the flurry of weibs that followed, including several which said 'Hey, that link is broken' or similar, and several more after that, which confirmed that Madison Webb's story had been taken down from the *LA Times* site. It had been up less than fifteen minutes.

He knew none of this until a call from Barbara Miller, whose new partner Steve – and 'new' he would remain, in Jeff's eyes at least, for several years to come – was quite the Weibo fiend. He had spotted the weib-storm brewing over Maddy. He had alerted Barbara who alerted Jeff. And now the detective was staring at his phone, scrolling down as he read what Madison had written. Handily, several bloggers had cached the piece from the *Times* site and reposted versions of it, which were now replicating themselves at viral rates, too fast for the *Times* or anyone else to keep up, let alone take down. As Barbara had put it when they spoke, 'The story's out there.'

He remained unsure as to the purpose of Miller's call throughout their conversation and even after it. Was she seeking to enlist his help in reining in Maddy, bringing her to heel? Unlikely, given Barbara's fairly accurate assessment of the relationship: she knew that Jeff's interest in Madison Webb was unrequited and that the chances of him persuading her to do anything she didn't want to were slim, typified by her consistent refusal to become his girlfriend. Or was Barbara simply on a fishing expedition, to see what he knew about Maddy and, most pertinently, whether he could shed any light on where, and from whom, she was getting her information? On this point, he insisted he had nothing, that Maddy was very definitely not keeping him in the loop. Miller's reply – 'Hmm' – suggested she was not convinced.

A clue to his colleague's motives came later, at around seven thirty am. In between scanning Weibo, talking to Barbara and watching the local TV news – which hadn't touched Maddy's story – he had not yet showered. He was about to when the phone rang again. It was his commander, Eric Sutcliffe.

'Jeff, tough call to make so I'm just going to get this over with. I need you to come downtown.'

'What's going on?'

His boss cleared his throat, telling Jeff all he needed to know. The commander said the words all the same. 'We need to reassign you. Traffic duties. Starting right away.'

'Traffic duties? Are you *kidding* me? What the—'

'Don't make this harder than it already is, Jeff.'

'Harder for *you*, you mean. What the fuck is this about?'

'We both know. You want me to spell it out?'

'Yes. Spell it out.'

'A certain story appeared on the *Times* website today.'

'I had nothing to do with that.'

'Well, the feeling is—'

'I don't care what the *feeling* is, Eric. I had nothing to do with that. First I knew of it was when—'

'Well, that girlfriend of yours didn't get all that information from nowhere, did she? Come on, Jeff. Don't be an asshole.'

'She's not my girlfriend.'

'All right, all right. I'm not going to delve into your underwear, Jeff. To be honest, I couldn't care less who you're banging. But you don't leak operationally sensitive information to—'

'For the last time, I did not leak!'

'Whatever, Jeff. Whatever.' Then, as if unable to resist, 'You're telling me she starts pointing the finger at the PLA all by herself?'

'Yes!'

'If that's what you say.'

'Eric, tell me the truth. It's bullshit, this whole China thing, isn't it?'

'It doesn't matter whether it is or it isn't. The bosses are very clear. You're reassigned. Come in and get your new instructions. You hear me, Jeff?'

The secretary nodded for Howard Burke to go in. He could see Goldstein fixed on her screen, spectacles perched on the end of her nose. She waited a second and then another before looking up, then rose and moved over to the set of chairs by the window. At least she didn't stay behind her desk, as he had feared: her sitting, him standing, as if awaiting punishment in the principal's office. As she gestured for him to take a seat, he launched right in, too pent-up to wait for her cue.

'I'm furious, Jane, I really am.'

'Shouldn't I be the one who's furious?'

'We *both* should be furious! What she's done is an insult to you, to me, to this pap—' He rapidly corrected himself, falling back into line with the approved corporate vocabulary. 'To this *news organization*.'

'Why don't you start at the beginning?'

'It's not that complicated, Jane. Madison Webb' – the full

name, as if he were talking about a criminal suspect or perhaps a fugitive in the news – 'sent me a story she had written which fell well short of *LA Times* standards. Of *any* standards. Hearsay, conjecture, blind quotes, unsourced claims and, of course, a glaring conflict of interest.'

'Her sister?'

'Exactly. I got there as fast as I could. Crack of dawn. I don't know if you know, but she keeps crazy hours. Really.' He put a finger to his temple, as if to signal that the person they were discussing was a lunatic, but the blankness of Goldstein's expression deterred him from making the full gesture. 'Anyway, I told her what I just told you. There was no way the *LA Times* could run such a story. No way at all.'

'And then she ran it anyway?'

'Well, I wouldn't say she *ran* it exactly. She *posted* it. Without permission.'

'Using access codes we gave her?'

'Well, yes, but years ago. And not for this purpose. It's a complete abuse of our system. It's an abuse of our *trust*.'

'I understand, Howard.'

'I took it down straight away, of course, but you know how it is out there, online. It's the wild west. There are no—'

'Howard—'

'They've copied it and copied it. Cached it, mirrored it, you name it—'

'Howard!'

'Sorry, Jane. It's just, I'm so—'

'What do you want to do about it?'

'About the story? We've already issued a—'

'About Maddy.'

At last, Howard Burke took a breath. And then let out a sigh. 'She has huge talent, there's no denying it. She's the best reporter I've got, by a mile. But she can be impossible, you know that. And she's just broken every rule we have. I mean, if we can't trust her, it doesn't matter how good she is, does it?'

'You think this story has caused us damage?'

'To our reputation? Huge. And with, you know . . . yeah, I'd say that was pretty lasting damage.'

'If she's wrong.'

'Even if she's right, Jane. You can't just take a flier like this. This is serious stuff, you don't say a word till you've got it nailed.'

'I know that, Howard.'

'Of course, of course. I didn't mean to . . . I was trying to say that you and I know this, but I'm not sure Maddy does. And until she does, I don't think . . .'

He let the sentence peter out. But they both knew what he meant.

'Howard, see that story there, the one in the frame, just behind you?'

He twisted his neck to see it. It was the splash from all those years ago. *US–Chinese Treaty looms, critics call it 'Surrender'.*

'Yes, Jane. I see it.'

'Do you know the funny thing about that story?'

He shook his head.

'The date on it is wrong.'

He looked over his shoulder again. The date looked perfectly right to him, the date every kid learned at school, the date that was in the history books. He gave her a quizzical look.

'The date's wrong because it should have been a day earlier.'

'I don't follow, Jane.'

'I had the story a day earlier. I filed it, I had it double-sourced. But the man who sat in this chair said no. He was getting calls from DC, pressure, you know the drill. He didn't believe it. Or maybe he thought it was too much of a risk. I don't know, he never told me. So he held it for twenty-four hours. Seemed the sensible thing to do at the time.'

There was a pause while he received her message. 'With respect, I think this is real different, Jane. Madison hasn't got one, let alone two real sources and—'

'I know. I'm just saying sometimes we can be a bit too quick to silence young, bright, female journalists when they bring in stories that shock us. This paper has a history of it.'

'I don't see what being female has—'

'I don't want you to fire Madison, Howard. She's too good and too special for that. Find another solution.'

Jeff Howe was too stunned to feel anger. He was in a state he had seen a hundred times in victims, but never in himself. He was in shock.

He left Sutcliffe's office staring straight ahead, conscious of the eyes on him as he walked through the homicide floor: the once rising star, now crashed to earth. He didn't want to talk to anybody.

It was by the elevators that he was eventually cornered. Gary Cole saw him and raised his eyebrows in a smile. It was clear even before he had opened his mouth that he hadn't heard about Jeff's 're-assignment'.

'So, buddy, how you doing?'

'Not bad, Gary. Not bad.'

'Gotta tell you, that friend of yours has done us a big favour. "Free at last, free at last, thank God Almighty, we are free at last!"' He grinned broadly.

Jeff chose to grin back, nodding enthusiastically but saying nothing, so that Cole would say more. It worked.

'I mean, we've been doing this thing in the dark for weeks now. And it's not getting results. I've been telling them, "We gotta get this out there."'

'In the dark?'

Cole lowered his voice. 'Now we've got Barbara and Steve on board, there's six of us on it. But all on the down low, even in here. Command demanded a total news blackout.

Brief the media that these were suicides, all files to be restricted access to prevent leaks, only a summary held by the coroner's office – the whole nine yards.'

Jeff was doing his best to project nonchalance, to look less interested than he was. 'Oh, I've worked on those. What was the reason this time?'

'Usual thing: serial killer craves fame and attention, don't give it to him. That's the official reason anyway.'

'So there's no doubt this is a serial.'

'No doubt at all. The guy's leaving a calling card. Seemed that way from the first one, but no doubt after the second.'

'The second being . . .?'

'You want to read your friend's story, buddy. Rosario Padilla.'

'And the first was Eveline Plaats?'

'Yup. Just like in the story. Which is why they're going apeshit up there. They assume your friend's got a source. I'm surprised they haven't hauled your ass in yet.'

'And Webb's sister is definitely the third?'

'Seems that way. Same signature as the others.'

'Jesus. And what about the Chinese thing? Is she—'

'Well, I can see why she's jumped to that conclusion. I mean, we're looking at that too.'

'Because the victims all had a connection with—'

'No. To be honest,' he dipped his voice quieter still, 'she had more on that than we got. We didn't even know about Plaats and the cleaning job.'

'So why were you—'

Still whispering, Cole said. 'The calling card.'

Jeff, now straining to seem cool and only mildly interested, raised his eyebrows.

Cole reached for the folder he'd been keeping under his arm. 'I'm only doing this because we're in the open now. Which is what I've been saying we should be from the beginning, but anyway. Here.'

Cole began to work his way through a sheaf of crime scene photographs, then a series of pictures from the coroner's office. Finally he reached the one he'd been looking for. 'That's Abigail Webb,' he said, as he let Jeff get a brief glimpse, before returning the photo to the folder and putting it back under his arm.

The picture showed a young blonde woman, stripped down to her underwear, lying on what Jeff presumed was a pathologist's table. She was unmarked, as far as he could tell: no wounds or lacerations.

Still, what Cole had called the killer's calling card was unmistakable. Tucked into Abigail Webb's underwear was a flower, laid in a diagonal, its stem poking out of the top on the right and continuing down past her thighs on the left. Even seen fleetingly, Jeff Howe found the image unsettling.

It took him a few seconds to say, 'And that was the same with the other girls?'

'That's right,' said Cole. 'All found the same way. Silk flower in the panties, right across the snatch. Even on Plaats, the first one, it looked like some kind of signature – so they kept that detail back.'

'Then Padilla confirmed the pattern.'

'Yep. Weird, don't you think? He doesn't put his fingers there, doesn't put his dick there. He just leaves a flower. Like, he's proving how Zen and self-restrained he is. Or maybe he's gay. I don't know. Anyway, look, Jeff, I gotta run. But, you know, any bright ideas, any leads, you know where to find us. We need all the help we can get on this one.'

Cole had already turned and begun his walk away, his arm raised in a wave, when Jeff called out.

'Hey, Gary. One other thing. What kind of flower?'

'What?'

'The silk flower. What kind was it?'

'Oh, didn't I say? Well, you can tell your friend she's no fool. The flower was a poppy. A red silk poppy.'

Chapter 26

Leo had counselled against this venue, but clearly he had not done so forcefully enough. He never liked breakfast events at the best of times, especially for donors. No alcohol, so you were starting at an immediate disadvantage – though that was less of a factor in LA where the rich drank nothing but wheatgrass smoothies anyway.

He glanced down at his phone. A weib from the official *LA Times* account. 'Statement from the *LA Times*,' it said baldly, followed by a link. He clicked on it to read a single paragraph.

The Los Angeles Times *wishes to apologize to its readers for a story that appeared earlier today under the byline of* Times *reporter Madison Webb. The story was unauthorized and as such did not go through the usual* Times *editorial processes. It was removed as soon as possible. Lawyers for the* LA Times *are working with internet service providers to halt its publication elsewhere online. The item represented a breach of* Times *protocol and should never have appeared.* LA Times *Executive Editor Jane Goldstein said, 'The* LA Times *wishes to apologize to all those who have been distressed by this rare lapse in* Times *standards. The technical defects that made this lapse possible are being addressed.'*

Oh, Maddy. She was tough and strong, he'd known that from the beginning. But he also knew that Madison was not quite as solid as she would have you believe: sometimes she needed another person to help carry that weight. For a while, that had been him. And now, just when she should be allowed to grieve for her kid sister, she had made an enemy of the mighty People's Republic and her own employer – all before most people had had breakfast.

He had gasped when he saw the original weib: *Latest on murder of Abigail Webb, possible China connection?* Literally gasped, out loud. Officially, he would say that there was nothing Madison Webb could do that would surprise him, that her knack for finding a line and promptly crossing it was so well-honed that her doing the unpredictable had become predictable. He might say that, but it would not be true. Somehow even he, who by now should really have got used to Maddy's disregard of all convention and accepted constraints, her absurd pig-headedness and the sheer size of her *cojones*, could still be shocked. This statement from the *Times* did not, by contrast, surprise him in the least: he had only had to read the lede on her story this morning to know that she had smuggled it online without permission. There was no way any editor of the *LA Times* would have let that through.

He wanted to call her. She'd be feeling the pressure now, no doubt about it. She'd landed herself in the deepest of deep shit before, but this was different. He couldn't remember a public statement, disavowing her. In fact, he couldn't remember the paper disavowing any of its journalists like that. It had never happened

And all this while she was mourning Abigail. More than once, he had wondered if Madison was borderline crazy.

Indeed, on one occasion, he had used that very phrase to her face, with results that were not good. But now he saw it as quite possible that, if Maddy did indeed walk that edge, the loss of Abigail had pushed her over it.

He thumbed out a text.

Can't imagine what you're going through. Here if you need me.

First line too saccharine, second line too cursory.

Maddy, I'm guessing you're having a very hard time just now. Is there anything I can do to help?

Didn't even sound like him. Too limp-wristed.

Maddy, I can see the hole you're in from here. Let's talk. L.

Fine when they were dating. Too flip now.

Finally, he stabbed out something inadequate but not disastrous.

I want to help. Call when you can. L

He spent another three minutes debating with himself whether he should put an 'x' on the end of that. Ubiquitous now, it could hardly cause offence. Though it was different coming from him. It was at once too much and too little. They had been lovers, their attachment too strong to be reduced to an empty 'x'. Yet, without it, that 'L' looked so stark. He finally pressed the button – leaving off the kiss.

He put the phone back in his pants pocket and surveyed the room. The only thing worse than a breakfast fundraiser was a breakfast fundraiser in a bad venue. Like this one. A basement ballroom in a hotel in Thousand Oaks, bland walls, dark carpet to absorb the stains, all flooded by artificial light. If you were going to haul people out of bed at this hour, at least let them see some sunlight. Leo counted the tables and made an estimate for the morning's takings – eighteen tables, ten donors per table, thousand per donor – checked the banner behind the lectern – *Forward, Together* – picked up a forlorn lotus-seed bun, sought to avoid conversation with any of the guests and waited for the candidate.

The arrival was well co-ordinated, Mayor Richard Berger doing a good job of 'sweeping in' rather than the simple 'walking in' achieved by mere mortals. It helped that the entourage was boosted by the presence of a camera crew. A San Francisco channel, shadowing him for the day, provided the bustle, as well as the halo of TV lighting, required to make a politician look important. Leo watched from the back of the room.

For most events, he would meet his boss beforehand, briefing him on the way, telling him whom to avoid, who required extra kiss-ass treatment. But for this event – early start, distant location – he'd let one of the infants do it.

Now he watched as Ross, an over-keen rising star in the communications shop, whispered into the candidate's ear as the latter rushed from table to table, shaking hands and kissing cheeks as if he had a plane to catch. All about creating the impression of urgency, even at an hour when no one – not even the would-be Governor of California – needed to be anywhere else.

Ross had conveyed whatever nugget he needed to impart and now, Leo observed, Berger had his fake face on, the one he wore to cover up some alarm below the surface. He kept up the flesh-pressing and back-patting, but the smile was too wide, the eyes unnaturally bright.

Don't tell me that idiot has actually told him.

Now, by way of confirmation, Ross was showing the mayor the screen of his phone, Berger breaking off from man-hugging donors to grab it with both hands, his eyes boring into the words displayed before him. This was a disaster. Leo couldn't believe what that upstart asshole had done. You don't knock the candidate off his game with seconds to go! If shit's brewing, you hold it back. Let the star do his star turn, then drop the bombshell afterwards. Leo had planned to tell him, of course he had. But he was going to wait till the opening remarks were done, then fill the mayor in during the applause – ensuring the candidate was forewarned before the Q and A. Basic tradecraft.

Leo abandoned his perch, leaning against the side wall, and marched over to the front of the room, hoping to limit the damage. The young aide clocked Leo's expression then scampered to the side, pre-emptively pushing himself out of the way.

'Mr Mayor,' Leo said, reaching for his boss's elbow. The candidate turned to him with a broad, dazzle-white smile, as if greeting a long-lost friend. Through his teeth, he said, 'Your lady-friend is brewing up quite the shitstorm, isn't she?'

Seconds later, after a gushing introduction from the perma-tanned lawyer who was hosting the event, the politician was at the podium, fluently running through his talking points. He would revive Californian business, dig it out of the slump in which it had found itself these last few years. He still remembered the days when California was an economic powerhouse, when it was the place people all around the world dreamed of – and he was determined it would be that place once more. He knew the mountain was steep and the road was hard. It was for all America. The jobs his parents' generation had taken for granted seemed to have gone forever. Once Americans could assume their economy was number one on the planet. Now it seemed hard just to cling on to its spot as number two. Some days you felt you were running in that global race and just watching as first one big country and then another came up on your shoulder and overtook you. But he believed in the people of California, in their ingenuity and enterprise. They would be strong once more. They just needed to join together, all of them – including those who had once been rivals – and make California what it had always been, the greatest place in the world. Thank you. Thank you so much.

So he had kept it in, Leo noted. That reference to *those who had once been rivals*. Was that just force of habit, a line from the pre-canned stump speech that just came out automatically? Or a deliberate show of defiance, sticking to his message of amity between Americans and their new Chinese neighbours despite the bomb Madison Webb had dropped this morning? Maybe he wanted to show he was not to be diverted, that he was a man of principle. But it was high risk. More likely, the mayor had simply not had time to absorb what he had heard from Ross and adapt accordingly.

Then it was time for questions. The permatan acted as moderator, picking out hands, naming those who were his friends. Two questions in and it came, a bald-headed guy who introduced himself as a 'Californian and a father', asking about the Webb story. He referred to 'reports on Weibo that a serial killer is on the loose and he's from the garrison'.

Luckily, that wording allowed Berger to duck the question entirely.

'Well, thank you for that question. I think I speak for everyone here when I say that our hearts go out to the Webb family on the terrible loss they suffered this week. I know that I am not the only Californian who has them in my prayers.' He made the slightest, almost imperceptible dip of his head, a nod towards reverence. 'Sadly, given my position, it would be irresponsible for me to comment on an ongoing police investigation. But of course we need to get to the bottom of what happened here. For the family's sake. For California's sake. We need to know the truth. But it won't surprise any of you to hear me say,' slight pause, 'I believe in letting the police do their job.' The voice rose for that final clause, bringing a small surge of applause. Berger glanced towards the moderator as if to say, *Next question*.

He was more effusive on everything else: jobs, education, whether Californian farmers had a moral obligation to ensure their produce went first to the domestic market, rather than being sold for more lucrative export to China. 'I know they're paying top dollar, I get that,' the questioner said, conceding that pollution, excessive use of pesticides and soil contamination had made the Chinese super-rich distrustful of their own homegrown food and understandably keen to buy in high-quality fruit and vegetables from north America. 'But I want more children to be able to taste oranges from the San Joaquin Valley or strawberries from Oxnard. American children, I mean.'

Berger was about to answer when a voice from another table called out, unbidden. 'And our land, too. There should be more restrictions on selling off our farmland. Pretty soon we won't have any left.' Leo noted the nodding heads around the room.

The mayor had handled it all fluently and deftly avoided making any unscheduled news. As he watched the room empty and the donors file out, the richest among them receiving another mega-watt smile from Berger, Leo considered that it had been a successful morning's work. The answer on the Webb case was sufficiently bland to have neutralized the issue for now. It wouldn't have worked at a press conference and he'd have to say more next time he was confronted by a journalist rather than pliant members of the public. But it would buy them an hour or two.

He had begun to say as much, as he and the candidate were led back to the holding room where there would be a couple of final hands to shake. It was shameless, but it worked on most politicians: flattery and reassurance to smooth and soothe. He needed to pre-empt the attack that was surely coming: *Now I'm accused of letting some Chinese psycho stalk the city killing our women!*

But Berger interrupted him.

'You spoken to your friend yet, Leo? The sister?'

'Not this morning, no.'

'Sounds like she's in a bad way. Hacking into the *Times* system, Goldstein hanging her out to dry like that. Christ, that woman can be vicious. She reminds me of my first wife. Do you think it's a menopause thing? You know, the compassion gland shrivelling up, along with the ovaries?'

221

Here we go, thought Leo. The mayor – whose public, pro-feminist stance on the issues had won him a one hundred per cent rating from the National Organization for Women – often defaulted to crude misogyny when under pressure. If anyone ever recorded or, worse, filmed even one of these outbursts, Berger's career would be over in an instant. Leo had thought of doing it himself, as an insurance policy. But this time he said simply, 'That's disgusting, Mr Mayor.'

'So you haven't spoken to Madison. Do you think there's something we can do?'

'I don't follow.'

'Perhaps we can help somehow. She could probably use some help right now.'

Leo hesitated, scanning his boss's eyes for a clue.

'Does she need some help grieving, do you think? Is that something you could help her with? Maybe she's pursuing this whole investigation thing as a way of avoiding dealing with that. Look, I'm no expert but this cannot be healthy for her. I think it would be really good if she stopped all this poking around. *Really good.* Why don't you see what we can do for her, Leo? Helping people, Leo. That's what I'm all about.' And he gave his best and brightest politician smile.

Chapter 27

Black-and-white, exterior shots of a chicken-wire fence, the camera panning across to find a padlocked gate. Gloomy, baleful music in a minor key. Cut to an image of a damaged road surface, pitted and potholed. Cut to a rundown street, smudged by rain, flashing red lights out of focus; in the foreground a stretch of police incident tape.

Then the voice, deep, gravelly and reliable.

'You hoped for better. But our factories are shuttered and our towns are falling apart. You know we can do better. But not with a political insider, a man who doesn't want to *beat* our enemies but to show them the white flag.'

Over those last words, the screen fills up with a grainy, too-close picture of Richard Berger addressing a rally, his hand chopping the air, his face caught in what looks like a dictator's grimace. An edited recording of his voice, played as if through an old, crackling radio says: *We should join with those we used to call our rivals.* There is an echo on the voice, as if the radio is playing in an old, abandoned warehouse.

The baritone voice continues. 'This weakness has gone too far. Now there are reports of a Chinese *serial killer* running rampant – and it's happening *on Dick Berger's watch*.'

The music builds to a climax now, the voice growing more intense:

'We're sick of being second best. It's time to end the decline. It's time to take back America.'

And then, on screen for less than a second, the ad's first appearance of colour. An image of a woman in a red suit, smiling into the middle distance, a powerful shepherd ready to lead her people out of the wilderness.

I'm Elena Sigurdsson and I approved this message.

Chapter 28

Maddy had half-thought about telling Katharine about this rendezvous, just in case. In case of what, she could not answer. Obviously, Howard Burke posed no physical threat to her. He was tired, overworked and unfit, a man who panted after two flights of stairs. But he had also turned up at her home unannounced just after daybreak, a move so unprecedented, so out of tune with *Times* custom, that she now believed anything was possible. Merely *writing* the story had prompted a dawn house call from Howard. God alone knew how he would respond to her disobeying his direct instructions and publishing the piece anyway.

So Maddy had responded warily to the bombardment of calls from Howard, screening the first three. She had tried calling Jeff Howe, but was repeatedly answered by his voice-mail. For a man who normally leapt on a call from her in a single ring, she could only conclude he was now wary of any association with her. It was hardly surprising: she had gone so far off the reservation, she was now toxic.

To be certain, she resorted to the technique tried and tested by everyone from undercover reporters to spurned lovers: she left it for ten minutes, then called him from a landline whose number would show up as 'Unknown'. If he really were avoiding her, rather than all calls in general, he would pick up. Which he did.

'Howe.'

'Hi Jeff. It's Madison.'

His voice fell to a whisper. 'I can't talk to you.'

'Why not?'

'Because they think I'm the source of your story. They've suspended me. I'm on traffic duty.'

'Jesus. But you weren't the source on—'

'I know that. But what does it look like?'

'That means I must have got it right.'

'I can't do this, Madison. I'm sorry. I can't afford to get fired.'

'Just tell me, does it mean my story was right?'

'Madison.'

'Just one word, Jeff. Yes or no. Am I right?'

'Please, Madison.'

'OK, don't say anything. But if I'm right, stay on the line. If my story's plain wrong, there's no connection between my sister and those other deaths, hang up right now. OK?'

She waited, listening intently to the dead air between them. There was no click. She let the seconds pass, counting in her head. *Eight, nine, ten.* At last she broke the silence. 'Thanks, Jeff. I appreciate it. And you didn't say anything. Not a word.'

'Bye, Madison.'

Soon after that, there had come the fourth attempted call from Howard Burke. Heartened by what she had just heard – or not heard – from Jeff Howe, she picked up and agreed to meet. But before heading out, she dipped into Weibo and other forums, taking in the reaction to her story. She had thrown a stone in the pool and had sat fascinated, watching the ripples spread further and further outward.

The first weibs were simply passing on the story, linking to it with minimal comment. A 'Whoa' or 'Jeez' or 'Big'. That was followed by a sudden surge of people noticing that the

226

story had been taken down, providing the link that led nowhere, only to an *LA Times* error message. Then a wave of media-related commentary, short weibs denouncing the *Times* for lacking balls and praising Maddy for 'having a pair'. Most, she noticed, were wary of discussing the actual substance of what she had written. For all their bravado, she thought, they were as twitchy around this subject as Howard and the paper.

But once the mirrored version of her story was up, a few voices and then a few more began to express their outrage. They demanded action from the LAPD, from the mayor, from the president. Several pointed out that there was nothing the US authorities could do. *Get it into your heads, numbskulls. That place is off limits. Ever since the Treaty, we can't set a foot in there.* Others, usually those whose accounts were under pseudonyms, vented what Maddy suspected was long pent-up suspicion of the Chinese garrison. *It's about time that place was opened up to proper oversight. What the hell goes on in there?*

Those were the coherent ones. There was also plenty of garbage, some of it plain racism. *The yello man wants white woman, drugging her and fucking her. Get them out!!* Several dwelled on the supposed sexual inadequacy, and physical proportions, of Asian men. The weibs were piling up, dozens turning into hundreds and, as the hours passed, thousands. And that's just counting the ones that mentioned her.

She called Katharine, the tone instantly confirming Maddy's fears. 'Oh, hi.' And then, 'You've been busy.'

'Yeah. It's been quite a thing. I didn't realize—'

'What? What didn't you realize, Maddy? That there are a fuck of a lot of people in this country who really hate Chinese people?'

'No, I mean, I didn't realize that the—'

'Look, Maddy. We all loved Abigail, you know that. And I will do whatever I can to help you. But I don't know what you're doing right now. I really don't. You can't just make wild accusations like that. You just can't.' Her voice was wobbling. 'It has an impact. What you say, what you write. It affects people.' And Katharine had hung up. Not so much in anger, but saving herself from breaking down completely. Or that's what Maddy told herself, at any rate.

So she didn't get to tell her friend about her planned meeting with Burke, right here in the café around the corner from the office – the same one where Katharine had hacked her way into CleanBreak's system. She didn't get a chance to explain that she had agreed to meet her boss chiefly because she didn't quite know how to refuse, not without risking him reappearing at her door at some creepy hour. And because she was curious to see how exactly he fired her, and whether he would admit the real reason or whether he would maintain the charade that news outfits like the *LA Times* could say whatever they want and offend whoever they want.

He was already there when she arrived, at a table, latte in front of him. Surprising: she had expected him to keep her waiting, make a statement.

He brought her a coffee and launched straight in. 'Madison, Jane and I have been talking. About what happened. And about you.'

'Howard, don't do the concerned, sincere shit. Really. It just comes over as simpering. I prefer you when you're punching holes in the wall.'

His face fell. She did not soften. 'Come on, Howard. Spit it out. Let's not make it any more painful than it has to be.'

'All right, Madison. All right. So here's the thing. I haven't yet run it by Jane, but I wanted to sound you out first. This is my plan.'

Maddy stiffened, her muscles growing rigid in preparation.

'As you know, the Chinese president is making his farewell state visit here next week. He'll be in DC from Tuesday.'

'I know.' She could feel herself frowning.

228

'So what I thought was, if you're so determined to keep on working, even though I think – we *all* think – you need to be taking time off to grieve, but if you're not going to stop, well, this could be a really good opportunity.'

Maddy stared at him, attempting to process what she had just heard. Burke apparently took her confusion to be indifference, because he moved into persuasion mode.

'This is a step up, Madison. Covering politics. It's going to be a big story. You can write a long thinkpiece. You know, *Is the special relationship with China still special? Does America punch above its weight in the world?* Or colour: *What gifts will their president give our president?*'

'Not a boxed set.'

'Exactly! You've got it. All that stuff. Besides, it'll be a chance to get away from all the, you know, unhappiness here.'

Maddy took a sip of coffee. 'That's really sweet of you, Howard. It really is. Very sweet.'

'Good. So that's arranged. I'll get Maria to book the—'

'No, I mean it's sweet of you to think I'd fall for that.'

'What? What the hell are you talking about?'

'The obvious thing to do is fire me. That's what I deserve. But then it becomes a censorship story. Which is actually even worse for the Chinese. "PLA gags journalist." Everyone starts saying she must have hit a nerve, no smoke without fire. No way they'd want that, especially on the eve of a presidential visit. So do the opposite. Make a big show of how great and independent the *LA Times* is: "See, we didn't gag her, we gave her this plum assignment." The *Times* looks strong, but the garrison, the PLA, they get to look cool and tolerant. And I'm out of the way. Win, win, win. Can't believe you thought I wouldn't see through that, Howard. I'm even a little bit offended.'

He paled.

'I'd have more respect for you if you just gave me the sack. You'd be right to do it. What I did was completely

229

unacceptable, against all editorial standards. But this isn't about journalism any more. If my story is right, this is way bigger than that. Way bigger.'

She stood up. 'But you know that. That's why you took the story down so fast.'

He began an effort at defence, 'I made that decision because you had acted in an unauthorized . . .' But he couldn't keep it up. He stayed in his chair, avoiding her eye.

'Thanks for the coffee, Howard.'

As she walked out, her phone was buzzing. *Caller unknown.* She watched it ring, then ring again. She had been screening all calls since Abigail's death and there had not been many: most preferred the less intrusive text or Weibo. But once she had posted the story that morning, it had become a bombardment. It had begun, curiously, with media-watching blogs, hunting for crumbs of *Times* gossip, fascinated by the newsroom intrigue that surely explained why a story that went up could come down again within a few minutes. Then came the LA news channels wanting her to come on and talk about 'the garrison killer'. In the last hour or so, the texts and emails had started arriving from national media outlets based in New York and DC. She had also had calls from a radio station in London and a news organization in Moscow. She had ignored all of them.

The phone was still buzzing. On a whim, with no logic she could explain, she pressed the green button.

'Maddy, it's me.' Leo.

'Hi, Leo.' Her voice sounded remote, even to her.

'I need to see you. Right away.'

'Why didn't you call me on your cell? Why does it say "unknown"?'

'Please. I'm at UCLA for the debate. Meet me here.'

'What's this about, Leo? I can't just drop everything, I have things I need to—'

'I have something you should see.' His voice dropped to a whisper. 'I've got the classified police report into the murder of Rosario Padilla.'

Chapter 29

Thanks, Dana. 'A thousand points of light,' they're calling it and you can see why. A vast crowd assembled here, each person clutching a candle, forming a kind of sparkling mass, steadily filling up this park. And they're still coming as we speak. We're told organizers did not anticipate anything like these numbers for this rally. The turnout has, according to one of those involved, speaking to me earlier, 'blown us away'.

But, as you can see – Jim, why don't you let our viewers see some of the banners and signs here. OK, there we go. Cameraman Jim Deaver helping us out here. That one says, as you can see, 'Keep our rules or get off our land!' And here's another one. Jim, you got that? 'Chinese troops out!' That's a very direct message. And some of these slogans, Dana, undeniably aggressive. Earlier I saw one that said, very starkly: 'You kill an American woman, an American man will come kill you.'

Sorry, Dana, I missed that. Can you repeat the question? Absolutely, Dana. That's right. Appearances can be deceptive. It looks like a kind of prayer vigil, but the message coming from here is pretty robust. Some would say hostile. You can probably hear some singing, not far from me. They're singing that old folk song, kind of a sweet and gentle song. But instead of saying, 'This land is your land', they're stressing that 'This land is our land.' That's the change they've made and that, in a way, is the message they want to send out from here.

Yes, Dana, that's right. The organizers originally wanted to protest on the sidewalk directly in front of the head office of the LAPD, right here in downtown. But, perhaps no surprise, the police did not allow that request. They refused it, pushing the organizers over here, a block away, in City Hall Park. And some of those organizers are no doubt very relieved things turned out that way. There'd have been no room at all if they'd stuck to LAPD headquarters. Not much room here, I gotta tell ya . . .

OK, Dana, let me give our viewers some of the background. We can't really speak about 'organizers' in the usual, conventional way. This was a pretty spontaneous event, I'd say. But yes, it began with a call issued on Weibo by Mario Padilla of Boyle Heights. Now, he's the brother of Rosario Padilla, who was found dead in the area some three weeks ago. Initially police reported that as a straight drug overdose, but you'll know – and here at KTLA we're being very careful on the details of this – but you'll know that Padilla was named in a story that began on the LA Times website, later taken down, suggesting that she and two other women might be the victims of a serial killer at large in the city. And the story, which I stress KTLA has not confirmed and cannot verify, suggested the culprit could be somehow connected with the garrison stationed at Terminal Island.

Mario Padilla, brother of the first victim named in this highly controversial story, used social media earlier today to spread word of the story – and issued a call for others to join him in a demonstration. That went viral and you can see the result all around us. Police sources telling KTLA the crowd here is already at least two thousand, but organizers saying it's many, many more.

OK, KTLA cameraman Jim Deaver is signalling for me to

get moving now – this is all pretty much happening on the hoof here – because I think the main speech is about to get started. So let's get right to the front, here we go. OK, just need to squeeze in right here. And yes, as many of us predicted, the main address is going to come from Mario Padilla himself. He's standing on what looks like an orange crate and someone's handed him a bullhorn. He's got a bullhorn in one hand, and he's holding a candle in the other. Let's listen in.

'. . . for coming. I can't believe it. Really. And I know this would have meant so much to Rosie. And I guess to Eveline Plaats and to Abigail Webb, too. We're here above all to remember them. That's why I suggested we all bring a candle here tonight. To keep their memory alive.

'They were beautiful young women who, we believe, did not die because of something they did, but because of what somebody did to them. Now I'm not saying we know who that person is, who did these things. We call on the police to find that person. That's all we ask. The LAPD need to investigate these crimes!

'Thank you. Thank you.'

This land is our land, this land is my land.

'Thank you very much. OK. Thank you. What we say is we want the truth! We want to get to the bottom of who did this to our families! And that means the police reopening the case of my sister and of Eveline Plaats and hunting down the killer of Abigail Webb. And not just these crimes. You go back through the record of the last few years, just take a look as I have, and you'll see – there's a whole lot of crimes that were traced to this place, this base, that were never punished, suspects never arrested, charges never brought. So we want those cases reopened as well.'

This land is our land, this land is my land.

'OK. Thanks. Thank you so much. Now a moment ago, I mentioned Abigail Webb. Now I want to say something about her sister, the journalist Madison Webb. Without her – that's right, yes. I applaud with you. I do. She's not here, but let's show the LA Times *what we think of Madison Webb and how much we respect what she did today . . . Yes, thank you. She was the one who blew the whistle on what's going on. She wants to get to the truth!*

'Now, it may turn out that these murders – my sister and the other women – were done by a citizen of the United States of America. OK, if that's how it turns out, then let's catch that person and bring them to trial. That's how our system always worked in the past and that's how it's meant to work.'

USA! USA! USA!

'OK. OK. But let's say someone else did this. Let's say the article, which the LA Times *took down because they were too cowardly to publish, let's say that article was right and the killer is someone in that base. You know what? We can't do anything about that! The people on that base, in the garrison, are not subject to American law. They're subject only to Chinese law. It's the same in San Diego and San Francisco and the rest of the Pearls. That's what it says in the Treaty. I'm a law student and I've read it. But it's not fair and it's not right. That's what's got to change!*

'So this is what we want. We want the police to find the truth about these women. They are our sisters and daughters and friends. They deserve justice. And we demand that that search has to find the truth, wherever it may lie. Even if the politicians don't like what it says. Because the law should apply to everyone. That's what we demand. Justice for Rosario and Eveline and Abigail!'

USA! USA! USA!

They had agreed to meet somewhere discreet: the parking lot would make sense. Madison had assumed he would give her precise co-ordinates by text once she got closer, but all her messages went unanswered. Now that she was here she could guess at the problem. Leo was inside some concrete-lined press room surrounded by ten thousand reporters and their cellphones and none of them had signal. It always happened in a cluster-fuck situation: too much pressure on the network. The usual solution was email, which would work so long as there was a wifi connection – except she knew that the last thing Leo needed was an email from her stored on the official City of Los Angeles system. Even texts were risky. It meant she would have to do what she so desperately had wanted to avoid.

She followed the signage indicating the debate venue – billed by the host TV network as 'The Showdown' – and walked through the lobby of the UCLA lecture theatre where Richard Berger and Elena Sigurdsson would confront each other in just over six hours' time.

She tried to ignore what her peripheral vision suggested were familiar members of the LA press corps who, if she made the mistake of making eye contact, would soon be over here, feigning condolence and angling for the lowdown on what had happened to her story. In the corner to her left, munching a burrito, she could see Burke's predecessor as news editor – a man the other women in the office had warned her about when she first arrived. The last thing she needed now was him pawing over her, oozing fake sympathy.

So she kept her gaze fixed firmly on the accreditation desk, locking onto one of the clutch of twentysomething women who were signing in journalists, handing them passes.

'Hello there! Can I have your name and organization?' She was young, blonde and, though dressed in a suitably sexless black pant-suit, the perkiness of that greeting popped an instant question into Madison's mind: was this woman sleeping with Leo? Maddy had no grounds for thinking it, no grounds besides Leo's personality and past behaviour, that is. He might never have met this woman, who probably worked for the university rather than the Berger campaign. But still her manner, the whiteness of her teeth and the trim outline of her shape had Madison thinking of it.

She had not been like this when they were together. She had not been obsessively possessive or jealous. They had had other problems. But here now, and in the Mail Room three nights ago, she had found herself feeling it. In some way she barely understood, she did not wholly dislike the feeling. It was an emotion normal people might have.

Madison explained that she had arranged to meet Leo Harris and watched as the woman went off to pass a message to him. This was another unfamiliar situation. Waiting for a drop from Leo. Other reporters had done it, usually at tourist destinations – Hollywood or Santa Monica pier – complying with Leo's rule that the best hiding place was in plain sight. But not Maddy. When they were together, he had never been much of a source. Part of it was practical: she did not cover politics, so there was a limit to how much use each could be to the other. There was more to it than that though. It was not quite a principle; certainly, neither was high-minded enough to use such a word. Rather it was a sense, never articulated, that they'd have a better shot together without letting work intrude. Still, she was not above asking him for an occasional steer from the mayor's office if a criminal case ever rose to that level. And he was not above giving it.

Leo was coming closer, eyes down, staring at his phone. She felt an unexpected pleasure at seeing him, a reminder of the very different charge she would feel when they first dated. Back then, it consisted chiefly of anticipation of what was to follow: fizzing conversation and sex. Now the pleasure she felt was quieter: the prospect of consolation, of speaking to someone she knew well, of spending a few moments with someone who might help.

When he looked up to see her, he gave her a quick hug then gestured for her to follow him towards a coffee cart stationed in the lobby, in the process passing her a magazine, almost absent-mindedly, with so little ceremony she barely noticed it herself. But she felt immediately the weight of stiff card within its pages, holding onto it while they waited behind the journalists, politicos and assorted hangers-on lining up for a shot of caffeine.

At intervals, they'd be interrupted, as colleagues, contacts and rivals came over to exchange gossip or wish his candidate good luck. She couldn't tell if Leo was relieved that there was no real chance for the two of them to talk or frustrated. Just once their eyes met, Leo looking deep into her with an expression of such tenderness, she had to look away. His eyes spoke of sadness at her situation, but also of regret and even shame. It startled her.

The interruptions continued. At one point, Leo made a show of groaning as he was approached by a big, ruddy-faced man in middle age. Leo offered up his palms in surrender.

'I'm sorry, Ted. I know, I know: I owe you a call.' He turned to Madison. 'Do you know each other? Madison, this is our sworn enemy, Republican legend and state chairman Ted Norman. Ted, this is the journalist Madison Webb.'

At that, Norman's smile dropped and he extended a firm hand. 'It's a pleasure to meet you, Miss Webb. On behalf of the volunteer members of the Republican party of California, I offer you condolences on your loss. I know what it is to lose someone too young,' he said, shaking his head at the tragedy of it all. The synapses were working slowly, but eventually Maddy made the connection: she had come across this man's name in her first sweep of overdose stories online. He'd lost his daughter. Maddy took his hand and held it a second longer than she needed to, the two of them sharing the kinship of the bereaved.

'I also want to offer my congratulations on the journalism you're doing,' Norman went on. Maddy nodded her gratitude, wondering if the redness around the rims of this man's eyes had appeared just now or was a permanent function of his complexion. Or had it only been there since his daughter died, a tattoo of grief that would soon be etched on Maddy's own face? 'That story you did took guts. Too bad the *LA Times* doesn't have the guts to stand by you. There was a time when an American newspaper would have been proud—'

'Don't get started, Ted,' Leo said. 'You need to save some energy for tonight.' Moving to wind up, Leo added, 'And I haven't forgotten your call. I'll get back to you.'

'I can explain it right now, it's real simple.' Norman turned towards Madison. 'Are we off the record?' She nodded her acceptance and he continued. 'I wanted to offer the mayor my help.'

Leo smiled. 'You want to help the mayor? Now what kind of "help" would that be, Ted?'

'You're too cynical, you know that? That's the trouble with all you Democrats. You think we're all like you, calculating and scheming. I'm serious. You know I have a software business, tracking technology and all that. I'm offering to put that at the disposal of the LAPD – free of charge – to find this killer.'

Leo moved his eyebrows into a gently quizzical expression. It said, *What's the catch?* Or even, *What's in it for you?*

Norman understood the unspoken question. 'I'm not looking for anything, no publicity, nothing. Not even from this young lady.' He gave his head an avuncular tilt towards Madison. 'That's why I approached you, Leo. I'm happy doing this privately. Whatever helps the investigation.'

'Have you discussed this with Doran?'

'No. Like I said, this is not some political ploy. I don't want you to look bad by saying no. I want you to say yes.'

Madison watched Leo scanning the older man's face, still looking for the trick he was missing. Eventually he said, 'OK, Ted. Thank you. I'll put you in touch with the relevant folks.'

While the pair exchanged a last few nuggets of smalltalk, Madison let her hands distract her. She probed the edition of

The Economist Leo had given her, establishing that wedged inside was a manila wallet. She stepped away from the coffee line, her back to the people in it and pulled out the contents of the file. She then lodged the papers back inside *The Economist*, so that she could read them and look as if she were simply flicking through a magazine.

When Leo joined her, two Americanos in his hand, she said, 'Where did this come from?'

He smiled, looked around and said, 'You remember the rules, Webb. You don't get to ask that. The only thing you need to know is, is it genuine?'

'And is it?'

He took a sip of coffee. 'It is. That's official LAPD documentation.'

'And whoever gave it to you—'

'Maddy.'

She dropped it, letting the obvious fact remain unspoken: that the Chief of Police was the direct and personal appointee of the mayor.

She assessed the wad of papers, felt its weight. It was thinner than she had expected. That meant that either Mario Padilla's instinct had been right and the LAPD had not pursued his sister's case very hard – plausible given Rosario's low ranking on the Los Angeles social hierarchy – or that what Leo had handed her just now amounted only to a selection of papers from the original dossier. The mere possibility of which was sufficient to make her pre-emptively angry, an emotion that always served as a set of jump leads when she was exhausted, sending ten thousand volts of electricity direct into her nervous system.

She scanned the first page, a bald statement of the known facts of the case: date and time of death, coroner's remarks, name of next of kin.

'Leo, there's nothing classified about this. This is all in the public—'

240

'Patience, Madison, patience. Keep reading.'

She turned to the next few pages. An exchange with the district attorney's office about whether there were 'circumstances likely to lead to criminal prosecution'. More internal LAPD correspondence culminating in a request from the spokesperson's office that they be allowed to brief the media that 'police are not looking for anyone else in connection with the death of Rosario Padilla'. The next page showed the homicide department signing off the request. Maddy opened out her hands in protest at Leo, only to be greeted by the same smile, delivered without eye contact while he continued to survey the political chatterers around them. 'Keep reading, Maddy.'

She turned the page to see a document that surprised her. It was a witness statement form, similar to ones she had seen in dozens of cases. But there were two details so odd, she read them twice to be sure that, in her sleep-deprived state, she wasn't seeing things. (It would not have been the first time.) The name at the top of the statement was Rosario Padilla. Except her name was entered not in the field reserved for the subject of the case, but in the line marked 'Witness'. And the date was not from this or last month, but nearly a year ago.

Maddy glanced up at Leo, who gave a smug lift of the eyebrows. *I told you it was good.*

She quickly ran her eye over the text, taking in the gist of it. Certain sentences stopped her:

At the beginning of this month, the messages became more frequent. On March 11 he sent me 118 texts, most of them of a sexual nature. He says what he wants to do to me, what he wants me to do to him. I called the phone company and they say they are taking action but nothing happened . . .

In the last week, I have begun to get really frightened.

*The texts and weibs are beginning to get violent. One
message said he was watching me all the time. He knows
when I go to work and when I come home. He watches
me and does things to himself. He says one day he will
have me for real, he won't have to imagine what it's like.
I have tried everything, but the phone company now says
the phone number that sent these messages 'does not
exist' . . .*

Maddy turned the page, seeing what she guessed was a printout
of the offending messages Rosario had received and submitted
to the police. Judging by the timespan, just a few hours, this
was a mere sample, even though it filled three pages.

*You visit the dry cleaners just now. I saw you drop off your
stuff. Why you need to get your skirt cleaned, Rosie? Had
it got stained from your wet pussy? I like imagining that.
I'm going to go jerk off now. I know that makes you wet
. . . Why do you not look my way today, Rosie? You know
I was watching you, so why not a little wave? Or maybe
a kiss from those lips, made to give me blowjob? . . . Just
one little reply . . . I don't care if you don't want it, we're
going to do it anyway. I'm stronger than you, Rosie . . . If
you don't like it, that's just going to make me harder. I like
it dry. And remember, no one will be able to hear you
scream when you have my dick in your mouth . . .*

Maddy thought instantly of Abigail. Had she been on the
receiving end of anonymous hate like this? Had she been
terrified in the weeks leading up to her death, fearing it was
coming? Lowlifes like this guy must have been a dime-a-dozen
at the Opium Den or hanging around outside. Had Abigail
been quaking with fear but too scared to talk about it, even
with her sisters? Or perhaps Quincy knew. Perhaps she had
known all along.

Maddy needed to stay focused. What was certain was that Rosario Padilla had been getting messages like this, at this intensity and volume, for, what, weeks? Months? How long did this go on for? Had she told her brother? He hadn't mentioned anything, even though it was surely highly relevant. Had the police mentioned it to him after Rosie's death? Surely they would. Almost the first thing you'd look for in the homicide of a young woman: after the boyfriend or husband, you'd search for any sign of a past lover, would-be lover or stalker. That was obvious. There was no reason they would keep that from the brother. Perhaps he was ashamed. Maddy pictured the crucifix on one wall of the Padilla home, a Madonna and Child on another. Maybe he didn't want to tell a stranger, Maddy, of such things. Maybe he had not told the rest of the family, keeping Rosie's ordeal from their mother and father. In life, Rosie had probably done the same.

Maddy looked up. Leo was paying her no attention.

No wonder these papers were classified. Jesus, the way these institutions behaved. Somebody stood to be badly embarrassed by the discovery that a murder victim had already complained to the police and no one had acted. Padilla had told them she was targeted by a violent man and she had been right. Yet, by the looks of things, the police did nothing (and then had the nerve to imply Rosie had taken her own life). Whoever within the police department had made that decision had blood on his hands – or that's how it would look on Weibo or the front of the *LA Times* or, most likely, both.

Maddy turned the page to see a written request from Rosario Padilla, seeking a restraining order. Except the name of the subject of the order was blank. On this evidence, it seemed she had not known the name of her tormentor.

As Leo sipped his coffee, Maddy flicked through to the next item. To her great surprise, it was a photograph. A straight-on, unsmiling portrait of a white man, aged thirty or so. The background was a dull grey. Was this a police mugshot, perhaps of a suspect?

No. She looked closer at the border of the picture to see the image had been cropped from a driver's licence, then blown up. Why would someone take the time to do that? Why not simply print out an image of the licence itself? And if they had the photograph, that meant they had identified a suspect. So why was there no mention of his name? Had they known but withheld that crucial information from the victim, Rosie?

She stared longer at the face, the hair short, the lips thin, the neck suggesting a man fit and strong. Could it be? The answer was yes, it could. Hard to be certain, given that this photograph had been taken front-on, while the CCTV in the Great Hall only ever caught him from the back or the side. But yes, this could be the same man – the last person ever seen with Abigail.

Chapter 30

She thanked Leo as warmly as she could manage. He lingered on their hug. Maddy could sense him breathing in the scent of her, his chin caressed by her hair. It felt good to be held by him too, to feel the muscle of his arms, to have the smell of him wreathed around her. When she pulled away, his face hovered close by. She could see he wanted to kiss her and part of her wanted it too. It had been nine months but the memory of their skin touching, of how they had devoured each other, had not faded. She remembered his tongue and his taste.

But she was serving Abigail now, no longer her own master. Thanks to Leo, she now had a serious lead, one the police had clearly put to one side. Her duty, the only thing that mattered, was to follow it.

From the inside of her car, she pulled out the phone with which she had photographed the key pages from the file. It had taken her no time at all to do it, while Leo had busied himself with sugar, stirrers and lids for the coffee. He would understand. In fact, he'd expect nothing less.

She drove ten minutes to a strip mall off Veteran where she found a bodega and for thirty dollars each bought three 'burners': cellphones with a pay-as-you-go SIM already installed. She paid in cash.

That move wasn't a precaution against being tracked. Katharine had worked her magic to disable that function in Madison's phone long ago: unlike most of these devices, it would not reveal her location. But that still left the risk of surveillance. The only way to guard against the eavesdroppers was to use a different phone altogether, one unknown to those keen to listen in.

Ten minutes later, she turned onto a side street, her eye briefly caught by a car she thought she saw make the same turn a hundred yards behind her. One minute it was there, its headlights on – not so unusual in this smog – the next, the lights cut out. She squinted into the rear-view mirror. Was it still moving, slower now and with its lights off? Or had it come to a stop, killing its lights as it did so? Or perhaps the car she was now staring at had been there all along, parked and stationary for hours. Which car had she seen? She was now confused. Had she watched a car turn that corner at all or was her mind seeing things that were not there? That was possible. Sleeplessness could generate its own dreams, even in the daytime.

Madison switched on one of the burners, its battery pre-charged as promised. Next to her, scribbled on a reporter's notebook, was a note of the number she needed. Normally stored in her phone, it was almost the first time she had seen it.

She keyed in the digits and drafted the text message.

Only do this if it's easy. But if you can tell me who this guy is, I'd be very grateful. M.

Katharine would know it was her and would know from the new phone number that something was up. She would understand the caution, given the story Maddy had published that morning. The only question was whether she would be forgiving enough to help.

The radio was on, playing that infernal ear-worm of a song, 'Shanghai Style'. The video had gone viral, every kid in America learning that funny little movement of the knees and

246

ass. The singer, a schoolteacher from Shanxi in her fifties, was the unlikeliest pop star; Maddy turned it off. She needed to think.

Now she selected the driver's licence image, attaching it to the text message. She checked the number one last time, to be sure it was K's. And then she pressed send.

Katharine Hu's response came an hour later, during which time Madison had driven around, bought a soda, checked her email, texts and Weibo, along with Abigail's Facebook page, and had between thirty seconds and ten minutes of sleep, a strange, convulsive spell of unconsciousness rather than a rest. Her legs had been twitching, a nerve behind her eye too. She had wondered before if this was how she would die, her nervous system reduced to a series of spasms and tremors until it eventually packed up. In all the hours she had spent online since this disease gripped her, those were two words she had never put together in a search: *insomnia death*. She didn't want to know.

The phone, on the new number, rang. *Unknown.*

Madison picked up. 'Yes?'

'OK. You need to say more than that so I know it's you.'

'Thank you for calling. When you didn't reply, I thought maybe you—'

'Don't thank me. I haven't done anything yet. You know I think this is crazy, right?'

'You're the one who always said, "Think like a paranoid."'

'Not the phone thing. That's sensible, given the shitstorm you've started today. *This.* This whole thing. For once your older sister is right. You should not be doing this. Enri—' She stopped herself, just in time. No names, no identifying details: those were the rules. That Katharine had forgotten them told Madison her friend was shaken by this situation. 'Certain people think what you're doing is a big mistake.'

'A mistake?'

247

'For you. For *you*. There's only so much a person can deal with. And you keep adding to it.'

'Did you look at what I sent you?'

'You're not listening to me, are you?'

'I am. But I have to do this. You know why.'

There was a pause, in which she could hear Katharine conceding.

'Look, I can't swear this is the guy. Online facial recognition software is good but not perfect. OK?'

Katharine spelled out the name, letter by letter. She gave a date of birth and a last known address, though that was three years old. She repeated that she could not be certain, though it looked a good match. She did not ask why Madison was interested in this man. Finally she said, 'And please. Look after yourself.' But the tone suggested she had little hope her plea would be heeded.

Tony Gilper, aged twenty-nine. Madison stared at the name in her notebook, trying to squeeze something from it. What was that, Irish? She looked back at the mugshot stored on her phone, staring back at her. So maybe she had been as wrong as Howard Burke said she was about the connection to the garrison. She thought back to her short, coded conversation with Jeff Howe. Hadn't he, through his silence, confirmed her story? She replayed their last, rushed exchange in her mind.

If my story's plain wrong, there's no connection between my sister and these other deaths, hang up right now. OK?

Only now did she realize her error. In the haste of that moment, she hadn't asked Howe to stand up the China element of her story and he hadn't. By saying nothing, he had simply confirmed that there was a connection between the deaths of Abigail, Rosie and Eveline. And Gilper could be that link.

She did an instant search. *Tony Gilper, chiropodist, San Luis Obispo.* A few clicks told her he had qualified in Pennsylvania long enough ago to be in his late fifties now.

Next came Tony Gilper of Eagle Rock. He was a father of three young daughters, which made her shudder. His age seemed to fit too. But his Weibo profile led to a personal site, complete with photos, which established that this Tony Gilper was an African-American.

She kept searching, hitting dead-end after dead-end. The only nugget she unearthed that looked to be of any value came from the Eastsider LA website, a paragraph recording that an Anthony Gilper of Huntington Park had been arrested and charged for a DUI nearly four years earlier. It gave his age as twenty-five. The story mentioned a street address that she knew, as soon as she saw it, was no longer valid. If you did this kind of work long enough you developed a gut instinct for such things.

Still, she made the journey, the 101 emptier thanks to the New Year. She fought the gentle pull to sleep, at its most seductive when sleep was impossible. She stared straight ahead, glancing in her rear-view mirror too rarely to see what was going on behind her. Even if she had, the smog would have made it hard to make anything out with certainty.

Once there, among the projects and abandoned stores, garbage piled high in the doorways, she walked quickly, anxious to get this over with. When you're going through the motions you want to keep each one as brief as possible.

Sure enough, when she got inside the building, climbing the stairs to the sixth floor, the nameplate for what had been listed in the DUI story as Gilper's apartment was covered by a sticker. The name on it, *Martin*, was crossed out. If Gilper had ever lived here, there had been several occupants since. Maddy looked at the plain, scratched door and the stained, threadbare doormat, searching for any identifying mark, but found none. She knocked once and, of course, there was no reply. She knocked again. Still nothing.

Now, from the foot of this concrete stairwell, there was a sound – not a series of footsteps so much as a single thump announcing a human presence, several storeys below. Instinctively, she called out: 'Hello?' But there was only silence.

She wanted to get out. She would check out this next apartment on the landing and be off. She rang the bell once, then tapped lightly on the door. Nothing. She was about to try one last time, when the door opened to reveal an elderly, slightly stooped Asian woman – Chinese, Vietnamese, Korean, Maddy was uncertain. Half the woman's face was covered by a face mask against the smog.

As she began to speak, explaining herself, it came again, that thump, like a single, heavy footstep from the stairwell. It was nearer this time. It stopped Maddy in mid-sentence, bringing a look of confusion on the face of the old lady. What had begun as a sensation in her gut was hardening into a certainty: she had been followed.

Maddy rattled out her question – *a man, Tony Gilper, maybe Anthony, white, twenties, next-door, do you remember?* – doubtless too fast for the woman to digest, presuming, that was, she spoke any English at all. Still stooped, she shook her head, blankly. 'So many,' she said eventually. 'So many.' Maddy took that to be a commentary on the transience of the population of this building, churning too much for anyone to keep up, but it hardly mattered. Her mind was now elsewhere.

Maddy thanked the woman and was about to head down the staircase when something caught her eye. There, at the other end of the corridor of the old lady's apartment, was the fire escape, invitingly accessible thanks to a back door, ajar even now on a mid-winter evening, despite the smog. Perhaps, in her confusion, the elderly resident thought it would somehow let in fresh air. Maddy glanced at the stairwell, source of those unexplained sounds, then back down the apartment corridor directly in front of her.

'Thank you so much,' Maddy said once more, hunching to look directly in the old lady's eyes, touching her arm as she did so in what she hoped was a gesture of softness signalling no danger. And then, a half-second later, she walked past her, as if it were perfectly natural, as if she were a girl visiting her grandmother and heading for the kitchen to fix herself some milk and cookies.

The Chinese woman was so stunned, it took her three or four seconds to call out – 'Hey, you!' – but by then it was too late. Maddy had already pulled the back door open and was on the narrow, metal staircase, swiftly descending, the soles of her shoes clicking against each rusting step.

Once at the bottom, six flights later, it took her a moment to get her bearings, to work out that she needed to do a half-circle around the block to get back to the street and her car. Now there, she slammed into first gear and took off as fast as she could, eyeing the other cars parked nearby, singling out a too-clean Lifan 620 as the likeliest suspect. This time she checked her rear-view mirror, but was too far away to be certain if the dark-jacketed figure she saw emerge from the apartment building was her pursuer or just someone who happened to live there. Just as she could not be sure the noises she had heard from the stairwell were not a faulty boiler, coughing its way through early February.

She headed a few miles west on the 10, pulled off at a random junction and dumped the car, hiding it down a residential road where, she hoped, it would not catch anyone's eye. She walked back to the main drag and, for the second time in as many days, did that most un-LA of things: she took a bus, getting off as it approached the Fashion District. Looking over each shoulder, she guessed – or hoped – she had given her follower the slip.

But she was no nearer finding Tony Gilper. She found a café, took a seat at the back and pulled out her laptop. She had tried this on her phone, but now she would be more methodical, looking for Gilper online. She went to Facebook, found several men of that name – and a woman called Toni – but none were him. She tried variations of the name, playing with Tony, Anthony, Antony and assorted combinations of numbers. AnthonyG plus the birth year, rendered in both two digits and four, TGilper expressed the same way, as well as TonyG, TG, AG and a dozen other variants. She added LA to some and CA to others. She searched for these imagined, virtual men on Weibo, on Renren, on Weico and other photo-sharing sites – anywhere she could think of. He was nowhere to be found, perhaps smart enough to understand that a man who sends violent sexual messages to women needs to remain out of sight.

Over a long hour and a half, the tables around her filling up and emptying and filling up again, Maddy monitoring the new arrivals, assessing them for danger, she sunk her drill into the ground only to hit hard, unyielding rock. Either nothing fitted or, if it did, a photograph established there was no match. She let her face fall into her hands.

From deep inside her bag, her phone rang. Quincy. Madison weighed the risk but she couldn't keep blocking her sister forever. She pressed the green button and closed her eyes.

'Christ, Maddy – like having one dead sister is not bad enough.'

'Hi Quincy.'

'Where *are* you? Where the hell have you been?'

'It's a long story, Quincy.'

'It always is, Maddy. It always is. Did it ever occur to you that you might be needed? That there might be things that have to be done? Things for Abby?'

'Yes, Quincy. As a matter of fact, that *had* occurred to me. Had it ever occurred to *you* that I might be doing things right now that are all about Abby?'

'I very much doubt that, Maddy. I really do. Whatever it is you're doing, I very much doubt it's really about Abby.'

'What the hell's that supposed to mean, Quincy?'

'And while we're at it, what's all this about a secret between you and Mom?'

Maddy could feel herself swallowing. 'What are you talking about?'

'I hear that at this moment of severe trauma for our mother, you rushed over there not to console her but to swear her to secrecy.'

Paola. Listening from the kitchen.

'Listen, Quincy. You don't want to be doing this and I don't want to be doing this. We've both got things to do. Why don't we both just do what we need to do?'

'Oh, here we go. You do this every time, Maddy, every—'

'I'm going to hang up now, Quincy.'

'Yeah, that's it. Just run away whenever it gets difficult. The moment things—'

'Goodbye, Quincy.'

She stared hard at the silenced phone, as if it too were about to rebuke her. Then she looked up, glad for the distraction of the café crowd, faces to look at who were not her or her sister. She needed to focus, to rejoin the train of thought that was advancing before the phone rang.

Come on, she told herself. *Think. Who was this guy? What do you know about him?* Only one thing. That he was a stalker, a sexual predator with an aggressive appetite and a taste for rape fantasies, if not worse. He'd have been a regular on porn sites, no doubt. But, hold on, that's not what turned him on. He got off on looking at, and terrorizing, real women, those he could see in person. And, of course, he would want women who would lack the obvious protection of a husband or boyfriend. How would he have found them? Perhaps he hung out at clubs like the Opium Den, but online that meant only one destination. How had she not thought of it before?

With new vigour, she hammered away at the sites she knew of, one of which Quincy had recommended, back when the animating purpose of her life had been to find Maddy a husband.

'I don't need some website to find a date, Quincy,' she had said, standing in her sister's cavernous, knocked-through kitchen. 'For Christ's sake.'

'I know you could *date* every night of the week, if you wanted to,' her sister had replied, making the word date sound strongly like 'fuck'. 'Perhaps you are, for all we know.' Always that 'we', implying, what, husband Mark and her? Or, Mom, Abigail and her, the three of them sitting together, denouncing Maddy as a slut?

'The point is, this is not about hooking up. This is about, you know, settling down.'

To humour her, Maddy had signed up for the thirty-day trial, created a profile (no photo), and a handle (middle name plus year of birth) and had even gone on two dates. One had become the source for a good story about corruption at UCLA; the other one, she had slept with for one night – the thrill enhanced by knowing that was precisely not what Quincy had intended.

She remembered her password, was pleased to see it still worked and astonished to see more than six hundred 'requests' left for her since she had last looked. But there was no sign of Gilper, under any of the permutations.

Truth was, he was never likely to be there. The same was true of Rosario Padilla. Dating sites were as stratified by class as everything else in LA. Quincy's recommendation had been one of those 'exclusive' forums, where not one degree but two was considered a must. But Maddy refused to be discouraged.

She worked through the more mainstream sites, first searching by name without success. That was hardly a surprise. If Gilper's intention was to find women to stalk, he was hardly going to advertise his identity. But the advantage of dating sites like these was that they demanded users posted a photo. That would have been hard to resist for Gilper: it meant he could check out his potential prey. And he couldn't easily post a fake picture of himself; these days, thanks to tagging, whoever's face he had stolen would have found out pretty quick.

So she scrolled through reams of male faces, three or four hundred she guessed even though she had filtered by age, before finally striking gold. TonyG and a recent year – perhaps the year he had joined the site – in two digits. There he was, the face unmistakable from his mugshot. The profile gave little away:

My name is Anthony, but everyone calls me Tony. I'm fit, athletic and an all-round good guy. If you love the Dodgers and want a guy who'll love you just as much, then you know who to call.

She had found him. A few more clicks told her that the account had been dormant for four weeks. He had stopped using it before the first killing. Maddy felt her palms grow clammy.

She texted Katharine and, within twenty minutes, her friend had cracked loveheartsusa.com wide open, extracting the address under which Gilper had registered. The tone of Katharine's reply – terse – left Maddy in no doubt that this was a kindness proffered to her late sister, not to her.

Maddy called for a cab to take her to East LA, arriving at the address twenty-five minutes later. She was, she noted, not far from Rosie Padilla's home in Boyle Heights, near enough for Gilper to have kept watch over her, at any rate. The building surprised her. Expecting a down-at-heel apartment block, she couldn't tell if it was instead an office or some kind of hotel. As she got closer, she understood. A sign announced 'The Bruce J Rhind Residential Facility for Military Veterans'. She knew of these places, sheltered accommodation they called them, often the sanctuary for those whose brains got mashed up in Iraq or Afghanistan or the second Korean war. That would explain the missing four or so years after the DUI conviction, during which Gilper had left next to no trace online. He'd been on a tour of duty. Maybe several. And come back to hunt young women.

Gingerly, she approached the reception desk, saying that she was there to visit Tony Gilper. (A mistake to ask for 'Anthony' if everyone called him 'Tony'; it would only arouse suspicion, marking you out as a stranger. The other way around carried less risk: if everyone there knew him as Anthony, no problem; she'd be implying that true intimates, from way back when, called him Tony. All this went through Maddy's mind in the half-second before she opened her mouth.)

'Tony? Oh, that's nice,' said the woman seated at the desk, an African-American, in her fifties and motherly. 'He doesn't get so many visitors. You family?'

'Friend of the family,' Maddy said.

'And what name shall I give, honey?'

'If you tell him Rosie's here to see him.'

It was a gamble, she knew that. Maybe even a reckless one. The name alone might prompt him to refuse to see her, though that would be an answer in itself. But then she had a better idea. 'Actually, I'd like to give him a surprise. It's been a while.'

'All right, then. Why don't you follow me.'

The woman levered herself from her chair, rested a home-made, cardboard 'Back in 5 minutes' sign on the counter, and set off down a corridor, through one set of double-doors, then another. There were paintings on the walls, the kind you'd get in a high-school art-room: amateurish still lives; prog-rock voluptuous fantasy women and winged horses; gloomy self-portraits. Infusing the air was the smell of institutional food.

Now the linoleum was replaced by carpet, signalling that they were away from the communal space and nearing the individual rooms and apartments. They stopped outside number thirty-one and the receptionist gave a light knock on the door.

'Who is it?'

Crouching slightly, as if communicating with a young child on the other side, she said, 'There's a visitor for you.'

'OK.'

The woman creaked the door open gently, yielding just a sliver of the room inside. In that wedge, though, Maddy saw enough to know that she had found him. Older, the skin greyer, the eyes smaller and harder, without the youthful arrogance she had seen earlier, there was nevertheless no doubting it: this was the face on the documents Leo had handed her, the face on the driver's licence, the face of the man identified by police as the stalker of Rosario Padilla. It was bathed in the sickly glow of the television directly opposite him.

Maddy felt a clutch inside her stomach, as if an unseen hand were squeezing her innards. This was the man who had tormented a woman and possibly killed her. And if he had done that, there was at least a chance he had done the same to Eveline Plaats and to Abigail. She was seized with a dizzying sensation: that she was about to come face to face with the man who had killed her sister.

Chapter 31

'We OK to come in?' the receptionist asked, seeking a second confirmation.

'Sure.'

The door opened wider to reveal a modest room, dominated by the big TV. A bed, two chairs, a small window and then another door leading to what Maddy guessed was a bathroom. At intervals, leaning against a cupboard and a back wall, were items of medical equipment. She only understood their purpose when she took a proper look at Tony Gilper.

He was in an armchair, remote control on his lap, wearing a loose Dodgers sweatshirt. It took Maddy a moment to absorb the information her eyes were giving her. The left sleeve was hanging loose and floppy. It was, she realized, empty. Only then did she register that there were no trousers to speak of because there were no legs.

She must have let out a gasp, or else her face betrayed her, because the receptionist laid a soft hand on her forearm. 'It's often a shock the first time, honey,' she whispered. 'You just take your time.'

The woman pulled out the second chair, patting it for Maddy to sit down and make herself at home. 'I'll leave you two young people to talk,' she said as she withdrew from the room and headed back to the reception desk. Maddy thanked her, noticing that, under the bed, were the disassembled component parts of a mobility scooter. Now she looked directly at Gilper, comforting herself that though this man had been capable of following a woman and torturing her from afar – and that having his body shattered in battle had perhaps filled him with enough rage and frustration to do it – he was surely not able to do much more.

Once the door was closed, Maddy introduced herself as Detective Madison Halliday of the LAPD, producing her badge for inspection. She was making inquiries into the death of Rosario Padilla and had seen a series of complaints relating to him.

He seemed terrified, as if he had dreaded this moment.

'I don't know what you're talking about,' he said.

'Yes you do.' She began reading. '"I don't care if you don't want it, we're going to do it anyway. I'm stronger than you, Rosie . . . If you don't like it, that's just going to make me harder. I like it dry." Ringing any bells? Or should I go on? How about this? "Why do you not look my way today, Rosie? You know I was watching you, so why not a little wave? Or maybe a kiss from those lips, made to give me blowjob?" You sent that to Rosario Padilla, who worked very near here, as it happens. Near enough for you to have seen her walk past your window."

'You've got no proof.'

'Oh yes I do. I have phone company records tracing these messages directly to you.' It was a bluff, but she held his gaze and he soon crumbled.

'Look, look, I told you guys already. I'm sorry, I'm really sorry.' He was shaking his head from side to side as he spoke. His left eye began to twitch. 'I never meant no harm by it. I mean, I didn't want to hurt her. I just, I just – sitting here, in this room, when you can't move and no girl will ever look at you again, it's hard. I'm sorry. I told you, I promise I won't

259

do it again. I won't.' She wondered if he was about to cry.

Torn between disgust and pity, Madison tried to repress both feelings. 'Rosie Padilla is dead, Mr Gilper.'

'I'm Corporal Gilper,' he said, his left eye now opening and closing as rapidly as a camera shutter. 'And I know she's dead. But I had nothing to do with it. I can barely wipe my ass, how the fuck could I kill anyone?'

She pressed him a little more, but her heart was not in it. Afterwards, she had a chat with the receptionist, asking her to check the diary to work out if other friends had been visiting Tony as often as they should be. Sure enough, the log confirmed Tony Gilper had been right here on the nights Rosario Padilla – and Eveline and Abigail – had been killed.

Maddy left the Bruce J Rhind Residential Facility for Military Veterans at first glum and then enraged. Glum at the horror that breeds horror, the war that had left Gilper so damaged and pained that he inflicted more pain on Rosie. And rage that she had wasted so much time, a full day chasing down a useless, blind alley. With that fury grew a suspicion. Whoever had set her haring off around this track, so soon after she had made trouble by raising the China connection, had known it would be futile. That's why they had done it. She had been set-up, deliberately distracted and taken out of the game. Someone had decided to do that. Leo or whoever had handed that file to him. But who was it?

Chapter 32

Bill Doran hit rewind for the ninth time.

They were beautiful young women, cut down when their lives should have been ahead of them.

That could work. Could even be the opening. He pressed play.

We want the truth! We want to get to the bottom of who did this to our families!

That would work too. He played the next bit, mentally doing the edit that would produce the workable bite.

Let's say the killer is someone in that base. You know what? We can't do anything about that! The people on that base, in the garrison, are not subject to American law. They're subject only to Chinese law. But it's not fair and it's not right. That's what's got to change!

Too long, but it was good. And the closer, this last bit: you wouldn't need to do much to it. The tiniest edit, here and there, nip and tuck. But it was all there, ready to go.

We want the truth about these women. They are our sisters and daughters and friends. They deserve justice. Because the law should apply to everyone. That's what we demand. Justice for Rosario and Eveline and Abigail!

He wasn't sure about the names. Maybe that diluted the

impact, plus Abigail at least was an ongoing case. They'd have to run it past legal. Wouldn't be a disaster to cut it. And you could still end on a high, with the crowd chanting. *USA! USA! USA!*

There were, Bill Doran concluded, endless riches to be mined from this seam. He had watched newcomers before. As a trained spotter of political horseflesh, he believed he had a pretty keen eye. He had picked out a candidate for city council in Lincoln, Nebraska, at the time not even elected to that lowly office, who before the decade was out was the state governor and talked about for the VP slot on the next Republican ticket. He could detect talent at a hundred paces and this guy, this Mario Padilla, had it by the sack full. Obviously untutored, a total novice, he was indisputably a natural.

It had been Doran's idea to ride the wave Padilla had unleashed. Besides the crowd that young man had pulled in with no notice, his campaign had gone wild on social media. It was exactly the kind of energy Republican candidates needed to tap but rarely did: young, grass-roots, real. He had suggested a rally – big, college basketball arena – where Padilla would be the guest speaker. Free media would be all over them: they couldn't get enough of this guy. Bill had even come up with a name for the event, which he pictured on a vast banner as the backdrop: *The Rape of California.*

He made a few quick edits on his computer, collected up his papers and headed into the conference room of the Sacramento headquarters of the Sigurdsson for Governor campaign and prepared to make his case.

'OK,' the candidate said. 'I get it. Downsides. Someone?'

There was the briefest of pauses, while Doran waited to see who would be first to throw a spear into the hide of the oldest rhino at the watering hole.

'I love the idea, Bill. I think it's bold. It's provocative.' It was Matt, young, keen and with a sharp nose for whatever doubts were brewing in Sigurdsson herself. Doran waited for the *but*.

'But my only worry is whether Padilla would do it. His strength is that he's nonpartisan. Why would he throw that away?'

'Because he's a kid. He's an amateur. He doesn't know about any of that stuff yet. He's a boy with a computer who's started an earthquake. He gets an invitation to speak to fifteen thousand people alongside the future governor of this state, he's going to say yes.'

'Maybe. But maybe *we* don't want to be associated with *him*. We don't know where his campaign's gonna go, do we? What if he starts diving into crazy? That then becomes us. "Ms Sigurdsson, you've appeared at a rally with this man who believes the United States should declare war on the People's Republic." There's a lot of risk.'

Doran could have come back with an answer, put that upstart in his place. But he had been watching the candidate, giving a slight nod of the head at intervals while Matt was speaking. At which point, the realization clicked into place. Of course. He should have seen it; he should have *anticipated* it. Sigurdsson was a decent speaker – a little one-note, rarely able to shift out of courtroom battler mode – but decent. But she was no match for Padilla. She lacked his emotional power, his passion, his electrifying sense of a man wronged. No wonder she didn't want to share a stage with him: she feared she would begin the rally the star and end it overshadowed.

'OK, fair enough,' he said, staging a tactical withdrawal. 'There are other ways to seize the same bit of ground. We could play in some VT from the first rally. In fact, that would allow us to do something else.'

'Yes?' The candidate sat up. All politicians were like that, suckers for novelty.

'What about an all-female line-up? Every speaker a woman. "We are the daughters, sisters and mothers."'

'Oh, I like that.'

Doran smiled. He knew what these kids had not yet learned. Come to a meeting with a good idea and, in your back pocket, an even better one.

'You'll top the bill, big rousing speech, pull it all together.'

'And what about the message?' It was Matt again, having a second stab at the rhino.

'What about it?' said Bill, relaxed now.

'I agree we want to ride the wave. Totally agree. Love that. We all do. "We demand the garrison open up." Perfect. No one's against that. Openness. Let the sun shine. Great.'

'But?' Bill, still in control.

'No buts. We demand the PLA co-operate with the police investigation. Again, who's going to argue with that? We close with slamming Berger for letting this happen on his watch. "Weak, weak, weak."'

Bill smiled. 'Weak, weak, weak' was the phrase that had made his name, deployed to devastating effect in a presidential four cycles ago. He had toyed with the notion of unleashing it in this campaign in the spring. Now, if he proposed that, he would look as if he was plagiarizing this kid. He was determined to show no irritation, just seasoned calm. 'I still sense a "but" in there somewhere, Matt.'

'OK. Maybe just a teeny one. The message is great, *but*,' he over-emphasized the word, bringing smiles from the sycophants around the room, 'we don't want to go much further than that. That's all I'm saying. Up to that line, but not beyond it.'

'For example?'

'Padilla has hinted at tearing up the Treaty, kicking out the Chinese. The Ted Norman folks would love us to climb onto that one, but we can't go there. Not a candidate for the highest office in the state.'

'I hear you.'

'I know you do, Bill. We're all on the same page here. We

want to ride this tiger, no doubt about it. We just gotta make sure we've got a good, tight hold of the reins. Because if we lose control, this thing could destroy everything in its path.'

Maddy knew she was doing it too often, that it was looking like a tic. But she couldn't help herself. Every ten or fifteen seconds, she felt the same urge to look over her shoulder. To see who was there, to see what had changed, to see whoever might be seeing her.

A break came on the first of the three buses she had taken. The back seat was available, enabling her to keep her head relatively still as she surveyed all those in front of her, assessing every passenger, weighing up whether they were a regular commuter or a fake – an agent of Terminal Island, carefully concealing his or her true mission, which was to watch her.

Even on the back seat, she couldn't rest, though. She found her eyes darting sideways, watching the young black man dozing in the far corner, listening to his breathing to determine whether his sleep was genuine or phoney.

On the second and third buses, it was worse. She had to maintain a three-hundred-and-sixty-degree view, scoping the entire vehicle, front and back. She knew she was arousing the suspicion of those sitting alongside her, that the repeated turns of the head looked manic. But she could not rest.

Not that she knew what she was looking for. She watched two men – one in his twenties, another, bearded, perhaps fifteen years older – whose studiedly distracted manner unnerved her. But then the younger one got off the bus before she did. Another took a call and proceeded to defend himself in loud, animated Spanish from an accusation that he had failed to pick up his youngest son from football practice: 'Honey, we never made that plan!' Maddy realized that any man she suspected was almost certainly above suspicion. It was probably the mumbling senior at the back of the bus or the mom with kids she needed to fear.

She broke her journey with two taxi rides. The first driver paid her no attention, but the second kept taking fleeting glances at her in his rear-view mirror. What was he looking at? Had he recognized her? She got him to drop her off two blocks early downtown, so he would not be able to tell his handlers her precise destination.

From there, she walked to the car rental place, paying in cash. The tactic struck her as useless even as she did it, for there was no ducking the requirement to show her driver's licence. If her pursuer had tracked her to Tony Gilper's place, then a car rented in her own name was not going to present too stiff a challenge. As she drove, this time using the paper smog mask provided with the rental car, she resumed her regular over-the-shoulder checks. The result was a near-collision with the Changan-Benni that came to a sudden halt in front of her when she was looking the other way. Which made her wonder if her pursuer was, artfully, in front of rather than behind her.

Exhausted by her own paranoia, she eventually arrived at Leo Harris's building in the Miracle Mile district a full two hours later than she might have done. She told herself that she had come here chiefly because it made no sense to have this conversation on the phone. She was less willing to admit that, after the chase through the stairwell in Huntington Park – and the encounter with the triple-amputee veteran of the 82nd Airborne and rape fantasist whose window Rosario Padilla used to pass on her way to and from work and on her lunch hour – Maddy also felt wary of returning to her own, empty apartment.

She pressed on the buzzer, the sound prompting an instant image of her ex-boyfriend hurriedly stuffing a woman's discarded underwear into a drawer as he picked up the entryphone. More paranoia, she thought, pushing the image out of her mind.

'Leo. It's me.'

266

'Maddy, what's—'

'Just let me in.'

She came up the stairs to see Leo standing by his front door, his arms open for an embrace, which Maddy shrugged off as she pushed her way in. Wasting no time, she said 'I've just spent the entire evening chasing – and being chased – down a blind alley, thanks to you.'

'Hold on, hold on,' Leo said, following her inside. 'What happened?'

'Oh, I think you know very well what happened. Exactly what you wanted to happen, that's what happened.'

'Back up, Maddy. I don't know what you're talking about. What happened?'

'That file you gave me led – surprise, surprise – nowhere. Or, to be more accurate, it led to a man with no legs and one arm. A man who, it's clear for all to see, had nothing to do with these murders.'

'Oh.' Leo looked crestfallen.

'All of which was obviously checked out by the, you know, *authorities* who would have cast this lead aside as utterly, fucking useless. That wasn't help you gave me, Leo. That was a big, exhausting, *deliberate* detour.'

Exhausting was the truth. You could stay afloat on adrenalin when there was a prospect of a breakthrough. But failure always had the same effect. Fatigue would flood the system, sudden, surging waves of it, the thicker and stronger for having been dammed up by hope.

She was unloading on Leo but she blamed herself more. Stupid, naïve, to believe it would ever be that easy. She had failed to ask the question every journalist was meant to ask of everything: *cui bono*, who benefits? A classified file does not just land in your lap unless someone wants it there. In her excitement, she had hardly thought about that, accepting that Leo had acted out of nostalgic kindness. He had done her a favour. Even he, she had thought, was not beyond that.

Had she got him so badly wrong? Was he as morally empty as he liked to pretend, ready to exploit her grief and send her into an exitless maze just to buy himself a few hours? Was his devotion to his boss and his political career so fierce that he would do that to a woman he had once . . . what? They had never said they loved each other.

Perhaps the hard-bitten cynic shtick was not a front. Maybe Leo really was ready to do whatever it took.

He was shaking his head, his eyes down, his fingers running through his hair. 'I had no idea, Maddy. Really. I thought what was in that, you know . . . I thought it was a lead.'

'Well, it wasn't, OK? How'd it work, Leo? The boss tell you to shut that crazy bitch down? Is that how this worked?' She had imagined that conversation in her head on her way over here, Dick Berger agitated by the Weibosphere buzz accusing him of allowing a Chinese serial killer to terrorize the streets of LA, ordering his lieutenant to change the subject. What better way than to get the author of the original story to chase another hare?

'You're right,' he began. 'The boss does want you shut down. There's only bad news in this story for him. But that's not what was going on here, with that . . . information.'

'So what exactly is going on here, Leo? What? Can you tell me? Can you?' He began to open his mouth but words were still falling out of hers. 'I mean, can anyone tell me what the fuck is going on here? I'm running around this city and no one is helping me. My older sister hates me, my mother doesn't know what day of the week it is and my baby sister – my baby sister—'

'Oh, Maddy,' Leo said, stepping forward to hold her. She moved to push him out of the way, but this time he would not be shaken off so easily. He reached for her wrists: he would force her to accept a hug from him, if that's what it took. Her resistance continued, Madison writhing in his arms, her fists beating on his chest.

'Get off me,' she was saying. But he was enveloping her, the way he always used to. Her head was against his chest, his arms were around his shoulders. She looked up, so that their eyes met. 'I mean it,' she said.

'I know you do,' he said. And the gaze held for a second longer than it should, a second past the point where one or both had always looked away. And a second later their lips were touching.

Leo kissed her gently but the first taste of his lips on hers flooded her with desire, a craving for his mouth, his tongue, for as much of him as she could consume. She tugged the shirt from his chest, breathing deeply, taking in the scent of him. She knew her voraciousness was a surprise to him; it was to her, too. But now that it had been unleashed, it could not be stopped.

Still kissing him, she wrenched off her shirt and, before he could remove her bra, fell to her knees, unbuckling his belt, pulling down his shorts, taking his cock in her mouth, sucking on it as if it would nourish her. She heard him gasp. Pushing him back onto the couch, she climbed on top of him, felt the familiar surge of him inside her. Her desire thundered in her ears.

An hour later and she was looking at Leo's face. He was asleep in the bed they had reached eventually. With his eyes closed, he looked as she had remembered him after sex: younger and, however improbably, more innocent. She closed her eyes and saw him again, a few hours ago when he had watched her read through the contents of that file in the UCLA lobby.

She was trying to analyse the expression he wore, the image of it frozen under her eyelids, ready for study. Leo had been pleased, no doubt about it. But his was not a smile of cunning

269

satisfaction that she had taken the bait. There was something different in his eyes, she had seen it. They were warmed by the idea that he was helping, that he was doing good. There had been no gags, no bluster. In his own way, he had been sombre – sombre, she reflected now, at the loss of Abigail.

She could not prove it. She would simply have to trust her intuition, even in its current, unreliable state. And her intuition said Leo had given her those documents in good faith. Her mistake had been not to press further at the moment of handover. She had asked how he had got the file, but she had got no answer and had not demanded one. She castigated herself for not learning this lesson long ago: it was not enough to understand your source. You needed to understand your source's source. On this one, she was in the dark.

The inescapable fact hovering over the bed they had just shared was that Leo Harris served at the pleasure of the mayor; it was Berger whose bidding he was commanded to do. Is that how this happened, Maddy wondered. Had the mayor presented Leo with the documents, along with instructions to get them to Maddy? Leo would not have agreed to that if he had thought it a trick, a deliberate exercise in wasting Maddy's time. If her gut was right about Leo, he must have been assured he was handing over something useful. Which meant either his boss had lied to Leo or the mayor had himself been lied to.

The former was certainly possible: that politicians lie was hardly news. But a candidate lying to his closest advisor? Rare and beyond reckless. It strained credulity to believe Berger's career had come as far as it had – and he had just won a competitive primary race to become the Democratic standard-bearer in California – if he was capable of that. And Leo had always been a sharp judge of character: he wouldn't work for Berger unless he trusted him.

But if it hadn't been Berger lying to Leo, it must have been someone else who had set her chasing after Gilper. She opened her eyes. She didn't like being played. Not ever and definitely not at a time like this.

Gingerly, she levered herself away from Leo, replacing the arm that had stretched across her. She collected up her underwear and shoes, finding stray items all the way from the bedroom to the living room to the hallway, and let herself out. She was aware that she was not the first woman to perform this ritual – probably not the first one to do it this week. She did not say goodbye and she did not leave a note.

Once back in her apartment, she resisted the urge to fall into the sofa and sat at her desk instead. The long, circuitous journey she had taken home had given her time to think. Leo, she had decided to accept, for now at least, had been telling the truth. As for the mayor, she could be much less certain. He was probably a lying snake. For all that, she could not realistically envisage either scenario – the mayor lying to Leo or the two of them explicitly conniving in a diversionary tactic. For now, she believed Leo would have refused. Surely it was most likely, despite Berger's determination to shut her down, that the mayor had no direct part in it.

Which pointed the finger elsewhere.

She fired up the computer and keyed in the name of the Chief of Police, Douglas Jarrett, personal appointee of Mayor Richard Berger four years ago. She called up the long profiles first, scanning the details of his past service in Chicago and, earlier, in Hawaii. Most of the pieces were glowing, including a recent extended magazine profile that said Jarrett had won admirers in Washington for policing Los Angeles 'tactfully'. She read on:

Where others have stirred the complex racial and ethnic brew of the west coast's biggest city, Jarrett is credited for letting things go from a boil to a simmer. Policing LA was always a complex business, even before the Treaty. But now it involves managing relations with an area over which the Chief is not chief. The Port of Los Angeles and Terminal Island, with its Chinese customs officers now protected by their own garrison of People's Liberation Army personnel, is off-limits to Jarrett. Yet his fellow officers as well as city and state politicians note how he has, as one puts it, 'elegantly finessed' that fact. He keeps a close eye on his Chinese counterparts, 'making sure their authority is not too "in your face"', says one City Hall source, who spoke on condition of anonymity. 'If the PLA wants to act, Doug always makes sure there are LAPD guys present and visible, so it looks like a joint effort, even if it isn't. He understands the optics.'

More praise for his blameless private life: an attractive wife, Rachel, seen at the opening of the Sinopec Museum of the Arts in Brentwood, two adult daughters. A cop his entire life, from his very first job, walking the beat in Cedar Rapids, Iowa.

She looked at the pictures accompanying the articles. He was in his mid-fifties with salt-and-pepper hair and a decent build. Looked like he played squash. Solidly Midwestern, reliable and dull.

Here was one from the summer before last, when the heat was insufferable. He was out in Koreatown, praising shop-keepers who had doused a situation before it could turn into a riot. He was in chinos and a polo shirt. As fatigue enveloped her, muffling and smothering her brain, she stared and stared at the photograph. It might have been a minute, might have been an hour. She found she was not looking at Jarrett's face but his wrist.

On it was a solid Patek Philippe watch. She enlarged the

image and took a closer look. It was substantial and jewelled, the kind you'd see advertised in the international magazines left behind in business class on the LA to Beijing flight. She could see the weight of it, even from here.

Idly she Googled it until she had found a price. The first figure she saw she deemed so absurd, she presumed she had identified the wrong watch. But site after site suggested otherwise. To her amazement, the item was sold for between eighty-five and one hundred thousand dollars.

Now she widened the search, looking for any other images she could find of Jarrett. In each case, she looked only at his wrist. But it didn't yield much; in too many cases he was wearing a jacket or shirt cuffs that obscured the view. But her blood was up now.

She reached for her tablet, equipped thanks to Katharine with a VPN gizmo that kept her IP-address secret by substituting it with another one. This was the machine she used for probing the othernet, when the pickings offered up by the regular internet were too slim. K had never admitted it outright, but Maddy had long suspected her friend had been part of the original othernet community, even perhaps that she was still active now. Those pioneers had started beavering away below radar when Beijing, backed by Moscow, started getting its way on tightening the global rules governing the internet. With the US no longer strong enough to resist, the Chinese authorities set about pruning the internet of anything it deemed damaging to state security, 'national honour' and – the justification used most often and broadly – the safety of children. They started with the wilder fringes, but bit by bit the censors' shears turned into chainsaws, hacking down the woods and forests of the internet, slashing away at anything they deemed too unkempt. Katharine-types had cached much of what was lost and migrated it over to a realm they constructed themselves: the othernet. Before long, dissenters posted there first, many of them abandoning the original internet altogether. The othernet came under attack day and night, Katharine's comrades playing a constant game of cat and mouse, jumping from hidden deep-sea server to remote Icelandic relay station and back again, as they sought to avoid the blade coming down on them. Maddy's relationship with it was less noble. She was a user. Or a 'parasite', in K's language: taking out but never putting in.

She typed in Jarrett's name and hit 'Search'. Now the screen filled with more images. She could see a couple of exposed wrists immediately and, on one, another heavy watch. She zoomed in and saw that it was as heavy as the other one, but in a different shade: a brown strap this time and a silver face, TAG Heuer the brand. This one too was comfortably in the high five figures.

Now Maddy went over to Weibo, the mirrored version that existed below ground. There she put out a simple message, issuing a call for help the way she had on several stories in the past. She attached the Patek Philippe picture.

Chief Jarrett seems to have an expensive taste in watches. Any other examples besides this one?

She sat back and waited, hoping the late hour would bring at least a slight delay in the bolt of fury that would, inevitably, be hurled her way by Leo and, no less certainly, Howard Burke. What she needed was for the little cogs of the human flesh search engine to turn. It was crowdsourcing at its very best, thousands of unseen individuals digging at their own little patch of virtual dirt, turning up whatever they could on an individual – scouring every link, reference, article and, above all, photograph, that had appeared on every conceivable forum or platform. A human flesh search would scour magazine pieces but also Renren and Weibo entries, including those a dozen degrees of separation away from the subject. If Jarrett had been at a hotel bar in Redondo Beach at the same time as a wedding reception six years ago, snapped in the far background of the family group shot, the search would find it. When the ants of the online colony started crawling over you, examining every pore of your skin, they missed nothing.

Maddy went to her bathroom cabinet to look for amphetamines: she would need to stay alert for this next hour. She found three and knocked back all of them. She caught her reflection in the mirror: her neck was still flushed red, the way it always was after strenuous sex. She went back to the machine, hit 'Refresh' and realized she was still wearing her coat.

She clicked on the weib she had posted to see that it had already been re-weibed, passed on, seventy-eight times, in just the last few minutes. Of the many imports from China, the human flesh search was, she reflected, her favourite. The spontaneous collaboration was a joy to behold, the enthusiasm and eagerness of the searchers always surprising. In China the habit took hold because it was one of the only effective ways the public could spot wrongdoing in their bureaucratic overlords. Americans had taken to it more slowly; maybe they preferred working solo. But now they were hooked – and quite good at it. One hundred and thirty-three re-weibs and counting.

The results were trickling in too. Here was Jarrett at a crime scene in Watts, in what looked like the early morning. His mien was grave, suggesting a homicide. On his wrist was a watch, solid and hefty. But the angle was side on; there was no way of telling what he was wearing.

Another link arrived, this one accompanied by a message.
What you working on now, Madison? Will this be in the LA Times – or will it be taken down? ;) Anyway, hope this helps.

She clicked on the link, which turned out to be a webpage containing several images in a sequence. The Chief was reviewing a passing out parade, smiling at new recruits. The third picture had him offering a playful salute. This time the watch on his wrist was crystal clear, a Rolex, the gold of its face catching a gleam of sunlight.

Maddy sat back in her chair. If anything, this third apparent example made her confidence wobble. What man owned three watches, let alone three expensive ones? Maybe they weren't precious at all, just street-corner knock-offs, churned out by those underground factories in Alabama or Kentucky in the few days they got to operate between police raids. Maybe Jarrett was vain, choosing a different fake for each occasion. Lame, but no crime.

She replied to the two users who had posted pictures.

Are we sure these watches are genuine?

Answers came rapidly, not confined to those to whom she'd directed the question. Others came on, people who even at this hour – and it was the middle of the night on the east coast – had enlarged the images and submitted them to detailed, if not forensic, examination.

Note the grooved winder, said one of the Patek Philippe. *Very hard to replicate that semi-herring-bone pattern. See photo of fake here and note difference.*

Madison did as she was told and could not argue; the attached photo of two watches, one fake, one original, side by side appeared to settle the matter. What Jarrett had been wearing on his wrist was the real deal.

Now more replies were coming in, most offering the same evidence: the same photos of the same events. Finally, there came a fresh sighting of one more watch, a vintage piece this time – 1930s, if she had to guess – and therefore hard to value instantly. It was Swiss with a face cast in two tones of grey. The picture was the clearest yet, the watch front and centre in a shot of Jarrett at a grip-and-grin, shaking hands with some city bigwig at an event to mark the anniversary of his appointment as Chief. The cop was mugging at the camera, his jaw set firm. To Maddy's amusement, the picture came from *LA Policing Today*, the cops' own house magazine.

She was no expert, but this one looked really precious. Five minutes later someone who had been following her Weibo timeline popped up to let her know that a similar watch had come up for auction in London recently and been sold for one hundred and sixty thousand dollars.

Still, though, she was unsure. It seemed such an unnecessarily risky thing to do; almost daring someone to notice. It was true that plenty of these alpha types in top jobs craved danger and created it for themselves if there was too little of it. One of her earliest reporting assignments had been the discovery that the City Comptroller of Oakland had been using prostitutes, cruising in his car on the corner of 50th Avenue and East 14th Street to find them. Of course he could have arranged discreet, if expensive, liaisons but that, Maddy came to realize, was to miss the point: he wanted the thrill of risk. Maybe Chief Jarrett was the same.

There could be alternative explanations. She scanned the profiles again, to see if she had missed an alternative source of wealth. But no: his parents were modest hog farmers, no money there. His wife had been his college sweetheart from Des Moines; she was a school librarian. And he'd only ever worked as a cop. There had been no lucrative, five-year spell as a 'private security consultant', raking in the corporate cash. The only salary he had ever earned had been from the public purse: decent money, for sure, but not Patek Philippe, TAG Heuer and Rolex money.

Madison stood up, went to the fridge, found some Greek yoghurt, spooned it from the tub and then poured herself a Scotch. Her body, the series of tastes in her mouth, reminded her where she had been an hour or two ago: for a second, her skin tingled at the memory of it. In reply, her brain told her it had almost certainly been a mistake. She and Leo were chemical elements that, no matter how drawn together, could not mix. She could picture Quincy delivering her verdict, shaking her head in condemnation of what her reckless sister had done – and at a time like this too.

Back at the machine, there was a Weibo alert in the corner of the screen.

Nothing on watches, I'm afraid. But nice vacation . . .

Attached was a picture that looked pleasingly amateur, a vacation snap. In the background, a vast swimming pool with artificial waterfall, waiters in white and palm trees. In the foreground: Doug Jarrett in shorts and lobster-red chest, his arm around his wife on one side and another woman on the other, with a second man at the end. Two middle-aged couples on vacation.

She replied to the sender, who appeared to be an accountant in St Louis.

Where?

His reply took less than thirty seconds.

Glasses.

She went back to the photograph, now zooming in on the low, poolside drinks table that she had barely noticed. There were three glasses, each resting on a coaster, and a fourth that had been drained. A gold pattern was visible: a logo, circled by three words. *Dominion Hotel, Macau.*

The briefest of searches confirmed that this was the plushest resort in the former colony, now administered by China, boasting six stars and prices to match. When, an hour later, another searcher produced the evidence that Jarrett was not only a visitor, but a paid-up member (albeit discreetly, in his wife's name) of LA's Tang Polo Club, a spin-off of its ultra-exclusive Beijing counterpart, the matter was settled.

The Chief of Police was living way beyond his means – or rather way beyond his publicly disclosed means. Either someone was giving him serious hospitality – six-star vacations and memberships of the most upscale outfits in the city – or they were giving him the cash to pay for it himself. Either way, it could only mean one thing: Jarrett had been taking bribes. And almost the only people in LA who could afford to pay bribes these days were the Chinese.

She sat back for a second to absorb what she had found. So was this why the Chief had been so adamant that his detectives focus only on Abigail's case? Did he know that if they linked her death with others, it would bring his benefactors embarrassment?

As for the file, she did not know how the mechanics had worked precisely: how Jarrett had got the dossier to Leo or how he had persuaded Leo to take it, whether directly or through a trusted, and perhaps equally duped, intermediary. But she could guess at the sequence. Maddy's story had appeared, pointing at the garrison. Jarrett had determined to shut her up, if only for a while, by sending her to chase a goose that was not only wild but triply amputated. Had he done that on the orders of his Chinese paymasters? She doubted it. In her experience, such arrangements were rarely so crude. They 'looked after' him, as they surely put it, and in return he knew what to do without needing to be told. That was why they called it corruption: it corroded you from the inside.

And not just him. If she was right, the entire LAPD, which followed Jarrett's direct orders, could not be trusted. Jarrett had been ready to do whatever it took to stop her. So, therefore, had the entire Los Angeles Police Department.

The irony of it did not escape her. She had written that story in a stupor, drunk with tiredness, armed with the sketchiest facts, in a state, the shrinks would say, of mental and emotional turmoil. Her sister had died just seventy-two hours earlier. When Howard had arrived to tell her it was a crock, that it passed none of her own standards, let alone those of the *LA Times*, she knew he was right. Part of her had been glad he had taken it down from the site: it was not good enough.

Yet now, with his heavy-footed attempt to close her down, Doug Jarrett had stood up the most radioactive element of her story as firmly as if he had summoned the media to West

1st Street and announced it was true. By throwing her the severed bones and damaged psyche of Tony Gilper, he had achieved the very reverse of his objective. In his determination to divert her away from the China connection that linked the deaths of Rosario Padilla, Eveline and her sister Abigail, Doug Jarrett had just proved it.

Chapter 33

There was nothing she could do now, even though the temptation to try was intense. She needed, she knew, to get at least an hour or two of sleep. Or if that proved as impossible as ever, then at least some rest and some silence, sixty or one hundred and twenty minutes when her brain might fall still.

She began the drill, the one that was meant to work. She ate something, microwaving some surviving pasta from the back of the fridge. Carbs make you sleepy, the books said. Sometimes that was true, sometimes it wasn't. But it was worth a try. She closed the lid of the laptop and set the other machines to sleep. She dimmed the lights and resisted the urge to put on the TV, knowing that that way lay the evening news. Instead, she put on a radio station playing music that, it claimed, came 'straight from the chiller cabinet'.

The last stage would be a shower, another one of the allegedly failsafe, but usually futile, steps towards a good night's sleep. She headed into the bathroom and slipped off her clothes, the sensation instantly reminding her of the frenzied rush with Leo a few hours earlier. Except now in the mirror she saw the bruises she had sustained in her escape from the sweatshop that might as well have occurred several years ago. She wondered if Leo had noticed them.

She looked at her naked self in the mirror, baffled once again at how, despite everything, she retained her shape. She was still trim, her waist still narrow, even though regular exercise had become a stranger to her. She made a three-quarter turn, looking back at herself over one shoulder. Her ass was firm, with a roundness of muscle hardwon from that now-abandoned routine of squats. No obvious cellulite on her thighs, no dimpling of fat. Not yet, not in this light, at least.

She turned back, the memory of her visit to Leo's apartment still fresh. She closed her eyes, remembering how he had laid her down on the couch and found her with his tongue, how he had explored her. She realized her earlier hunger had not been fully sated. She began to touch herself, opening her eyes so that she could watch in the mirror.

Afterwards, she stepped into the shower, letting the hot water run for a long time, the water soothing on her skin, washing away both the pleasures and terrors of the day – both the scent of Leo and the stink of the apartment block in Huntington Park, the pounding fear of that flight down the fire escape, the ordeal of preparing to face the man who might have been her sister's murderer. She closed her eyes, cradling herself in the heat of the water, savouring the fact that she was home. The bathroom was enveloped in steam, wrapping itself around her. Suddenly the shower was as hard to leave as a bed in the morning: it felt warm and safe.

Only the hope that she was now so faint from the temperature she might at last fall asleep pushed her out. It was a wrench to turn off the water, but she did it, stepping out to grab a towel. The room was a cloud, a dense fog of steam, the walls dripping. She had lost track of how long she had been in there. But then, as she towelled herself dry, shaking off the droplets on her thighs, she noticed something that stopped her.

The entire room was covered with condensation, every last surface beaded with droplets of water – save the mirror. The

282

glass was pristine, the slightest blurring at the very edges, but otherwise unaffected. Her reflection was sharp and clear; the anguish now engraved on her face entirely visible.

Nothing like this had happened before. A reliable part of her morning ritual involved emerging from the shower to give a big wipe of the mirror, clearing a face-sized window in the steam. It was the same every day. She had an extractor fan, but it rarely made a dent. In her bathroom a glass as clear and untouched as this was unheard of.

That it defied physics was obvious. She had no idea how to explain it, except for the iron certainty that it was no accident, coupled with a nagging and sickening suspicion.

Still clothed only in a towel, she opened the bathroom door and headed for the kitchen drawer where she kept a handful of tools. She found a screwdriver and returned to the bathroom. Now she examined the mirror more closely, but there was nothing she could see. She pressed her head into the wall, closed one eye and looked at the backing. She could make out a small stretch of wire dangling from the back. But this was the first time she had ever looked back here; it was possible the wire had been there before.

Now she set to work, first gingerly probing the fittings until she had worked out how and where the mirror was attached. With screwdriver in hand, she began to remove it, a teenage memory returning. Once her father was gone, it had fallen to her, aged just fifteen, to be the handyman of the house. The division of labour was never formalized or even spoken about, but that's how it was: Quincy would put food on the table and pack Abigail's lunch for school, Maddy was the one who knew how to restore a dead car battery or get the DVD to work. So she knew one end of a screwdriver from the other.

As it turned out, she didn't have to do much to get confirmation. In her palm were the first fittings and screws she had taken out; they were brand new, not caked in paint and accumulated dust and grime like the others in this bathroom.

Some kind of installation had been done that day, she was certain of it.

It made sense. The one thing that would thwart a surveillance camera concealed in a two-way mirror would be steam, misting up the mirror and obscuring the view. To prevent that, you'd want one of those dinky heating pads on the glass, working like the demister on a car's rear windscreen, keeping it forever clear. This mirror had never had such a feature before. Which could only mean that someone had taken the time to install one today. It probably came with the camera, working automatically.

Which meant that the lens had been in place, silent and unblinking, as she had stood there naked. Everything she had done to herself, it had seen.

Maddy returned the mirror to its place then took a towel from the rail. She gave her reflection a long hard stare, announcing to whoever hid behind it: 'Show's over.' Then she threw the towel over the glass, hoping to block out the very thought of it.

Still, she could not stop thinking about the men who had put it there, padding expertly around her apartment today, their shoes off, their movements noiseless. She would find them, of that she was determined. And she had a good idea where to start.

Chapter 34

Across town, at the same time, Katharine Hu was making a rare submission to weakness or need. She prided herself on being able to carry on under pressure, to stay up when those around her were knocked down. Quietly, and almost never voiced, she put this strength partly down to her heritage. Of course she hated it when her parents used to talk that way, especially her father. 'Remember, the Chinese people are the greatest nation in human history,' he had told her, quoting his own father. She argued with him about it, bracketing it with the garbage he talked about Africans, whom he had once called 'monkeys', later claiming all he had said was that they 'lack innate intelligence and skill'. It was racist and vile and stood alongside his medieval attitudes to sexuality as a measure of the distance between their generations and between them.

Still, *hǔ fù wú quǎn zǐ*, as they used to say in the old country. A tiger does not father a dog. An immigrant to the US when she was just eleven years old, an American citizen and proud of it, some of what she had been told must nevertheless have got into her marrow, because there were times when she found herself thinking just like the old man. She did not share these thoughts with anyone, not even Enrica – especially not with Enrica. Her wife would be appalled (though Enrica had plenty of similarly indefensible attitudes of her own). All the same, she could not help but feel it. The laziness of these Americans, their sense of expectation and entitlement, still shocked her, even after all these years.

The way they believed that working from nine till six or seven elevated them into heroes, when to her such a short working day looked like luxury. The way they saw leisure and entertainment as a right, to be exercised daily. The hours they spent in front of the TV, the meals in restaurants, the weekends at ball games, the barbecues, the surfing, the hiking, the computer games, the gym, the celebrity magazines, the dance classes, the therapy, all the countless things they did that were not *work*. They were like children, endlessly seeking fun, fun and more fun. It was even in their constitution: the pursuit of happiness. When she first heard that phrase, she assumed someone was teasing her, mocking her as a foreigner. Of course such a thing could not have a place in the country's basic law. It could not be, and yet there it was. No wonder they had lost their position at the top. It was a miracle they had stayed there as long as they had.

She was sounding like her dead father, may the angels guard his soul. But what could she do? If he was a tiger, she could be nothing else.

At this moment, though, she lacked her usual superior confidence. She identified with the Americans and their weakness. She was tired of all that had happened. The loss of Abigail Webb was a blow, of course, but it was not immediate and she could have borne it. But the events since then – Maddy's using her; the suspicion of her demonstrated by the news editor Howard Burke, who clearly believed Katharine was in cahoots with her uncontrollable friend; and, above all, the roiling, festering pot of ethnic hatreds Maddy had stirred with her latest story – all these were too much to bear.

In the nearly eighteen hours since Maddy's report had appeared and then disappeared, Katharine had felt worse than

286

at any time since the Treaty was signed. Those had been painful months, make no mistake: the impotent rage of Americans, particularly American men, had exerted a daily terror on Katharine and everyone like her. A brick had sailed through her parents' shop window; Chinese restaurants had been set ablaze, a whole district of Chinatown torched. In the worst attack, three Chinese students had been stabbed in Palo Alto. In that period, Katharine had found herself speaking all the time and loudly, even when walking down the street, pretending to talk into a dead phone if necessary. It was a defensive measure, designed to ensure anybody within a fifty-foot radius knew she was an American first, whatever modifier came before the hyphen. She would will strangers to hear her accent before they saw her face. She was not proud of that.

And now she was having to act that way again, thanks to the great Madison Webb. The demonstrations, those Sigurdsson political ads, the venom spilling out of Weibo – it all added up to a climate of febrile, sulphurous hostility. Sure, they were all at pains to say their issue was with the garrison, the PLA, the government in Beijing, anybody but the Chinese community of LA. But Katharine had been around long enough to know that, while that distinction might make sense on the *LA Times* editorial page or in a Stanford seminar room, out here, on the streets, it didn't travel.

So she had succumbed, feeling the rising need to have a drink and finally waving a white flag in its face. Here she was, on a stool at Poppies, sipping her third whisky of the night. And she had only been here twenty minutes. No point denying it, she was defeated.

Around her were the usual crowd: lonely business travellers and men whose wives had left them. She spotted, on his own at a table at the back, that cop Madison repeatedly rejected – what was his name? Jim? Jeff?

Only then did she become aware of someone in her

peripheral vision, on the stool two away from hers. She glanced over to him: early forties, stubbled, business suit, tie loosened. He gave her a look of weary empathy, then raised his glass. A gesture of solidarity among losers.

She nodded back then drained what was left of the honey-coloured liquid, resuming her straight-ahead gaze over the shoulder of the bartender. She let herself be mesmerized by the different labels on display, enjoying the names: Tanqueray, Taaka, Seagram's, Hendrick's, Boodles. *Boodles*, she thought hazily. *Boodles*. She remembered a lover in college, a Virginia girl who talked about 'oodles of love'.

'Can I get you another?'

She turned to see the stubbled man, looking her way. His eyes were a clear blue; he was handsome, the kind Maddy liked. He seemed lonely. She was in no mood to talk, but saying no seemed too much like hard work. 'Sure,' she heard herself say.

'Same again,' Stubble instructed the barman. 'For both of us.'

As the barman complied, Katharine noticed the man slip without effort onto the stool next to hers. She was too woozy to talk but he began and he had a nice voice and it was easy to listen to him, to drink and to listen and to drink some more. She nodded and sipped and nodded and soon enough she was doing some talking herself.

He explained that he was in town from Atlanta, that he had just done a presentation for a big client which he'd messed up. Ever since his divorce this had been happening a lot. He needed to be focused on work, but he was still thinking too much about, you know, everything else – about the stuff that really matters: family, love, real life, you know what I'm saying?

Katharine did know. Friendship mattered more than anything, but not everyone seemed to understand that. Some friends acted like friends, but they weren't really. They liked you for what they could get, you know what I mean? Not all of them. And not all of the time. And maybe she was being hard on Maddy. After all she'd been through a lot. But that's what life was like. It was hard. There were tests. You were tested all the time. She had been tested her whole life. And sometimes, just sometimes, it would be nice if your friends could pass, you know? Pass the test.

It was getting late, but the conversation flowed easily. She barely noticed her glass getting empty, let alone being refilled. An hour earlier she had resolved to drink some iced water and call Enrica, let her know where she was. But she had never quite gotten round to it.

'I really should be going,' she said, the words loose rather than slurred. She began to manoeuvre herself off the stool, but it was harder than it looked. Stubble had to take her by the elbow, guiding her down. His grip was strong.

'You really should not be driving anywhere.'

Katharine was not so drunk that she didn't know he was right. Her car was valet parked, but she was in no fit state to drive it. 'Could you call me a cab?'

'I can go one better,' he said, his hand still lingering on her forearm, his eyes now probing deep into hers. 'I have a suite at the Wyndham, just across the street. We could go there. You could rest a while.' The hint of a smile was playing on his lips, his face now fractionally closer to hers.

Katharine paused, the information winding along her neural pathways at a sluggish half pace. By the time it reached her brain, where it was processed and converted into the realization of what was happening, she gave the only reaction she could. She smiled and then began to giggle, the sound of which only made her laugh more. The man smiled back, his eyes twinkling at first and then uncomprehending.

'I'm sorry,' she said, in a voice wobbling with laughter. 'I'm really sorry. You're very handsome. And I'm sure most of the women here would be very glad to go back to your suite.'

That word, *suite*, nearly set her off again. 'But I have a wife at home who's waiting for me.' She dug into her purse, found a fifty and put it down on the bar. 'That's for the whisky.' Then she leaned forward and gave the man an unsteady kiss on the cheek, her lips recoiling somewhat from the bristles on his face. That too made her laugh.

As she stood outside among the valet parkers, waiting for the taxi they had ordered for her, the wintry air blew away some of the Scotch fog. She smiled, both amused and, it had to be said, flattered. Nothing like that had happened to her since college. If she had been feeling benign towards herself, she would say that that was because she had long radiated dyke vibes, warding off men at a hundred paces. When she was being less charitable, she would say it was because, for all her brilliance, she wasn't that much to look at. But tonight a rather handsome man had come on to her. It was silliness itself, he was probably drunk. But after a rough few days, it was a pleasant boost all the same.

Her earlier anger was fading, diluted by alcohol and the little ego lift kindly gifted to her by Stubble. She had been too harsh on Maddy, who was obviously going through a hell she, Katharine, had never experienced. She shouldn't have dissed her friend to this stranger; it wasn't fair. Maddy was being a good sister. Not for the first time, Katharine wondered if she had failed to understand sibling love because she had no brothers or sisters of her own.

She dug into her purse and took out her phone. Coughing against the smog, she dialled Maddy's number. If nothing else, she would get a kick out of telling her the Stubble story. Though the look of incomprehension on that man's beautiful face was slightly wasted in a phone call. This was a story that needed to be told over raucous drinks on a Friday night with the girls in the Mail Room.

'Maddy? It's Katharine.' Giggling as she got closer to the punchline, she proceeded to unfurl the story of the hot man who had propositioned a gay woman, making him as gorgeous as a movie star in the telling. To her delight, Maddy chuckled in all the right places, the first time she had heard her friend laugh since . . . since. Then Maddy's tone altered.

'And you say this has never happened before? Nothing like it?'

'Don't rub it in, Madison.'

'You're lovely, Katharine, you know that. But, you know, a *man* coming on to you. That way. You know, leaving no doubt what he's after. That doesn't happen often?'

'That's the whole point, Madison.' The laughter was seeping out of her voice. 'It never happens.'

At the other end of the phone, Maddy was digesting what she was hearing, dismissing the thought as paranoid and self-absorbed, then coming at it once again. She was sitting on the window ledge in her apartment, every mirror in the place now covered, her laptop snapped firmly shut. The curtains were drawn, save for the small gap through which Maddy gazed down at the street below. She had been doing this for an hour or so, watching the human traffic on both sidewalks as well as the cars.

Just because I'm paranoid doesn't mean they're not out to get me.

The old stand-up joke was playing back to her. Someone had concealed a camera in her bathroom and had now set an admittedly ill-conceived honey trap for one of her friends. And even though they had made a basic error in the execution – doubtless discovering in their research that K was 'married' but drawing the wrong conclusion – the intention was not stupid. They had chosen wisely, rightly divining that Katharine Hu was not just a friend but a crucial collaborator. That would not have been too hard to work out: you simply had to have watched Maddy these last three days, following her, monitoring her calls, staring at her computer screen.

She shuddered. These people, whoever they were, were

inside her apartment and all over her friends. She looked at the burner she'd been using. She ought to call Quincy, tell her to scrap the old number – not even to dial it once, lest her sister find herself on their radar – from now on to use only this new, disposable one. She could imagine the reaction: 'You sure you're not imagining all this, Madison? You know, it isn't always about you.'

Down on the street, the people and cars were still moving. Perhaps they were hurrying to the supermarkets, to pick up the now-staple roast-duck-in-a-bag or preserved fruits for the big New Year dinner. Lots of people were doing those now, a kind of Christmas reprise with a Chinese twist. Winter was long, especially in the smog; people needed treats to break it up.

There! White male, early twenties, six-two, maybe one hundred and sixty pounds, hoodie and gangsta headphones. This was the third time in the last fifty-five minutes he had passed by this building.

She checked her watch. If she was right, the thirtysomething black woman with braids carrying a courier's bag over one shoulder would soon appear from the other direction. Maddy waited and waited, not wanting to look away even for a moment. Nothing.

Maybe Quincy was right. Maybe Madison's ego, inflated by lack of sleep, was playing tricks with her. For all she knew, it was possible the landlord of the building had installed steam-free mirrors in every apartment of the—

Bingo. There she was, Mrs Braids, completing her own circuit. A few minutes late, but unmistakably her and unmistakably walking in a loop.

They were onto her friends, they were in her bathroom and they were on the street. They had followed her on the dead-end trail of Tony Gilper too. Whoever they were – and she had an inkling – they were watching her, inside and out. They were after her. And now she was after them.

Chapter 35

Politics Live Blog, Thursday

11.02am *Signal's a bit in-and-out here on Terminal Island, but I'll be doing my best to cover the latest event organized by activist Mario Padilla. Today's demo is called Encircle the Base and it's his most ambitious yet. Crowds are already building up. Padilla says he hopes to start at noon. I've already been slapped with a sticker saying, of course, Encircle the Base. Will post a pic shortly.*

11.11am *Other reporters are here too, including Eli Haddin who's just weibed this rather good question:*

For an amateur, Padilla's a master. Hastily organized, yet already he's got bespoke stickers printed. They're not cheap. Who's funding him?

Gotta admit, I have wondered the same thing. There was a rumor that Elena Sigurdsson's campaign had put some dough Padilla's way, which would figure, given how hard she's been running on the serial killer/Berger's watch meme. But it's still only rumor.

Hundreds of people arriving, by the way. Forgive shaky grip on this pic.

11.18am Padilla himself has just DM'd me:

There has been no question of direct funding from Elena Sigurdsson's or any other partisan campaign. Our effort is 100% independent and outside politics. It comes from the grass roots.

Anyone else notice that use of 'direct' there? Sounds like Mr Padilla speaks lawyer.

11.22am Ben Portman of LA Politico has spotted GOP state chair Ted Norman in attendance. Norman says his presence does not signal formal Republican backing for Padilla campaign and that he's here 'in a personal capacity'.

11.24am. Padilla back again. Says one of the donors to today's event was the catering firm his sister Rosario used to work for. They paid for the stickers apparently.

11.36am Slogans spotted on placards. 'This land is our land', obvs. Also: 'Don't Tread on Me', 'Live Free or Die', 'Go back to China.' Personal favorite, if slightly lengthy: 'You commit the crime, you do the time – in an American jail.' Be interested to know if there are events planned in other Pearl cities. Let me know if you hear anything.

11.48am The encircling is properly underway. Hundreds, maybe thousands of Angelenos, hand-in-hand, linking up and forming the human chain around the base, as promised. There are stewards with bullhorns, attempting to choreograph the process, corralling people, shepherding them into single file etc. They're as close to the base as they can get, which means essentially that they're going to form the chain directly in front of and along the perimeter fence. There are LAPD officers facing them the whole way, standing between them and the fence itself. Maybe they're worried some stunt-artist will bring out the fence-cutters and try to break into the base. I'll be on hand to record that if it happens. Will be interesting to see what Chinese security do with them at the main entrance. I'm heading over there now.

11.53am Replying to my question above (see 11.36am), Janice Plum in San Diego says activists there have 'no specific event planned at present' but are keeping 'a close watch' on LA and wish 'Mr Padilla and other proud Americans' the very best of luck. I'm picking up similar noises from US nationalist groups in San Francisco too. Seems like all the Pearl folks are following this one.

11.55am OK, at the main entrance: it's all LAPD out front. But you don't have to look too hard to see uniformed PLA military police or guards (weib me exact title, please, anyone who knows) right behind them. Pretty stern-faced bunch. Can't see how they're armed, but other reporters here assure me they will be. So it's weirdly like double security here. A line of LAPD, right in the protestors' faces. Then, maybe ten yards back, by the entrance gate itself, it's all PLA. Think of it as the thin green line behind the thin blue line. No way any protestors could break through that. Not that I'm saying they planned to, mind. (In case Mr Padilla is reading this!)

11.57am Crowd estimates are in. Police say they believe three thousand people are here. Organizers say they believe the figure could be as much as TEN times that. My own impression – and I am horrible at doing this – is that the base is so big, it's not humanly possible for three thousand people to encircle it all. Yet Weibo tells me the whole thing now has *a human ring all around it. No gaps. Some achievement, given access to Terminal Island is not easy. Kudos to Padilla: impressive.*

11.58am What a time for battery running low!

11.59am The chanting and singing is now full throttle. No surprises, they're doing the chorus of 'This land . . .'

11.59am Now they're doing a countdown to noon. Ten, nine, eight . . .

Noon. Big cheer as the bullhorns broadcast a recording of a clock striking twelve. Sounds like a cathedral or something. Spooky, chimes of midnight vibe.

12.05pm I wasn't near enough to see before, or maybe they've only just appeared, I'm not sure – but I now have a clear view of one of the watchtowers. Inside, facing the crowd, are a pair of (it could be three) Chinese snipers, their guns clearly trained on the crowd. Geez, that is quite a sight. Can anyone confirm they're seeing that at the other watchtowers?

12.07pm From the southwest corner, via Weibo:

We're seeing the same thing. Chinese guards aiming weapons (sub-machine guns?) towards the crowd. People singing the national anthem.

12.09pm I can confirm the anthem thing. Very charged, hearing that sung right here, in this situation. Big throaty push when it comes to the final line:

Oh, say does that star-spangled banner yet wave
O'er the land of the free and the home of the brave?

12.17pm Finally, right by the entrance, Mario Padilla has appeared, lifted on the shoulders of two fairly beefy supporters. They're resting him on one shoulder each, as it were, holding him steady. He has a bullhorn.

12.18pm He thanks everyone for coming. Says the size has surprised everyone.

12.19pm Says no one wants any trouble. Urges people to protest peacefully.

12.21pm Urges the Chinese authorities to listen to what the people of Los Angeles are saying. That they don't want revenge, they just want justice for the people they love. They just want the Chinese to co-operate.

12.22pm Padilla says if the people in charge of the base have any knowledge that could lead to the capture of the man who killed Rosario Padilla, Eveline Plaats or Abigail Webb, all they have to do is hand that knowledge to the LAPD. That's all.

12.23pm Says they must do it. It's their duty.

12.25pm Now ramping up the rhetoric. Padilla is quite the speaker. Amazing intensity. His words being relayed via other bullhorns and makeshift speakers. Slight delay as word gets passed along the ring. Only makes it more powerful somehow.

12.26pm Now he's giving a direct message to the PLA in charge of the garrison. 'If you are harboring a fugitive from justice, the time to hand him over is now. Be open. Do not hide behind these fences and barriers. If you have nothing to hide, be open. You don't need these men and these guns to protect you. Be open. And if you love justice as we believe you do, then tear down this wall. Tear down this wall! Tear down this wall!'

12.28pm The entire crowd are still chanting it. They won't stop. The words are encircling the garrison. There's no way the men inside can't hear this message. 'Tear down this wall! Tear down this wall! Tear down this wall!'

They were in the car, on their way to the launch of a new children's literacy initiative in Santa Cruz. Leo looked at the briefing note resting on his lap. 'Book It!' the scheme was called, and it involved giving a free book every semester to every child in the district, paid for from the estate of a local boy who'd gone on to make a fortune in Silicon Valley. Leo turned the page to see a potted bio of the late donor. He'd asked Ross, the upstart asshole, to check for any landmines and he'd said there were none. But Leo ran his eye over the bio anyway, looking for signs of any rogue affiliations or past donations that could cause problems. In politics, it was always best to trust no one but yourself. Not just in politics.

Berger was on the phone, smooth-talking an early backer who needed some reassurance. The mayor wasn't asking him for money this time. Instead, he was keeping the benefactor sweet, offering him the illusion that he was being consulted. Illusion it most certainly was. At one point the candidate pulled the phone away from his ear and hit the mute button, allowing him to speak to Leo while the donor kept right on talking to him.

'You got the numbers yet?'

Leo realized he could stall no longer. 'When you've finished your call.'

Berger clicked the un-mute button on his phone. 'Adam, I think the argument you're making is too important to wait. I'm going to take it to my senior staff right away . . . That's right . . . We have a meeting now, in fact. It's going to be top of the agenda . . . No, it's me who should be thanking you . . . I'll keep you posted. Love to Cindy and the girls.' He put the phone on his lap. 'OK. What have we got?'

Leo was balancing a printout on his knees, directly below the Book It! papers and the design of a proposed new campaign flier: a shot of Berger and his gorgeous blonde wife against a backdrop of giant redwood trees. But he had to maintain the pretence that the data had only just arrived. He looked at his phone, recalling the numbers from memory. 'Remember, these are raw numbers. They haven't been weighted or adjusted for—'

'For Christ's sake, Leo, just give me the fucking numbers. I'm not a child.'

'You're down eleven on last week. Berger forty-four, Sigurdsson forty-two.'

'Jesus, that's within the margin of error.'

'Yes.'

'It's a statistical tie.'

'Yes.'

'This is California, Leo. Democrats are not meant to tie with Republicans in California IN FUCKING FEBRUARY!'

The driver looked over his shoulder. Leo gave him a 'don't worry' expression.

'I know, Richard. But this is a temporary blip, brought about by unforeseen and extraordinary events. This will pass.'

Berger swivelled to face his aide directly. 'How exactly is this going to pass, Leo? Hmm? How?'

'Well, we—'

'I've become the pro-China candidate in this race. That's what Sigurdsson and Doran are putting on me. It's political death, Leo, that's what it is. I'm the guy who's let some psycho with a needle on the loose because I won't stand up to the garrison, because I'm too far up the PLA's ass. That's the message. Every day Sigurdsson sucks Padilla's dick, that's the message: vote Berger and it's a vote for the People's fucking

299

Republic. If you don't like secretive Chinese killers and if you don't like a big fucking Chinese base in the middle of LA, then vote Republican. I mean, how the hell do we fight that, Leo?'

Leo allowed himself a short exhalation of breath, cutting it shorter lest it sound like a sigh. 'We need to get out in front of this issue. We could try again to have a meeting and a photo with Padilla. No harm in that, but I think you should go substantive. Plays to your positives, hints at Sigurdsson's negatives. You're the heavyweight in this race, remember.'

'Substantive?' Berger said, quieter now. 'Like what?'

'You do a big, set-piece speech, maybe in DC. Council on Foreign Relations, National Press Club. You know, statesman-like. You go through the history, the context, all that cr— . . . stuff. Then you float a commission. Bipartisan. Former senators, couple of governors. Some big-swinging dick professors.'

'To do what?'

'To renegotiate the Treaty.'

'You're kidding, right?'

'No,' said Leo, now facing the mayor, their knees touching. 'Why not? You're jumping ahead to the heart of the matter, ten moves ahead of Sigurdsson. You leave her way back, still whining and bellyaching about the garrison. Meanwhile, you're going big, focusing on the solution. It's classic Eisenhower. "If a problem cannot be solved, enlarge it."'

'The press would kill us. Everyone knows we can't change the Treaty. It just can't be done. It's an open question whether the President of the United States could do it, even if Congress wanted him to. The Governor of California can do nothing. Not on his own. And I'm just the mayor of Los Angeles! Can you imagine what the press would do with this? It would just advertise my own impotence.'

'I think you'd start a debate in the prime—'

'I don't want to start a debate: you can leave that to NPR. I want to win this fucking election.'

300

'It makes you the big picture guy, the geopolitical, strategic *leader*. She's a complainer, on the same level as the street protestors. You're above that. You're planning for a better future.'

It wasn't getting through, Leo could see that. Politicians liked the long term in theory; they made speeches about it, especially when they were campaigning. They always hoped and planned to govern for the *long term*. But the brute reality was they cared more about right now. And 'now' was getting more immediate all the time. Leo could recite Doran's lectures on the subject: 'When I started out in this business, it was all about the next morning's newspaper headlines. And everyone complained *that* was too short.' Then the news cycle got shortened, Doran would say, 'It became about that night': what pictures you got on the evening news, the daily tracking polls. Now the old twenty-four-hour news cycle seemed an impossible luxury, a pace of near-academic slowness and deliberation. These days it was all about the next thirty seconds on Weibo. If a politician contemplated a horizon beyond that, he was instantly branded far-sighted and cerebral.

Leo understood his boss did not want some high-minded plan for the future that might take weeks to bear fruit politically. He wanted a quick fix to get his numbers back to where they had been a matter of days ago, leading Sigurdsson fifty-five to forty-five.

'There is something more immediate you could do,' he began, reaching for an idea he had had that morning but had hoped not to have to deploy. 'Just to establish your anti-garrison *cojones*.'

Berger had returned to his prior position, leaning back into his seat, once again staring straight ahead. 'I'm listening.'

'This would be something you could do, rather than just say. In your capacity as mayor.'

'OK.'

'Parking fines.'

'Oh, come on.'

'I mean it. Remember the estimate we got from Jack? Tens of millions of dollars in unpaid fines, unregistered vehicles, speeding infringements.'

'Which the garrison refuse to recognize. Extraterritoriality, diplomatic immunity, all that bullshit.'

'Yeah, yeah, I know. Yadda, yadda, yadda. The point is, you've let that go quiet. That's one reason Sigurdsson's able to whack you now for being soft on the Chinese. And the polling was always very strong on this stuff, you'd be surprised. That's what people resent. That the garrison get to drive as fast as they like, park anywhere, behave like they're above the law.'

'Which they are.'

'So why not serve them with a legal notice for the money they owe?'

Berger shook his head. 'Because it will make us look pathetic, that's why. Make *me* look pathetic. They're killing our women and I'm worried about a few boys driving through a red light? We'll look like fleas on an elephant's ass.'

Now he leaned forward again, his face so close to Leo's, the aide could smell his aftershave. 'You were gonna close this down for me, Leo. Remember? I told you. "Shut it down." That's what I needed you to do. I don't want me or my name within a thousand miles of this case. You need to keep me out of it.'

'I understand, Richard. And I have ensured that—'

'Don't "Richard" me, Leo. I'm not gonna be soothed and calmed like I'm one of those interns you're boning. No way. I don't wanna be soothed and calmed. I want action. I want you to solve this problem by cutting it off at source, like I asked. And if you have "personal reasons" for not wanting to do what I ask, then I'm afraid your time on this campaign will be done. Do I make myself clear?'

Leo nodded. But Berger was not finished.

'And when I say "at source", are we clear what I mean? Or rather *who* I mean?'

'Yes.'

'We're clear about that?'

'Crystal.'

'Good.' The mayor settled back into his chair, gazing out of the passenger-side window. At that moment they passed a crop of Sigurdsson for Governor lawn-signs. 'Then get it done. Now.'

With dread, and a rising sense of failure, Leo Harris reached for his telephone.

Chapter 36

Maddy had tried to leave her building long ago. She walked into the side street where she had parked the rental car she'd picked up the day before and took a while to absorb what she saw. She had been clamped, a bright yellow 'boot' immobilizing the front wheel on the driver's side. The windscreen was covered with an oversized sticker, fully obscuring the view and announcing that she was in violation of parking restrictions for the City of Los Angeles. She cursed herself. Her idiocy for parking in a residents' zone in a car that had no permit. Except, once she studied the signs, she saw there were no such restrictions here. She looked around. None of the other cars, equally lacking in permits, had been clamped. Only hers. She filed it away along with the fruitless hunt for Tony Gilper as a tactic her opponents were using to delay and derail her. And to signal that they knew exactly where she was and what she had been doing. This was their way of saying that, for all her attempted evasions yesterday – and her stop at Leo's apartment – they had never let her out of their sight.

She could not afford to let that cow her. That was what they wanted and she would not give it to them. She would do what she needed to do and if they wanted to watch, they could damn well watch.

So Madison had walked a few streets, sticking to the busy ones, then used her phone to summon a cab. Even though she was using one of the burners, which she hoped had not yet been tracked by her pursuers, she took extra precautions. She called three taxi companies, one after the other, rejecting the first two that arrived just in case. She reasoned that those who had been stalking her were well-resourced – the two-way mirror, the three-person, plain-clothes surveillance team on the street corner, the false suitor despatched to woo Katharine – and that they might well stretch to having a fake cab standing by. But even they would be unlikely to have three. When the third car pulled up, giving the name she had given to the dispatcher, she nodded and got in. 'To Terminal Island,' she said.

And now here she was, having arrived just after noon – in time to catch the beginning of Padilla's speech. She held her notebook in front of her, not that she planned to use it. She was not here to write. But it helped to have something to do with her hands. It separated her from everyone else here, too, which she liked. Most reporters took notes electronically these days, tapping into their phones. But Maddy stuck with pen and paper, clasping her notebook like a shield.

All around the crowd were chanting. *Tear down this wall! Tear down this wall! Tear down this wall!* They kept it up, as if they believed the words were an incantation, an open sesame that would suddenly and miraculously see the fence disappear and the gate swing open, the Chinese garrison exposing itself to the wintry daylight. They were enjoying it, this crowd, high on their own self-righteousness, their shared mission, that sense of momentum you feel at a big rally, the conviction that the tide is turning, that soon nothing will stand in your way.

Padilla had played them beautifully, no doubt about that. He was a natural; you'd think he'd been working crowds all his life. He stood at the front, perhaps twenty rows of people

305

between them, slightly raised on a homemade platform and with a bullhorn in hand, joining in the chorus. *Tear down this wall, tear down this wall.*

He had, Maddy assumed, finished his speech; there was no way he could top that climax. Yet his posture indicated he had something else to say. Finally, he spotted a dip in the chanting and brought the horn to his lips. 'We're going to stay here all day, our hands linked around this base until our voices have been heard.' A big cheer. 'Before I finish, I do want to thank some folks who have made today possible.'

He thanked the police, which brought an ironic round of applause, praising them for keeping things orderly. A couple of police officers near Madison raised their hands in appreciation: ironic or sincere, it was hard to tell. Next Padilla thanked the stewards, 'all volunteers who came forward in the last twenty-four hours because they love this town and its people'. And then he said, 'I want to single out just one person, though. I'm not sure she's here today, I can't see her, but if she is, I hope she'll give us a wave so we can express our thanks. Because without her, I don't think all of you would be here. I know I wouldn't. It was her reporting, her refusal to give up, her determination to get to the truth and to let all of us know about it, that started this movement. She is, like me, one of the bereaved. Like me, she lost a sister. Please, let's give a big hand to Madison Webb.'

She was suddenly enveloped in a roar, so loud the air around her seemed to vibrate. Someone started a chant: 'Madison, Madison.' From the front, Mario was back on the bullhorn. 'Come on out front here, Madison, if you're here. These folks want to see you.'

The noise was solid, a thick wall encircling her. She considered a wave and shake of her head, a modest brush-off to Padilla, but realized even that would draw attention she did not want. She remained frozen, with no intention of going up front. Wading through this crowd would be impossible for

306

a start; they were packed in so tightly, she could barely move. More to the point, the very idea appalled her. She was a journalist, not a politician. She wanted to know what was happening, that was all. She didn't want to make things happen, just understand those that did.

What Padilla chose to do was his business, but she found the idea of being cheered and applauded for being the sister of a murdered woman appalling. Abigail was dead. That did not make Maddy a movie star.

So she stayed fixed to the spot, willing Mario to drop it and let the moment pass. She stared down at her feet, an anonymous, unrecognized face in the crowd, hoping the lack of eye contact would somehow make her disappear. It was in that moment that she felt herself shoved in her left side, a move that pushed her two or three paces rightward. There must have been a surge from that part of the crowd, she thought, as she tried to keep her footing. But a second later there was another jostle from behind her. More forceful this time, she lurched forward, almost losing her balance. She stuck out her right foot to keep herself upright but it was too late. There was more pressure from behind – it felt like a pair of hands at her back – and a second later she had fallen to the ground, landing on her knees.

Instantly, she felt a boot-heel on her fingers, sending a sharp stab of pain up through her arm. The crowd seemed to be closing around her. She could see legs, feet, knees. She tried to get up, worried she was about to be crushed underfoot in a stampede. But the crowd around her was too tight. There was no space for her to lever herself upward.

It was at that moment that she felt a sudden and sharp kick to the base of her skull, just above where the head meets the neck. 'Hey!' she called out uselessly, still believing that she was caught up in an accidental crush. The pain was bright.

Another foot on her hand, her right this time. If only she could get to her feet. But the knot of people around her was becoming tighter. It was dark on the ground. She could see no sky above, just a thicket of legs. Far away, she could hear Mario Padilla's voice. But he was on the shore and she was several fathoms below the ocean surface.

Now another kick came, landing directly on her throat. She let out a sound that was part gasp, part vomit. An instant later, from another direction, a boot arrived on her thigh. Then, as if correcting its aim, the same boot made a direct hit on her groin, the shock of being kicked in that intimate place almost overriding the pain of the sensation.

There were three more blows, the last apparently targeted with expertise at her head. As always, her brain refused to switch off. She found herself thinking that the people around and above would assume that what was happening was a terrible accident, if they were aware of it at all. They had probably not seen the two or three men who, she suspected, had formed a ring around her, deliberately preventing anyone else gaining a glimpse, each taking turns to administer their punishment. They must have been standing close by and on either side of her, waiting for their cue. Nor would anyone else have noticed these men walking away once the job was done, each in separate directions, melting into the crowd – performing their disappearing act at the very moment Madison Webb passed out.

Chapter 37

Doran surveyed the room. He knew these people. He knew the churches they went to, the names of their daughters, the TV shows they watched, the cars in their driveways. He had met none of them before. But they were county chairs of the state Republican party, a breed he knew as intimately as his own family. In fact, given that his parents were both dead and his ex-wife and son lived in Maine, he knew them more intimately than his own family.

In the diary, this meeting at the campaign HQ in Sacramento was scheduled to be sticky. For the GOP, the February meet in a statewide California race always was. The oldest among them still remembered, or at least had heard of, the glory days when Ronald Reagan was comfortably winning consecutive terms in the state en route to national office. 'Why can't we have some of that now?' they'd bleat, in their nylon trousers and oversized glasses, although not in so many words.

But this time was going to be different. Thanks to the *LA Times* and that ferret of a journalist, the garrison protests had Elena Sigurdsson neck and neck with Berger, a phenomenal achievement for a Republican so early in the cycle. The danger now was that it would go to the candidate's head, that she would start believing she had something special, that it was down to her unique appeal and charisma that the numbers were shifting. Hard to break it to them that they were just a can of beans whose sales went up or down depending on the vicissitudes of the market. But he would do it if he had to.

No need to do that now. This was to be a happy, breezy occasion. Matt had even invited a camera crew in for the occasion, doubtless for a feelgood item on surging morale in the Sigurdsson camp. Not a bad idea, Doran was grudgingly ready to concede. He took up his position on the side wall.

After an introduction from state chairman Ted Norman – his face even redder than usual, the rims of his eyes apparently raw, he was all but glowing – the candidate launched straight in, giving her assessment of the race ahead, why there were no grounds for complacency, it all depended on your support in getting out the vote, but California was ready for change and, with your help, that's what we're going to do in November!

Then it was time for questions, the first a softball lovingly moulded from cotton wool and candy floss. 'I'm so proud of you and this campaign. Do you really believe you can win this thing?'

That brought applause and the pleasingly predictable, 'I wouldn't have entered this race if I didn't believe . . . as I've always said, I'm in it to win it!'

If anything, the questions got mushier. What is your opponent's greatest weakness? What more can we do, out there in the field, to bring home victory? What will be your first act as governor? Funny, Bill Doran reflected, what one good poll number can do. Without it, these activists would be demanding more of this, objecting to the inclusion of that, and generally Monday-morning-quarterbacking the entire campaign strategy, convinced they knew better than these hired guns who didn't understand California politics the way they did. Instead, they were putty.

Then Sigurdsson gestured at a persistent hand at the back; Doran had to twist his thick, linebacker's neck to see him.

He clocked the questioner's morose expression, automatically setting this man apart from the true believers crammed into the room, all of them cheerily knocking back the Kool-Aid.

'I want to thank you for your campaign too,' he began. 'Especially your courage. It's about time someone had the *cojones*' – he pronounced it with a hard 'j' – 'to say what needs to be said in this country. What's *needed* to be said for a long time. I wouldn't have guessed it would be a woman who had the balls to do it – excuse me – but there we are. That's just how things work out sometimes.' A barely perceptible ripple of discomfort passed through the room.

He went on: 'But someone had to start telling the truth about what's happened here. About the menace we've allowed into our country.'

Doran stiffened.

'Now I know we're not allowed to talk like my daddy did – about the "yellow peril" and all that. That's not *politically correct*. But sometimes you need to tell it like it is. And right now, peril is exactly what it is. They're right here. With *their* boots on *our* ground. So excuse me if I'm not too polite.'

By now Doran was standing tall, his chin raised. He had made strenuous eye contact with Matt, issuing a glare that said: disaster. He reinforced the point by tilting his head towards the cameras. *This will look bad.* Worse still, Norman was nodding visibly and within the camera shot, adding to the impression that this wingnut represented the true, if repressed, views of the party faithful.

But Doran hardly needed to worry. Sigurdsson had enough instinct of her own to know she needed to step in. She talked over the questioner for the time it took Matt to locate the technical guy and get him to cut the microphone. The man was still speaking, crying out to be heard, but she was amplified while he wasn't, so she had the floor.

'I want to be very clear. There is no place for racism or xenophobia in this campaign, none whatsoever.' When the

311

inevitable applause came, she wisely carried on speaking through it. Even if she was not saying much – 'No place at all, let me be clear about that . . .' – it was an effective, if ancient rhetorical trick. It created the illusion that the speaker was all but drowning in applause, struggling to wade through the flood of approval that was enveloping her.

Doran nodded his assent. The candidate was both growing into the role, he reflected, and growing in his esteem. He was too hard-headed to be a gusher, to let emotion cloud his judgement. He would always rely on the stats; he would not get carried away. That said, even hired-gun political consultants needed to feel the moment sometimes, to feel what the folks felt. If you stopped getting turned on yourself, then you'd have no idea how to turn on others. And right now he was allowing himself to feel what, he was ready to swear, every county chair in this room was feeling: that this woman really could win in November. That she could be the next Governor of California and after that, who knew?

What she did next only confirmed that impression. She pulled off a subtle two-step, not easy for a relative novice. First, she strengthened her attack on racism, nicely appealing to moderate voters (especially suburban women, aged thirty-five to forty-five). 'My message has always been one of good, old-fashioned patriotism, the kind my parents instilled in me: America belongs to Americans – *all* Americans, every one of us, no matter where we come from.'

And then a neat little nod to the base, lest they think she was going soft. 'All of us who love America feel the same way about this. We want the American people to be strong again, to be proud again, to be the independent nation our Founders dreamed of. Friends, join with me in sending a message out from this campaign to California and beyond: It's time to take back our country!'

Thursday 10.10pm

The first sensation, before the realization of pain or the intimation of the bright, overhead light, was surprise. The experience of a long, sustained sleep was so unfamiliar to Madison Webb that to emerge from it was striking. It brought a strange kind of pleasure, though that was fleeting. The instant she moved even slightly, any comfort was scattered and dispelled by pain.

Her head was throbbing at its base, sending out the image of a spreading stain, like a tattoo of a grey cloud, on her neck. She could picture it, contracting and expanding in time with the hurt. She tried to turn, but that only started up the discordant orchestra of the rest of her body: the agony of bruised ribs and pounded muscles. She let out a sound that was part cry and part gasp. She still had not opened her eyes.

She heard him before she saw him, his voice soothing and calm. He placed his hand on hers. 'Take your time,' he said. Jeff Howe. Patient, quiet, preparing her gently. Acting as if he were a family member, as if he were her lover.

That made her rush to open her eyes, to find out what the hell was going on. She saw the white walls of a hospital room; stretching directly in front of her, the rumpled sheets of a hospital bed. She was tilted at an angle, even though she was certain she had not lifted herself up. It took her at least thirty seconds to work out that the top half of the mattress had been raised to create this gradient, but it was nothing to do with her. She moved her left hand under the covers, to check that she could. Her right too. But this hand was resting close to her most private parts which, she remembered, had been made agonizingly tender.

Her dream came back to her now, the gobbling sense of being swallowed, as if she had been sinking into a soft marsh. Except this bog was made of people. She had been standing still and then the ground had opened up, devouring her before closing over her. Once below the surface, demons had prodded and poked her with hot irons and heavy clubs; she had fallen and they had kicked her, punching her crotch. She had seen two of them, or perhaps she had sensed them – her attackers, initially flanking her like discreet bodyguards, determined to protect her. But when the boots and fists rained on her exhausted body, seeking to soften and batter it like a cut of meat, she had never got so much as a glimpse of their faces.

'I had a very bad dream,' she said, even the words draining her. She was trying to focus, but the light was so bright.

'Yes. It must have felt like a dream.'

'You know about my dream? That's funny.' The act of offering a feeble smile seemed to tug on several muscles, all of them rent and shredded.

'I wish that's all it was, Madison.'

Now, in the haze, the word 'painkillers' presented itself to her, as if emerging from a smoggy cloud, still wreathed in fog. That's what this was, that was why she had slept.

Then came the other realization, the same one that had greeted her each 'morning' – or, more accurately, after each short interlude of sleep during these last few days – the realization that it was not some night terror of the imagination that had killed Abigail. That it was real, a hard boulder of fact that would not be shoved out of the way. It would still be there tomorrow. And Abigail would be gone.

Only at this moment did she look directly at Jeff, leaning forward in a modest wooden seat at her bedside. A dark line was etched under each eye.

'What's happened?' she said lamely, attempting another wan smile.

'Lots, Madison. Lots has happened.'

She raised her eyebrows, a manoeuvre which hurt much more than it had any right to.

'Starting with you. You were at Mario Padilla's rally, do you remember that?'

Maddy made the slightest of nods.

'Things turned pretty nasty. They kinda got out of hand. A scuffle broke out near you. Somehow you got caught up in it. I don't know how. Knowing you, you were trying to interview both sides while they were fighting.' He gave her a wide smile. She was struck by the whiteness of his teeth: even in her stupor, she could see he was trying to be charming, trying to charm her.

A thought was taking a long time to form, uncoiling slowly like a sleepy worm. She had no firm idea of the shape of it, except that it did not agree with what Jeff had just said, though she could not say exactly how. Still, long before she could think how to convert it into words, he was speaking again.

'But there's something else that's happened, Madison. That's why I'm here.'

She summoned the energy to say, 'Go on.' The sound the words made was a whisper.

'We've got him, Madison. We found him and we've got him.'

Chapter 38

Maddy let her head fall back into the pillow as Jeff explained how the prolonged exercise in facial recognition had finally brought a match to the man spotted at the bar of the Great Hall on the night Abigail had been killed. Given the poor angle, it had required a team of highly specialized computer forensic analysts to generate anything that could count as a positive ID. Tellingly, bar records showed that the suspect had paid in cash that night, leaving no identity trail. He had also arrived alone, so there had been no obvious witnesses to interview. He had been unusually difficult to trace which, in Jeff's unofficial view, counted as grounds for suspicion in itself.

'He was careful,' he said.

'What about the others?'

'All the men who'd been interviewed have been released now. He's the one, we're sure of it.'

'No,' she said, frustrated not to be able to talk faster. 'The other women.'

'I think the team are taking it one step at a time,' he said, letting the words hang in the air for a while.

'So who is he, this—'

'Justin Brooks.'

316

She nodded, saving herself the effort of repeating the name. 'Who is he?'

'White Caucasian male, twenty-eight years of age; army veteran; resident of Long Beach, occasional visitor to LA; unmarried; record mostly clean, except for two cautions for domestic violence. Used to work in house removals; last known employment was driving a cab.'

'Domestic violence?' The words seemed to have more syllables than Maddy remembered; they took so long to say.

'Yep. I think that kind of clinched it for Barbara.'

Maddy paused, letting her eyes close as she swallowed. Barbara Miller, the detective. An earlier, unanswered question tugged at her. With effort, she said it out loud. 'Is there any connection between,' she swallowed again, 'between this man and the others? Between him and Rosie? Or Eveline? Anything at all?'

Jeff checked his watch. 'Christ, Madison. The doctors told me I shouldn't talk to you for more than thirty seconds.' The bright white teeth were showing again.

'Just answer my question.' No longer a whisper, but slurred. As if she'd just come from the dentist.

'Madison, I'm not on this case, remember?'

'Barbara would have told you. She told you everything else.'

He stood up, as if to go. 'You need to rest, Madison. Please. Forget what I'm asking you to do. Your *body* is pleading with you.'

He let his hand rest on hers, a gesture capable of more than one interpretation and chosen for that reason: it could be platonic if that's what she wanted. He was almost at the door when she spoke again.

'I thought they reassigned you. To traffic duties. Punishment for helping me.'

'They did.'

'But here you are. In the loop.' The phrase was hard to form, her mouth full of cotton wool.

'They switched me back.'

'How come . . .' She swallowed at the effort of it. 'How come they switched you back?'

'What can I say, the Chief of Police always liked me. Now get some rest.'

The room was quiet, save for some beeping coming from an unseen and, to her, mysterious machine. There was a red button attached to a cord resting on her lap. She wondered who would come if she pressed it. Which prompted the return of the worm that had not managed to uncoil while Jeff Howe had been facing her: her disagreement with his account of what had happened at the rally. There had been no scuffle. There had been no fight. She had been pushed to the ground and attacked. Why had he pretended otherwise?

And Jeff was back in his old job, his punishment over before it had begun.

What can I say, the Chief of Police always liked me.

Jarrett himself had intervened to overturn the suspension. Why would he do that? Just because he liked Jeff? And, and . . .

Her brain was fogging up again, like the inside of a car on a wintry morning. *Think*, she told herself, but even that instruction moved through her slowly. Jeff had just invented some bullshit story designed to conceal the fact that she had been beaten up in broad daylight, as plainly as she had been followed and, she now remembered with nauseous horror, watched by a camera hidden in her bathroom. Her friend and closest colleague had been subject to a crude honey trap. Her car had been unaccountably clamped. And all of it had happened straight after Maddy had published a brief piece putting the garrison in the frame. Why would Jeff be covering for even part of that effort?

What can I say, the Chief of Police always liked me.

She moved fractionally, which brought signals of pain from her ribs and between her legs. She touched herself there again, to explore the soreness. She had been hit very hard and very deliberately, the manner of the beating designed to send a message: that once roused, the forces behind the garrison could follow her, watch her and hit her where it hurts. They would show no delicacy just because she was a woman.

She needed to stay focused. What did she really know of Jeff Howe? That he had long been keen on her, persistently so. What else? That he was ambitious. And that his ambition was justified: when she was on the crime beat, the LAPD gossip had regularly tipped Howe for promotion, eventually even as a future Chief of Police. Somewhere small to start with – San Luis Obispo, say, or out of state – but afterwards, who knows? He looked the part: forty, salt-and-pepper hair, good with the media. So if it came to a clash, her wellbeing or his career, what would he choose?

The conversation was not hard to imagine, Jarrett promising to get Howe back on track in return for his help smoothing over a wrinkle created by a particularly stubborn reporter. 'You may even know her a little bit. Anyway, will you help me out, Jeff?' The detective might have known of Jarrett's corrupt relationship with the garrison, he might not. He certainly didn't need to have been complicit in it. The fact that the Chief was asking him would have been reason enough to say yes.

It was hard to keep her eyes open, but she did not want to sleep. She'd been asleep too long already. She needed to know what was happening, out there, beyond these four walls. With great effort, sending red flashes along her sides, shooting through her neck and radiating hotly from her groin, she stretched for the TV remote. She clicked until she found local news.

She had to sit through an item on the Winter Olympics. *Yet more disappointment for Team USA, as America's golden couple crash out of the figure skating competition – and the medal drought continues.* Then a business story about yet another audacious foreign bid to buy up a quintessentially US brand: *Now even the ketchup on your burger is not American.* Finally, they had what she was waiting for.

Let's return to our main story here on KTLA News at Eleven, the arrest of a suspect in the Abigail Webb murder investigation. A twenty-eight-year-old man, named tonight as Justin Brooks, is in police custody. Brooks was perhaps fatefully caught on CCTV at the bar of the Great Hall of the People restaurant and club where Abigail was last seen on the night of her death. Earlier, KTLA correspondent Janice Rossi caught up with Mario Padilla, who's been leading a high-profile campaign on the issue and who believes his own sister Rosario was murdered last month.

'*I welcome the arrest of Justin Brooks. My family and all our supporters will now let this investigation run its course and we look forward to the findings of the police and the courts. Thank you very much.*'

'*Mario, will you be suspending your campaign?*'

'*Right now, we're going to give some time to the authorities to do their work. All we and the other families have ever wanted is to bring the killer of our loved ones to justice.*'

'*But everything you've been saying . . . the demonstration outside the garrison?*'

'*Like I say, I want this investigation to run its course. Let's get to the bottom of who did these terrible crimes. If it's proved there was no link to the garrison, I will be the first to apologize. I'll have no problem with that at all.*'

'*And the rally you were planning outside the base for next week?*'

'*That's on hold. Thanks. Thank you.*'

Mario Padilla there, talking with KTLA's Janice Rossi. Let's get a weather update. Al, can I put away my hat and gloves any time soon? Whatcha got for us?

Madison clicked on the remote, cycled once through all the available channels, stopping at what had become the number one sitcom, a show set during the height of the Cold War about a suburban dad obsessively building and then equipping a nuclear bomb shelter in his yard, his wife and kids shrugging, sighing and generally mocking his delusions about leading the American resistance the day the Russians invade. All the comedies seemed to be like that these days: hapless American men, with absurdly grandiose dreams. She watched for a few minutes, managing a painful chuckle or two, clicked a few more times before falling into a fitful sleep, one powered by codeine and punctuated by dreams of smog and bombs and men sitting at bars, their faces always just out of view.

Maddy did not know it, but she had been asleep for more than six straight hours when the words on the TV seeped into her consciousness, like floodwater coming in under the door. At first, they simply mingled with her dreams: 'body' and 'police' and 'midnight' fitting effortlessly into the tales spinning at REM-speed through her brain.

But something in the repetition of them finally winched her up from the bottom of the sea and forced her awake. It felt like the dead of night though it was in fact dawn, as she heard the sunrise anchor on KTLA speaking his peculiar news dialect.

Again, details sketchy now, the picture emerging as we get it. But Los Angeles Police Department sources telling KTLA this hour that the body of a woman has been found in the Burbank area, the woman having suffered an apparent heroin overdose. She is thought to be in her early twenties, found at home in the early hours of this morning by her boyfriend, who was returning, we're told, from a late shift. KTLA has learned that he found the woman laid out on the floor, with drugs paraphernalia nearby.

Maddy tried to sit up, but the mattress had been lowered. Instead she widened her eyes and stared at the screen.

Let's cross live to senior crime correspondent Valerie Walker. Valerie?

Standing by a line of 'Do Not Cross' tape, the indigo sky of dawn broken by flashing police lights, Valerie Walker proceeded to repeat everything the anchor had just said, almost word for word. But as the words sank in, Maddy heard something new.

'Now, of course, no word on this from the LAPD yet – but the way in which this woman was found will inevitably lead to speculation that this is another victim of the so-called "heroin killer" said to be behind three unexplained deaths in the city in the last few weeks, including of course the murder of Abigail Webb, found dead just four days ago.'

Maddy felt herself do an involuntary wince, like a twitch. The casualness with which her sister had become public property still shocked her, even though she had no doubt that there were plenty, Quincy for one, who would say she had added to it.

'There are some details which KTLA is still trying to verify but which would suggest what forensic experts call a "signature" used by the killer – a signature apparently found once again in this case. Confirmation of that as and when we get it. Scott?'

And is this something the police are telling you, Valerie?

'Not officially, Scott. LAPD officials giving us very few details. But, and I must stress KTLA has not been able to independently verify this, some of these details are now emerging via social media. There is a Weibo account, apparently in the name of the dead woman's boyfriend and he, incredibly, has been weibing some key facts of the case. He went onto Weibo within an hour and a half of discovering his girlfriend's body. The weib from him, or apparently from him, reads: "This is what they did to my baby. Just like they did to that other girl."'

Maddy could feel the first inklings of adrenalin release into her system. Valerie was still talking.

'Now we must stress, this is not confirmed yet. We need to verify that for you here on KTLA and we'll be doing that as the morning goes on. Some very disturbing photographs now coming to light, which we are also hoping to check. But the claim that this is the latest in a series of killings, that's certainly what we're picking up on social media sites and we expect the police to be facing questions on that just as soon as they call a press conference later in the morning. Scott?'

But what are police saying about the fact that this death – this murder *perhaps – happened just hours after their prime suspect for the so-called heroin killings was arrested and taken into custody?*

'Police saying nothing about that, Scott. But that's gotta be a big question as this story develops. As you know, LAPD officials were very upbeat last night, one briefing journalists that, "We've got our man." And now this. It'll be a big blow to morale at the LAPD, little doubt of that. As we've been reporting on KTLA, this has been a high-profile, high-priority case for the Department: from the top down, they've wanted this case resolved. There's been political fallout, as you know, so stakes very high for the LAPD. But if this latest death is indeed linked to the others, and that means the heroin killer is still at large, well, that means the man currently in police custody is not who the LAPD thought he was – and it means much more besides. Scott?'

Almost noiselessly, the door opened to reveal a woman in whites wheeling in a trolley. She had a kindly face, maternal, even if she was probably no more than five years older than Maddy. If she'd had to guess, Maddy would have identified the nurse as from the Philippines or perhaps Vietnam.

'Ah, you're awake!'

'Have I been asleep long?' Maddy replied, her voice thicker than she expected.

'Quite long. Since your husband was here last night, fast asleep!'

'He's not my husband.'

'I forget. No one in LA get married. Everyone wait! If I have handsome boyfriend, I get married!'

'He's not my boyfriend.'

'Oh.' She seemed crestfallen. 'Maybe he wanna be your boyfriend? Hold on, I take your temperature.'

With that, she jammed a white revolver into Maddy's ear, or at least that's how it felt. The thermometer made a brief popping noise before the nurse withdrew it for inspection. Once that was done, Maddy asked the nurse if she'd mind bringing over her phone, which lay on the night table charging. Madison had no memory of putting it there.

The nurse did as she was asked, her smile now gone. Perhaps she'd wanted a chat; Maddy worried she'd offended her. But there was no time. As the nurse brusquely placed the blood pressure sleeve on her arm, Maddy read the pair of texts that greeted her. Three from Quincy, the first a terse *Where are you?*, the second a more concerned, *I hear you're in hospital. I'll be there right away.* The third said, *Planned to come visit. Nurses said you were fast asleep and not to be disturbed.* And one from Katharine: *Oh darling, I heard what happened. I'm so sorry. Enrica says enough is enough. You have to stop running, come here and let us look after you. She's made soup.*

Maddy opened up Weibo where, just as KTLA had said, the early morning chatter was about the discovery of this fourth corpse in as many weeks. Much of it was marvelling at the sheer strangeness of the dead woman's boyfriend weibing so soon after discovering her. It was another Weibo milestone, wrote the *LA Times* columnist who had set himself up as a sage of the medium.

Maddy scrolled past all that. Like most reporters, she hungered for facts not commentary. To her amazement, there was a huge amount of what purported to be concrete detail. It seemed the boyfriend had indeed posted pictures of the immediate scene, before the police had arrived to take charge. One picture had been repeatedly removed but, Weibo being Weibo, it would simply pop up, reposted, elsewhere. It took patience – a double dose of it, given how slow and clumsy Madison's fingers had become – but eventually she found it.

It showed the body of the woman the man had found, the photo cropped at the neck, which at least gave a measure of anonymity if not dignity. She had been wearing a dress buttoned down the middle and either the boyfriend had opened it or he had found her this way, but the dress was undone, exposing the woman's naked stomach and legs, bra and under-wear. Madison saw instantly why the boyfriend had both photographed it and posted it.

At the centre of the image was a single red poppy that appeared to have been tucked carefully into the woman's underwear, so that it lay at a diagonal across her private parts. It was a confusing image, at once both gentle – like a long-stemmed rose, placed on a lover's pillow – and a violation, for it represented an intrusion into the most inti-mate place.

All Madison could think of were the words she had heard on the TV news. *What forensic experts call a 'signature' used by the killer.* She knew all about those. They were the distin-guishing characteristic of any serial case.

The reporter was obviously referring to this photo, but what had she gone on to say? *A signature apparently found once again in this case.* Once again. Meaning that the reporter had reason to believe this same signature, the poppy in the underwear, had been found on the bodies of the three other women – including Abigail.

Amy Alice, Mario Padilla and Jessica had never mentioned a flower, poppy or otherwise. But why would they? The dead women they had found had been clothed. The poppy was a calling card that would have been found by the police or coroner only, once they came to undress the deceased. It would have been a secret message from the killer to his pursuers. And they had kept it secret.

Her thoughts were too fast for her still-sluggish brain, the engine was revving but the wheels were just spinning. She tried to take it stage by stage. If she was right, the police had known what she had been working so hard to prove: that they were confronting a serial killer. Why would they keep that quiet from the very start?

She wanted to say it was because they – like everyone else in this city – was terrified of the China connection and the trouble it could bring. The red poppy was all the warning they needed. Jarrett, thinking of his paymasters, would have issued his edict and the LAPD would have fallen into line.

Or perhaps it was like any one of half a dozen cases she had covered, legitimately subject to a news blackout. Sometimes the cops did that, purely as a tactic: starve the killer of the glory he was after, see what move he made. Publicity would only reward him – and spread panic through the city.

So it might not have been craven fear or corruption that explained why the police had apparently refused to see what she had seen. But it made her angry all the same. The effort, the pain, they could have spared her if they had only shared what they knew.

She went back to Weibo, now filling with word traced first to 'rumour' and then, from a clutch of credible journalists, to 'LAPD sources'. They quoted police insiders confirming that, yes, there had long been a 'dark team' working on the assumption that they were confronting a serial killer.

But that was not the main focus of online interest. More attention was devoted to the other pictures taken by the bereaved boyfriend. There was enough there to draw out every wannabe forensic scientist with an internet connection. One showed a hypodermic needle and various drug-related bits of kit which, the armchair analysts decreed, appeared to have been abandoned in a hurry. It was turning into the LAPD's worst nightmare: a crowdsourced homicide investigation.

Madison skimmed over most of it, her first priority to discover the identity of the victim. Thanks to the boyfriend's stance of full disclosure, that was not difficult. Within a few clicks, Maddy was looking at a picture of her. Blonde and twentysomething. Next to Abigail, Eveline and Rosario, she could have been a cousin – or a sister.

Then she went back through the Weibo feed, to look again at one message from an amateur expert that had barely registered first time around. She wondered if she had read it wrong. But there it was. She clicked on the profile of the sender: he was not a nut.

The nurse had stopped her ministrations, removing the blood pressure cuff. Maddy attempted a smile. 'Sorry about this,' she said, indicating her phone. 'Just some family members I need to tell. You know, that I'm here.'

'Oh, you no worry. Everyone busy in LA. No one have time to talk.'

'Can you tell me something? Where are the painkillers coming into me?'

The nurse pointed at the cannula on the top of Maddy's right hand, while she packed away her testing equipment. 'It working, yes? It help you sleep?'

'Yes. Thank you,' Maddy said. 'I might try to sleep now.'

'You no want breakfast?'

Maddy shook her head. 'Just some sleep.'

Once the nurse was gone, Maddy stayed put with her eyes closed. Give it ten seconds, she thought, in case the woman comes back. Maddy counted up to eight but could wait no longer. She reached immediately for the tube and then took an educated guess, based largely on watching Charlie Hughes's medical show, on how to remove it. Once it was disconnected, the machine at her bedside sent out an electronic cry of pain but she had only to press the 'cancel' button to halt it. Next came the saline, entering her via her left arm: same process. Finally, and most painfully, the catheter. She prepared herself by putting the corner of a pillow in her mouth: she would bite down hard rather than let out the whelp of pain that she knew was coming. She closed her eyes, gave the tube a tug and let her teeth sink deep into the cushion.

Madison knew that she needed several hours' rest, both to recover and to let the codeine wash out of her system. But there was no time. In the torrent of speculation, RIP messages and half-rumours she had scrolled through on Weibo, a single line had stopped her. It meant that she had to get out of here. And it told her exactly where she needed to go.

Chapter 39

Getting out of bed had required an enormous effort of will, her legs barely answering to her command. Her limbs were impossibly heavy one moment, apparently drifting away from her the next. Somehow she got to the other side of the room, where her clothes were still in a closet. She dressed standing up, clutching hold of the door handle. Journeying to the bathroom would have demanded, and wasted, too much effort. She cursed her jeans as she pulled up the zip, so tight that she was reminded of the shocking place those boots had struck.

She emerged from her room, hobbled past the nurses' station staring straight ahead, summoning all her will and energy to walk in a straight, purposeful line. Her prime objective was to avoid all eye contact. A voyage that felt as long and exhausting as any she had undertaken brought her to the elevator. She pressed the call button and finally allowed herself to breathe out.

'Miss?' A voice, female, calling out from behind. One of the nurses. 'Oh, miss?'

Don't turn around, she thought. *Don't turn around.*

'Miss Webb, is that you?' The voice was getting nearer, coming towards her on the corridor.

Come on, come on. She could see the cables twitching and

moving behind the glass of the elevator shaft. At last, it was there. She stepped in, her fingers finding the close button: she kept pressing it until at last the doors drew together, leaving just a parting glimpse of a nurse she had never seen before. Maddy looked away as quickly as she could, but not soon enough she feared. Chances were, the woman had seen her face. Still, she got to the ground floor where she called a cab and lurked in a locked stall in the ladies' room until it arrived, announcing its presence by text message.

Once in the back seat, she read out the address on Hollywood Boulevard she had retrieved from the phone. Thank God they still made movies in this town, she thought, at last allowing herself to sit back and breathe.

To guard against interruption, the anti-smog mask she had snaffled from the hospital remained glued to her face. It was a reliable rule: when you wore it, taxi drivers were less eager to talk. Conversation was such an effort – each word muffled, requiring constant repetition – that most didn't bother. She could stay still and quiet and concentrate.

In truth, such a feat seemed impossible. Her body seemed to be suspended in a flotation tank; she imagined herself enveloped in a viscous liquid, containing the nutrients she needed to survive. Being halfway between wakefulness and sleep was not unusual for her. But this sensation was different: the heavy dose of codeine was urging her to shut down her brain and let the drug do its work. It wanted her to float away.

She looked back at her phone, staring at the short message, barely more than a hundred characters, on Weibo that she had kept open, as if fearful it might vanish if she clicked away from it. A postgrad at Berkeley had seen the weibed image of the latest crime scene and had noticed something amongst the paraphernalia: the discarded bag that had apparently contained the lethal drug.

Only one type of H comes packaged like that. Prepared to wager that the killer used #3.

That meant nothing to Maddy first time round and nothing, it seemed, to anyone else on her timeline. No one had picked it up. But even through the thick analgesic cloud, a distant bell had rung. Something she had seen in the early hours of Wednesday morning, when she worked through the night, reading and reading and eventually writing the story that Howard Burke had taken down after fifteen minutes. The reference had come in an extended piece that had appeared on one of those quasi-literary, high-end websites, journalism dressed up as art. She could see the headline: *Strangers Among Us*.

The writer had spun an imagined, interminably long account of life in the LA garrison, the facts few and generously spaced. The most memorable passage was about drug use on the base, how it was officially forbidden, punishable by death or extended imprisonment, yet was said to be surprisingly widespread. Not among the regular soldiers, of course, but among the officer class elite. The drug of choice was cocaine, but some heroin leaked through too. It was not bought on the street market, but smuggled in via the shipments that came to the garrison each week from the home country. Heroin #3 was Beijing heroin. It was found nowhere in the United States except in the string of pearls, the PLA bases along the west coast, chief among them Garrison 41 at Terminal Island by the Port of Los Angeles.

They pulled up on Hollywood and Hudson. Maddy had checked the store's opening hours and she was in luck. Better still, it was too early for tourists: later on in the day and a shop like this could be heaving. Right now, the neighbourhood – of pizzerias, tacky murals on shuttered storefronts and signs promising 'maps of the stars' homes' – was just waking up, the cheap coffee barely brewed. She took the driver's cellphone number and told him to keep driving around the block until she called. She then took a few slow, ginger steps and went inside Hollywood Wigs.

The shop was cramped and crammed, like the toy stores of her childhood, each shelf filled with an identity parade of mannequin heads, all frozen in the same, wide-eyed stare suggesting vague alarm. But Maddy wasn't there to look at the Barbie-doll faces. She wanted to look at their hair. Wild, Medusa-style snakes of red and yellow on one, Marilyn-style platinum on another, geisha black on the third. There were crazy purple curls, and Betty Boop bobs, untamed auburn and Princess Leia brown. Madison was disappointed. Her internet search had promised a specialist wig service, regularly used by the movie business; this looked more like a novelty shop, the provider of comedy hair for Hallowe'en.

'Can I help?'

Asking the question was a short, older woman in thick glasses, her hair so daringly unfashionable that Madison wondered if she had lifted it from one of her dummies. She was wearing a housecoat, as if she had just come in from her kitchen. Now that Maddy thought about it, perhaps she had.

'I want to be blonde,' Madison said quickly. 'As convincing a blonde as I can be.'

The woman gave Maddy a glance up and down, followed by a grandmotherly look of concern as she assessed her face. Then, in a gesture whose tenderness caught her by surprise, she reached up and touched Maddy's hair. 'This is because of the treatment, yes?'

The feeling of an older woman's fingers on her hair, the gentleness of her voice, made Maddy's eyes prick. She had stroked her mother's hair in recent years, but she could not remember the last time her mother had done the same for her. She felt movement behind her tear ducts. But it went no further, dammed up by the drugs or the need to get on, it didn't matter which.

'When did you start?' the woman said, still assessing Maddy's hair. It felt wrong to lie about such things and especially to a woman like this, but she was not going to complicate matters by correcting her.

'I've just come from the hospital,' is what Maddy said. 'And I need a wig.'

'Well, dear. Take a seat and I'll show you what we have. You can look at textures and lengths and then we can make up a—'

'I'm afraid I don't have much time.'

The woman nodded, her lips forming a shape of resigned sympathy.

'No, no,' Maddy said quickly. 'I mean I don't have much time this morning. I need to have a wig right now. One that's ready-made.'

'Oh, but, dear, for this situation it's better to have one that looks like your hair. And that takes time.'

'I need to be blonde. And I need to make the change now.' Maddy held up her hand, blocking any further protest. 'I'm sure it's crazy. But it's what I need right now. Please help me.'

The woman retreated to the storeroom, her eyebrows raised and her palms up in surrender, the whatever-you-say gesture people make when complying with the demands of the unhinged. It was a gesture Madison had seen often.

She emerged seventeen minutes after she had gone in, her hair a close-cropped blonde. As she levered herself slowly back into the cab, she caught a glimpse of herself in the rear-view mirror. The woman looking back at her seemed older but, unexpectedly, somehow sexier too. The shorter hair was less innocent, more knowing. She could not have said why.

The driver was talking to her. 'Where to now?'

She thumbed through her past emails until she found the office address of the only person she could think of who might be able to get her where she needed to go. That he was also a doctor was a bonus.

*　　*　　*

333

Charlie Hughes shared his practice with two other physicians on Wilshire and Crescent in Beverly Hills, a building wedged between upscale boutiques and a Maserati dealership. The instant Maddy walked into the reception, she half-regretted giving him even the distracted, eyes-glazed sympathy she had provided at least half a dozen times over the years. All his whining, you'd have thought he was waiting tables or shining shoes while he waited for his big Hollywood break. Instead, he was clearly making a mint treating the aches and pains of the Beverly Hills set.

Still, it was only a half-regret. Had she not been a rare, friendly face to him, most recently at the Mail Room that night, the gambit she was about to play would not have had even its current, wafer-thin chance.

She thought of giving her name at the desk, but seeing the waiting room already filled, at nine in the morning, with the surgerized faces and manicured nails of half a dozen ladies of leisure, she changed her mind. She sent a text instead.

Charlie. It's Maddy Webb. I'm in your lobby. That might work, she thought. But just to make sure, she added three more words. *Hollywood is calling.*

Fifteen seconds later and Charlie emerged, dressed this time as a doctor rather than a pining movie wannabe. Set against his white coat, his dark hair and thick-rimmed glasses now looked impressive rather than nerdy. She noticed the evil looks she was getting from the mannequins: *how did* she *get to jump the line?*

'Maddy? Is that you? You look awful.'

'Thanks, Charlie.'

'I mean, you don't look well. Here.' He led her to an empty consulting room where, to her relief, he invited her to sit down on the examination bed. 'What the hell's going on? I've been hearing all this stuff about you. And what's with the hair?'

334

She gave the most potted version she could manage. She didn't need to do much more, given that the key elements had been on the news.

'I should have called you about Abigail,' he said finally. 'I just didn't know how . . . there's been so much going on . . .'

You mean you're so self-absorbed the idea never crossed your mind, Maddy thought but didn't say. Instead she replied, 'What, with *Devil Monk*? They gonna make your film?' She heard her own feigned enthusiasm and thought it didn't sound bad, considering.

He shook his head. 'I love that you remember that project, Madison. It proves I'm right: audiences will fucking love this movie.' His face clenched on the word 'love'. Then he remembered himself. 'But I'm sure you didn't come here to talk movies. Not at a time like this.'

'As it happens . . .' She did not want to ask him for help. She doubted that would work. She had another approach she would try first. 'There is something that could come out of this.'

'How'd you mean?'

'Put it this way, this news story is already pretty dramatic, right?'

'Sure.'

'When that piece of mine appeared online, and was taken down? I don't want to say too much, but when that happened there was some . . . *interest*.'

Charlie Hughes's eyes brightened. 'You mean . . . ?'

She nodded.

'Like a major studio?'

She nodded again. 'All I'm saying is, it's not like it hasn't happened before. *LA Times* stories have become movies. Some reporters like to write the screenplays themselves. But some like to, you know, hand it over to an experienced screenwriter.' Her eyes bored into his. 'Someone who knows what they're doing.'

335

He gave her his serious face, as if to say 'I won't let you down.'

'But there's something the story needs, Charlie. If it's to work. And truly you're the only person who can make it happen.'

Chapter 40

He gave her something for the pain, something that would, he said, help her more than codeine and without making her woozy. He was not specific about the name and his tone suggested dubious legality. She suspected a Chinese import but was too tired to probe.

'Now,' he said, pulling up a seat in the consulting room for the first time. 'What's the plan?'

She walked him through each step. What he would say, what they would say in response, what he would say next and what he should do if anything went wrong. She explained her role and how it would relate to his. She offered a modest backstory, including responses to any possible objections. She was methodical, imagining and addressing the range of possible scenarios in a way that would, she understood, astonish anyone who knew her physical state. Charlie, for one, appeared stunned. But what Maddy knew about herself was that such calm, forensic rigour did not represent some kind of remarkable defiance of her medical and emotional situation. It was confirmation of it. This was how she reacted under extreme stress: like the control room of a nuclear power plant, she would cool automatically under pressure. It didn't make her feel any better.

He heard her out, asking some shrewd questions. But, troublingly for Maddy, they had a common theme: fear. 'It's a little risky, Madison,' he said after five minutes. 'I can't do it,' he said after fifteen.

Madison had prepared for this. Indeed, she had expected it, considering it far likelier than a yes. She had readied her response.

'OK, are you absolutely sure about this? That your final answer?' She gave a weak smile.

He nodded.

'OK,' Maddy said. 'But you're still going to do it.'

'No, Maddy, I'm not,' Charlie replied, offering a mirthless smile of his own. 'Maybe I wasn't clear. Your scheme is way too dangerous, especially given my position. I'm not going to do it. No way.'

'No, Charlie, you will do it. Because if you don't I'm going to write that you've been identified by police sources as the likely supplier of illegal drugs, including heroin, to the garrison and possibly to the killer himself.'

'What?'

'You heard me.'

'You've got to be kidding. There's no way you'd write that. The police would deny it in a second.'

'Not a second. It would take at least fifteen minutes. That's how long my story about the China connection was up on the *Times* website before it was taken down. Long enough for it to go right around the world, long enough for it to trigger one of the biggest mass demonstrations this city has ever seen. Want one of those outside this office, Charlie?' She made a show of tilting her head towards the front entrance, as if she were imagining the thousands gathering outside at this very moment.

The doctor was paling, his skin beginning to match his coat. 'You wouldn't dare. It would, it would . . . ruin your reputation, making up shit like that.'

'Oh sure, I'd weib a correction a few hours later. I reckon people would be pretty forgiving. Stress of the situation and all that. I might even offer an apology.' She fluttered her eyelids, a picture of sweet innocence. 'But the damage would be done, by then. To you, I mean. What do you think they'd be saying in there?' She nodded towards the waiting room. '"No smoke without fire," they'd say. "And that girl from the *LA Times* has been right about everything else. She's got all those awards. Must be something to it." Maybe we'll go see Dr Cohen instead.' She smiled again.

He shook his head, his eyes kept firmly on his feet. 'You know, it's true what the guys say about you, Madison.'

'Oh and what's that, Charlie?'

'That you might be a great fuck but you're one messed-up, crazy bitch.'

'Well, now you know at least half of that is true, don't you, Charlie? So get your car keys. We've got some people to visit.'

Before they left, Charlie sent Maddy off to what he insisted on calling a 'fitting' with one of the nurses. He made clear this was not any kind of favour to her. Rather he was engaged in 'risk-minimization'. When Maddy emerged, she was dressed in white cotton trousers with a jacket that buttoned at the side. She caught a glimpse of herself, bruised and exhausted, in the mirror: she looked like a beautician in need of one of her own treatments.

They went in Charlie's car, an Audi convertible. As she walked unsteadily across the street, a childhood memory of Fords and Chevys floated into her head. How long ago that seemed. These days, if you had money, you wanted a European import. If you were on Maddy's kind of income, you drove Chinese.

She gave one last look over each shoulder, concluding that whoever had been pursuing her before, including the men who had beaten her, had apparently been thrown off the scent. The blonde wig and the nurse's outfit might have helped.

As they drove down the 405, Charlie demanded they go through the plan one more time, saying each element of it to himself, committing it to memory. He had not come around to it; he remained hostile to the very idea, convinced it was suicidal in its risk. Even once he realized he had no choice but to comply, he did not give up hope of persuading Madison that her plan was doomed and that she should think again. But she would not budge.

Motivated solely by the desire to save his own skin, he worked through with her the possible defects, Maddy doing her best to insure against them. Intermittently her mind became as clogged and cloudy as the smog-filled air all around them, but as they headed south on the 110 she decided she could do no more. This was the best she could come up with.

As they got nearer, Charlie's fear hardened and solidified. If he could have backed out, he would. But together they had concocted a story that, with refinements and in the absence of any alternative, he glumly accepted as sufficiently plausible to try.

Charlie was known to the guards on the gate, his car was on their system, which was an advantage. But it didn't mean he could just stroll into the garrison whenever he chose. Usually he would come for a specific appointment, his patient letting security know in advance that he was to be admitted.

That had been Maddy's first thought. Charlie should call one of his patients, saying he was concerned about recent test results: having looked at them again, the doctor would say he had detected what he believed was an alarming pattern and it would be best if he came over right away.

'That's unethical on so many levels, Maddy.'

'Afterwards, you can say it was a rogue test. The worrying

340

numbers turned out to be wrong. Don't tell me that doesn't happen all the time.'

'It happens. But not *deliberately*.'

'You mean you might get a summons to the LA medical board on a minor ethical violation? That would be *terrible*.'

That hushed him. Next, with a great show of reluctance, Dr Hughes enunciated into his in-car microphone the name of the patient from the base he had seen most recently. It was the Princeling he had waved to at the Mail Room that night; it turned out the young officer had come in for an examination earlier that day. It was ideal; his test results had only just come through. Dutifully, the Bluetooth device dialled the number. They waited as the phone rang.

There was no reply. Maddy shook her head at leaving a message. 'Call another one.'

Hughes tried half a dozen patients among the garrison's officer corps, all without success. 'I think their access to cellphones is restricted during the day. Or maybe they're on, you know, manoeuvres or something,' Charlie offered. Maddy came up with an alternative that she explained in the briefest terms.

'That's even worse than the first idea,' he said. 'I'll get struck off.'

'Which will leave you more time for writing. Come on.'

As the car nudged through the traffic, the fumes thickening the winter smog, they went over each possible scenario once again, what Charlie should say and, more important, what he should not say. The more they discussed it, the more Maddy's confidence waned.

She must have dozed because suddenly they were there, slowing down as they crossed the Vincent Thomas Bridge to Terminal Island and approached the outer perimeter of the base. There was a checkpoint to clear first, the traffic funnelled into a single lane, two LAPD officers on either side of it. One was carrying a scanning device which he aimed at the Audi's licence plate. The other beckoned Charlie to inch forward, then asked him to wind down his window and present his photo ID.

'How y'all doin' today?'

'We're OK,' Charlie replied, solemnly. Oh no, thought Maddy. This had been her greatest worry about Hughes. That he would start *acting*. He was playing the part of the concerned doctor, weighed down by the grave news he was about to deliver.

'And who's this with you, Dr Hughes?' the officer said, returning the ID.

'This is Nurse Kelly Michaels, who works with me,' he said, too emphatically, as he handed over the ID card he had requisitioned from the most junior of the three medical assistants he employed. Maddy smiled from behind her smog mask, which she pointedly did not remove.

The officer took a look at the picture, then back into Maddy's eyes. His next words made her throat seize up.

'Can you remove your mask for me, ma'am?'

She did as she was told while, at the same time, holding out her hand. She had not planned it. The move was pure instinct. But as she lowered the mask to reveal her face, habit made him hand back the ID card. When he looked at her, he compared what he saw – blonde, thirty years old, give or take – to his memory of the face he had just seen. It was a classic case of priming, the brain seeing what it expected to see. Without knowing he was doing it, the LAPD officer made the face in front of him comply with that of Kelly Michaels. He decided they were close enough and waved the car through.

Charlie let his relief show by breaking into a wide smile.

'Not yet, Charlie,' Maddy hissed, her mask now back on.

They drove on until they reached the main, sliding metal gates. Now the guards wore a different uniform and a more severe expression. They were soldiers of the People's Liberation Army. Once again, Charlie wound down the window and handed over the ID cards, both of them this time. As they had agreed he would, he began speaking to the guard in Mandarin.

He was effusive, talking away as the guard swiped his way through the electronic pages of his tablet, apparently checking their names against a list. Smiling and dipping his head in a show of courtesy, Charlie appeared to be explaining that his nurse was new to the base. She couldn't be sure: his Mandarin was better than hers. But the doctor's charm seemed to work.

They were asked to step out of their vehicle, while two more PLA guards appeared, one carrying a boom with a circular mirror at one end. He proceeded to probe under the car, looking for any explosive devices. The second soldier asked Charlie to open the trunk. Once it was cleared, a third soldier materialized, took Charlie's key and drove the car away, to a secured and guarded lot. Neat twist on LA valet parking, Maddy thought.

They were led next into a security hut, the entrance consisting of two airlock-style doors, the second only opening once the first was closed. More guards here, who mimed for them to stretch out their arms to be frisked. A female PLA soldier stepped forward to do Maddy, her face blank, refusing any sisterly eye contact. Meanwhile, Charlie's medical bag went through the scanner. No beeps. Finally, the guard manning the central desk, a kind of square island with a raised counter on all four sides, asked them to hand over their ID and cellphones.

Shit. Why had Charlie not mentioned that? Maybe he had and, in her codeined stupor, she had missed it. One look at the contents of that phone would blow her cover in an instant, to say nothing of the light it would shed on her investigation, in which every possible sign now pointed to this place.

She pretended to search for it, asking to look inside Charlie's bag. She opened the bag wide and, as deftly as she could, slipped the phone from her pocket inside. While continuing her fake rummaging, she removed the back cover of the device and, using her fingernails, popped out the SIM and micro SD cards. 'It's here!' she said, raising it aloft, showing off its lit screen as requested – thereby proving it was no fake concealing an explosive device – and finally handing in a phone that was safely neutered.

After that, they were released from the other end of the security hut, where yet another soldier offered to escort them to their destination. Maddy threw Charlie a look: *Are we going to be chaperoned every minute we're here?*

He said nothing, immersing himself instead in his role as the dutiful doctor. He had asked to be taken to the medical facility as soon as possible and he would offer no sign that he was here for any other purpose. Maddy's job was to walk as fast as she could manage and reveal no hint of the howling pain coursing through her nervous system.

She looked around. The place was vast. Charlie had told her that it accommodated a brigade of seven battalions plus support units. Those terms meant less to her than a fact she already knew: that with around seven hundred officers and men in each battalion, the PLA presence in Los Angeles amounted to nearly six thousand troops. And yet she had pictured something more compact, certainly not this, a sprawling complex that stretched as far as she could see. There were sheds, storing vehicles and equipment, but also large, empty spaces. They passed through an avenue of trees, flanked by flowerbeds. Now they came to what was either a small farm or an oversized vegetable patch. It was not for show: Maddy could see the winter vestiges of a potato crop.

The pain was intensifying; this walk seemed to be taking forever. She could see hardly any buildings, let alone the clinic they were looking for. She wondered if they were being led into wasteland.

Then a shot. And another. Involuntarily, and in a sudden

movement, she turned her head over her right shoulder, sending a flash of hurt down that side of her body.

'Firing range,' said Charlie, quietly. 'Behind the assault course.'

It was distant, the view poor thanks to the gauze of smog, but she could make it out, in a field to her right: the hurdles and climbing walls, the curtains of webbing and wide troughs of muddy water, surmounted in succession by khaki-clad men in twos and threes. And then, a short distance later, more noise, this time from an asphalt square that functioned as a parade ground. On it were rows of young Chinese, arranged in perfectly ordered lines, shouting in time with each other as they appeared to engage in unarmed combat with an invisible opponent, throwing neatly choreographed punches into the air. At the end of each sequence, they instantly began running on the spot, the combination of so many fit, trained young feet pounding on the ground at once making a thunderous drumroll. None of the officers caught their eye, even though Charlie and Maddy appeared to be the only outsiders around. The soldiers looked right through them.

Charlie was tilting his head leftward, urging Maddy to glance over toward the other side of the path. There, perhaps fifty yards away, stood a billboard-size TV screen, lit in the brightest high-definition red. Suddenly a string of Chinese characters appeared in luminous yellow. Charlie made an instant, whispered translation: *Patriotism, Innovation, Inclusiveness, Virtue*. That familiar slogan dissolved, replaced by another. Charlie told her this one called on the soldiers of the PLA to renounce 'the four types of decadence: formalism, bureaucratism, hedonism and extravagance.' Despite everything, Charlie looked like he was enjoying himself, playing the tour guide. He liked knowing something she didn't.

As their journey continued, they glimpsed yet more of these electronic hoardings, dotted at intervals around the base. One showed heroic images of the Army in action: columns of men

345

marching to war, tanks advancing through clouds of smoke. Another seemed dedicated to a dissolving slideshow of archive photographs in black-and-white: past heroes of the regiment, according to Charlie.

Meanwhile, one parade square had given way to another. This time the men were not shouting or shadow-fighting. They were moving through the fluid, graceful movements of tai-chi, executing them with synchronized perfection. Just like the dancers in Circle Park. Maddy felt a pinching sensation in her heart. She could see her mother and her blank, faraway face. The idea that she was in the same city, at this very moment, seemed absurd. Maddy felt as if she were ten thousand miles away.

'We're not far now,' Charlie said.

At last she could make out buildings that were not for storage or maintenance but for human occupation. As they got nearer, she could see the larger of the two. A column of soldiers was filing in through the double-doors of its main entrance, two-abreast, like children at elementary school. (For a passing instant, Maddy saw Abigail leading her pupils on a trip to the zoo.) From inside came the sound of a mass, communal lunch, a clattering, metallic din. Their uniformed guide ushered them in.

She had never seen a dining hall so huge, filled by three tables as long as a running track. Each soldier faced an identical steel tray-like plate, divided into compartments for each item of food, along with a separate steel bowl, containing soup or rice, Maddy couldn't quite tell. A group at the end of the table were talking animatedly, until they noticed the two Americans close by. They stopped, their eyes falling on her. She hardly believed it, given how rough she felt and the ridiculous nurse's uniform she was wearing, but she recognized the gaze: they were checking her out. Their tentative smiles suggested they liked what they saw. So this was what it was like to be blonde.

Their escort was beckoning them to follow him, down this endless refectory, with its echoing clang of steel cutlery. They did as they were told, Maddy avoiding the eyes she felt on her, until, halfway down, he guided them to an exit door. They were into one corridor, lined with posters depicting more regimental heroes from the 1940s, then another until finally she saw a symbol that assured her they had arrived at the garrison clinic. 'He took a short cut,' Charlie whispered. They had been walking for nearly twenty agonizing minutes.

Mercifully, the clinic opened up to them easily. The staff there recognized Charlie and greeted him properly, if not warmly. A minute or two later, someone Maddy guessed was the senior medic on duty appeared and shook them both by the hand. In his fifties, with thinning dark hair and eyes that suggested curiosity, he introduced himself as Dr Lei and showed them to his office where, at last, Maddy could sit down. His English was fluent, spoken in a strangely hybrid, trans-Pacific accent.

'What seems to be the trouble, Charlie?'

Charlie did what Maddy hoped he would not do, shooting a nervous glance in her direction, like an actor hoping for a prompt. She dipped her head, as if to remind him that he, not she, was in charge.

'I came here right away,' he began, 'because I think we may have a problem.'

'What kind of problem, Dr Hughes? I'm afraid I've been out of the country for the last month, I'm not up to speed.'

He sighed. It was nerves but, thankfully, it came over as doctorly anxiety at the scale of the trouble he had unearthed. 'I've seen some alarming data, relating to several patients of mine. Patients here, I mean. In the garrison.'

'What kind of data?'

'Test results. Which suggest a presence of strychnine in the blood. I saw it in one man last week and was going to recall the patient for further—'

'Strychnine? How on earth would that get there?'

'Precisely the question I asked myself, Dr Lei. There is almost no history of that element being found in patients on the continental United States. In fact it rarely arises anywhere. The only case I could find was in the People's Republic. In Beijing.'

'I think you have something you're not saying, Dr Hughes.'

'The only time strychnine has been found in humans – the only case I can see anyway – was in Beijing. It came through a tainted batch of heroin. The "three" variety. I have now found three young men who exhibit a trace of that same element. Three men from here. The only conclusion I can come to is that they have been using—'

'Can I see those results, please?'

'I didn't bring them with me, Dr Lei. I decided they were too . . . sensitive.'

'You could have anonymized them.'

'With respect, I don't think it's the individual names that are sensitive. People know I treat patients here. They could put two and two—'

'I understand.' The military doctor rubbed his forehead. 'And what is it you propose to do?'

'Well, Dr Lei,' Charlie began, before an involuntary gulp swallowed the sound. His nerves were jangling, Maddy could see that. Especially because he knew he was coming to the key line. 'The money shot', he had called it on the way over here. 'We're both thinking of the safety of the men and women on this base. That's our number one priority, as it should—'

'What do you propose to *do*, Dr Hughes?'

'I think you need to think very hard, and very honestly, and draw up a list of the people on this base you believe might be users of this drug. I know that's going to be tough. And awkward. But I think we both know the drug is expensive. That only a very limited group of people would be likely to have access to such—'

'*Wuh tsow*,' Dr Lei said suddenly, more to himself than to anyone else. '*Wuh tsow.*' Even Maddy knew what those words meant. They did not yet threaten 'fuck' in English, but in California they had entered the language as a handy alternative.

'We can do this discreetly,' Charlie continued. 'But we need to start with the probable heroin users. Those likely to be paying for an imported cut. We need to test them. Because if they are carrying this element in their system, they need to be treated—'

'I know, I know. And we can test them here?'

They had planned for this. 'I don't think that's such a good idea. Then there'll be a record of the test on your system. Your nurses will have to be informed. I'm trying to minimise the risk of . . . embarrassment. For the garrison. I suggest we keep the circle of knowledge pretty tight.'

'So how then?'

'Back at my office. We can make appointments for all the men involved. Nurse Michaels here will do it. Quickly, with minimal fuss. I'll process the results and then you and I can decide what our next move should be. If those earlier numbers were wrong, then good. No problem. But if those results are positive a second time . . .' He let the sentence trail off, knowing the danger he had conjured would linger.

Lei now had his elbow on his knee, the better for rubbing his forehead more intensely. 'I should inform the Political Commissar,' he said quietly.

'You *could*,' said Charlie, now ad-libbing, since this had not been in their script. 'But, you know.' He made a ring of his fingers. 'The circle of knowledge. Tight.'

Dr Lei nodded and it required all of Maddy's energy not to empty her lungs of air in relief.

It took forty-five minutes for the doctor to assemble this gathering. De Lei had had to call in junior officers from across

349

the base, several of whom had pulled up in just the last few minutes in buggies that resembled golf-carts more than Jeeps. They were meeting in their accommodation block.

En route, Maddy had seen the difference. The regular blocks, for the regular conscripts, were spartan, functional buildings, three or four storeys high, with few concessions to comfort. The dormitories themselves were long and free of decoration, filled only by steel-framed bunk beds. Each one was identical: the bedding folded and squared away, no personal touches or mementoes to separate one from another.

Superficially, the junior officers' quarters looked similar. But the beds were single rather than bunks, the bedding fuller and thicker, each equipped with a bedside table and small closet rather than the single locker allocated to the other recruits. The bathroom was still communal, but was more generously appointed with proper light fittings rather than the exposed bulbs she had spotted in the main blocks. If the conscripts' barracks resembled a low-security prison, these reminded Maddy of the freshman dorm of an under-resourced college.

She waited along with Charlie while Dr Lei used his phone to co-ordinate the ingathering operation. To her relief, he had asked her nothing, all but ignoring her. She was just the nurse and he wanted to talk, doctor to doctor, only to Charlie. The longer she could remain exactly like this, silent and all but invisible, the safer she would be.

Twice though she had stepped forward to murmur something to Charlie, when he threatened to deviate dangerously off script. She noticed his hands were clammy.

Steadily, the young officers began to arrive, in two groups as far as she could work out. One had been pulled out of a lecture and were dressed in uniforms that were neatly pressed, the creases sharp as blades. The other came in out of breath and wearing khaki, their faces filmed with sweat. She guessed this group had been out supervising the men on the assault courses she had seen. After a few minutes, there were fourteen of them, all standing by their beds.

Her gaze moved from one face to another, studying each as carefully as she could without appearing to stare. She wondered what she should feel. It was one of them, all the evidence said that. These were the men suspected of having ready access to heroin and specifically the #3 batch which had been found a matter of hours earlier by the dead body of the woman now confirmed as Mary Doherty, trainee chef at the Cinematheque, a restaurant and movie theatre that was a favoured haunt of the Princeling set, not least because it showed first-run Chinese movies. Given everything else she knew, the probability was great that the killer was here, in this room. She looked from face to face. But all she could see was a kind of languid complacency, a fearlessness common to all of them. They were standing, but it was hardly to attention. It was in deference to the fact that Dr Lei was a captain and technically their superior, but their posture emphasized that it was only technically. They were recognizably the group she had seen at the Mail Room and elsewhere around Los Angeles: the spoiled sons of the Chinese elite whose default expression was boredom.

They were listening to what she assumed was Dr Lei's explanation of the situation, punctuated by gestures in Charlie's direction. The latter had gone very pale. He was petrified at what he had started, she could tell. He had not bargained for this. He had pictured a chat with Dr Lei, the handing over of a list of names that he could take with him, quiet dummy tests next week and then the whole prank could conclude and be forgotten. But a room full of young, powerful Chinese officers lined up by their beds, staring straight ahead as they now faced a serious disciplinary action that he had triggered? No, this was much more than he had signed up for, even under duress.

Maddy knew it was getting out of control as soon as Lei

started working the phones, despatching orders to bring in those he had deemed suspects. But there was nothing either of them could do. Though Charlie did try.

'There's really no need to disrupt the men's day immediately, we can—'

'No, Dr Hughes,' Lei said, raising his palm to demand hush. 'You said it was urgent. That means it's urgent.'

With that, the doctor had returned earnestly to his task, summoning the men he believed might have smuggled heroin into the base. Madison realized then that she had no idea what the punishment might be for such a crime. Now, her head dizzy with pain, tiredness and the thought she had just released, she guessed it would be extremely severe.

Then, as if performing another drilled exercise from the parade ground, they turned on Dr Lei's command in unison and walked the three paces to their bedside closets. More or less in time, they punched in the numbers that unlocked the cupboard doors. When those sprang open, they revealed what had been missing in the other barracks: photos, posters and stickers, marking each man out as an individual. The young officers stood to one side, like sentries, ready for inspection.

Dr Lei first walked through the aisle that ran down the centre of the dormitory, between the rows of beds, turning his head left or right as he did so, as if expecting to see a giant sack of heroin in one of the closets, so big it couldn't be missed. It took Maddy a while to realize that this was an exercise in intimidation – surprising in a small, cerebral-looking man, but intimidation all the same.

As he walked, Maddy did a survey of her own. Rooted to the spot, alongside Charlie, she could only glimpse the decoration on the first few doors. The one nearest to her on the left had family snaps from back home: a picture of the young man as a cadet, flanked by two beaming parents and what she guessed were four proud grandparents. There were postcards too, images of the Chinese countryside mainly. The inside of the closet door on her right was kitted out entirely in the red and white colours of an English soccer team.

But she stopped at the next one along from that. It was plastered with semi-naked images of women, cut from magazines. Some were topless, most were in bikinis or underwear, all were curved and gorgeous. But that was not what Madison noticed. It was that every woman photographed had the same distinguishing feature: pristine pale skin and long blonde hair.

Now she looked hard at the junior officer standing to attention by his locker. What lay behind that superficially bored face? There, was that a movement of his Adam's apple? Was that a nervous swallow? What was he hiding? What did he fear was about to be discovered in his closet?

Madison kept her gaze fixed, waiting for the reaction of her innards, expecting them to heave at the possibility that here, no more than three or four yards away from her, stood the man who had killed Abigail. She pictured him at her sister's apartment building, silently climbing the stairs while Abigail was in the elevator, waiting in the gloom, patiently counting the seconds – then stepping out and, from behind, placing his gloved hand over Abigail's mouth, forcing the front door of the apartment open, then pressing her to the ground, all the while aroused by the sight, the smell, the texture of Abigail's hair. She had run this sequence through her mind a hundred times, torturing herself with the pain of it, making herself see what she dreaded to see.

In her imagining, he was a strange, abstinent kind of pervert: motivated by a warped lust that he kept repressed. The police had been clear in each case, Abigail, Rosie, Eveline and, as far as she could tell, Mary. The women had not been sexually assaulted. The killer took a different kind of pleasure; the climax for him had come in seeing these women die.

The officer could feel Madison's eyes on him, the heat of her stare making him glance up. He was not frightened of her stare, but returned it, able to look as steadily into her as she had been looking at him. It was she who blinked. Yet when she glanced back, she thought she saw the faintest tremor of his hand. He was hunted and, Madison told herself, he now knew it.

Dr Lei began inspecting each locker, moving the contents around to get a proper look, removing some items and placing them on the bed. Weekend clothes: shirts, jackets and shoes. Music equipment; tablets; car keys. The odd book. He looked inside each shoe, he unzipped each wash bag. He went through the same performance fourteen times, but found nothing.

He resumed his position at the head of the room, Charlie and Madison standing to one side, as if he were the commander and they his faithful lieutenants. He addressed the men in Mandarin, his sentence prompting a sudden inhalation from Charlie. 'Christ,' he whispered, too loudly.

'What?' Maddy said, but there was no time for a reply. Dr Lei turned towards them and said in English, 'Dr Hughes and Nurse Michaels will now take bloods from all of you.'

'But I thought—' Charlie began.

'No. You have raised the alarm. It is important that we resolve this speedily. We have not been able to do so as I would have wished, so now we need to try a more direct method. Junior Officer Wang, please step forward.' The doctor looked at Maddy. 'Nurse Michaels, will you please bring us two chairs from the adjoining room.' He gestured towards a door just behind them.

She went through to discover a kind of communal living room, basically furnished. A few stiff-backed chairs, a table piled with magazines with more past military heroes on the cover. There was no TV set, but there were two computers in the corner. She grabbed a couple of plastic chairs and went back inside.

Waiting for her, his jacket off and stripped down to his khaki tank vest, was the very man she had suspected, the junior officer apparently obsessed with blondes. Had Lei seen her staring at him? Did Lei have grounds of his own to suspect this Wang? Why else would he pick him to be tested first? As calmly as she could manage, Maddy set down the chairs and gestured for him to sit in one of them. She waited for Charlie to sit in the other. Right now he was hunched over his medical bag, his right leg visibly palpitating through his pants.

Dr Lei spoke again. 'Dr Hughes, could I have a word, please?'

Charlie pretended he couldn't hear.

'Dr Hughes?'

Charlie looked up. He was holding a syringe and a vial. He was wearing latex gloves. 'What, you want to have a word *now*?'

'Yes, now. Leave Nurse Michaels to take the blood.'

'But, I was going . . . I mean—'

'That's what she's here for, isn't it? Now please.'

Maddy stepped forward, willing the last wisps of codeine fog still inside her head to clear. She took the equipment from Charlie's trembling hands. His eyes glared at her in fervent panic. She noticed his upper lip was damp.

Unprompted she peered into the medical bag to find another pair of gloves and put them on. She then sat alongside Wang.

She stared down at the syringe in her hand. All she could think of was what she had seen in the movies, doctors holding the needle up to the light and squirting out a small measure of liquid. But surely there was to be no liquid in this one. She was not injecting in, but taking out. That meant pulling the plunger out, rather than pressing it in, didn't it? But how did you start that? And where exactly were you meant to put the needle? And how did you attach this little bottle? Her own fingers began to wobble.

Charlie was staring at her, standing next to Dr Lei but not listening. She fussed some more with the syringe, catching the eye of Wang for just a second. The irony of this moment

355

seemed to catch her somewhere in the throat. Hadn't he plunged a needle into Abigail's right arm just five days ago? Now she was about to do it to him.

Her hands were shaking, both of them. She watched them, as if they were not hers. She willed them to stop, her brain sending a direct command. But it made no difference. Her fingers trembled wildly as she tore open the tiny packet containing the wet square of material, infused with antiseptic spirit, that she guessed was to be used as a swab on the site of the injection. She chose the deltoid muscle, at his shoulder; that, after all, was where she had got a shot back in high school. She wiped the swab on the area twice, afterwards letting the moist square fall onto her lap.

Now she removed the plastic cap from the syringe. The needle was just a few inches away from his skin. But it was oscillating in her fingers, her grip so unsteady. She moved closer and, in a single movement, closed her eyes and firmly drove the needle into the muscle.

What happened next happened so fast, afterwards Madison could barely break it down into its constituent elements. They all seemed to occur at once, in a matter of seconds. It began with a howl from Wang who, shocked at the brutally inept way his muscle had been pierced, instinctively reached for the syringe and pulled it out of his arm. That released a spectacular jet of blood, spraying a sash of red on Maddy's white uniform.

A second later, Charlie rushed forward, crying out as he did so. With his gloves still on, he attempted to cap the blood fountain coming from Wang's arm, simultaneously calling out over his shoulder to Dr Lei as his hands turned red.

'She's not a nurse! She's a fake! This was her idea, she made me do it. I didn't want to, but she made me. That's not even her real hair, it's a wig. I can tell you who she is!'

Chapter 41

She had no idea of the dimensions of the room. When she coughed, the echo gave nothing away. It could have been a tiny concrete box, no bigger than a closet. Or a space as large as that vast canteen. But the walls and the floors had been treated somehow to make them soundless and dead. She might have been inside a coffin.

The darkness was complete, thanks to the blindfold clamped onto her face, its seal tight. Instinct made her want to touch, to probe, to feel the hardness of the floor or the nearness of the walls. But that too was impossible. They had tied her hands behind her back and made her squat, so that all the pressure – and the pain – was in her legs.

In the dark, she could imagine how she looked. She had seen this posture before. It was a so-called stress position, perfect for this purpose. The victim would suffer, rapidly plead for mercy, eventually telling his captors whatever they wanted to know – or whatever they wanted to hear – whether it was true or not. And afterwards, there would not be a scratch to see. Total deniability. The American army had used it against the Viet Cong; Maddy had seen photographs in a college psychology textbook.

Right now, the pain was concentrated on the balls of her

feet; they were taking the strain. But given the battering she had taken at the rally, every part of her ached. The muscles had already been abused; now they were being stretched and torn all over again. Yet she refused to cry out. She knew it was pointless in this soundproofed cell. And she knew that, if anyone heard it, the noise she would make would sound like defeat. And she was not going to give them that.

Besides, endless time in the dark held little terror for her. Solitude, silence, the constant whir of her own thoughts – this was normal service resumed for Madison Webb.

One surprise was her lack of anger at Charlie Hughes. When they had led her away, the man was a wreck. He had collapsed into a chair, his body shaking as he sobbed. He had not even needed to be asked. 'She's that journalist, Madison Webb. She blackmailed me. I'd never have done it, I swear.' After that, the babbling continued in Mandarin.

He was weak, she knew that when she first thought of using him. If she had known anyone else with a line into the garrison, she'd have approached them. But she had no one. And he had let her down, the way most people let you down. And so they had brought her here, into the chamber she guessed the People's Liberation Army used to punish their own offenders. She wondered if she was the first American to have been brought here. If she was, this was an exclusive she could have done without.

How much time had passed, she had no idea. Judging time was never one of her strong points; sleeplessness had long ago rendered her inner clock faulty. Mainly she was focused on the throbbing pain coming from her ankles. She tried to distract herself thinking of Abigail. But she could not conjure up the face or voice of her sister, which was what she wanted. She opted for the next best thing, returning herself to the bedroom she had stood in just a few days ago. She pictured the pile of schoolbooks, waiting to be marked. She saw the creases of the bed, dimpled into the shape of Abigail. She imagined herself lying down on that empty bed, finally able to rest.

Next Maddy called herself in for questioning. Why had she not seen more of Abigail when she had had the chance? Why had she not visited the school where she taught? Why had she not heard her play guitar for, what, three years? Five? All this energy devoted to finding her killer; if only she had given even half of it to Abigail when she was alive.

There was a sound of a door opening. No change in the light; the blindfold was too heavy for that. But a voice. She recognized it as Dr Lei's. Thank God. She was desperate to be released from this position, before there was any lasting damage. She would ask him to examine her wounds from the beating at the rally too.

'Apologies are due, Miss Webb.'

'I'm sorry about misleading you. I can explain everything. I just need you to—'

'No, not from *you*,' he laughed at the absurdity of it. 'From *us*. It's awful, holding you this way. I don't like it. Not at all.'

'Well, your colleagues wanted to teach me a lesson. OK. Job done. If you just untie my hands and let me stand up.'

'Yes, yes, absolutely. Please.'

She cocked her head up, which in this squatting position pained her neck, as she waited for the doctor to come over and cut the cable ties that were binding her hands. The prospect of release, of being able to uncoil her legs and stand up, of feeling the blood flowing through her once more was delicious. Any second now . . .

Yet when he spoke again he was not where he was meant to be. He was not bending down, armed with the scissors or blade that would spring her free, as she had guessed. He was still several paces away, standing up while she remained down here. 'We must get you out of this position as soon as possible. Just one or two questions.'

Now the darkness seemed to enter her, bleeding through the blindfold and into her eyes. What was happening?

'Who sent you here?'

'What?'

'It's a simple question, Miss Webb. Who sent you here?'

'No one sent me here. What Charlie – Dr Hughes – said is right. I'm a journalist. My sister was murdered this week and I'm looking for the person who killed her. I've published most of what I know. You must have seen some of it. It's been on the news.' When there was no response, she continued, 'All the signs point to someone on this base. Sorry, but that's the truth. Someone on this base who uses heroin three.'

'And you do all this all by yourself?'

'Yes. Please untie me, I can hardly—'

'All these campaigns, politicians, demonstrations? Tens of thousands, maybe hundreds of thousands of people, screaming outside this base? Republican candidate for Governor of California, "Tear down this wall"? One girl on her own does all this?'

'I didn't *do* all that. I've never met the Republican candidate for governor; I had nothing to do with organizing the rally. They're just *responding* to what I wrote. Look, at least take off this blindfold.'

'Yes, of course. No need for you to wear a blindfold.'

She waited, once again looking forward to the small comfort of opening her eyes, even if only to see more darkness. But it didn't come. Dr Lei stayed where he was.

'Let me put it another way. You are at the centre of a very large campaign of opposition to the garrison. You do not do this alone. You are a woman. You are just thirty years old. You don't work like this alone. It can't be just you.'

'And it can't be just you either, Dr Lei. You didn't put that camera in my fucking bathroom on your own, did you? You didn't send some asshole to fuck my best friend, who's a lesbian by the way, all by yourself, did you? Just like it wasn't

360

you who kicked me in the shins and punched me between my legs. That was people who work for you. The difference is, no one works for me. I'm on my own.'

'Enough of this. Enough.'

She jerked back at that, an involuntary reflex that sent sharp currents of pain through her neck and down her spine. It was the shock that did it. For those last four words were not spoken by Dr Lei, but by a new voice. And it was coming towards her.

Chapter 42

She was relieved to feel the presence of another human being near her. Her hands could not move. She had tried to shake off the ties on her wrists, but they were tight and unbending; only the help of another human being would bring her relief. When she caught the smell of a man, and heard the rustle of his clothes, she couldn't help but let out a bleat. 'Please.'

'Yes. You need a change from this. So you can think. Here.' The age of the voice was hard to place. Chinese, most certainly. The accent stronger than Lei's. But older or younger, she could not tell. That he was in authority was clear. His cry of 'Enough' had established him as Dr Lei's superior.

She felt movement by her hair. At last, they were taking off this blindfold. Who was this man who was coming to help her? But it didn't matter, so long as he helped her. The muscles in her legs and thighs seemed to be tearing; she could almost see it happening. She didn't know how much longer she could bear it.

Except the blindfold was not off. Instead something was happening to her ears. They were becoming enclosed, wrapped in some kind of hot fabric. And now she could feel a strap tightening around her head. Were they planning to strangle her? Or was this a noose and they planned to hang her, right here in this dungeon? With horror she realized the Treaty might even allow it. If she had committed a crime – they'd probably call her botched blood test an assault on a member of the People's Liberation Army – she had done it here, on what was Chinese territory in all but name. They could do what they liked.

But the strap was not placed horizontally around her neck but vertically around her skull, beginning under her chin. It clamped her mouth shut but also, she now realized, kept in place a pair of headphones that had been placed on her head and which could now not be shaken off. In a second or two, she understood why.

Instantly, her brain was filled with the loudest noise she had ever heard, a high piercing tone, combined with static and the sound of crashing metal, all at once. The urge to block her ears was intense, but her hands remained immobile. She screamed but it made no difference. It was as if someone had placed a jackhammer into the side of her head and was now using it to drill inside her skull. She wondered if her ears were bleeding.

It was impossible to differentiate the sounds. There might have been an electric guitar, perhaps a howl of electronic feedback. In truth she could hear nothing. The circuits of her brain were flooded and all they could register was pain, pain, pain.

And then it was gone. The sound was turned off as suddenly as it had been turned on, though the ghost of it lingered, ringing inside her head. The memory of it seemed to wax and wane audibly in her ears, still producing different frequencies. Now the second voice spoke to her again, directly to her, inside her brain. It was coming through the headphones.

'Are you ready to talk now?'

She nodded reflexively, ready to do anything rather than be subjected to that hellish noise ever again. She wondered if they were still here or whether they were speaking to her from some distant control room. Maybe they had never been here. Maybe she had only ever heard voices on a loudspeaker. Perhaps that smell of male and sound of fabric had been a hallucination. She had no idea.

'So tell me again. Why did you come here?'

She did not sigh or show exasperation. Partly, she did not want to anger them. And partly she did not feel it. She was relieved to talk. Every second she spent telling her story was another second they were not hurting her.

'And this drug that killed the last girl. You say that drug is here on this base? Who tells you that?'

'I read it. In an article about the base.' Her words were slurring. Her head wanted to loll forward, but the tension of her wrists tied behind her back would not let it. 'I checked it out. Online. The only mention of that drug is in China. It's never come to the US. Except at the garrison.'

There was a silence. Her body stiffened, the muscles in her legs becoming taut and cramped. The silence was alarming. She was bracing herself for more pain.

'And you're certain that the killer is on this base?'

She gave a small, painful nod. 'I believe so, yes.'

'And you know who it is?'

'No. I don't know who it is. That's why I came here.'

'You have a suspect though, yes? One person you suspect, more than any others?'

'I wish I did. I don't know one person on this base . . .' She was running out of breath. 'From another.'

With no warning, the noise came again, as loud as before, making her brain seem to judder in its skull, like a hazelnut inside a shell. This time she saw it more than she heard it, bolts of harsh white light behind her eyes, like an electrical storm. For the first time, she believed that it would be easier to die than to endure any more of this. She began wishing it would happen.

And then it was over. And the second voice was back inside

her head, delivered via the headphones or in person, she could no longer tell. 'Now I ask you again. Why did you come here?'

Automatically, surrendering to the pain and to their command, she went through it all one more time. When she was finished, she braced as best she could for the sound that would rip her head off.

But it did not come. Instead, the voice spoke one last time. 'Your story remained consistent, even under extreme stress. I am satisfied that you are telling the truth. I am letting you go. Dr Lei will take matters forward from here.'

The first man now spoke again. 'Thank you, Colonel. Miss Webb, in a moment I shall remove these restraints. This will mark the end of the interview.'

'Interview?' she said mirthlessly, immediately regretting her show of disrespect.

'Yes. Our interview. That is how, if asked, we shall describe it. We shall say nothing of these . . . techniques.'

'And if *I* do? If I tell the world what you did here, to an American citizen?'

'We shall say you are a liar. That you make up stories. Fantasies. You will have no proof. Yes, it's true that you're bruised here and there. That's most unfortunate.'

'"Most unfortunate!" Like you had nothing to do with it!' Maddy couldn't help herself.

'My point is,' the voice continued, ignoring her. 'You looked like this before you came here: there are medical records from your stay at the Long Beach Memorial hospital that prove that. There is not an additional mark on you. Remember, we are not like you Americans. When we have to engage in an, um, enhanced interrogation we are careful. And we most certainly do not take photographs of the occasion. We do not need souvenirs.'

'But I can show people the camera you fitted in my bathroom.'

'You'll find that that will be gone when you get home. Miss Webb, if I may. You have done all you could. You have earned a good rest. You need to let your body recover. If I were you, I would go to bed and have a good long sleep.'

He must have given some kind of signal, because a moment later there were hands at her wrists, untying her and lifting her to her feet. They unbuckled the strap and removed the headphones. Supported on both sides by guards or nurses, she couldn't tell, she hobbled out of the room. Her eyes remained covered.

They remained that way even as they put her in the back of a vehicle, perhaps one of those buggies. The blindfold was only removed once their journey was over. In a flood of daylight, she discovered that the earth had carried on spinning while she had been deep in the underworld. She was back at the security hut at the main gate. By the time she had blinked and adjusted, her escorts had disappeared. She was wearing a nurse's uniform, similar to the one she wore before – but this one carried no trace of blood.

The guard behind the central counter presented her with her phone. 'Thank you for visiting us,' he said, in heavily accented English. 'Goodbye.'

And with that she was suddenly on the other side of the gate. She looked at her phone, dead and dumb with no SIM or media card. They were, she assumed, where she had left them, unseen among the detritus at the bottom of Charlie Hughes's bag, their presence unknown even to him. As for her purse, containing all her cash, credit cards and ID, that was hidden under the passenger seat of Charlie's car. She had nothing. Except for the single, tiny morsel her torturers had, without knowing, given her.

Chapter 43

There was a back elevator and she took it. She could not face walking through the newsroom, not like this, not today. She had discovered this route by accident a year or so ago, after happening to share the elevator with her boss one morning. This was Jane Goldstein's way of getting to her office without running into any needy colleagues.

Madison left the cab she had eventually flagged down – a mile's painful walk from the base – idling outside. She had no cash to pay the driver and she owed him a lot. She had got him to drive first to Katharine's, but nobody was home. With no money, no cards and no phone, she didn't have many choices. She had thought about Quincy but rejected it: her sister would not understand any of this or, if she did, she would only be angry.

Besides, coming here made sense. She needed to see someone who knew from the inside what it was to pursue the truth, someone who at the start of her own career had also been regarded by colleagues as obsessive, if not outright nuts. She needed to see a true journalist, someone who, unlike Howard Burke, had balls.

Madison raised a hand in greeting to the assistant whose desk was supposed to deter visitors from approaching the editor-in-chief and, registering the aghast look on the woman's face, walked right past her and into the office. Jane Goldstein, who had been standing by her desk, stabbing at her keyboard, all but fell into her chair with surprise. 'Madison?'

'Hi.'

'What's happened to you? What's going on? Why are you—'

'Not sure I can do it in one hundred and forty characters, but I'll try.'

She went through it all, naming Dr Lei and adding her strong conviction that 'the Colonel' he had referred to, in perhaps his only slip-up, must have been the garrison commander, Chen Jun. 'There's only one person of that rank on that base,' she explained. 'And he's the man in charge.'

Goldstein sat throughout, nodding at intervals, utterly absorbed in the tale Madison was telling. Her reaction gave Maddy the confidence known to any reporter who pitches a story and senses their editor is buying it.

'Everything about their reaction suggests the Chinese know they have something to hide. They're not stupid. They know what we know. The first three victims all had links to the garrison; the fourth was killed by heroin you can only get on that base.'

'Sheesh,' Jane said, shaking her head in shock at the whole thing and scribbling a note. 'And they said that to you? "We'll deny everything?" After this . . . this *torture*, had stopped, that's what they said?'

Maddy nodded.

'Do you think they know who it is, Maddy? The actual individual?'

She paused at that. Her interrogators had put a version of the same question to her. 'I don't know. They released me as soon as they realized I didn't know. Maybe they were relieved. Now they've got more time to spirit him out of the country.'

'If they know.'

'Yes, if.'

'And you were telling them the truth? You really don't know who the killer is?'

Maddy shook her head.

Goldstein glanced at her computer, distracted for a second. 'And why didn't they just keep you there, in that cell you described, the one that could have been tiny or could have been huge?'

'Harder to explain why a US citizen, who was last seen entering the garrison, goes missing for a few days than one who's gone a few hours, I suppose. That would be hard to explain, wouldn't it? Isn't that abduction?'

'Hmm.' Goldstein looked towards her bookshelves, as if she were considering the legal definition of the term. 'You certainly look like you've been through a helluva'n ordeal. But you say you had all these cuts and marks before you went to the base. From when you got beaten up at the rally, am I right?'

'Yes, but that's the whole point of these stress positions, Jane. They don't leave a mark, that's why they're so clever. Remember that story years ago about the LAPD . . . Listen, I don't know how they do it. I just know that I'm tired of doing this on my own, Jane. I need the back-up of this place to complete the story, to nail this. I need other reporters, I need editors, I need Howard. I need you.' The pain in her leg and thigh muscles was total.

'And this nurse's uniform: they gave you that?'

'Yes. The one I was wearing got splattered with blood. This one was clean.'

'But you're not quite clear when. Or how they got you dressed.'

'No. They blindfolded me, they took me somewhere on the base. It's possible I blacked out for a minute or two. I can do that sometimes.'

'Black out?'

'Yes. It's a long . . . you don't want to know . . . I have trouble sleeping. Nothing to do with this, I've had it for years.'

369

'Oh, my ex-husband used to have that. And you sometimes fall asleep at weird times, right?'

'Right. So listen, Jane. I'd really like to work alongside Katharine Hu on this one. And Howard to edit. I know he's been sceptical, but that's good. That'll only make the story better. And if perhaps—'

'Look, Madison. This is one helluva story. It really is. But a story this big, you can't afford to slip up. I mean, every last detail has to be one hundred per cent iron-clad. One t that's not crossed, one i that's not dotted, and it's my tit that's in the wringer. And this paper with it.'

'I get that, Jane, of course I do. That's what Howard can—'

'I don't mean the words on the page, Madison. We need to make sure the source of this information is completely, wholly reliable.'

'But *I'm* the source of this information, this happened to *me*.' Maddy paused a moment. 'Oh.'

'Here's what I'm going to do,' Goldstein said, nodding as she spoke. She reached for her purse, on the floor by her chair. 'First, I'm going to give you five hundred dollars to pay for that taxi outside and to get you some clothes and back into your apartment.' She handed her five notes. 'And next I want you to take this.'

She handed Maddy a scribbled note. It read *Dr Alex Katzman, Analyst* together with an LA phone number. 'What's this?'

'Alex Katzman is my brother. He's also the best therapist in LA. I think you need to see him.'

'Christ, Jane. I don't need a fucking *shrink*. I've just been held in a dungeon by the P-L-fucking-A. I need you to help me on *that*.'

'I think the loss of your sister has left you very disturbed indeed. I know from experience that people with extreme insomnia can suffer from hallucinations which—'

'This wasn't a fucking hallucination!'

'—which feel very real. And I'm not saying this *wasn't* real. But we need to be sure – entirely, comprehensively sure. Now, please, Madison, let Alex help you. He's a good man and you're a talented, beautiful young woman who has suffered a terrible trauma.'

'I don't believe it. They've fucking got you too.'

'Madison.'

'I always knew Howard's nuts shrank at the first fucking mention of the garrison. But I thought you were . . . I thought you were stronger.'

Madison stood up, desperate to throw the five hundred-dollar bills back in her boss's face. But she resisted that urge: she had no other way home.

Instead, she quietly turned and walked out – of Goldstein's office and out of the building. The editor's message could not have been clearer: Madison was on her own.

Except she wasn't, not completely. There was one last place to turn.

Chapter 44

Bill Doran had given up on the 'ideas memo' years ago. As a form, it was badly flawed. They only ever leaked, they only ever gave you trouble. Better to do what he was doing now. Grab ten minutes with the candidate, then write up what had been agreed and circulate it. The good memo was not a tactic for victory, but a proof of it.

Which is why he was here now, in the back of the car with Elena Sigurdsson. He had spent the first three minutes preparing the ground, explaining that her numbers were 'softening'. The freak lead she had gained over Berger had stalled and was now beginning to roll backwards.

'It's not rocket science,' he explained. 'You pulled ahead when the China thing was front and centre. When it fell away, with the arrest and all, the lead went with it.'

'So I need the China story back in the news?'

'Exactly.'

'How do I do that? They arrested that guy.'

'They did. But that story's unravelling, as you know. As soon as he was in custody there was another victim. Within hours actually.'

'So it should be back up and running, "the heroin killer" and all that?'

'It *should*, Elena. It definitely should. But the *activistas* are holding back. Padilla's not out there, no one's heard from the reporter who'd been leading on it, there are no rallies planned.'

'How come?'

'Our intel on Padilla says he felt he got his fingers burned with the arrest. He was on TV saying we're suspending the campaign, blah blah. Now he loses face if he goes back out there five minutes later. He wants to see how events pan out, hang fire till he knows what's happening.'

'Smart boy.'

'For *him*, sure. Very smart. Not so great for us.'

She sighed and looked out of the window, one of those fleeting moments when the TV face of a politician vanishes and you can imagine them as a regular person. He and his fellow consultants always talked of trying to bottle those moments, the ones they saw backstage, when the candidate was real, and showing them to the voters. That was the holy grail of every TV spot, every interview. But it almost never happened. And after a while, those moments became rarer. The mask eats into the face and all that.

'So what can we do, Bill?'

'I suggest that if the story doesn't come back all by itself, *organically*, as Berger would probably put it, then we help it along.'

'I'm listening.'

'The outgoing Chinese president is visiting Washington next week, which is a very big hook. You could tie the issue to that.'

'Make some demands.'

'Precisely. Very specific information the people of California need to hear.'

'Kind of, "The questions he needs to answer before he comes to America."'

'Yes, Elena. I love that. That's great. Ted Norman's volunteers will lap that up. *The questions he needs to answer.* Shall I get one of the guys to draft an op-ed on those lines?'

The candidate nodded as she took a call. Bill Doran leaned back in his seat and glanced at his phone, scrolling through to the place where he had saved his draft of the memo he planned to send out after this conversation. And there it was, his main action point. *Candidate to author an op-ed: Ten questions the President of China must answer if he's to be welcome in America.*

Always make the client think it's their idea. The golden rule of all political consultancy. Lead them to water and they shall drink – but only if they think they put the goddamn stream there themselves.

He polished off the memo, beginning as ever with the bulletproof opening: 'The candidate has just instructed me to do the following . . .'

They would be back in the comfort zone within the next few hours, training their guns on Richard Berger by aiming for the more immediate target: the Chinese military presence in Los Angeles.

Leo had lost track of how many times he had tried to call. Upwards of three dozen, along with perhaps twenty texts and a dozen emails. It wasn't Maddy's usual style. She could be a door-slammer and a shouter, but never a non-speaker. She was either unprecedentedly furious with him (possible after the piece-of-shit file he had given her), consumed with regret after they had slept together (not just possible, but likely) or she had gone to ground. At his lowest moment, he had thought about calling that cop with a crush who was always hanging around. But he couldn't bring himself to do it.

He was staring at his phone, as if mere willpower could make it spark into life, when a text arrived. It was from Berger: *KTLA now*.

Leo already had it on, albeit on mute, but now pushed the volume button on the remote. It was Sigurdsson being interviewed on the set of the evening news, a departure from the usual grammar of both TV and politics.

'. . . published tomorrow, and you're saying you want answers from the very top.'

'That's right, Dana. My campaign is making no accusations. But Californians want to know, have the senior team at Garrison 41 been as candid with our law-enforcement authorities as they should have been?'

Shit. They should have seen this coming. Truth is, they should have done it themselves, got in ahead of Sigurdsson.

'We want to know very simply whether commanders at Garrison 41 have done a full search of the base for any evidence which could be relevant to this inquiry. Bottom line, do commanders there know who is behind these killings? Are they harbouring a fugitive from American justice?'

Shit, shit, shit.

'The people of California have a right to know these things. So tonight I'm calling on the president to make clear that he wants answers to these questions from his Chinese counterpart when he visits our country next week. I know my opponent believes in staying quiet and bowing politely, if you will. But we've tried that approach and the verdict is in: it doesn't work. I have more respect for our Chinese friends than that. I know they respond best to people who are as proud and strong as they are. Mayor Berger thinks bowing and scraping gets results. Well it doesn't. I'm tougher than that. And in November, if I have the privilege of serving as Governor of the great state of California, you, Dana, the people of this state and our Chinese friends are all going to see that for themselves.'

'Elena Sigurdsson, thank you for being with us here on KTLA. Appreciate it.'

The phone was already ringing. On the screen: 'Unknown.'

'Mr Mayor.'

'Did you hear that, Leo? Did you fucking hear that?

"Bowing politely." "Bowing and scraping." Did you hear what she just did there? She's trying to make me out to be some geisha girl who's getting fucked in the ass by the Chinese. *Bowing!*'

'That's not even a Chinese thing,' said Leo, regretting the words as soon as they left his mouth.

'It doesn't fucking matter, Leo. She's killing me on this. Now she's "calling on the president". Who the hell does she think she is? I tell you, I'm not going to take this any more, Leo. I'm fighting back, you hear me?'

'Yes, sir.'

'Listen, Leo. I want a strategy meet tonight. At the residence. OK? And listen, I need you to bring my phone. I left it at an event. One of the girls has left it on your desk. OK? Leo. I need you on this, man. Need all that Ivy League brainpower I'm paying top dollar for, every last ounce. OK? We good?'

Leo hung up, noticing for the first time the padded envelope placed on his desk. He ripped it open to see his boss's phone inside. He put it in his breast pocket, then pulled it out again, punching in the numerical combination he knew would unlock it: the most important date in Berger's life. Not his wedding or the birth of any of his kids. But the date of his first election victory.

He scrolled through the texts and emails, half of which were from him. He read the ones from Ross, scanning them for any signs of conspiracy or betrayal. One of them included an attached photo, which Leo clicked on: a proposed new-look logo for the website. Hmm, no one told him about that.

It brought him to the 'gallery' section of the phone, where Berger had stored a handful of downloaded images. What Leo saw there filled him with dread. Staring out was a series of faces of young women, all blonde and attractive. Oh, Christ no, please no. Not a bimbo eruption. That was the last thing this campaign could handle, not now.

But as he enlarged the images, the third one especially, Leo

376

felt his body temperature lower. For what he was looking at, stashed away on the private phone of the mayor of Los Angeles, were close-up, apparently intimate portraits of Rosario Padilla, Eveline Plaats, Abigail Webb and now, joining them, Mary Doherty. The four victims of the heroin killer, at their sexiest and most alluring in life – and now secretly preserved in death.

Chapter 45

In her apartment Maddy felt as watched as she had in that lightless cell. The camera in the bathroom mirror seemed to have gone, just as Dr Lei said it would. She tested it, running the shower for five unbroken minutes and filling the room with steam. This time the glass misted over as thoroughly as it used to.

Still, that offered scant reassurance. It probably just meant they had hidden their lens somewhere else. So she avoided the shower, filling the tub instead, foaming it up with bubble bath and remaining covered up until the last moment, primly stepping out of her robe and into the water like a nun at the seaside.

As it happened, it helped. The hot water soothed her aching, pounded flesh. Her ankles were raw with pain, though their outward appearance suggested little of the agony within. Her thighs, shins and stomach were all bruised and were now purpling. Everywhere else, including between her legs, remained tender.

She stayed in the tub for nearly an hour, topping up the hot water regularly, allowing herself to drift into sleep for fleeting naps, never more than thirty seconds at a time.

Once out, she felt readier to return to battle. She picked

up her landline phone, its shape unfamiliar in her hand through lack of use. The display told her there were approximately thirty missed calls from a number she recognized as Leo's. Quincy had called just as often. She pressed the voicemail key, pre-emptively jabbing at the volume control so that the messages would not be overheard by any electronic ears. A futile gesture, she knew: as if they wouldn't have had a tap on this line the instant she posted the initial story naming the garrison. The first message began to play.

Where are you, Madison? When I didn't hear from you, I went to the hospital but you weren't there. They said you'd discharged yourself. What's going on? Please tell me where you are. Mom really needs you, I need you. There are a hundred practical things to do. I don't want to have to go to the funeral home alone.

The next six or seven continued in that vein, sympathy laced with guilt-trip. But then the tone began to change, gradually at first, culminating in the most recent one, left barely an hour ago:

Maddy, I'm sorry. Please forgive me. Please just talk to me. I'm going out of my mind with worry. Just let me know you're safe. I'm worried that something's happened to you. Please.

And then, through tears:

I can't lose you too.

Madison went into the kitchen, reaching into the very back of the oven, where she had hidden the pay-as-you-go phones, in the hope that was one place where her PLA stalkers would not have thought to check. She thumbed out a quick message to Quincy.

I'm OK. I was off radar for a bit. I wish I could explain and I will, soon. But I'm doing what I can for Abigail. She deleted that last sentence, knowing it would look strange. But it was only the truth. *I'll be in touch soon, just as soon as I have this cleared up. Don't try replying to this phone or my usual one or my landline: I'm afraid I'm not using them for a while*. She typed out the words, 'Much love' but couldn't do it. She changed it to 'Speak soon, M'. Next she added an 'x' in recognition of the hand her sister had reached out towards her in her last, pleading message, before dumping the phone into the trash can under her desk.

Now she went to an old laptop she kept in a drawer. She built a stack of books around it, hoping to obscure the view of the screen from almost every angle but hers. Next she connected the machine not to her own wireless router but to the one next door, remembering the password her neighbour had given her on that day last summer when her own device had apparently melted from the heat or, more likely, sheer pressure of use.

Thankfully the inertia principle so often cited by Katharine Hu – people never, ever change their passwords unless they are forced to – held good. She was connected. Next Maddy routed herself through a VPN, not failsafe but the closest you could get to wearing a mask and gloves online. Whoever was following her would, she hoped, find it a tad harder now.

So equipped, she plunged into the othernet, heading immediately for the underground version of Weibo. Jane Goldstein was nearly right: Maddy was almost entirely alone. But there was one last ally she could turn to: the human flesh search engine.

Her request broke the regular pattern, she knew that. Usually, you threw in a name and the worker bees got searching, turning over every stone relating to that one person. This request would necessarily be vaguer.

Anything on the Princelings, the elite junior officers of Garrison 41? Names, résumés, history of specific indivs, esp. anything, um, suspect?

Within a few minutes it was spreading, re-weibed into the furthest reaches of the othernet. She sat back in her chair. How strange, she thought. She could not trust her colleagues or her boss or her ex-lover; she could barely talk to her mother

380

or her surviving sister. But somehow the people of this unseen crowd felt like allies. She had faith in them.

She whiled away the next hour attempting to turn the detritus in her fridge into food. She ate toast, some tuna out of a can and a soya yoghurt once recommended by Abigail. She savoured the taste of each mouthful, marvelling at how recently, at the start of this week in fact, her younger sister had been alive.

When she returned to the machine, pulling a towel over her head to further obstruct any view of the screen, she was gratified to see that there had been a fairly decent flow of replies. Mainly, though, these consisted of links to photographs of passing out parades, whose captions featured long lists of names; or gazetted records of military commissions, again packed with names. There was one odd nugget about a junior officer who had been pulled over for speeding, but let go thanks to diplomatic immunity and the principle of extraterritoriality which, the article helpfully explained, held that Garrison 41 was sovereign Chinese territory, entirely beyond the reach of US law. But that one individual apart, there was next to nothing specific.

She scrolled back to the top where a new weib had arrived. *Can you follow me so I can DM you?*

This was common enough; not everyone wanted to communicate publicly. Maddy did as she was told, then opened the private channel by sending a direct message. *I'm here.*

A minute passed and then a reply, sent just to her.

Here you go. Lots of links to come. May be more than 140 characters, so be patient.

Madison waited as a half-dozen DMs arrived in quick succession. Each one contained a link, which led her to a mixture of websites and PDF documents, which opened up instantly.

She only had to read for a few moments to be stunned by what she saw.

Chapter 46

The first was a link to a Chinese dissident website operated outside the country in both English and Mandarin. The story was dated two years earlier and told of the son of a leading party official who had been out driving in Beijing late at night. The nineteen year old had swerved into an oncoming car, damaged both vehicles and badly injured the other driver. When the police came, he had tried to get away but was so drunk he fell over. Surrounded by motorists and onlookers, he started screaming at the police, telling them it was no good trying to arrest him because of his powerful father. He kept shouting his father's name, again and again. The story had spread by word of mouth among young Chinese and especially on social media, capturing perfectly the arrogance of the Princeling class.

The next item was a PDF of a letter, apparently written by the young man's British-born tutor and addressed to his direct superiors at the prestigious Tsinghua University. The tutor was complaining of 'serious disciplinary issues', which, understanding the need for discretion under the circumstances, he would not spell out. Suffice it to say, he had found compelling evidence of 'inappropriate' behaviour towards female students, especially towards those on the overseas programme, including young women from the United States and Europe.

He has shown an over-zealous interest in several students,
who allege that he has followed them to and from classes
or appeared suddenly in their accommodation quarters.
He is causing them great discomfort. I am aware of his
family's high standing, but nevertheless suggest that he
be issued with a formal reprimand.

Next came a page that had been screen-grabbed from Weibo, which Maddy strongly suspected had been taken down within minutes of appearing. The messages were in English, but that was no surprise. Plenty of Chinese thought they had a better chance of slipping past the censors if they did not write in their mother tongue. The weibs were all variations on a common theme, expressed through different euphemisms. The gist was the allegation that this same young man, who had already had problems with drink, had also developed a liking for other, harder 'substances'. Several dropped coded references to heroin.

The last link led to another underground site, though this one had a trashier, more celebrity design. In its 'whispers' section, it reported the rumour that the same Princeling, now twenty-one, had crashed a black Ferrari outside a Beijing nightspot, killing one of his two young, female passengers. 'Insiders' had told the website the driver had become distracted because one, or even both, of these two women were engaged in a 'lewd act' with him at the time. He had not been prosecuted for this fatal accident, however. Instead the young man had been quietly packed off to one of China's many military bases around the world, though no one was saying which one.

Something tells us that, with the guanxi *this young man*
has at his disposal, he won't be digging trenches in Angola
or doing a hundred press-ups in Mali. We suspect he'll
have found a cushier place to make the transition from

drugged-up road pest to respected officer of the People's Liberation Army. Officially though, it remains a mystery where exactly in the world this young tearaway is doing his military service.

But not a mystery to Maddy. There, in the last DM, was a link to a PDF. The first page was the original, in Mandarin, complete with the grand, martial emblem of the PLA. The next was a translation, which confirmed that the Princeling in question, having completed a spell at an elite military college in Beijing, had won a place among the officer class of Garrison 41 at Terminal Island, the Port of Los Angeles.

All of which would have been fascinating enough. Here was a man who fit the profile she had been building up, piece by maddeningly elusive piece, ever since Abigail had been found dead. He was a drug user and a stalker, with an obsessive interest in American and European women. At that moment, she'd have been ready to wager good money that every single one of those foreign, female students who had complained about him to their tutor was white, fair-skinned and blonde.

But that was not what had left her agape. It was not what he had done but who he was that stunned her. She returned to the tab open with the first story, of the drunk driving episode, and read the key sentence again and then again. But the letters on the screen had not changed. There it was, as shocking as when she read it the first time.

He fell over and was then heard shouting, 'Arrest me if you like, it won't mean anything! My father is Yang Zheng!'

There it was again in the string of screen-grabbed weibs. They had been coy about mentioning heroin, but not about naming the suspected drug user. He was Yang Zhitong, son of Standing Committee member and then rising star, Yang Zheng.

The name stared at her from the screen the way it would

have stared at any person on the planet who kept even half an eye on the news. For Yang Zheng was set to take over the most powerful office in the world in the once-a-decade transition due later that year. He was the man universally tipped to become the next President of the People's Republic of China.

Chapter 47

She snapped shut the lid of the computer and stood up, anxious to escape the cocoon she had made for herself. She went to the kitchen, then back to the desk, then back again, trying to make sense of what she had just seen. It was impossible to believe and yet it explained so much. Of course the Chinese had followed her, had her beaten up and given her the full 'enhanced interrogation' treatment, supervised by the base commander himself. To them, this story, her story, could not have been more menacing. It went to the very top.

Maddy wanted to go to the window, just to see the sky. But she knew there would be eyes down there, eyes on her. Even a flicker of curtain would alert them. Not that it made much difference. There were almost certainly eyes in here too.

She paced some more. The very idea of it, the Prince of the Princelings, son of the soon-to-be Emperor of China, pursuing the women of this city, hunting them down, then filling their veins with the very drug on which he himself was hooked. Was it a sexual thing? The placing of the poppy suggested it was, though the coroner's department were adamant that none of the women had been touched. Now that she knew who had made it, that gesture seemed as much political as perverted: a kind of symbolic rape, a Chinese intrusion into America's innermost place.

Was that the way to view these killings, as a bizarre act of political revenge, the Chinese finally doing to the West what the West had done to them, poisoning America's daughters with heroin the way the British had addled China's sons with opium two centuries earlier? Was this payback, a child of Beijing's ruling circle visiting on the Occident a taste of the humiliation the Orient had suffered for so long, and doing it in, of all places, the latter-day Treaty Port China had exacted from a supine United States?

She had to stop herself writing the story there and then. She needed to focus, but questions kept intruding. Was this why Jane Goldstein had given her the brush-off, pretending she was going nuts? Because the Chinese had leaned on her, knowing they had to protect the reputation of their incoming leader? What, Madison wondered, had they given Jane in return? A weekend at the Dominion Hotel in Macau, perhaps at the same six-star suite enjoyed by Doug Jarrett? Or something more permanent? A car? A house in the hills?

There would be time for that later. Right now she needed to work through what she had. Starting with the origin of this cache of extraordinary documents.

Madison went back to the machine, reopened it and clicked on the name of the sender, which predictably revealed precious little. The Weibo handle consisted of the word 'Messenger' and the current year. He had no followers and had sent a total of one weib: the one addressed to her, *Can you follow me so I can DM you?* The profile was empty, as was the space for a photograph. Nor was it a surprise that the account had only been set up in the last hour.

So someone had seen her appeal for information and decided now was the moment to pass on this radioactive material. Were they a whistleblower, an insider on the base who was privy to this stuff and had become sickened by the cover-up?

Maybe. But they could have come forward so much earlier. Why not make contact the day of Madison's first story implicating Garrison 41? Or if not then, why not during Mario Padilla's mass demonstration, when the crowds were circling the garrison and the story was at its most intense? Wouldn't that have been the moment?

Cui bono? Come on, Maddy, that's always the question. Any leak, any move whatsoever, just ask yourself who benefits and you'll soon understand. So who benefits here?

Not the garrison, for whom this was only a public relations disaster of epic proportions. She went back to the computer and read through the DMs again, to see if she had missed anything.

Here you go. Lots of links to come. May be more than 140 characters, so be patient.

It sounded like a native English speaker. *Here you go.*

She got up and paced some more. Think, think. *Cui bono?*

For distraction, she clicked on the TV remote. No news, just ads: Tylenol, Tropicana juice, Sigurdsson for Governor, Mercedes car. She went back to the fridge, only to see nothing that could even generously be described as food.

Hold on. Hold on a damn moment. She rushed back to the computer, still wedged between the towers of books. She went to the Sigurdsson website and saw the main window was filled with video of the candidate's anti-garrison speech from a few days earlier. Alongside it, her latest op-ed, *Ten questions the President of China must answer if he's to be welcome in America.*

This was their issue, the first and perhaps only way a Republican could make headway in California. They needed to keep this story going, of course they did. And who was a more obvious conduit for that strategy than the journalist who'd first made the link between the murders and the base? They'd have probably leaked it to her eventually anyway. But once she'd issued an appeal for information, they had the perfect cover.

She could picture it, some Leo equivalent in Sigurdsson HQ tapping out the DM, from an internet café. *Here you go. Lots of links to come . . . be patient.* That's exactly how those people talked; she could imagine Leo sending that very message.

Did it matter? If every reporter worried about the motives of their sources, they wouldn't write a word. It might be serving their sources' political purposes, but that's life. What this leaker had given her was a huge lead. For the first time, she had a name. One that went to the very top.

And then another message arrived.

Chapter 48

It was from the same sender. And this time it consisted only of an instruction: *Go to Dropbox*, followed by a username and password, both of which were the same as the Weibo handle: Messenger and the year.

She did as she was told, logging into the storage service through which people could either back up or share big files. The photographers on the *LA Times* used it all the time.

There were four files displayed. She selected 'Download All' and in a matter of moments, they were sitting on her machine. She clicked on the first one, represented by the reassuringly familiar icon of a PDF document. It sprang open to reveal what appeared to be a list of just over a dozen Chinese names, written in Roman characters, with a long string of digits by each one.

Most of the names she did not recognize, though one inevitably stood out. Third from the top was Yang Zhitong. She identified one or two of the others as Yang's fellow elite junior officers from the garrison, including the young man who had been mentioned in that story about a speeding offence.

But the numbers were harder to work out. She counted the digits. Thirteen for each one, too long to be a phone number.

And also too long to be a zipcode for some address back in China. Were these bank accounts perhaps? She looked for any identifying markers on the document. It seemed to be vaguely official, but the proportions suggested the page had been cropped, perhaps removing the letterhead from the top. All she had were the names and these opaque numbers.

She went back to the other three files she had downloaded. She let her cursor hover over the first one, her heart rate accelerating at the prospect of what she guessed would be a damning photo or photos, linking Yang indisputably to one of the killings. She braced herself for what she feared: a CCTV image of this playboy prince with her sister. She clicked.

Nothing happened. She waited and still nothing happened. Eventually the screen displayed an error message:

/Users/madisonwebb/Downloads/UNKNOWN_ PARAMETER_VALUE could not be opened, because an unknown error occurred.

Try saving to disk first and then opening the file.

She followed that vague instruction, but without success. She tried the other files, but they returned variations of that same error message. She tried opening them with a whole range of applications, but none worked. The files just stayed there on her screen, each one a blank rectangle, closed and unknowable.

There was only one person guaranteed to be able to help in this situation. She picked up one of the disposable cellphones she had bought, checked the time and texted Katharine's number.

Katharine, I know it's Friday night and you're probably out running right now, but there's been a very big development. Huge. I have a few files I need to open. Go onto Weibo as me – you remember the password, right? – and check out my DMs. Follow the instructions and see if you can crack it. I'm on my way. You'll understand when you see the stuff. M x

She removed the battery from that phone and took the last virgin one she had left. She threw the old computer, the one she'd just used, in a bag and went downstairs, avoiding the elevator. When she saw the black thirtyish woman with the braids, nodding convincingly along to beats playing through what were doubtless mute headphones, she almost felt like waving. Bus, cab, bus. That's how she would do it.

Madison walked as fast as she could, though with the bruising all over her body it was not easy. It was also unfamiliar. These were streets she had been on a hundred times, but always by car. Only now, on foot, did she appreciate their scale. The width, the space between blocks – they were not really designed for humans at all. Indeed, in the old days, you'd almost never see anyone walking in this kind of area – except for the army of Latino domestics, arriving to clean the houses and tend the gardens at dawn and leaving at dusk. That sight had not vanished. In Crestwood Hills, Quincy's neighbourhood, that twice-daily human migration in and out was as regular as the tides. But here in Silver Lake and in places like it, not nearly so much.

She was still a good three blocks away when she saw the flashing red and blue lights of an LAPD squad car. *What were they doing here?* As she got closer, she saw there were not one but two cars, as well as an ambulance. They were at the junction of Silver Lake Boulevard and a turning, Berkeley Avenue, and whatever had happened had clearly taken place in just the last minute or two because the police had not yet sealed off the road. A couple of cars were backed up, unable to get past, and people were beginning to come out of their houses. Around the paramedics, a small crowd had formed, blocking Madison's view.

A road accident, no doubt, though there was no sign of any wrecked cars. Tragic, but Maddy had to press on. She had all but passed the scene, walking north towards Effie

Street, when she took one last look back. She squinted to be sure she wasn't seeing things. But there, kneeling on the road, at the centre of the knot of people, was someone who looked very much like Katharine's wife, Enrica.

It was hard to tell. Enrica was always so glamorous, while this woman was hunched over, wearing sweatpants, her hair loosely tied back. Now that Maddy looked properly, there was no doubt about it. And the woman's back was trembling, as if shaking . . .

At that instant, Maddy just ran, pushing past the neighbours and strangers until she was standing by Enrica's side. When one of the police officers tried to push her back, she pulled his hand away and said, 'No, I'm her friend.'

That made Enrica look up and, for a second, Maddy caught her face, her eyes red, as if they had been grated by shock. But it wasn't Enrica she was looking at. It was Katharine Hu, flat on the ground, wearing running clothes but making no move. Her arm was splayed at an unnatural angle, the hair on one side of her head matted with blood. Her skin still had some colour. But it was draining away.

Chapter 49

The rest of the night went by at a tempo that was both slower and faster than regular human time. The minutes seemed to become thicker, each moment viscously full of meaning and emotion and pain. And yet it was also sped by adrenalin, the seconds surging and hurtling past them. When it finally came to say goodbye it had somehow become midnight.

They allowed only Enrica into the ambulance with Katharine, but Maddy had followed in the police car behind. Once inside, she asked the lead officer if there had been any witnesses. One had seen a car accelerate very fast from the scene; another had heard what they believed was the moment of collision. There were tyre marks, which were being examined. 'I'm afraid this looks to be a classic hit-and-run accident, ma'am.'

'Looks' is the operative word, Maddy thought. What about the fact that Katharine had done this same run along the same route at the same time every Friday night for years? That she was always almost neurotically careful, that she never wore headphones or any device that might have impeded her ability to hear the car that had slammed into her? Or that she was an experienced runner and nothing like this had ever happened before?

But she said none of this. She would have liked to pretend

that she was sparing Enrica's feelings: better surely that Enrica believe the woman she loved had been run down through a tragic mistake rather than a deliberate attempt on her life.

That sounded plausible enough, but Madison knew it was not the truth. She knew that Katharine had caught the attention of the Chinese authorities, to the extent that they had – ineptly – sought to entrap her with some male bait. Of course they would have monitored her phone, picking up her text messages even before she did. How naïve Maddy had been to think she did. True, she had not revealed her password (and she and Katharine had set up an elaborate verification process that made that very hard to hack) but she had revealed that there was *something* there, even if she had not spelled out what that was. She had, in other words, protected her information but exposed her friend.

This was what she could not say to Enrica, even as she sat with her outside the operating theatre at the Silver Lake Medical Center, holding her tightly, waiting for news. That that car had not come out of a clear blue sky, or even a smoggy February one, by sheer, unlucky coincidence. It had gone there on a mission, to take out Katharine before she unlocked whatever was in that file. Garrison 41 clearly understood its significance even if Maddy did not. And they had known what to do, to find Katharine out running in her neighbourhood, because Maddy had, unwittingly and via a careless text, told them.

This was what Madison could not say, even though she felt it so keenly. 'I'm sorry', she could manage, with its bland ring of generic sympathy. 'I'm so sorry for making this happen' – that she could not say. But she felt its truth drilling into her, into that same part of her heart that had had to grow hard all those years ago.

* * *

395

It was time, surely, to give up. Whatever good she once thought she was doing was outweighed, if not cancelled out, by this possibly fatal blow to her kind, generous, whip-smart friend Katharine Hu. In the space of a week, Madison had lost her sister and now, perhaps, her closest friend. She had asked too much, making one pay the price for the loss of the other.

It struck her that she had failed in a basic, elemental duty not once but two – no, three – times. She was meant to have been Abigail's protector. But she had failed in that task as badly as any person can ever fail. And Katharine? She was Madison's friend and most loyal co-conspirator. Again and again, Katharine had kept Maddy out of trouble, saving her skin, professionally and, more than once, physically. Tonight was the one time when it fell to Madison to do the same. And she had done the very opposite: she had placed her friend directly in the path of lethal danger.

She should leave this whole business alone, retreat and let the police find the monster responsible for all this hurt. Yes, it was true that in Chief Jarrett they were led by a man in the pay of Beijing, a man who had bent the entire Los Angeles Police Department to match the shape of his own corruption. He had somehow diverted the homicide squad away from the truth, preventing them from making the connections between the deaths of Rosario, Eveline and her sister, the connections that would lead them to the killer. But somewhere in the LAPD, there would, surely, be at least one good person who would refuse to be corrupted. Maybe, who knows, it was Barbara Miller. Or perhaps her partner. All it would take was one member of that whole, rotten organization determined to find the truth.

But she was not persuading herself. She knew that, even if such a person existed, someone as determined as her, another one or two or more women might die before that individual finally began to look in the right place. Meanwhile, the rest of Jarrett's crooked LAPD would doubtless try at least once more the manoeuvre that had unravelled in the last twenty-four hours: finding someone else and pinning the blame on him. That could keep happening, each time the killer taking another victim just to prove the police had got the wrong man.

No, she couldn't leave this, even though she was so tired her body was crying out for surrender. Back in her apartment, back in her feeble cocoon of books and papers, with her puny attempt at encryption, she would have to try doing alone what she had needed Katharine to do with her.

How strange that they had acted so fast to stop Katharine, yet they had – so far at least – refused to do the same to her. They'd had ample opportunity. It wouldn't have taken much to make that beating during Mario's demo fatal. But they had held back. The same with her 'enhanced interrogation'. Indeed, they had gone to some lengths to leave even the assault on her wholly deniable. They must have concluded that she had become too high-profile a critic to eliminate. After that initial story of hers was published, however briefly, it became impossible for her to disappear or be found dead, even in a car accident, without Garrison 41 facing the charge that it was killing its opponents on US soil. Whatever trouble they were in now, that was an escalation they did not need.

Maybe it was an illusion, or a delusion, but it gave her a kind of comfort as she got to work. She had DM'd the self-styled Messenger, asking for help but had had no reply. So, for the next hour or more, she searched and scoured both realms of the internet, above and below ground, visiting forums and online support sites, reading her way through the gobbledegook and tech-talk. She read about file extensions and compressions, compiling and disassembling, at every step hoping to hear the voice of Katharine, guiding Madison to what was important and what could be safely ignored, until she could see a way of cracking open the first of these opaque parcels that had been sent to her.

At last, she followed the steps her research had suggested, installing one bit of software, then another, before making the crucial click.

No error message, but an encouraging delay. After a few moments, the file did indeed send out the graphic signals that suggested it was buckling under her sustained pressure and preparing to expose itself. After another delay, a new window opened on her machine – but it was filled with sequences of numbers.

At first she assumed this was yet more garbage, the strings of indecipherable nonsense offered up when she tried to display a music file or a photograph as just plain text. Except these looked like actual numbers, rather than meaningless lines of symbols. They were punctuated only by specific groups of letters, which appeared anything but random. After ten digits, there would be an *SSW* or an *NE* or an *NNW*.

She had just an inkling of what she might be looking at when she remembered one of the earlier user help sites she had consulted. She went back to it now, typing in its suggested commands as slowly and deliberately as a seven year old on her first computer. To her astonishment, the computer opened a video application and began to display what seemed to be a short, animated film on a mini-screen. Except that it was nothing like anything she had seen on a computer before.

It was a sequence of satellite navigation images, the kind you'd see on any GPS device in a car, unfolding in real time. Maddy watched it and felt as if she were driving, the arrows suggesting a right turn here, a change of lane there. The display showed the time remaining to destination, the miles elapsed and, crucially, the street names. The current image suggested there were twenty-one minutes remaining.

She clicked on the controls and fast-forwarded to the last two minutes of the journey. East on Whittier, south on Soto

Street, coming to a stop between Seventh and Eighth: Boyle Heights.

In this empty apartment in the dead of night, alone with a glowing screen, Maddy felt the adrenalin thump through her system. For the first time since her sister had died, she was certain she had found the man who killed her.

Chapter 50

Boyle Heights was the neighbourhood where Rosie Padilla had lived and died. Now Madison knew what she was looking for. She opened up the third of the three files she had been sent, instantly fast-forwarding to the final thirty seconds. This GPS sequence ended in Alhambra, where Mary Doherty had been found dead less than twenty-four hours ago. She took a deep breath and clicked on the second file, the one she had been avoiding.

There was no mistaking it. The little chequered flag graphic that popped up in the final few frames, the one usually accompanied by a voice saying 'You have reached your destination', appeared now on the downtown location of the Great Hall of the People and the Opium Den, the last place Abigail was seen alive.

Frantically now, Maddy clicked on every possible icon or button, hunting for more information. Remembering everything Katharine had taught her, she eventually right-clicked to produce a menu called 'Properties'. There, amid the technicalia, was a date and time: eleven thirty last Sunday. According to the police estimate of the time of Abigail's death, that would fit with what was almost certainly the last hour of her sister's life.

Maddy checked the timings on the other files too, each one fitting the date and time of the victim's death. This car had been at or close to the scene of the killing in three of the four cases, never more than an hour before the presumed time of death. Tellingly, there was no file for Eveline Plaats, perhaps because her last hours alive had been spent on the base itself.

Now Madison studied the Properties more closely and saw that the hieroglyphics contained one long number set apart from the others. Her right hand trembled with excitement as she went back to the first document that had been left for her in Dropbox. She ran her eye down that list of names until she found Yang, doing her best to remember at least part of the thirteen-digit number alongside it. Then she went back to the Properties on the GPS video. She let out a long, focused breath.

It was the same number. She now understood that those three little videos she had been sent were computer animations of the movements of Yang Zhitong's car, based on tracking data. She had heard about these tracker devices, installed into cars as an anti-theft mechanism: wherever the car went, its movements were transmitted to a computer that stored them minute by minute, a detailed record of precise co-ordinates. The films were just those numbers translated into graphics, made to look like regular satellite navigation.

That list of names and numbers left in Dropbox must have been produced by the tracking company that ran the service for the garrison or perhaps by the garage that maintained the cars of the junior officer elite, each vehicle allocated its own, unique, thirteen-digit code. It made good sense: if that Ferrari story was true, these privileged young men had expensive tastes. Were one of those cars to be stolen, you'd want to know where it was.

But it had proven to be Yang's undoing. There it was, hard data that put him close to or at the scene of three crimes. It was incontrovertible.

401

Her mind was speeding now, each thought completing an electric circuit that started another, lighting up bulb after bulb. This time it was the word *tracking*. It triggered a memory, one she had to work hard to dredge to the surface. But there it was. The man Leo had introduced her to at the debate venue, the Republican big shot, Ted Norman. He had castigated Leo for failing to respond to his repeated offer of help. She closed her eyes and recalled his exact words. *You know I have a software business, tracking technology and all that.*

So that's where these files had come from. It meant her hunch had been right. She had been sure the source of this help, 'the Messenger', was the Sigurdsson campaign, eager to maintain the anti-China drumbeat that had seen their candidate advance so rapidly. This confirmed it. Norman was not only chairman of the Republican party in California but the owner of the company that had, it seemed, tracked Yang's car. Norman had doubtless made his data available to the Sigurdsson campaign team – who, thanks to Madison's story, knew exactly where to look.

A window was still open on her screen from one of the dissident sites. She went to the story of the road accident, when Yang had demanded he be allowed to get away with driving drunk and crashing a car simply by shouting his father's name. A photo accompanied the story. It was snatched and grainy, showing several faces, none looking directly at the camera. But at the centre, with a head of jet-black hair, slicked back off his forehead like an old-school movie star, was Yang. He was not smiling, but had his lips pursed in an expression of . . . what was it? It took Madison a while to realize that it was a look she had seen often on those born into power and money. It was impatience.

She went to the bathroom and was about to put the light on when she stopped herself. She stared instead, in the gloom, at the mirror, wondering if they were still looking. What could they see in the dark like this? Nothing? Or maybe they were gazing at her now through a night-vision lens, her body a mere ghost of white lines. She looked over her shoulder, at the empty wall above the bath. Maybe they were looking at her from there. She bent over, feeling the ache in her sides and her ribs, splashed some cold water on her face and, as she pulled herself back up to full height, she resisted the urge to whisper into the mirror, 'I've got you.' But she felt it all the same.

Madison returned to her desk. She checked her phone one more time: no word from Enrica. The last message had come an hour ago, saying that a nurse had emerged to tell Enrica, 'That woman of yours is a true fighter.' Every minute they were still operating or checking or scanning, Maddy could breathe.

Back in her chair, she repressed the fatigue winding itself around her like bindweed and got to work. She would not allow herself to think of Katharine as anything but alive. She would not allow herself to think of Abigail. She would not linger on their faces. But she would do this for them. It was time to make her move.

Chapter 51

'Sorry to turn the tables like this, Howard.'

'Madison? Is that you?'

'Yes.'

'It's – what time is it?' She could hear a woman's moan, irritated rather than erotic. 'Maddy, it's six o'clock in the morning. On the weekend.'

'Actually, it's just past six o'clock. And I'm sorry. But I wouldn't have come here unless I'd done what you told me to do.'

'Madison, where are you?'

'I'm outside your front door.'

'Oh, for fuck's sake, Madison.'

'Can I come in?'

'It's the . . .' There was a rustle. 'Yes, I'm dealing with it. Go back to sleep, darling . . . Madison, I'm coming down.'

She continued her slow jog on the spot, keeping herself moving. In her eagerness to get here as soon as she deemed acceptable, and in this she took her cue from Howard Burke's dawn appearance at her own door, she had come out without a coat. Even in LA, six am in February was cold. Especially for insomniacs who occasionally forgot to eat. She could feel her nose turning red.

There was the sound of one then two locks being turned and the door was open. Filling the frame was Howard Burke, haggard in a dressing gown, the kind she thought no one wore any more. He looked drawn, his stubble apparently growing in real time. 'Madison, what the fuck is this?'

'You told me the problem with my first story was that it was vague and unsourced. You were right. So I now have the real story, with documentary proof. And it's way stronger – and way bigger – than I ever believed.'

Reluctantly, his face still a picture of scepticism, he pushed the front door wider, allowing Maddy to step inside without actually inviting her to do so. She went past him, while he remained static, still gazing straight ahead.

She made straight for the big table in the living room, setting up her battered old laptop.

'Not there,' he said. 'Kitchen.'

She did as she was told, following his heavy, sleepy steps into the room, waiting for him to turn on the light. She noticed the children's drawings stuck to the fridge and decided in that instant that Howard had probably tried, despite everything, to be a good dad – a thought that nearly undid her resolve. She needed to stay strong.

Howard pulled up a chair and nodded for her to do the same. They were both at the kitchen table. She brought out the laptop but he put his hand on hers before she could open it. 'Is this about Katharine? I heard you were there.'

Maddy wanted to say that of course it was about Katharine, it was about everything, it was all connected and surely he didn't think Katharine had been hit *by accident*. But she remembered the piece of paper that she kept in her pocket for this exact purpose, the note from Jane Goldstein. *Alex Katzman, Analyst*. She would not do or say anything to add to that impression.

'How is she?' he said, trying again.

'She's breathing on her own. She's alive.'

'But will she . . .?'

'I don't know. Enrica says the brain scans are not yet definitive. So we don't know.'

He nodded, a cue to get to the business in hand.

She proceeded to walk him through what she had, step by step and in a voice of studied calm: the evidence that four women had been killed by lethal drugs overdose; the failure of the police to investigate properly and the strong indications that the Chief of Police had been receiving bribes; the association of the drug used in the murders with Garrison 41; the GPS data that linked one specific junior officer with the location of those crimes committed off the base and at the relevant times; the chequered past of that one individual. And finally, the revelation of his identity.

'Jesus Christ,' was what Howard said, putting his hand over his mouth. 'Christ almighty. Christ alive.' He stood up and then he sat down again. 'Jesus.'

Maddy said nothing. There was no need. The facts said it all.

Finally, Howard asked her to step outside and wait for him in the family room. He needed time to think. He closed the kitchen door and there were a few moments of reflective silence. And then Maddy heard Howard's voice, low and intense, speaking on the phone.

Had he called Jane? Or was he going to cut out the middleman and talk to his handler on the base direct? Too crude? How did it work then, she wondered. Clearly Howard Burke did not rely solely on his own instincts, using his judgement alone to determine what would or would not be acceptable to California's Chinese guests, or else there would have been no need to make a call. Obviously self-censorship only went so far. On the big occasions, there was no 'self' about it.

Maddy prepared herself for the 'no' that was bound to come at any moment. She was ready for it, with a back-up plan. And if she had to open that particular parachute, she would do so with a clear conscience, knowing she had tried the alternative. No one could say she hadn't tried.

Howard emerged from the kitchen, carrying two cups of coffee. He put them down on the table and said, 'You're going to need that.'

Maddy looked up at him, disbelieving.

'Why?'

'Because you've got a story to write.'

Leo Harris looked at the menu and concluded there was nothing at this or any other restaurant he felt like eating. Each word on the menu – diner food: oatmeal, pancakes, cream – nauseated him. There was still time to get up and leave. Bill Doran would come here, look around and figure he'd been stood up: a small, but satisfying humiliation.

But Leo knew he would not do it. He had asked for this meeting; he had been desperate for it. Within a few minutes of Madison's story going live, he had decided this was one of those days when you break the glass and pull the red cord. A state of emergency.

He hadn't told Berger. He had barely known how to look at him after he found those photographs of the dead women – including Abigail Webb – on the mayor's phone. Suddenly everything about his boss had unnerved him. Leo found himself studying that election flier photo of Berger and his wife, noticing for the first time how very blonde she was. Was the mayor some kind of fetishist, capable of God knows what darkness? It had taken Madison's bombshell of a story to dispel those fears.

Except larger, more rational fears had simply taken their place. Which was why he was here and why he had not breathed a word of this meeting to Berger himself. Keep the candidate out of it, maximum deniability. Also, he knew the mayor would disapprove. No negotiating with terrorists, no negotiating with Republicans. It meant weakness.

And now here he was, the old boy swinging through the glass door, pot belly first, in a rumpled, shapeless blue jacket, looking around to find Leo, then giving a raised hand of greeting – the hand clutching a dog-eared file. You'd know Doran was an old-school political consultant from a hundred yards away: shabbily dressed, unhealthy pallor, always clutching reading material.

'Hi there, boy wonder,' Doran said, taking the opposite seat in the booth. 'How's the sorcerer's apprentice?'

Same joke every time. Different wording, but the same intention: a reminder of who was once a kid who knew nothing and who had taught him all he knew. Not that long ago either.

'Thriving, Bill, thriving.' Leo tried to smile brightly, but it was an effort and he knew Doran could see through it. People – Madison included – always asked him why a certified political genius like Leo hadn't gone into politics himself. 'You're smart, you're talented. You know all the moves. Why aren't you the candidate, rather than that jerk?' Well, this, right here, was the reason. You'd have to eat a plateful of shit and smile like you'd won the Superbowl. That was the job. And moments like this were a reminder to Leo that he couldn't do it. He wasn't a good enough actor.

'So to what do I owe this pleasure, a late breakfast with the child prodigy of California state politics?'

'You've seen the *Times*?'

'Yep.' Doran made a show of looking at the menu, denying Leo eye contact: the non-poker player's alternative to a poker face.

'The story's moved to a new level now, I think we'd agree.'

'Oh yes, I'd agree with that.'

'It's not a joke any more, is what I mean, Bill.' He reached across the table, touching Doran's hand. He immediately regretted the gesture: it made him look desperate, like a dumped girlfriend pleading that they give it one more try. But now Doran was looking him in the eye.

'It never was a joke, Leo.'

'Sure, but we're playing with fire now. We both care about this state too much—'

'Save that for the ad, Leo. What's your point?'

'My point, Bill. My *point* . . .' He took a sip of the iced water already placed on the table. 'There could be riots. There could be pogroms. People now know this city's been terrorized by the . . .' he lowered his voice, though given that this was now the most widely circulated news story on the entire internet, it made no sense, '. . . son of the Chinese fucking president-to-be. There's going to be rage, Bill. People are gonna need an outlet. A target. We're hearing shops are already closing in Chinese areas. They're frightened, Bill.'

'You mean Chinese-*American* areas. Unlike you to slip up on that stuff.'

'OK, very funny, Bill. You can make a joke of this if you like. I think we have a responsibility—'

'Like I said, Leo. Save it. What do you propose?'

'A joint initiative.'

'A what?'

'The two candidates meet and announce that they jointly agree not to fan the flames of tension at this difficult time for the state of California.'

'They call for calm.'

'Exactly. "This is beyond politics. And both my opponent and I agree we will not exploit it for petty, partisan advantage."'

'I get it. Where?'

'Could be on the steps of City Hall.'

'My dead body. Gotta be neutral.'

'We could find a venue downtown, it could—'

'Not in LA at all. That says Berger's in charge.'

'All right, then,' said Leo breezily, surprised this was going so well. 'Sacramento. Steps of the statehouse.'

'Goatfuck?'

'Exactly. Joint goatfuck, the two stand together.'

'Who goes first?'

'We can iron out the details later.'

'Who goes first?'

'I don't know, we'll flip a coin. Are you in?'

'No.'

'What?'

'No, I'm not in.'

'Is this about going first? Because if it is, I'm sure we could sequence—'

'No. It's not about going first.'

'Venue? Timing?'

'None of those things, Leo. I was never going to say yes. I wanted to hear you out, was all.'

'For Christ's sake, Bill. I thought—'

'Look, there's nothing in this for us. Plenty in it for you, I can see that. But we're killing you on this China stuff. Public opinion is moving before our very eyes. Not just LA, but all the pearls. You seen the numbers in San Diego? You're even crumbling in San Fran-fucking-cisco. How often does that happen? The tectonic plates are shifting in this state, maybe even in the goddamn country. And it's happening *during* a campaign. That's really rare. And very big. Norman's foot-soldiers are having a collective orgasm. Why would we give that away for nothing? You're asking me to pull out my fangs and hand them to you.'

'Just as they're beginning to bite.'

'Correct. You've heard me say that before, haven't you?' Doran's voice softened a notch. 'Now put yourself in my position, Leo. You'd do the same, wouldn't you? Least I hope you would, else I didn't do my job properly.'

A waitress came over with a glass jug of coffee. Doran waved her away, rising to his feet and tucking his wad of documents back under his arm.

'And what job is that, Bill?' Leo asked, knowing the answer.

'Why, teaching you of course.' Standing, he extended a hand downward and Leo took it.

'May the best man win,' Leo said, attempting to sound cavalier, as if this little gambit he'd tried had been worth a shot but mattered no more than that.

'Or the best woman,' said Bill. And he was gone.

Politics Live Blog, Saturday

4.05pm The KTLA feed is now showing a large crowd massing at the gates of the garrison. No sign of Padilla yet, though he's said to be on his way. After the initial rally and Thursday's ring-the-base event, organizers are said to be planning a 'virtual blockade' until the suspect named in today's LA Times *story is handed over to the US authorities. One campaigner close to Padilla weibed:* We want to stop anything – and anyone – getting in or out of that base. #ArrestYang

4.17pm Presser at City Hall due to start soon. Will bring you key quotes just as soon as it gets underway.

4.21pm Mayor Richard Berger begins. As predicted: he's flanked by the Deputy *Chief of Police, Rene Hernandez, not Doug Jarrett.*

4.23pm Berger: 'The time for waiting has passed. There can be no excuse for delay. We call on Colonel Chen and his fellow commanding officers at the garrison to hand over this man and let him answer all charges.'

4.25pm Berger: 'I reject utterly the notion that the election campaign has played any part in this process. Protecting the people of California is my only priority.'

4.26pm 'Finally, I regret to announce that Douglas R Jarrett has been suspended with immediate effect from his role as Chief of Police. He will face disciplinary charges.'

4.27pm Deputy Chief Hernandez to become Acting Chief. 'We had a brief swearing-in ceremony in my office before we came here today.'

4.29pm Acting Chief Hernandez: 'We promise that Yang Zhitong will receive the same basic rights as any other suspect. If he wants to clear his name, he needs to help the Los Angeles Police Department with our inquiries. Starting today.'

4.31pm A reporter (off-mic, so I didn't catch who) asks Acting Chief Hernandez if he owes 'a debt of gratitude' to Madison Webb and the LA Times. Replies, 'Let's wait and see.' Berger jumps in and says, 'If you're asking whether this city needs great reporters who work at getting the truth, then I think everyone, whatever their views, owes a debt to Madison Webb and the LA Times today. As many of you know, I've always been a great admirer of her work.'

5.15pm White House press secretary just weibed that Prez will be giving brief 'remarks' when he lands at Andrews AFB shortly.

5.21pm No sign of POTUS yet.

5.23pm Two minutes, according to our DC folks.

5.28pm Here he is.

5.30pm Money quote from the Prez: 'The United States of America is a nation of laws. While it endures, we are bound and will be bound by the Treaty that ties this great country to the People's Republic. But there is also a higher law, the law of natural justice. And natural justice cries out for this man to answer to the charges before him. I call on the Commander of Garrison 41 to arrange for the suspect to be interviewed by the Los Angeles Police Department forthwith. Until we have a positive answer to this request, I'm afraid next week's summit between myself and my Chinese counterpart will inevitably be called into question.'

5.33pm Huge news there on the summit. Big.

5.36pm Lots to unpack in the POTUS remarks. Several on Weibo noticing the words, 'While it endures . . .' Was the Prez hinting that he might move to scrap the Treaty someday? Or was that just a bit of empty, populist crowd-pleasing?

5.37pm Credit to folks who noticed a difference between the demands made by the president and demands earlier by the mayor. Prez said an LAPD 'interview' with Yang will be enough: no reason why that couldn't be on the base. Mayor called for a 'handover' of Yang, suggesting he has to physically leave Garrison 41. Expect some back and forth 'clarification' on this as the evening goes on.

5.39pm More reax. Sigurdsson: 'We welcome the statements by the president and mayor. This is not the time for partisan politics. Instead it is gratifying that our repeated calls for action are finally being heeded. If only Mayor Berger had acted earlier, we might have avoided this drastic situation.'

5.55pm Pictures from outside the garrison gates suggest a huge crowd. KTLA saying it's swelling by the minute. Chants alternating between 'Tear Down this Wall!' and 'Give Him Up!'

6.33pm Sudden movement behind the gates at the base. Pictures are not clear, but we hear there are several vehicles preparing to exit.

6.35pm The crowd are surging forward. PLA guards struggling to push them back. This could get nasty.

6.37pm Crowd are repeating their promise not to let anything in or out till they get Yang.

6.39pm Rumor spreading that Yang is in one of those vehicles.

6.43pm Mario Padilla has appeared at the very front of the demonstration, right by the gates. Starting to speak now.

6.44pm Padilla calls on crowd to let the vehicles pass. Says no more than that.

6.47pm The crowd have withdrawn a bit and now the gate swings open. Looks like four, no five vehicles are emerging. Black SUVs, windows tinted. Does one of those contain the man at the center of these extraordinary events?

Chapter 52

Howard had cleared his own office for her use, poking his head around the door at intervals, bringing her coffee and assorted snacks. He was excited, fussing over the video team as they uploaded the three GPS animations and the rest of the documents that would accompany Madison's story. He had assigned a couple of reporters to write backgrounders on Yang, drawing heavily on the links and other material that the unnamed 'Messenger' had sent via Weibo about his past back in China. They had to drop the story of the girl in the Ferrari, killed after she had reportedly 'distracted' Yang while he was at the wheel, causing him to crash the car. Published on a flaky gossip site with no proper sourcing, it didn't pass the 'LA Times test', as Howard put it. But everything else – the past harassment of western, female students, the drunk driving, the evasion of justice by invoking the name of his powerful father – all that went in. It was a comprehensive takedown of young Mr Yang.

As it happens, Maddy had already written the story when she turned up at Howard's door: that's what she had been doing through the sleepless hours of the night. So in the morning, sitting at his desk, she had time to check the details, rephrase some of the sentences and think. At any moment she expected Howard or, if not him, Jane to come in and break the news that, on reflection, they thought it best to hang fire, to give it more time, to see how things played out. And yet, Howard remained gung-ho. At one o'clock, not long before the story was due to launch, she admitted to her boss that she was pretty astonished by his reaction.

'This takes real courage, Howard. I'm really, I don't know—'

'Surprised?'

'Yes. And impressed.'

'Well, you got the goods, Maddy. We run the story – and Yang can sue us for libel in a California court if we're wrong.'

What Maddy did not say was, 'What the hell happened in that phone call?' But she thought it.

The story went up, under a simple but devastating headline: *Suspected heroin killer is son of future Chinese president* and it was as if she had lit the blue touchpaper under the entire city, if not the country. When the President of the United States came on TV to react to the story, the newsroom broke into spontaneous applause.

At seven pm, Jane Goldstein and Howard Burke summoned the editorial staff to meet by the newsdesk. Someone had produced a bottle of champagne.

'This is a proud, but bittersweet moment,' Jane began, holding a glass. 'This last week began with a tragedy. Abigail Webb lost her life. I'd like us to take a moment to remember her.' Goldstein dipped her head, which prompted everyone to do the same. For a few seconds, far less than a minute, the newsroom fell silent, save for a distant TV set, still carrying pictures of the rally outside the base. Maddy observed the silence but did not dip her head. Instead she stayed focused on Jane and Howard, watching.

Then Goldstein spoke again.

'Yesterday the *LA Times* family very nearly suffered a second tragedy. As you know, the great Katharine Hu was knocked down in what seemed like a fatal hit-and-run incident. I'm

416

glad to tell you that we've just had word from the hospital and, in the last hour, Katharine has regained consciousness.' There was a burst of applause. 'It seems she's going to be OK.

'But in between those two devastating events someone very close to both of these wonderful women made some history. Madison Webb pursued the truth. It was her persistence which got to the truth. And what a truth, a story that went right to the very top of the world's leading superpower. She has done this organization proud and – something I suspect matters to her much more – she has got justice for her sister. I raise my glass, and I take off my hat, to Madison Webb.'

'To Madison Webb!'

Somebody, an intern she guessed, pressed a glass into her hand and looked at her with what she would have described, in a hurried text across the newsroom to Katharine, as sex eyes. Funny to think that just yesterday the editor-in-chief was politely ejecting her from the building as a potential lunatic and here she was now, feted as the star reporter and newly hot property. Fickle business, journalism.

She took a sip of champagne and returned to her desk, buried under an avalanche of paper. What with the sweatshop investigation and the madness of this week, she hadn't sat here properly in well over a month. She checked her email and Weibo to see a flood of congratulatory messages. She didn't read them.

Elation would not come. With Abigail gone and Katharine comatose until an hour ago, numb was the best she could manage. But, as she glanced up at the TV, she knew there was more to it than that. It wasn't only because she was in mourning that she could not find it within her to celebrate the story of a lifetime, the story that would probably be the greatest of her career. If she ever had a wall like Jane Goldstein's, this would be the story, framed and cherished, at its centre. And yet she could barely muster any pride or satisfaction. The usual buzz was missing. Something didn't feel right.

A Reuters snap passed across the top of her computer screen, followed a second later by a cry from across the newsroom: 'Jesus Christ!'

Chinese state news agency reporting an important announcement concerning the future of Yang Zheng to be made shortly.

She checked her watch. It was midday on Sunday in Beijing. Whatever was happening there was happening very fast.

And now on one of the TV monitors, KTLA were crossing live to the base from where Colonel Chen had emerged to give a few remarks to the cameras and reporters waiting outside.

'On behalf of the People's Liberation Army,' he began, apparently reading from a printed text he stiffly held in front of him, 'I wish to confirm that today we have voluntarily complied with a request that Second Lieutenant Yang Zhitong meet the Los Angeles Police Department to answer their inquiries. We do this . . .'

Madison closed her eyes, just to be sure. No doubt about it. It was the same voice. Less than twenty-four hours ago, she had been bound in a stress position in front of this man, her hands tied and her legs in screaming pain, while he interrogated her. And here he was on TV in his olive-green uniform and wide, peaked cap. He looked older than he had sounded. Perhaps in his late fifties, he seemed to be a man utterly in charge.

'. . . evidence advanced by the *LA Times* is clearly very disturbing and much of it was not known to us prior to publication. The People's Liberation Army was not aware of the troubled record at Tsinghua University or of the fatal road accident involving a young woman. As a result, we shall be conducting an internal inquiry into admissions procedures for elite officers. Let me reassure the people of this state that our partnership is built on a platform of mutual trust . . .'

Had she heard correctly? Or was she imagining things? While she would never forgive Goldstein for what she had said yesterday, the editor wasn't completely wrong: insomniacs' minds played tricks on them all the time. Madison quickly found a digital feed of the KTLA coverage on her computer and rewound the Colonel's impromptu presser.

The People's Liberation Army was not aware of the troubled record at Tsinghua university or of the fatal road accident involving a young woman . . .

OK, so she had heard that correctly. Now she went to the *LA Times* and clicked on her story, currently stripped with a banner headline across the front page of the site. She had read through the piece two dozen times, but had that line got through? She had included it in her first draft, but hadn't she and Howard discussed it and pulled it out? She read the story one more time, line by line. It wasn't there.

Perhaps it had slipped into one of the backgrounders that made up the package. She hadn't written all of those herself, though she had briefed the reporters and read through what she thought was the final copy. She read them again. Not a word about the Ferrari incident that had left a woman dead. Plenty on the separate 'Yang Zheng is my father' episode, which was richly sourced and well-documented. But though a car had been damaged, that accident had not been fatal and the *LA Times*'s coverage gave no impression otherwise.

It could only mean one thing.

Chapter 53

Cui bono? Cui bono? She had thought about it, but not hard enough. She had accepted the explanation she had given herself in the dead of night when those Direct Messages detailing the life and misdemeanours of Yang Zhitong arrived: that these leaks were the work of Leo Harris's counterparts, and deadly rivals, in the Sigurdsson campaign, using her to stoke up the anti-garrison fervour which had served them so well. But she hadn't pushed that thought further. There was no excuse. It wasn't as if she hadn't made this mistake before. In fact she had made it very recently, over the police file Leo had given her. It was not enough to understand your source. You needed to understand your source's source.

If she had asked that question, she would have realized the gap in her assumptions. If it had been California Republicans who were feeding her the dirt on Yang, then where were they getting their information from? OK, the tracking data came from the party chairman. But how on earth would the equivalent of Leo – his one-time mentor, Bill Doran, or someone working for him – have known the rest of what the Messenger had known? Yang's antics back in Beijing, OK. Maybe a very smart search on the othernet could have yielded most of that. But what of the private letter from his tutor at Tsinghua University, complaining of 'serious disciplinary issues' and 'inappropriate' behaviour towards female students? Or the equally confidential document stating that Yang was to be transferred from military college in Beijing to Garrison 41 at Terminal Island, the Port of Los Angeles? How would the Sigurdsson campaign have got hold of those?

That would have taken an insider. She would never have guessed it would have been one so high up, but Colonel Chen Jun had just outed himself. He had attributed to the story a fact that was not in it. People did that all the time about facts that were in the public domain, assuming they'd read it somewhere they hadn't. But this was no ordinary fact and it was certainly not in the public domain. Indeed, Chen had just stressed that he and his colleagues had not known anything about the fatal accident 'prior to publication'. Trouble was, on the specific matter of the fatal events involving Yang, the women and the Ferrari, there had been no publication at all, certainly not by her or the *LA Times*.

That proved Chen was lying about the garrison's lack of knowledge of Yang's track record: in itself a minor scandal, but no more. What mattered was his assumption that the Ferrari episode had been in Madison's story. There was only one way to make sense of that. The Colonel assumed Madison had used that morsel because *he* had fed it to her.

Now she thought hard about the timing. How to make sense of Chen all but torturing her one moment, using the full menace of the PLA to ward her off the story, then acting as her crucial source the next? It made no sense at all.

She rubbed her eyes, trying to zone out the newsroom murmur all around her. She opened her eyes to see that intern guy – or maybe he was one of the new video journalists she hadn't met – scribbling a Post-it note, which he then unabashedly placed on her screen. *Drink later?* She peeled it off and threw it in the trash.

She needed to concentrate. Hounding her the way the

garrison had hounded her – spying on her, stalking both her and her friends, throwing her into a dungeon once she strayed onto their territory – was perfectly logical. Her story threatened the base's interests very directly, fuelling an anti-Chinese surge in public opinion that could have made – was already making – life impossible for Garrison 41. So why then start helping her?

And if they had made a decision to help, why try to kill Katharine? Madison had no doubt that was what had happened, that they had got to her friend before she did, determined to prevent her decoding those files. Why give Madison the files with one hand, only to attempt to take them away, or at least render them useless, with the other?

Unless . . .

Her head was banging, images of a left and a right hand flashing up unbidden. She went to the *LA Times* database and raced through the last profile that had been written on Chen Jun, 'the secretive colonel who is the most powerful Chinese official in Los Angeles.' It was an embarrassingly moist piece, one of those 'at home with . . .' articles that reeked of controlled access and copy approval. It had appeared in the weekend magazine a while ago, back, Maddy noted, when Howard was its editor: the man had the spine of a jellyfish.

Having gleaned nothing of value there, Madison read the coverage on the day Chen's appointment as garrison commander had been announced four years earlier. It told how he was a favourite of the then-president, tipped for great things within the PLA. There was some general background on the enduring rivalry between the Army and the Party, how the two remained distinct, with their own bases of power. The president who had promoted Chen was unusual among Party men, the article said, because he maintained good relations with the men in uniform.

An idea was forming. Madison opened a fresh tab and

searched for similar pieces about the new man, Yang Zheng, due to replace the current president in that autumn's transition. Lots of detail on his record of economic management but it was this paragraph that leapt out:

. . . he made his name as a reforming governor of Guangdong province, building a reputation as a scourge of corruption. In one clash, he faced steep resistance from the People's Liberation Army over a dispute relating to taxation. Party insiders say that wound has never completely healed and that relations remain strained between Yang and the military . . .

So that was her mistake. Just because China was a one-party state did not make it a one-faction state. There were rivalries and turf wars there, the same as anywhere else: every place in the world had politics. Including, it seemed, Terminal Island.

No wonder Chen had been only too happy to feed her the damning evidence on Yang Zhitong: he saw an opportunity to derail the rise of an antagonist, the anti-Army, Party apparatchik set to be anointed president. And what more effective way than by exposing his son as a murderer?

He had done it alone too, she was sure of that. It must have been a subordinate, still believing his orders were to thwart Madison's investigations by whatever means necessary, who'd sent a car to take out Katharine Hu last night. If Chen had known about it, he'd certainly not stopped it. He needed to keep his own plan hidden.

The Reuters snap was still zipping across the top of her screen. *Chinese state news agency reporting an important announcement concerning the future of Yang Zheng to be made shortly.*

He would soon be gone, his presidency aborted. All thanks to Chen Jun – and thanks to her. That was why the Colonel had pressed her so hard during the interrogation: he needed to know exactly what she knew and what she did not know.

She had revealed that she suspected a Princeling, but she did not know which one. Which had given him his opening, the chance to direct her to the man he wanted to expose.

Madison sat back in her chair and stared at the ceiling. How long had the Colonel known, she wondered. Had he let Yang carry on killing, the more completely to destroy his father? Had he deliberately let one of his young officers kill woman after woman, just to defeat a political rival? To think that was why Abigail had died: collateral damage in a battle of Beijing factions played out on the streets of Los Angeles. Madison drew no satisfaction in exposing it. Because, she understood now, her big scoop had simply enabled one side to move against another. In the power game that had claimed her sister's life she had been an unwitting accomplice.

She looked at Chen's face on the screen. How pleased he must be with how his scheme had worked out. It had operated flawlessly, everyone, including Madison, playing their assigned part.

Or rather, almost flawlessly. There was one defect in his plan – and it was her.

Chapter 54

'I think it's time I bought you some dinner.'

Madison looked up, with the blinking eyes of someone emerging from the movie theatre on a sunny afternoon. It was Jane, freshly made-up, standing over her desk with her coat on. At her side, as bright-eyed and eager as a paid escort, was Howard. She half-expected to see him carrying the boss's bag.

'Actually, there are a few things I kind of need to—'

'Oh, come on, Maddy. No more work now. You worked harder than anyone in this building even *before* this week. Let me treat you.'

She had to think. 'Tell you what. Why don't I just make these calls – you know, to my sister and my mom – and catch you right up?'

'Well, I don't really think that's good enough,' Goldstein said, pursing her lips slightly in a feigned expression of hurt. 'But we'll be at Vidalia. I think we should have a conversation about *you*.' She gave Madison a friendly poke in the shoulder with a newly varnished nail, signalling that she had good news and was in a hurry to impart it. She thought of Jane Goldstein's own career: big story followed by big promotion.

'Be right there,' Maddy said, flashing her best, if most confected, smile.

Once they were gone, the rest of the newsroom began to empty out.

The mention of Quincy and her mother, offered up as an excuse, left Madison with a pang of guilt. She reached into her bag, found a phone and did the old Katharine trick, setting up a divert on her old number so that unopened messages left there now came here. After a few seconds, the machine went berserk, with texts and voicemails. She didn't bother with the latter – too time-consuming – but waded through the others. Plaudits mostly, including a sheepish text from Charlie Hughes: 'I'm glad it all worked out. Well done.' Countless congratulations, including one from Leo that she read twice and then once more: *I already knew you were the best reporter in America. But I underestimated you. L x*

There was a string from Quincy, the older messages pleading with her to get in touch, then one from earlier that afternoon, around the time her story had been posted, saying, *Is this really true? Do you really think you've found the man who killed Abigail?* And finally, *Please call. Am with Mom. She's doing her Sudoku right now, but she'd love to see you. We both would. Q x*

Madison smiled and knocked out a quick holding reply, stood up, paced a while and sat back down. She didn't like this feeling, of being used. It offended her to think she had been so easily manipulated, Chen sitting there inside his well-protected base, pulling her strings. It annoyed her that she had not been more sceptical.

She needed to return to first principles, to retrace each one of her steps of the last week. In the rubble of her desk she found a fresh sheet of paper and a pen and set out, in the baldest note form, what she knew.

Each one of the victims had had some kind of association with the garrison. Eveline had worked there, Rosie had just visited there on the day she was killed, Abigail performed for men from there. The drug that killed them was associated with the base. That was not manipulation. Those were just the facts and they pointed inescapably at Garrison 41.

Now she looked at it again. What did she know of the way the women had been killed? For one thing, though the LAPD had sought to keep it hidden, the killer had left a calling card, the single silk poppy in the underwear. He had wanted to leave no doubt that the women had been murdered and that they'd been murdered by the same killer. In the most recent case, that of Mary Doherty, he had also left crucial evidence behind: the drugs paraphernalia, including the telltale bag of heroin #3 that had led ineluctably to the base. Did that mean Yang had become less careful as time had gone on – or did it mean something else?

Maddy had half-contemplated the question before but not made too much of it. Based on her experience covering homicide cases, she knew that some serial killers became more skilled as they went on while others became over-confident and started making mistakes. But this felt different.

She sprang up out of her chair and began to pace; the synapses were firing now. Something else she knew: serial killers were often attention-seekers who could grow irritated if denied credit for their work. How infuriating it must have been for Yang that his poppy signature was kept secret, that publicly at least Rosario and Eveline were not even regarded as murder victims at all, but as suicides. Is that why he had left behind the heroin bag after killing Mary, so that there could be no doubt? It pointedly directed the police and Madison to the base – and to him.

Now she thought of the four victims, not only sharing a link to the garrison but all attractive young women whose deaths had sparked the outrage of the American media and public. Whose deaths were, in fact, *bound* to spark outrage. And all of it leading back not just to any Chinese recruit or official, but the elite of the elite, a culprit at the very top – one with a proven record of alarming aggression towards women.

427

The smarter homicide cops downtown used to talk about an 'orgy of evidence'. Jeff Howe had used that phrase once, about a case where the crime scene included so much that was incriminating, he suspected some of it had been planted. The words popped into Madison's head, and then out again. This was not quite an orgy; each element of it had a quite plausible explanation.

No, what Maddy was thinking about was her mother, hunched over her Sudoku puzzle, excitedly coming up with what looked like a solution, hurriedly writing in the numbers, which added up this way and that, fitting perfectly – only to discover that they came unstuck. It had happened a hundred times, her mother finally sighing the same, resigned sentence: 'It's too good to be true.'

Still standing, Madison clicked back to the *LA Times* website and then on a whole lot of others. Her story was on the front page or leading news bulletins all around the world: the BBC, *New York Times*, Al-Jazeera, the *Guardian*, even, after a fashion, the *China Daily* and Xinhua.

Her head was pounding. The son of the Chinese future president exposed as a serial killer of American women, his method of murder freighted with historic and symbolic significance for the two countries? She knew what her mother would say. And, Maddy feared with a rising sensation of nausea, her mother would be right.

But if the story she had sent around the world was wrong, what was the truth? The inkling she had was so faint, she hardly knew how to pursue it.

Chapter 55

She spent the cab journey working over the same facts, again and again. Try as she might, she could not find a new configuration. She was stuck in the same groove.

As she stared out of the window, Madison sought to imagine an alternative to what would remain the working hypothesis till something better came along: that Yang was a killer with an ego, who had left a trail of evidence pointing to him because he somehow craved the credit. If it was not Yang, there had been a deliberate attempt to frame him. But who was behind that? And, much more importantly, if Yang was not the killer, who was?

Logic suggested the answer to one question would be the answer to both. Yang had been at the scene of every death; the GPS tracker established that. It was absurd to think that a lucky triple or quadruple coincidence. No, the probability was that the killer had committed his crimes exactly when and where he knew Yang was close by. To do that would have required an intimate knowledge of Yang's life, with the ability to follow and predict his movements, who he would meet and where he would go. It would have needed familiarity with Yang's past, the understanding that the spoiled, obnoxious young officer would be easy to cast as a man capable of killing women.

There was only one person who checked all those boxes. For a moment, she summoned the memory of Dr Lei, the man of medicine, utterly familiar with needles and skilled in using them. It was easy to imagine him harbouring some pathological obsession with blonde women or else the desire to set up the privileged Yang for a fall. But then she remembered: he had been out of the country for the last month, away when at least three of the four murders had taken place.

That left only Chen Jun. He was in a position to know whatever he needed to know about Yang, who was under his direct command. He merely had to follow Yang, watch where he went, find a suitable victim – and know that the GPS record would go a long way towards convicting the young officer.

But that row of numbers did not add up either. *Too good to be true.* She only had to think of the lengths Chen had gone to, at least at first, to keep her from discovering Yang, doubtless leaning on the pliant Chief of Police, blocking the path of his detectives, making sure, by whatever intermediary, Maddy ran headlong down the blind alley that led to a wounded and physically harmless army veteran.

Chen's reaction to her first story mentioning the base had surely been alarm, worried about the political damage a killer on his patch would cause. At that time, he had striven hard to steer her away: tailing her, stalking her, intimidating her. That effort, she guessed, had culminated in Chen sending those thugs to beat her up at Mario's rally outside the base, his clearest instruction to back off. He only changed tack, leaking the critical information on Yang's past, once he was assured she had no other suspect in mind. He was as ignorant of the killer's identity as she had been. Her performance on the base with Charlie had given him a hint, pointing him towards the Princelings. He'd obviously made his own inquiries, checked the GPS numbers and seized his chance to damage a major political rival.

Chen had originally wanted to block her – until he realized she could be nudged into advancing his interests. His action had been thoroughly opportunist. If she was right and Yang had been framed, someone else had done the framing.

She paid the cab and was glad to see the lights on in the Padilla house. As she got nearer, the sound suggested the house was full too.

One of the countless cousins opened the door, her face registering surprise before she flung her arms around Maddy. 'Thank you so much, Madison,' the woman said into Maddy's neck. 'Thank you so much. You brought justice for our Rosie. I didn't think we'd ever see it.' She held her tight, until Madison felt her neck turn wet from the woman's tears. She was reminded again how this outcome suited absolutely everyone: the bereaved, including Quincy and her mother, the *LA Times*, Jane and Howard, Colonel Chen, Leo, Berger and the Democratic party, the President of the United States – pretty well everyone, in fact, except the young jerk called Yang Zhitong, who was about to spend his life behind bars (or worse), and her, the girl who never learned to leave well alone.

'Is Mario here? There's something I—'

'Mario!' the woman shouted, as if they were still kids in their mom's house. 'He'll be right down.'

Mario appeared from the kitchen at the end of the corridor, wiping his lips.

'I'm sorry,' Maddy began. 'You're eating. I didn't mean—'

'No, just a quiet family dinner.'

'For fifty people.'

He smiled. 'Something like that. Join us?'

'I'd love to, Mario,' and as she caught the smells of hot, home cooking, she meant it. 'But I just need to ask you something.'

'OK. But let me get you a beer. I owe you one.'

431

They went to the room where they had spoken a few days ago, though it felt as if years had passed since then. She held the bottle of beer Mario gave her, but did not drink.

'Mario, something you said at the rally the other day.'

'Which one! I've almost lost track.'

'You said there were other cases which needed to be reopened too. "Go back through the record of the last few years, and you'll see crimes that were never punished, suspects never arrested, charges never brought." You were talking about the base. It sounded like you'd found something.'

'Yeah, I did some research.' He took a swig from his bottle. 'You really want to get into this now? It's Saturday night, Madison. The bad guy's in jail. You got him.'

'I know. Just indulge me. Did you go through the records?' Mario nodded.

'And what did you find?'

'There's quite a lot of shit there, Madison.'

'Are we talking about more murders?'

'No, we're not. I found a few cases of drunk driving. Just waved away with a warning. No prosecution. Some fights, you know, in a bar. And several rapes.'

'I remember hearing something about that.'

'You won't have heard much. They hushed those up pretty good. Usually just a blanket denial and the suspect quietly flown back to China.'

'But?'

'But some are easier to keep quiet than others. Some victims keep talking, filing complaints.'

'And those are the ones you picked up in your research?'

He took another chug of beer, nodding as he did so.

'And do you have a record of all that? Could I see it?'

He looked wary. 'What's this about, Madison?'

'I'm not sure yet. I just want to be . . .' She thought about telling him what she was thinking, how the Yang story was too neat, how at every step the evidence all but invited

432

investigators to look for the culprit on the base, but she held herself back. 'I think there might be an opening,' she said instead. 'The taboo has been broken. For the first time, the base has been forced to respond to public pressure. Thanks to you.' She smiled, to reinforce the compliment. 'I think we might be able to get more action on these other cases.'

'What, now?'

'No, not now this minute.' She smiled again, as if to say, *I'm not that crazy*. 'But we need to move fairly fast. Before this window closes again. You know, for the sake of the other families.'

'All right,' he said finally. 'I'll show you where I got to. Then will you have something to eat?'

He went out of the room, returning a couple of moments later with his laptop. He fired it up, tapped in a password and then another one to open a locked file, then angled the screen so she could read it. It was a list: name of the victim, nature of the crime and, where available, the name of the probable suspect.

She searched through the last column first, finding Yang's name twice – both for driving offences, one involving alcohol. Then she went through the list of victims, only half-knowing what she was looking for, not wanting even to think it out loud lest the scarcely formed notion dissolve. She scanned the list once and then a second time and saw nothing.

'OK, thanks,' she said, somewhere between disappointment and relief. Well, it was a hunch, she began to tell herself. Only a few of those ever paid off.

'You got that?' Mario said. 'OK, here's the next page.'

'The next page? I didn't realize . . .'

But Mario had already pressed the button to scroll down, generating more names, more crimes, more suspects. There, in the list of victims, was a name she recognized.

Mario got to his feet, preparing to guide Madison into the next room to meet the extended Padilla clan, including his parents. But Maddy was too fast for him. She was already making for the hallway and the front door. After what she had seen, there was no time to do anything else.

Chapter 56

The American flag was flying, though it barely rippled on this windless night. The lights were on and she could hear a TV blaring, the loud laughter of a game show. She rang the bell.

There was a delay, followed by some fussing on the other side but eventually the door opened. A ruddy face looked at her, open in its surprise.

'Why, it's the woman of the hour.' He called out over his shoulder. 'Margaret! Madison Webb is here!' He didn't wait for a reply. 'What brings California's greatest reporter to this part of town on a Saturday night?'

The directness of the question caught Madison by surprise. She was not quite sure how to answer. Ted Norman seemed unbothered by her hesitation. 'Come in, come in.'

He ushered Maddy through a spacious living room of armchairs and an L-shaped sofa, the mantelpiece crowded with assorted patriotic paraphernalia, a couple of trophies, a vase of silk flowers, the petals faded with dust – and lots of family photographs. It took a second for Madison to realize that the room was not empty: still and silent, facing the TV, was a woman, her hair grey and lank. She might have been Ted's age, she might have been twenty years older. But what struck Maddy was that, though the woman's eyes were open, she was not watching the television at all. She was simply staring straight ahead, catatonic.

'Let's go on through to the kitchen,' Ted Norman said, making no mention of his wife. 'Now what will you have to drink?'

Maddy was still looking behind her, at the human statue in the armchair. 'Erm, nothing, thank you.'

'Nothing?'

'Water. Please.'

Soon they were seated at a white, circular table. It would once have been fashionable, but now it was just shabby. The surface was chipped. Much of the rest of the kitchen was in a similar state.

'So, Ms Webb. Congratulations.' He raised a glass, half filled with whisky. 'One helluva story.'

'Thank you.' She raised her water glass to her lips, but did not drink.

'So,' he said again. 'I suppose you're here about the tracking technology. The PR guys said this would happen. "Huge opportunity," they said. But I'm not interested in publicity. I'm just glad that our product could play a part in solving this thing. I always said it had the potential to be a tool in the crimefighters'—'

'No, Mr Norman, that's not why I'm here.' She swallowed hard. 'I'm here because I know what happened to your daughter.'

Ted Norman said nothing for a while, taking his time knocking back a second, longer swig of whisky. He drained the glass. Finally he looked at Maddy directly, allowing her to see that the flush had gone from his face. 'No, you don't.'

Maddy spoke gently. 'I know that she was raped. That the suspect for the crime was a junior officer at Terminal Island. That, in fact, you believed the suspect in question was Yang Zhitong. Am I right?'

Norman shook his head. 'I said, you don't know what happened. Only me and Margaret know that.'

'You mean she wasn't raped?'

He slammed his fist down hard on the table, the glass still in his hand. It shattered on impact. Blood appeared instantly in rivulets between his fingers. 'For Christ's sake, don't keep saying that word.'

Without meaning too, Maddy felt herself recoiling, her back pressing into the seat. The colour had returned to his face.

'You people keep calling it that, using that *word* . . . and you think you understand it. You put that word on a file, you give Jennifer that label, and then it's all squared away. Well, that's bullshit, Miss Webb. One word does not even *begin* to explain what happened to my daughter. You don't know the first thing about what happened to her.'

'No. I don't.'

'He beat her first. Hard punches to her face.' Norman simulated a punch, meeting his own jaw. The blood from his fist dripped onto his shirt: the same deep red as the silk flowers she'd passed on the mantelpiece, flowers she now realized were poppies. Eventually he reached for a napkin, which he wrapped around his hand. It darkened within seconds.

'Then he burnt her. With cigarettes or something else, I don't know. Then he suffocated her, long stretches of that. Then he beat her some more. Hour after hour. And all the time he was . . . using her. Like she was . . .' He couldn't complete the sentence, though it was clear he could see what he was describing. His eyes seemed to grow larger, as if they were engorged. 'You see, you didn't know any of that, did you?'

Madison shook her head, silenced by what she had heard and the fear that was spreading through her, like ink through water.

'Oh and he was not the "suspect in question". There was absolutely no doubt it was him, Yang Zhitong. The police knew. It's all in a file somewhere. But you'd have to know where to look, because they've hidden it away, haven't they? They're good at that: you've seen that yourself, haven't you?

Good at hiding something they don't want us – the victims – to know. That's what they call "an inconvenient truth". Inconvenient to the people who run this God-forsaken country.'

'You told the police everything?'

'Me? No. *Jennifer* told them. She went to the police. She forced herself to do it, describing it, describing him. Like he was doing it to her all over again.'

'And nothing happened?'

'Oh, plenty "happened", Miss Webb. But the police did jack, if that's what you mean. Lawyers and meetings and more lawyers, but jack shit. "Impossible to bring proceedings" or some bull.'

'But you said "plenty happened"?'

'Yes.' His voice dipped again. 'Plenty happened to Jennifer. And none of you know about that either.'

Maddy paused, waiting for him to continue. Eventually, she said, 'What don't I know?'

'You don't know what it did to her. How it changed her.'

Maddy told herself to stay quiet.

'No one knows that. How it made her hate herself. How she stopped eating. She didn't eat, she didn't talk – like Margaret now.' He nodded towards the living room and his wife, rendered mute and unmoving by grief. 'All she wanted was to fill herself with that poison.'

'Heroin?'

He gave a tiny nod. 'I know what that does to a person. I'd seen it myself. Destroyed two friends of mine. Fine men, both of them.'

'And no one was ever tried for her . . . for that crime, were they?'

'No one.'

'And you made lots of complaints, wrote letters to the base, to the LAPD?' Maddy was guessing, remembering how Mario had compiled his list.

'Like I told you, no one wanted to know. Even my great friends in the "Grand Old Party of California". What a joke that is. No one cared about Jennifer except us. Jennifer knew that. That's why she . . . that's why she did what she did.'

'I looked you up. Just now, on the way here,' Maddy said, pulling out her phone, by way of explanation. 'You're a veteran. Two tours in Afghanistan. I'm guessing that's where you lost your friends to heroin.' He closed his eyes, barely longer than a blink. But it looked like confirmation.

She went on. 'You were in satellite comms. That's where you got the idea for the tracker business. You supply every big car fleet in the state, including the garrison.' She gave a tight smile, trying to convey calm, to herself as much as to him. 'Your company would have known every time Yang got in his car. It wouldn't have taken much for you to access that data yourself – everyone says you're a "hands-on CEO". You could see where he went, street by street. You probably watched him on your phone.'

Ted Norman's expression didn't change as he got up, went to the counter and filled a glass of water. He then opened up his wife's handbag, looking over his shoulder to explain: 'I need to give my wife her medicine.' He disappeared with a portable medical kit as well as the water glass, and returned three or four minutes later.

'In some strange way, I find it quite moving,' Maddy began, unsure where she was heading. 'A father who loves his daughter so much, he's ready to go to such extreme lengths to avenge her death. You must have followed Yang for months, watching him day after day, driving where he drove, having a drink at the bar or waiting across the street. And then spotting a woman you knew he had seen or met and then killing her, just like that – just so you could frame him for her murder. And then doing it again and again, until people took notice.'

Norman's gaze remained fixed on the table between them. His face was turning redder.

She continued. 'And was it just random? Did you pick out my sister and the others just because they happened to be on Yang's route?'

He said nothing, though the words seemed ready to burst out of him.

'Is that what I'm meant to live with? That my sister died just because she was in the wrong place at the wrong time?' She waited, each second of waiting longer than the last. Finally she slammed her fist down on the table. 'Say something for Christ's sake!'

'I had nothing against your sister or any of those women. It was nothing personal.' He looked at her. 'It could just as easily have been you.'

With a great, almost muscular effort, Madison calmed herself and tried a different tack.

'It must have been hard for you, having to be so near the man who had inflicted such pain on your daughter. Following him around like that, walking in his footsteps.'

'Like you said, Miss Webb, I'm a soldier. I'm used to facing the enemy.'

'Corps of Engineers, wasn't it? I'm guessing that's where you learned about cutting surveillance cameras and all the other stuff. You did a professional job.'

'I wanted to see that man face justice.'

'For crimes *you* committed.'

'How dare you!' He raised his bloody hand. 'I wanted justice for the crimes *he* committed. For destroying my daughter.'

Maddy was undeterred. Her own blood was up now. 'And it worked so well, didn't it? Finally California – finally America – felt the outrage you felt, felt the anger you'd been feeling for so long. Demonstrations, rallies . . . at long last people were talking about getting rid of the base altogether, scrapping the Treaty. You'd woken them up! And you could use your position in the party to keep up the pressure, to make sure the candidate kept banging the drum. The timing was perfect, the lead-up to a big election. And in Yang you had the perfect target for all that rage: a sleazeball who was right at the very top, just to prove that this fish rots from the head.'

'Maybe not so perfect,' Norman said suddenly. 'They'll just throw his father overboard and it'll be business as usual.' He paused, as if reflecting further. 'You publish this and even that might not happen. The man responsible for Jennifer's death will go free – and we'll be stuck with them here forever.'

'No,' Madison said, full of certainty, though in truth this was the first time she had even contemplated the possibility. 'He'll be tried for the . . . for what he did to your daughter.'

Norman raised his eyebrows in a mixture of disbelief and fury. 'Are you kidding me? Don't pretend you're that naïve. You've seen what they do when their boys get caught. They put them on the first plane to Beijing – first class – to get a little slap on the wrist back home. "Disciplinary proceedings" they call it and it's bullshit. Yang'll be no different.'

'But his case is too . . . it's too well-known for that now. They can't just let him go free.'

'You don't think so? Even after you prove he didn't murder those girls, that someone else did it? Who'll believe he did anything to Jennifer? It'll be my word against his. And my word will be worthless.'

Maddy's head was throbbing. 'You said you wanted justice. Justice isn't punishing Yang for crimes he didn't commit.' She waited for a reaction, but there was none. 'He'll die, you know. In California, for these murders, they'll put him to death.'

Norman lifted his eyes, bloodshot and bulging with rage. 'Am I meant to feel sorry for him, for that animal? After what he did?'

Madison sighed, trying to see through the bubbling red smog of anger and frustration and confusion that was filling her head. 'No. I'm not asking you to feel sorry for him. I'm just trying to remind you of what you said to me. Yang should be punished for what he did to Jennifer.' She swallowed, the motion hard in her throat. She spoke again. 'Not for crimes you committed.'

He was staring at the table. 'You're so certain of everything, aren't you, Miss Webb? So sure of yourself.'

'I've just realized your biggest mistake,' Madison said, ignoring him. Her anger was now outrunning her confusion. 'Those women you killed were just like Jennifer.'

'What the hell is that supposed to mean?'

'They had people who loved them.'

Only now did he let his eyes meet hers. They were hot red but also, she now saw, glistening and damp.

'You want revenge too?'

Maddy paused a while, holding his gaze. She didn't know the answer. Eventually she said, 'I just wanted to know who killed my sister.'

He nodded at that as well. They were both silent for a while. Then he spoke. 'It won't mean anything to you, I know how much bullshit people talk. Especially these days: it's all bullshit. Land of the free, Independence Day. Crap, all of it. But still, for what it's worth: I'm sorry for what happened to your sister.'

'That sounds like a politician's apology, not a soldier's.'

At that, he raised his head, as if to attention, and said, 'I'm sorry for what I did to your sister. And for those others.'

'Thank you,' Maddy said, feeling a blend of relief and shock flow into her veins. She glanced at the phone on the table, a silent witness.

'Maybe you'd like to talk to your wife, before . . .' She let the sentence trail off, deciding it was best to avoid saying the word 'police' out loud.

'There's no need for that,' Ted Norman said with a sigh. 'Her suffering is over now.' He reached over his shoulder, pulling his wife's handbag off the counter and onto his lap.

'But I saved one more.' And suddenly, resting between the thumb, fore- and index fingers of his right hand, was a syringe and hypodermic needle, its chamber full and ready.

Chapter 57

Maddy froze in her chair, her nervous system suddenly flooded with fear. He had killed four women, he had just killed his wife and he was about to kill her. Resistance was pointless, her instinct told her that. This man was old, but he was a former soldier. He would be able to pin her down as easily as he had pinned down her sister and the other women.

'They'll find you in the end,' she managed to say, her voice a thin rasp. 'You can't keep running.'

'I know that,' he said, still calm and steady, as if they were discussing the weather or a train timetable. 'Which is why I want you to help me.'

She desperately wanted her limbs to move, to show some sign of life. But they were ice. 'Why would I help you? You're a murderer.'

'That's exactly why you *would* help me. To see justice done. That's what you want, isn't it? Justice? Here,' and he thrust his hand forward, 'take it.'

It took her a long second to realize that he was holding out the syringe, offering it to her. 'Please, take it. Do to me what I did to your sister. To Abigail.'

Hearing her name come from his lips prompted a curtain

of redness, bright and hot, to fall before her eyes. He was the man who had murdered beautiful, sweet Abigail. These were the hands that had grabbed her baby sister and covered her mouth and tied her and terrified her and extinguished the life from her. This man in front of her, not some name on a police file or an online search, but him, here, now, offering his death to her like a gift. She pictured Abigail's lifeless body, cold and still on the coroner's slab. She pictured the bed in her apartment, the creased sheets where she once lay, the children's exercise books, the life stolen.

Madison snatched the syringe from his grasp and, with trembling fingers, arranged it in her hand. He was right: he did deserve to die and she wanted to see it. The police and the courts and the politics were all too uncertain; she had always known that and she had seen the evidence all too clearly this week. The wheels within wheels, the bribes, the competing interests – the risk that nothing would happen, that Norman would somehow wriggle free, was too high. She should do it now, grab what was rightfully hers.

He had rolled up his sleeve, exposing his left arm. He left it there, the flesh of it just inches away from the needle in her hand. 'Go on,' he said. 'Do it. I deserve to die.'

And then, as if she had been plunged in frozen water, the heat inside her head dissipated as quickly as it had come. She would not do this, she would not give him what he wanted. She would not do this in the dark. She would not bury another secret, so that it lay rotting in the ground, forever mined by worms and maggots. She wanted this to be in the open, where everyone could hear it and see it and know what happened. Somehow, in that instant, she knew that this was the only way she would ever be rid of it, the only way she could bring it to an end. 'No,' she said at last. 'Not this time.'

He gave another small nod, grabbed the syringe from her

and, with swift and expert skill, plunged the needle into his own arm. His eyes closed and, by the time a carriage clock in the next room had chimed ten, he was gone.

Chapter 58

Quincy and Abigail were always early birds, but her mother, like her, was a night owl. When Madison knocked on her front door, she was relieved to hear the burble of the television set, on even at this late hour. She knew it drove Paola to distraction.

She waited, allowing herself to breathe for what felt like the first time in nearly three hours. The wait at Ted Norman's house for the police and paramedics to come, the explanation of what happened, the playing back of the recording of his confession, the giving of a preliminary statement and then the call to Jane Goldstein and Howard Burke, interrupting their dinner and telling them they needed to take the story down from the site and remake it as soon as possible – all of that had allowed no time even to exhale. She needed to collapse. But she needed to be here more.

The carer answered the door, her face a picture of genuine surprise. 'Well, look who's here, Mrs W.'

From the door, Maddy gave her mother a little wave and then, once she was by her chair, a long hug. 'Where have you been?' her mother asked twice and then a third time. 'Shhh,' was all Maddy could manage by way of a reply, said gently, while she stroked the hair by the older woman's temple.

Madison looked up. 'Do you think we could have some private time, Paola?' Once the room was clear, Maddy pulled up a chair, close to her mother's. She took the older woman's hand.

'I think Abby can rest now, Mom, you know?'

Her mother said nothing.

'I hope I've been able to do that for her. It's not been easy. In fact, it's been very hard. But I think she can rest.'

Her mother looked at her intently, but whether her expression was full or empty, Madison could not tell. She kept hold of her mother's hand, enjoying its coolness. After several moments, perhaps a minute, the older woman spoke.

'You look sad.'

'Mom, I need to ask you about something. Something that happened a long time ago.'

For the first time, her mother looked away. 'It's all gone now.'

'I know. I know, Mom. But I need to know one thing. About my father.'

Her mother's face darkened. Maddy responded by squeezing her hand. 'It's OK, Mom. It's just one thing. That night. After he'd hurt you so long. I need you to tell me what happened.'

'It's gone now.'

'The thing is, Mom, with Abigail gone . . .' The sentence dried in her mouth. She tried again, 'Without Abigail, you and me are the only ones who remember . . .' The falsity of that last statement, the futility of it, made her stop for a second time. She leaned back, letting out a sigh. This was surely pointless; her mother remembered nothing. But then she heard her own voice speaking again. 'At least, I think I remember. I think I can see it and then it . . . it gets so hazy.'

'Shhh,' her mother said.

Maddy gave the older woman a sad smile. 'That's what I always said, didn't I? I told you to stay quiet. I told you not to tell.'

'Shhh.'

'"Our secret." I must have said the same to Abigail. Maybe not those words, but she must have known. That none of us was ever to say a word. That was hard, wasn't it? On her, on you. On the three of us.'

Her mother was looking at her intently. Was she waiting for Madison to say more?

'But we can talk to each other now.' Madison paused. 'Because I need to know.'

Her mother looked down, at the floor to the right of her chair.

Madison took a deep breath. 'He didn't just fall down the stairs, did he?'

Her mother's gaze remained fixed downward.

'He was shouting at you, wasn't he? Same as always.'

The older woman winced.

'I can see him standing over you, yelling into your face. He grabbed you by the shoulders. He started shaking you. Hard, so your head was rocking backwards and forwards and—'

'Shhh,' her mother said, still looking at the ground.

'And you were by the wall, remember that wall on the landing, the one where we used to mark how tall we were getting? And he was shaking you so hard, he smashed your head into that wall. I'd just come out of my room, and I saw you there on the landing, kind of crumpled. I thought you were dead. And that's when I noticed Abigail. She had been there the whole time. She'd seen the whole thing.'

'Madison, shhh.'

'And she was so little, Mom. She was such a little girl. And I remembered what had happened the last time. Was it a few weeks before? Maybe a few months, I can't remember. But it had been the same thing: the shouting and the shoving and the rage and Abigail had got in his way, or got too close, and he had hit her. Do you remember that, Mom? He hit her. And she didn't even cry. That's what I remember most. She went white and still and didn't make a sound, like she was too stunned. She was six, Mom. Six years old.'

Her mother looked up at her for a second. Her eyes seemed to be swimming.

'And when that happened, I didn't do anything. I was just too scared. I watched him hit my little sister and I didn't do a thing. I just stood there.'

'It's gone now.'

'But that night, on the landing, it was different. I wasn't going to let him do it again, not to Abigail. All that anger in me made me strong.'

Her mother's eyes were closed now, whether to shut out the memory or to witness it again, Maddy could not tell.

'And then he raised his arm, like he was going to hit someone and that's when I did it. I took a few steps over and I pushed him. Didn't I, Mom?'

A silence held between them, maybe for a minute, maybe longer. In those moments, the last several years seemed to pool and collect between them, all the silences heaped together into one. Eventually her mother spoke. 'It's gone now.'

'But it hasn't, Mom, not really. I know we tried to make it go away. And you did so well, you did exactly what I asked. You kept our secret, Mom. God knows what it did to you, but you kept our secret. And so did I. Even from myself. But I pushed him down the stairs, didn't I? From that landing, right down the stairs. We told everyone he fell but it was me, wasn't it, Mom?'

Now her mother placed her right hand over her daughter's. 'Shhh,' she said, though her eyes seemed to be searching for words.

Madison nodded, unable to speak. It seemed her head, her eyes, her chest were filling with water.

'I didn't mean to kill him, Mom. I was trying to look after you. I was trying to look after Abigail.' The mucus in her nose and in her throat was making it hard to speak, but she forced out a few more words. 'I was her sister. I was meant to protect her.'

She was not sure her mother heard. By now Madison's face and her body were shaking, every part of her involved in the act of weeping. She rocked back and forth, the sobs sending a cascade of tears down her cheeks, onto her chin and down her neck. The more they flowed, the more came to replace them, a tide of floodwater pent up for years. In the tide were tears for Abigail, tears for her mother, tears for all the horrors she had seen. But as her mother tried to soothe her, stroking her hair and telling Maddy, 'Shhh, it's gone now', her eyes pricked with those tears that had stayed at the very bottom of the well, dark and unstirred for so long – the tears for herself.

It was late by the time she was back in her apartment. There had been more calls to make, and a further statement to draft for the police. The messages had piled up, too. She deleted most of them, including several from Jeff Howe, but saved the one from Leo, listening to it twice, enjoying his voice.

For once she did not listen to the radio, switch on the TV or check Weibo. Instead Madison Webb had a long bath. No candles, no oils, no aromatherapy, just hot water. She listened to no recommended music and attempted no ancient meditation. She wore nothing special and she did not so much as notice what she ate or drank or when she ate or drank it. Instead, she simply dried off and got into bed.

She couldn't say what happened next; later she would joke that that was, perhaps, the whole point. Perhaps she read for a few minutes; she might have listened to music. Or she might have been thinking of something, a fleeting memory of friends or a faraway place or maybe even her sister Abigail. All she could say with any certainty was that that night, for the first time in fifteen years or more, she closed her eyes and fell into a deep, deep sleep.

And so she missed the first, unconfirmed reports that, in a plea bargain agreed between the prosecuting authorities and lawyers for Garrison 41 – and in the light of the latest *LA Times* revelations confirming the guilt of the late Edward Norman – Mr Yang Zhitong was due to travel imminently to Beijing, to face 'disciplinary proceedings'. Nor did she hear the second lead on the overnight news bulletins: a statement from the White House looking forward to the upcoming state visit of the Chinese leadership and expressing confidence that the special relationship was now 'firmly back on track'.

Madison Webb slept through all that. She slept as the temperature dropped below zero and as a frost settled on Los Angeles, coating the trees and their dangling red lanterns in a sparkling white dust – a reminder from nature itself that it was still winter in America.

Acknowledgements

This book is only partly a product of the imagination. It is also the fruit of extensive research in both China and the United States, a process which was dependent on the kindness and generosity of many others.

First thanks are due to Tania Branigan, then Beijing Bureau Chief for the *Guardian* who not only allowed me to pick her brains but introduced me to others equally willing to suffer the same fate. Among them were Professor He Jiahong and Professor Shi Yinhong of Renmin University, along with Jeremiah Jenne and Eric Abrahamsen, all of them distinguished scholars and thinkers on China. Stephanie Kleine-Ahlbrandt, then in Beijing with the International Crisis Group, deployed her formidable intellect to answer a series of 'What if...?' questions from me. As did a group of outstanding British diplomats, including Jeremy Page, Henry Bell, Giles Montagnon and John Edwards. The latter was especially insightful on questions of language and culture, while Brigadier Duncan Francis OBE was no less helpful on matters military. Journalists Jamil Anderlini and Leo Lewis were enthusiastic sources of inspiration, while long conversations with Martin Jacques, author of *When China Rules the World*, and Mark Leonard, Director of the European Council on Foreign Relations, proved invaluable. I am indebted to Kathy Gao who acted as both patient guide and shrewd interpreter in Beijing and beyond, and to Steve Coombe, always wise on the dark arts of security and surveillance. DJ Collins was no less generous with his ample knowledge and experience.

Jonathan Cummings has long been the most reliable companion on these journeys: his talent for excavating the crucial fact or insight still fills me with awe. Jane Johnson is the very model of an editor; her empathy and understanding is what every author craves. Rhian McKay proved to be a sensitive copy editor, while the support of Kate Elton, Sarah Hodgson, Kate Stephenson and the rest of the tireless team at HarperCollins made a huge difference. As for Jonny Geller, he may well be weary of hearing it from me by now, but he is not just the best literary agent in the country, he is a good and constant friend.

Finally, a word about my wife Sarah and our two sons, Jacob and Sam. Their love and support is the foundation on which everything else is built. If this book is about a third woman, Sarah is the woman who comes first in my life, now and always.

Jonathan Freedland
London, 2015